D0201846

Ellora's Cave Publishing, Inc

Discover for yourself why readers can't get enough of the multiple award-winning publisher Ellora's Cave. Whether you prefer e-books or trade paperbacks, be sure to visit EC on the web at www.ellorascave.com for an erotic reading experience that will leave you breathless.

www.ellorascave.com

Ellora's Cave Publishing, Inc
PO Box 787
Hudson, OH 44236-0787

ISBN: 0-9724377-1-1

ALL RIGHTS RESERVED
Ellora's Cave Publishing, Inc, 2003
"Oath of Seduction: Seducing Sharon" © Marly Chance, 2002
"The Switch" © Diane Whiteside, 2002

This book may not be reproduced in whole or in part without
author and publisher permission.

Edited by Cris Brashear, Martha Punches and Tina Engler
Cover art by Darrell King

Warning:
The following material contains strong sexual content meant for
mature readers. *The Best of Ellora's Cave Volume I* has been rated
NC17, erotic. We strongly suggest storing this book in a place
where young readers not meant to view it are unlikely to happen
upon it. That said, enjoy…

The Best of Ellora's Cave
Volume I

Oath of Seduction: Seducing Sharon
by Marly Chance

The Switch
by Diane Whiteside

Oath of Seduction: Seducing Sharon

Marly Chance

Dedicated to my family, for always believing

Chapter One

It seemed like a good idea at the time. Now all of these years later, she had to laugh at the sheer perversity of fate. He was sex personified. She was just a small town librarian.

Standing in front of her, dressed in a black silk shirt and leather pants, he had to be six feet seven inches of sculpted, mouth-watering, sexy muscle. He was the kind of guy mothers warned daughters to avoid, and best friends advised, "Sure, enjoy the ride while you can, but he's gonna break your heart eventually."

His hair, cropped close to his head military-style, was pitch black. His face was all masculine angles. He was beautiful in a warrior kind of way. He looked about thirty-five years old, with quite a few of those years tough ones. This was no pretty-boy, sensitive, in-touch-with-his-feelings man. This guy was total danger. He was completely out of her league.

She was pretty much cotton gowns, a good book, and a cheery nightlight. He was sweaty, forbidden, no boundaries sex in the dark. As her gaze met his fully for the first time, she saw that they were a searing, penetrating blue. Within that gaze, she saw the blue flame of intense desire and possession. He wanted her, no doubt of that, but even more frightening, his gaze roamed her body as if he had already claimed it. Repeatedly. Intimately.

Sharon felt like she'd stepped off of a cliff. Her heart was pounding, her skin was flushed, and she had an impulse to scream. She dropped her gaze to the carpeting in pure panic.

This had been a really big mistake. Maybe doing her duty and registering had not been a good idea. Maybe she'd just paste a smile on her face, look him in the eye and say, "Look, I know we're supposed to be getting engaged, but could you maybe find another fiancée? I can't have screaming sex with you. I'm just a librarian, for goodness sake. I'm not really adventurous. I don't really want to live on another planet or meld minds or whatever alien activities are required. I'll just be running along now..." With a deep breath, she raised her gaze to his and felt the words become trapped in her throat.

He was smiling. In fact, he looked on the verge of laughter. The sudden amusement softened his features a little, making him more approachable. She wasn't fooled. It made him even more dangerous.

With a little annoyed sniff, she squared her shoulders. Okay, she was scared, terrified even, but if he was going to keep laughing at her, he was going to be sorry-she'd find a way to make him pay. She took a deep breath. Her hands clinched and she aggressively leaned toward him. Her knees might be knocking, but she would show him that she was not afraid of any big, smirking, sexy, annoying guy. Ever. He'd better understand right now that she was no pushover.

* * * * *

Liken looked at the little beauty standing so scared and defiant in front of him, and felt his heart rejoice. She was perfect. Her five-foot, eight-inch frame was practically vibrating with nerves and outrage. She was both beautiful and courageous. He appreciated the beauty, but she would need the courage in the times to come. She was fighting his effect on her now, but that would change. He would make sure of it. First, though, he had to get his own arousal under control.

She had long, black hair that dropped just past her shoulders. Seeing it in person, rather than telepathically, made him ache with the need to run his hands through it. He wanted that hair spread across his pillow. Or better yet, across every inch of his body. Her eyes were like *mer* stones, deep green and seemingly lit from within. Her face was not classically Shimerian beautiful. The mouth was a little too full, the nose a little too pert. The overall effect on his senses, however, was devastating.

He wanted that face looking at him with desire, with need. He wanted those full lips swollen and tender from his mating or rather, from his lovemaking. When on Earth, think like a human, he chided himself.

Yet even with that thought, his gaze drifted down the rest of her body. Full breasts, the nipples hardening beneath his gaze, were heaving with her rapid breaths. The tips were little defiant points underneath the traditional white blouse. It was fitted to her body, but not tightly. The scooped neckline showed the upper swell of creamy curves. He could tell she wore no undergarment, and those tight nipples were stiff and visible.

Going lower, he saw a small waist, tapering outward to full hips. He felt his hands flex with the need to sink his fingers into those curves and pull her toward him. The white ceremonial skirt fell all the way to the ground. What would those long legs look like? And what would they feel like wrapped around his hips?

Calling on all his discipline, he again raised his gaze to hers and felt the jolt to his soul. She would be his. He had no doubt. Attempting to ease her fear, he said, "Do not fear me, Sharon. I am merely invoking our oath. I am your pactmate, Liken da'Kamon. I would never harm you."

"I'm not afraid of you," she said a little too quickly. They both wondered if she meant to convince him or herself. "Why would I be afraid? This is just the ceremony. I don't think we'll be at all compatible. I think we should just say our words and then when it's over, you can go your way and I'll go mine. At the end of the knowing period, we'll just meet back here and file incompatible."

"You are mine. You will leave with me." The words were out of his mouth without any thought. Seeing her eyes widen, he fell back on Shimerian strategy. Timing was crucial to gaining any objective, particularly with females. "We will speak no more, Sharon, until after the ceremony. We should not be speaking now. Go to the Pactmaker and wait for me." With those words, he turned and walked to the other side of the room.

He might as well have said "Get thee to a nunnery!" like some classic Shakespearean character. Sharon, shocked speechless at his arrogance, stood there until she felt a slight tug on her arm.

Turning, she looked into her friend Kate's face and said, "I am *so* out of here. No way can I go through with this. How dare he order me over to the Pactmaker like I was some child to command? What was I thinking? Kate, we have to find a way to get me out of here."

Kate, her friend since elementary school, knew her only too well. "Shar, what did he say to you? You look scared to death. Did he threaten you or something?"

Turning back toward the other side of the room, Kate leveled a glower toward the Shimerian males gathered there. Finding the one who had frightened Sharon, she gave him a look meant to kill him on sight. To her disappointment, he merely raised an eyebrow.

The male he was in conversation with, however, grinned widely at her and gave a mocking little nod with his head. He was arrogantly gorgeous and his hot gaze, as it raked her body, felt incredibly familiar. He looked enough like Sharon's looming problem to be his brother.

She felt a shot of unease, and immediately turned her back on him. Shaking off the disturbing feelings, she asked Sharon, "What happened?"

Sharon, wrestling her own demons, missed her friend's exchange with the other warrior. She shrugged and said, "No, he didn't threaten me exactly. He more or less told me to shut up and go stand by the Pactmaker. I can't do it, Kate. I know when we registered we thought we were doing the right thing. But now, I'm freaked."

She struggled for calm as she remembered the beginning of this mess. "You know, when you're eighteen, you think you know everything. You have such high ideals. Registering seemed so simple. It was my duty. All of us felt like that. I don't think any of us really thought about what would happen if the Shimerian male showed up to fulfill the pact. I mean, what are the odds? Only about one in twenty thousand is ever called to fulfill the pact. I know it's my duty as a human to go through the ceremony and observe the customs, but I don't think I can."

Kate, feeling sorry for her friend, felt helpless. What could she say? All of them had registered in an idealistic rush of patriotism and duty without really counting the potential costs. Now her friend, the girl she'd literally grown up with and loved like a sister, was being legally and morally tied to an alien being who might remove her from all she held dear. Sharon would have to be intimate with him. She was such an innocent in so many ways. It was frightening and upsetting. Sharon didn't have many choices unless..."Have you really thought out all the options?"

With a shake of her head, Sharon said, "There wasn't really time to think. The two Pactmaker reps showed up at my door in uniform and told me to come with them. They didn't even let me grab my purse. The whole thing scared the crap out of me! I just couldn't believe it was happening, you know?"

She could feel her body begin to shake as reality really hit. "I mean, it crossed my mind when I turned twenty-nine last week that the claiming age would be over in a year. But, it just seemed so unlikely. They brought me to the city pactbuilding and gave me these clothes to put on. Now I've got twenty minutes to figure out what I'm going to do. I don't even know how they knew to get you here. Since I don't have any immediate family, I guess they picked you to stand with me."

It seemed logical, but Kate knew they needed to focus on what was happening now. She was the lawyer here. She ought to be able to fix this situation. She had to find a way to help Sharon. "Well, we can talk about the fun experience I had with the pact reps some other time. Right now, we've got to figure out what you are going to do. You only have three options: Seduction, Challenge, or Capture. Each has its own set of rules and problems. How much do you remember of the customs course?"

Mind racing, Sharon searched her memory. "If I choose seduction, we recite vows, go to his planet, and then live together for three weeks. He..." Her voice faltered a bit but she spoke up deliberately after only a second, "follows the Courtship Rules of Seduction. That means he's allowed certain intimacies with me at certain times. Kind of like baseball...first base, second, like that. He can go further than the prescribed intimacies only with my permission."

Sharon felt her panic rising as she tried frantically to remember what they had been taught. "God, how long before total intimacy, Kate?! I can't remember!"

Kate thought back and then said, "Damn it, they wouldn't give me time to get my copy of your paperwork." Her expression indicated someone would pay for that fact later. "I can't remember. Maybe two or three days at the most."

Three days. It wasn't long enough. Sharon didn't think two or three years would be long enough to make her comfortable with the idea of sleeping with that man. Still, at worst, after a few weeks of living together, she could file for incompatibility and never see him again. "What about Challenge?"

Kate sighed and said with careful calm, "You recite the ceremony and make the oath, but you are basically challenging him to seduce you into staying with him. You have to cooperate with anything he orders you to do sexually, but you can ultimately refuse to have intercourse with him. He can keep you for two weeks. It's his goal in that time to overcome your objections and make you want to stay. If you give in and actually have intercourse, you are ineligible for an incompatibility filing. I don't know, though, Sharon. Shimerian males are supposed to be so dominant in bed..."

Sharon thought of Liken being able to do whatever he wanted for two full weeks except intercourse. She shuddered. There was excitement at the thought, too, but she didn't feel that she could challenge him sexually with her level of experience. She'd only had two lovers, both of whom had been rather dull and unimaginative. Sex had been warmly intimate, but not exactly earthshaking.

This guy was a walking Kama Sutra. She didn't think she could hold her own in that kind of fight and come out on top for sure. "Nope. No way. He's way out of my league. That only leaves Capture. I'm leaning toward that. I say the words and all, but then I get to leave. I have one full day's head start. If I can evade him for one month, I can file incompatible then." She was starting to feel calmer at the thought.

Kate frowned. "Yeah, but if he catches you, you're in a fix. He gets the rest of the month of full sexual obedience. He can do anything he likes, short of seriously hurting you. He doesn't need permission at any time for anything, including intercourse. He has to be guided by your sexual likes and dislikes, but he doesn't have to play fair at all. The rumor is that they're telepathic or mentally gifted or something."

Kate's voice caught as her imagination leapt at the possibilities. "I don't know what that means exactly, but he can probably read your mind. If he picks up on something you would like, but would never admit to liking, he'll use it ruthlessly. He can't actually make you do anything that would be sexually repulsive, but he would push your boundaries pretty hard I'd imagine. We've all heard rumors and stories about the Shimerians' incredible sexuality. It might be pretty intense. You're not that experienced. It would be pretty frightening for you."

Frightening? The thought was enough to make her want to run from the room right now. There had to be some way to deal with this situation. Thinking hard, she quietly said, "But if I break the oath…"

Both women sighed and looked away. There were legal penalties for not fulfilling oaths-"long years in a penal institution with some very uncomfortable companions" kind of penalties. Besides, the guilt and shame of it would be awful. Each woman registering had made an oath of their own free will at the request of their government.

The Shimerian population was in trouble. They had a great disproportion of males. There were not enough females to mate with males and make families. Of the children born, a large percentage was male. It was a downward spiral, and the Earth government had agreed to help, ending with the signing of the Friendship Treaty.

Earth provided potential mates for Shimerians. In return, Shimerian resources and technology were fully available to Earth. Already, amazing cures for some of the worst Earth diseases had resulted from the cooperative knowledge provided by Shimerian scientists to Earth scientists. All kinds of positive advances were taking place.

The Earth government, making clear it was not prostituting its people, agreed to provide a register of potential mates and carefully agreed upon Courtship Laws. Since the Shimerian males' version of courtship leaned toward kidnapping and seduction, the Earth government had been very specific that the program would be voluntary and follow prescribed rules. If, after the knowing period, the Earth female did not want to continue the union, she could file legal paperwork that the union was incompatible and should be dissolved.

When the treaty had been signed some eighty years ago, there was hesitation by Earth females and only a few actually became Shimerian mates. However, as the positive breakthroughs in technology and medicine began to become widely felt, the Shimerian government pushed hard for a public relations program in colleges to promote registering.

These "culture classes" explained the process in glowing terms and encouraged young women to register. The classes had a very idealistic slant with just enough excitement to entice. "Help your fellow human beings and Shimerians, too," they persuaded, "while having an adventure."

More Earth females registered and were mated. Then, rumors began to surface about Shimerian men and their sexual abilities. Women spoke with sighs of their physical attributes, but a lot of information remained unknown. There was just enough mystery to intrigue and entice even the most hardheaded of women. More and more Earth females registered.

After a while, the overwhelming response meant that for every twenty thousand Earth women registered, only one would actually be called to Oath. Most would go on to fall in love with a man on Earth. When she married, or reached age thirty, her name would be removed from the register with thanks from her government for her willingness to serve.

Sharon sighed. Breaking Oath wasn't really an option. She had made a promise to her world, and for that matter, to his world. She might be a lot of things, but she wasn't the kind of person to break her word.

Kate's eyes were soft with sympathy and worry. "What are you going to do?"

"Make the best of it, I guess. Take the oath. Go with him to Shimeria. It's only three weeks, right? And he's not a total troll either. So I'll get to know him. Then, I'll come home and file incompatible. My life is here. Maybe my job isn't the greatest.

Maybe my little life isn't the most exciting. But it's *mine*. I'm not giving it up and moving off planet for some guy." She was going for defiant, but her words came out shaky instead.

Kate knew that was her cue to lighten things up. "Not a total troll, huh? Now there's an understatement. That man is *hot*. You'll be doing your duty *and* getting great sex. At least I assume it'll be great if he's as good as he looks!"

"Exactly." Sharon began to smile a little as her sense of humor rose to the surface. "Besides, a little interplanetary nookie won't kill me. They're basically humanoid. Their society is very similar to ours, just a little more advanced. It's pretty male-dominated, but I guess I can live with that for a few weeks. I don't know about the telepathy thing but I don't think they can read minds all the time or anything. I guess I'll find out..."

Determined to keep smiling and make the best of it, she headed toward the Pactmaker. "Come on," she called to Kate. "Might as well get it over with. We wouldn't want Mr. Tall, Dark, and Arrogant to get his drawers in a twist."

Laughing at that image, the two women headed to the other side of the room. Shimerian male heads turned at the sound. Watching the two beautiful women appreciatively, hearing their laughter, many of them felt a little envious of Liken. Liken, on the other hand, was feeling too eager for the ceremony to pay much attention. His brother Tair, sensing that eagerness, had to laugh.

He said mockingly, "You should have claimed her a year ago, Liken. Then maybe you would not be so impatient today."

Liken shook his head. "You know I was giving her time. She will be making a lot of changes. Best that she grew restless with her own life before facing Shimerian marriage. It will be difficult for her."

Liken thought of his cautious little librarian's reaction to his culture and mentally grimaced. She would not react well. There were good reasons for keeping Shimerian ways a secret from prospective mates.

"You are sure that she has no idea of the merging and linking? We are taught to be careful, but there have been some rumors on Earth from time to time." Tair had heard some pretty outrageous things, although some of them had some truth to them.

"No, I do not think so. She seems afraid of me in an emotional and physical sense, but I have not brushed her mind with mine yet. Except for my initial recognition a year ago. My mind touched hers then, but only briefly."

Tair shook his head at the thought of what his brother would need to explain. Humans, especially females, could react very strangely to the oddest things. His voice was dry. "Just be sure to secure her. It is quite convenient that my pactmate is her best friend. I think Kate will be much more amiable when I invoke the Oath if she knows Sharon is happy."

"So, I am to ease your way?" Liken said with a half-smile. He nearly snorted at the thought. Kate would challenge Tair at every turn. She was perfect for him. "I believe your knowing period will not be that simple. The look she sent me earlier could have felled me. I do not think your pactmate is the sweet, gentle type."

Tair's dark eyes gleamed with laughter. "Now what would I do with sweet and gentle?"

Suddenly, the Pactmaker, a rather small man dressed in his ceremonial robes of black and white stepped forward to address those gathered. "Will Liken da'Kamon and Sharon Glaston please step forward to take the Oath?" There was a murmur throughout the room at the sound of his words.

Most of the Shimerian males present were single and waiting anxiously to make arrangements for invoking their own oaths. They were lined along the wall waiting for their turn with the official Pactmaker representatives. All were dressed casually in different colors and styles of pants, shirts, and boots, but one thing was common to each and every one. There was a palpable sense of impatience and sheer male power exuding from each of the males. They were eager to conclude their business, but they were curious about the oath ceremony. For many of them, this ceremony would be the first one they had seen. Coming so close to their own pactmaking arrangements, the ceremony gained a certain significance.

Liken strode to where the Pactmaker waited. Sharon took the last steps remaining between them and came to stand at his side. Tair stood in the background to Liken's left, while Kate waited on Sharon's right. Tair's gaze met Kate's fuming gaze for one long moment before they turned to watch the other couple.

The next twenty minutes of the ceremony were a blur. Sharon heard the droning voice of the Pactmaker and responded whenever prompted. The actual words seemed to be coming from a great distance and she couldn't really grasp the meanings. The only thing she could hear clearly was the pounding of her own heart, which seemed to be coming out of her chest.

She kept her gaze on the Pactmaker and kept repeating to herself silently, "Liken, his name is Liken. I'm gonna have sex with the guy, so I should try to remember his name. He's an alien. I wonder if sex is the same? I'm not gonna get hysterical. I can do this. I have to do this. It's no big deal. It will be fine. I can do this..." Sharon hoped that if she repeated the words over and over again, she might convince herself that she was doing the right thing.

She could feel the heat of Liken's tall presence standing strong and still beside her. Only once did his big body grow stiff with tension. The Pactmaker repeated the words, "Your choice, my dear. You need to state it clearly...which oath do you choose, Seduction, Challenge or Capture?" The room was silent as everyone present waited for her reply.

She took a deep breath. Her mind spun with confusion like a top. What should she do? What could she do? She said in a quaking voice that was nearly inaudible, "Seduction." She felt ridiculous and mortified to even say the word. Feeling the tension leave him, she hoped it was the right choice. Putting some strength into her voice, she said more firmly, "I choose Seduction."

Sharon heard Liken state the rest of his vow in a strong, masculine voice. She knew he was speaking English, but she couldn't seem to absorb what he was saying. She felt disconnected from the entire scene.

Finally, the ceremony was complete. Liken held out his hand and said her name softly, then a little louder. "Sharon..."

Sharon suddenly realized he was waiting for her to put her hand in his. Trembling, she reached out. The hand that caught hers was warm and strong. She nearly shuddered at the contact. It felt good and scary at the same time. As his thumb caressed the softness of her hand in a soothing motion, she realized her own hand was trembling.

He gave her hand a gentle tug, making her raise her gaze to his face for the first time since the ceremony began. His smile was both satisfied and teasing. "You will be fine. You can do this...a little interplanetary nookie won't kill you..."

Sharon gasped softly as she heard him repeat her earlier words. "You were spying on us!" She felt angry and embarrassed. Her mind worked frantically, trying to remember what else she and Kate had said earlier.

With relief he watched the color come back into her face. She had gone pale and trembling during the ceremony, but anger was bringing her back to life. "Shimerian hearing is exceptional, *sherree* . Something you might want to remember in the future. We have all kinds of interesting qualities I'm sure you'll enjoy."

His smile broadened. "It's time to go to the portal. Say your farewell to your friend." He gently turned her in the direction of Kate and shook hands with the Pactmaker. Accepting the congratulations of the gathered males, he kept an eye on Sharon.

Sharon walked the few feet to Kate, who had angry tears in her eyes. She hated to see Kate so upset when there was nothing either of them could do to change things. She tried for a light tone. "It's only a few weeks right? I'll be coming back to file the papers and then it will be over. Life will be just the same as it was." Even she could hear the doubt in her voice.

Kate agreed immediately, a little desperately. "That's right. I'll meet you here when you get back. You'll be fine. We'll go to O'Tooles and have a little celebration. Get silly and drunk. Dance and make fools of ourselves." Thoughts of all the terrible things that could happen to Sharon were running through her mind, but she knew it wouldn't help Sharon to hear them. Sharon needed to believe it would be okay.

Sharon rallied. "I can tell you what it's like to sleep with the stud of the universe."

Kate gave a weak laugh. "Sleep? I don't see you getting much sleep." They smiled at each other. Hugging her close, Kate whispered in her ear. "Give him hell. Make him treat you right. If he doesn't, we'll both kick his ass."

Kate felt a touch on her shoulder. Startled, she looked back to find the Shimerian male who had made her so nervous earlier. He was even more gorgeous at close range. "What?" Her tone was hostile.

His grin only widened. "She will be fine. My brother will be good to her. They will be good together."

Her chin went up higher. "Yes, she will be fine. Because if she isn't, your brother will be sorry. You'll both be sorry. I'm a lawyer. I'm not threatening to sue you. I'm telling you my profession so you'll understand what a mean bitch I can be. I don't worry about playing fair. I just win. You understand?"

She looked ready to attack him physically if her friend came to any injury. His dark eyes gleamed with appreciation and some secret amusement. "I understand more than you think, *sheka* . And I look forward to playing with you." With those easy words, he turned and walked away.

Kate could only stare at him as his statements registered. He wasn't a bit intimidated by her. She wasn't used to that kind of reaction when she went into her "dangerous bitch mode." It was very effective, especially with men.

Sharon laughed. She couldn't help it. "I can't believe it...you threatened him and he seemed to enjoy it." Genuine amusement drained away a lot of her tension.

Kate made a small sound of disbelief. "I hate him." Shaking off all thoughts of the intergalactic jerk, she hugged Sharon one last time, hard. "Take care of yourself. I'll see you soon." Then, before she could get too emotional, she turned and walked out of the room.

Sharon watched Kate until she disappeared. Her heart sank as she realized that her final link to Earth had just walked out that door.

Chapter Two

Feeling lost and alone, Sharon looked around the pactroom. Liken was heading toward her, accepting congratulations as he went. Reaching her, he grabbed her hand again and started pulling her across the room toward the exit. She struggled to keep up with his long strides as they finally reached the hallway. Taking a quick right and then a left, he pulled her into a deserted office and backed her up against the wall.

Startled, she gasped, pulling her hand from his. Bringing both hands up against his chest, she pushed against him as he crowded her. He wasn't actually touching her, but there were only inches separating them.

Taking her chin, he raised her face so that their gaze met. "I cannot wait any longer." There was urgency in his voice and something suspiciously like need.

Sharon, feeling a wave of pure panic, choked out, "Don't!"

"It is my right..." Bringing both hands to cradle her face gently, but firmly, he lowered his mouth toward hers.

She expected a hard, devouring kiss. Instead, he played teasingly with her lips, lightly touching then withdrawing, then touching again. Her lips tingled and she felt like all the air was being drawn from her lungs. He kissed one corner, softly touching it with his tongue, then licked outward along the rest of her mouth. The soft wetness of his tongue, the gentle firmness of his lips made her feel restless, unsatisfied. She felt helpless under the gentle assault. His tongue kept inching closer along the seam of her mouth, seeking entrance.

"Open for me, *sherree* . Let me taste you..." His voice was sinfully soft and beguiling, as he continued luring her.

She could feel her lips parting with a sigh. He took immediate advantage, breaching her lips gently and then finding her tongue with his own. With that discovery, he ran his tongue along hers, penetrating her, mimicking the act both their bodies craved. He continued to thrust gently until her tongue began to parry. With her response, the kiss changed entirely.

Like a match thrown on gasoline, his body moved forward into hers. The hands on her face moved down to her shoulders and then slid around her body between her and the wall. He stroked her like a cat and then used those hands to pull her forward against the muscular length of his body.

Her nipples tightened. She felt the moistness between her legs. He felt so good against her. Every inch of him was hard. Cradling his erection between her thighs, she rubbed and felt a burst of pleasure. With a moan, she started to press herself even closer. With a moan of his own, he pushed his hips forward, pressing upwards hard and then teasingly easing back.

Then, she felt something else entirely. Like the tickling of a feather, his mind brushed softly against hers. The realization stunned her. Before she could react, the touch grew firmer. His mind was pressing against hers like their bodies were pressed against each other. She froze, every muscle locking up. Her hands, which had somehow been clinging to his shoulders like a lifeline, squeezed hard in protest. Pushing her head back against the wall, she said tightly, "Let me go. Now!"

Liken searched her face as he tried to bring his breathing under control. God, she was beautiful. She felt like pure pleasure under his hands. Every cell in his body ached to disregard her words and take her. His cock was hard, throbbing. Calling on all his discipline, he reminded himself that she was essentially a virgin when it came to Shimerian ways. Purposefully gentling his hands, he rubbed her back as he moved his hands up to her shoulders. He would have her soon, but he had to proceed with care.

"You are right, Sharon. We need to get to the portal. There will be time enough for such pleasures later." He could barely wait as images of the coming pleasure flashed through his mind.

Sharon blinked as if coming out of a daze. He looked hungry enough to forget about waiting and just take her, rules or no rules. Her cheeks began to burn with color and she said, "We are not doing this again. I don't know you. I'm not sure I even like you.

You can't just kiss me whenever you want. We need to set some guidelines here..." Her words faltered as his face grew harsh.

"You would go back on your oath?" He felt angry that she was threatening it when he knew she would do no such thing.

Sharon was surprised at his vehemence. "No, no I didn't say that," she said quickly. "I just need some time to get used to things, okay? I went to work at the library this morning. This afternoon, I took an Oath I had nearly forgotten about and didn't really expect to have to do. You yanked me out of the room and started kissing me. We need to slow down here..."

Liken shook his head. "There is no slowing down, only moving forward from here. Any intimacy we have shared can be repeated at your will or mine. I can take further intimacies at prescribed times in the days to come, but never forget: once you allow something, I can do it again at my choosing."

Her eyes looked angry. "Gee, thanks for the patience and understanding, big guy."

His voice gentled. "I can be patient and understanding, *sherree* . But I am also a demanding person. That cannot be helped. How can you expect to share such pleasure with me, and then ask me to forego it? I am merely being honest with you."

Sharon shook her head. "Whatever. Let's just get to the portal. I'm tired of being surprised and confused. Of not knowing what to expect from one moment to the next. I hate surprises. I hate this. Let's just go and get this over with."

Liken leaned down and placed a hard kiss against her mouth. It was over with before she could object. Taking her hand again in his, he strode out of the room and down the hallway. As they approached the lobby of the massive building, Sharon saw a sign indicating the portal for Shimeria was down two flights of stairs and to the left.

As they walked, she realized suddenly that all she had were the clothes she was wearing. She wasn't exactly prepared for interplanetary travel. She tried to slow her steps as she asked Liken, "What about my clothes, my things? I didn't even think about leaving right after the Oath."

Liken kept them moving forward as he said, "All has been prepared. I've known about you for a year, Sharon. You have all you need at my dwelling."

"Ohhh. Okay. Sure." She couldn't seem to focus. She wondered if her system had sustained too many shocks for one day. The pact reps, the oath, him, his kisses, his touch...

She needed to focus her thoughts and think about this whole thing in a more orderly, logical fashion.

As they walked, she considered what had happened in the deserted office minutes ago, trying to be more objective. It had been exciting. He had been forceful, but gentle. Things might not be so bad. That mind thing was weird, but he had stopped immediately. He might be predatory in some ways, but he had backed off when she asked.

She sighed unconsciously. There was nothing she could do to change things. Logically, it was childish and unproductive to sulk or fight with him constantly. She would do as she had told Kate. Make the best of it.

With a conciliatory smile, she told him, "I'm sorry. I don't know or remember much about Shimeria and its customs. The one class I had was years..." She stopped as what he said suddenly hit her. "A year? What do you mean you've known about me for a year?"

They had reached the portal and this was one discussion he hoped to avoid for a time. He used the distraction of the busy room as an excuse to not answer. There were Shimerians streaming through one portal on the right. They were showing ID cards to customs officers as they passed.

Sharon and Liken approached their own checkpoint for customs. Liken turned and handed her a Shimerian ID card. It had her name on it. She studied it in silence. Obviously, he really had made preparations for her. As Liken handed the officer his ID card and responded to his questions, Sharon waited impatiently. She wasn't going to drop this discussion.

The customs officer handed Liken back his card and then asked for hers. With a bureaucratic look of apathy that was recognizable on any planet, he glanced at her card and then handed it back. With a disinterested smile, he waved them forward. Sharon went a few more steps and then halted in awe.

She had been so focused on Liken that she had not noticed her surroundings. She gulped as she took in the two portals for the first time. She had never traveled off planet or seen one of the portals. Each portal structure was at least two stories tall. Made like an oval gate, the metal was unrecognizable. There were lever-like devices to the side that appeared to operate the opening and closing of the gate. Inside the open gate, was dense, flat blackness.

It would be like stepping into nothingness. She watched the other portal as Shimerians coming to Earth stepped through unharmed. They didn't appear to be missing any appendages.

Liken, remembering his awe and momentary fear when seeing the portal the first time, waited for her to begin walking again. In this situation at least, he would give her time.

Reminding herself logically that Liken had obviously survived it, she started walking. At the edge of the portal he stopped and looked down at her. "Sharon, we cannot go at the same time. Unpledged females such as yourself must arrive on Shimeria alone to signify you are coming of your own free will. I will go first. Once I disappear, step through."

She pulled her gaze away from the portal to look up at him. "You trust me to step through after you?" she said with some surprise.

"Of course," he said with a smile. "You have courage and will not break your oath. Besides, my mind brushed yours. I have some sense of what you feel. You have been through much today, but you are curious, too. I will be waiting on the other side, *sherree*. Once there, I will satisfy your curiosity. I will satisfy you in any way you desire." With a wink and a quick kiss, he stepped through. With one step, he was gone and Sharon was left staring into the dense blackness of the portal.

For about ten seconds, she considered proving him wrong. With a sigh, and a muttered "I *desire* to stay here, Mr. Tall, Dark, and Know-It-All" under her breath, she stepped through.

She had made her choice. What the hell.

Chapter Three

For a moment, time stood still. Sharon felt a numbing blackness pressing in all around her. Her lungs seized; she couldn't breath. Her body felt as if she was falling, but she couldn't see or hear anything. Then, before true panic could take hold, light blinded her and she felt air rush into her lungs.

She was standing on the other side of the gate. Liken quickly gathered her close, whispering softly, "Well done, *sherree*. The disorientation will pass in just a second. It is a little overwhelming at first. Just concentrate on your breathing. In, out, deep breaths…"

Sharon looked up at him and said, "I…don't…like…portals. I've just…decided." She gave him a weak smile. "That sucked." His arms felt warm and the weight of them around her felt comforting.

He laughed. "You will be fine." Gesturing with one arm to the room around them, he said more seriously, "Welcome to my world, Sharon." His voice was quiet, rather solemn.

Sharon looked around her. She didn't really know what she expected, but the room around her looked pretty much like the room they had just left. Even the bored customs officer looked the same, only his sheer size and that vague power the Shimerians seemed to have in common gave him away. He was gesturing with one arm for her to proceed. His voice carried strained politeness, although the undertone of impatience was clear. "Progress forward, *Isshal* . More passengers await."

Sharon's mouth dropped open. What an insulting planet! She heard herself say with quiet dignity, "No problem, asshole."

Liken gave a choked laugh. "He did not call you an asshole. You insult him, *sherree*. He was merely addressing you formally. *Isshal* is the Shimerian equivalent of ma'am."

The transport officer was looking at her with a combination of anger and shock. His face had gone red.

Sharon felt her own color rise along with her embarrassment. "I'm so sorry. Really. I'm new here and I thought..."

Liken laughed and said, "It is okay, Sharon. Let us move along."

She let him pull her through the room. She definitely wasn't on Earth anymore, no matter how familiar everything looked. Of course, she had expected something totally different for her first experience of another planet. Feeling somewhat disappointed, she followed Liken up two flights of stairs and into a large lobby area.

Liken, sensing her disappointment, said, "It is a way to help with the disorientation. Making both buildings look essentially the same makes the drama of the voyage a little more mundane. It is supposed to be calming. Being on a new world for the first time can be somewhat overwhelming. If you will notice, the signs in this building are in various languages. The top is Shimerian, but underneath are several Earth languages as well as other planetary tongues. There are differences here, but after the shock of the trip, it is best absorbed slowly."

Understanding the common sense of his remarks, Sharon remained silent as they walked through the lobby. There were no windows, just the bland walls of an office building, although they looked pink. She knew other people had to have left the building before them, but she couldn't see any exit doors. She let Liken guide her toward one of the walls. As they moved, she thought to ask, "What time is it here?" It had been late afternoon when they left Earth.

"It is early moonstime. Ahhh, I believe about eight o'clock in the evening, by your time. I should probably remind you that Shimerian moonslight is different." Liken pushed a large button on the wall. She watched in amazement as part of the wall opened and slid inside itself.

"Different how..." The words had no sooner left her mouth than she could tell he had opened a sliding door. Outside the building was a city street, similar to the streets where they had left. There were no vehicles or modes of transportation visible.

There were offices made of rocklike material similar to brick, but they were glowing in the moonlight. The light was pure silver. Looking up, she saw two large silvery moons overhead right next to each other.

Liken saw where she was looking in the evening sky. "Those are Tilus and Noman," he explained.

Stepping out into the light, she noticed her skin glimmering as if she had been dusted in mother of pearl. It was strange. Liken's skin remained the same color. "Why am I shiny?" It was bizarre, but kind of neat.

He said, "I do not know. I am sure there is a scientific reason, but all humans experience the same thing in moonlight. It is very attractive. Some Shimerian women even try to emulate it by applying glittering powder. It never looks the same." He could feel his body harden at the sight of her glowing in the moonlight. She looked delicate and beautiful.

"So, there are native Shimerian women here?" she asked. She had seen women travelers paired with some of the Shimerian men back in the portal room. The women had the same dark hair and intense charisma of their male counterparts.

"Yes, but very few." He sounded a little sad. Then, his mouth lifted in a smile, "Of course, if there were more, I might never have met you, *sherree*."

Visions of him kissing another woman as he had kissed her in the empty office came to mind. She didn't like the thought. She didn't like the feeling of jealousy that accompanied it, either. Resolutely pushing those thoughts aside, she asked, "How do we get to your home?"

Liken watched the changing expressions on her face. That brief flash of jealousy pleased him immensely. His little librarian was feeling possessive already. Things were progressing nicely. Not wanting her to guess at his happiness, he pointed to a sign that read " *shimvehi* ." There was a staircase leading downward next to it. "It is like your subway. We will be using it to get to *our* home, Sharon."

Shrugging her shoulders, she followed him down the staircase. Each step seemed to be difficult. Feeling strangely lethargic, she wondered about interplanetary jetlag. At the bottom of the stairs, there was something resembling a subway train. People, some native Shimerian, some obviously from other planets, were gathering in lines to get into what looked like subway cars. The individual cars had seats like benches inside where people sat.

There were no lone, unescorted females, although she did notice some women together in groups of two or three. The women were all dressed in outfits similar to the one she was wearing, although the colors were different. Some of the blouses were halter-tops and some of the skirts were much shorter. There were some women who looked like they were probably human, although she was having more and more trouble focusing on her surroundings. Fatigue was weighing down her body more with each step.

The cars formed a train that was pointed toward the gateway of a portal. Noting each side of the room had a portal, she assumed one was for coming and one for going. Looking at the portal the train was facing, she noticed it was smaller than the one back at the pactbuilding, but the eerie darkness was the same.

"Train ride to oblivion," she muttered to herself. "Great, just what I wanted, another portal to travel." Already exhausted, she wasn't looking forward to another trip through that blackness. As they entered the *shimvehi* and took their seats on a bench-like area, she found herself slumping.

Feeling her weight sagging against him, Liken put his arm around her and drew her close to his chest. "*Sherree*, you are crashing. Your body is adjusting to this planet's gravity and atmosphere. Your first trip through the interplanetary portal adds more stress. This portal merely takes us to a different city. Do not worry. Just relax. We will be home soon. You will sleep many hours. It is to be expected."

Before he finished the last word, he saw that she was sound asleep. Feeling her soft weight against him, he sighed. Finally, she was here.

Touching her hair with a soothing motion, he felt the *shimvehi* start to move. As his mind filled with images of the pleasures they would bring each other, he smiled.

Seduction had never promised to be so sweet.

Chapter Four

Where the hell was she?

Sharon looked at her surroundings and found nothing familiar. This wasn't her bed. This wasn't even her bedroom. Coming fully awake, she assessed the situation. She was lying in some sort of bed, although it was huge. The covers were quite soft but she couldn't place the material. It had the comfortable feel of cotton, but felt soft as silk. The walls were a light blue color. There were no windows and no doorway.

Was this a prison? If so, it was a comfortable one. There were pictures of strangely alien, but beautiful landscapes on three of the walls...

Alien.

With that thought, the events of the previous day came back to her. Startled, she sat up. Realizing she was stark naked, she immediately yanked the covers up around her. Oh, boy. Today was the first day of the rest of this farce.

Feeling energized, she looked around for some kind of clothing to put on. Her clothes had better be close by. As the wall slid open and Liken walked through, she had the mortifying realization that he must have undressed her. Oath or no oath, she didn't appreciate it.

Liken entered the room to discover Sharon sitting up in bed, bedclothes barely covering that naked body, cheeks rosy, eyes shining with outrage. In an instant, he was hard. He wanted to climb onto the bed and make her beg. Voice gruff, he asked, "How are you feeling, *sherree*?"

It was hard to be angry and maintain your dignity while stark naked under the thin cover of bedsheets. "Fine. Where are my clothes?"

"You will find garments in there," he replied with cautious gravity, although his amusement leaked through. She was shy, but he would change that inhibition. If he had his way, she would spend the rest of her knowing period naked and eager for him.

Sharon noticed the large bulge in the front of his pants. She knew if she didn't hurry, he would be joining her on the bed. Following his pointed finger, she saw a button off to the right. She assumed it opened a closet. "I'll meet you in a minute after I'm dressed." Her stomach growled.

Liken could hear the soft noise from the doorway. He smiled. "We will eat and then I will show you our home." He headed back out of the room. At the last second, he paused and turned back to her. "Regardless of what you choose to wear, *sherree*, you could not look more beautiful than at this moment." With that, he walked away and the wall slid shut behind him.

He was charming; she'd give him that. Smooth. She had the feeling that the charm was only one layer, though. Underneath it, she sensed a hard resolve. His desire was obvious and barely held in check. He would try to get something by charm, but if charm didn't work? She shivered a little at the thought.

Carefully crossing the room with a sheet wrapped around her, she pushed the button on the wall and watched as it slid open. It was a closet, just as she had thought.

She examined the clothes hanging there. There were numerous blouses and skirts. All were quite beautiful. They were made of a thin, silky material in different hues of colors. Some colors were like nothing she had seen on Earth. Blues and greens were more vibrant. The silver was especially lovely. There were even tiny panties with string ties. Looking everywhere, she couldn't find any bras. Just great. That silky material was going to outline everything.

Resigned, she selected a blouse and skirt of shimmering silver with tiny panties of the same color. There were strappy sandals to match. Putting everything on, she looked down at herself. The thin fabric of the blouse outlined the thrust of her nipples. The skirt was loose but hit just above the knee. Reluctantly, she wandered out into the hall.

Seeing a button on her right in the hall, she pushed it to reveal what was obviously a bathroom. It had a recognizable toilet, which she used gratefully. Seeing a stall to the side, she opened that door and discovered a shower with one handle. Feeling grubby, she decided to give it a shot. Removing her clothes and shoes, she set them on the floor and then turned the knob.

She was expecting water. She gave a little yelp of surprise as bright red liquid flooded from the nozzle high up on the wall. She reached out with one cautious hand and touched it. The temperature was hot, but not overly so. It felt more slippery than water, a little heavier. Weighing her grubbiness against the unknown, she decided to try it.

Stepping under the pouring liquid, she was surprised to discover it was like quicksilver. She hoped she didn't get dyed lobster red. The liquid poured over her skin, but when she stepped out, she was nearly dry. Grateful her skin hadn't turned the same hideous color, she put her clothes back on. Walking out into the hall, she kept going until she spotted open archways to the right and left. She could hear movement in the room to the right and turned toward it.

Entering the kitchen, she was surprised at the similarities to Earth kitchens. There was a long counter running along one side of the room. There were cabinets above it, although they had buttons she assumed would open each one. One wall was completely bare except for what looked like a small computer panel. It had a lot of buttons that presumably opened the wall or provided food transport maybe.

There was a mural carving of some kind on one wall that showed a waterfall. It was quite beautiful. In the center of the room, was a square table with four chairs. They could have come from any Earth kitchen. She was surprised to see that the table was already set. There were two settings, one on each side of the table. She saw plates and cups along with napkins, but no eating utensils.

In the center of the table sat a couple of bowls filled with oddly shaped fruits or vegetables, she guessed. There were some oblong dark green things, small orange shiny things that looked like berries, some larger purple things that were lumpy-looking, and even some bright yellow things that were almost square. She figured her first experience of exotic cuisine was about to start. Oh joy.

Liken set the last bowl onto the table and turned to smile at her. "Please do not assume I can cook. I am a guardian by profession. This is merely fruit." He moved and held out a chair for her to sit.

Pleased with his manners, she took it, watching as he sat down opposite her. "A guardian? What does that mean?"

Casually gathering an assortment from the various bowls, he began to put things on her plate. "A guardian is similar to your police officer. What do you call them? Cops? We protect those in need and prevent loss of life and property," Liken responded easily. It was nice to know that she was curious about him and his work.

Staring at him, she could see it. He did look like a cop. He could be gentle, but that underlying ruthlessness was there, too. "So, are you going to work today?" she asked hopefully. She shifted uncomfortably as she saw his gaze wander over her in appreciation. This outfit was no protection. She wanted as much distance between him and her tiny panties as possible. He couldn't seduce her if he wasn't around.

Looking amused, he shook his head. "I would not get assigned during my knowing period. I do not report back until after we have pledged." Breaking open a light purple fruit, he handed her half.

Eyeing it skeptically, but willing, she took a small, cautious bite. The sweetness burst in her mouth and she smiled with pleasure. She relaxed and continued to sample the different fruits. Making a face at the sour taste of the yellow one, she made a note to avoid it in the future. Very casually she said, "Yeah, I guess they've taken care of my job, too. I'm a librarian. After the noncomp papers are filed, I'll probably have a ton of stuff to catch up on." She waited for his reaction.

He had been eating his way through the fruit on his plate while she spoke. He paused. His face was still amused, but reproving. "There will be no noncomp papers, *sherree*." Reaching across the table, he took her chin in his hands, gently. Using his thumb to wipe the juice from her lips, he brought it slowly to his mouth. "We are very compatible. You will understand this quite soon."

Feeling the trail of heat left behind by his thumb, she swallowed the piece of fruit. She watched as he licked the juice from his thumb with sensual pleasure.

Her appetite for the fruit died and she looked away. Visibly gathering her composure, she tried reason. "Look, it doesn't have anything to do with you, okay? I like Earth. I have friends. I don't want to be a planet away from them. I have a job, an apartment, and responsibilities. A life. Mine. I've heard about this place. I don't remember much, but I do know that there are no unattached females over twenty. It's very male-dominated. Very old-style warrior mentality. I'm too independent to suit you or this place. I need different things. Trust me." She didn't hear the unconscious plea that had crept into her voice.

Liken studied her face during her oh-so-reasonable speech. Her eyes were sincere. She honestly believed she could not be happy here. "Maybe I can change your mind about what you need, *sherree*. Maybe I should start now." Rising, he came around the table and squatted next to her.

In alarm, she moved back against the seat as far as she could. "I didn't mean… Don't start messing with me again, okay?"

He smiled and raised his hand to her cheek. "Give me your mouth, *sherree*."

She shook her head and pressed into the cushion behind her.

Grabbing her hand, he pulled her slowly from her seat. "It is time. Come with me." Tugging her along behind him, he kept going until they reached the hallway and passed through the other archway into a living area. There were chairs and a couch along with a lot of buttons on the walls.

Gesturing her toward the long cushioned furniture, he went to a square structure coming out of one wall. Pulling out a drawer, he walked back across the room and handed her a small hand-held device, like a personal computer. It had a small screen at the top.

She moved closer to one side as he sat down beside her. "What's this?" She felt crowded by the weight and heat of his big body beside her. Even the big couch seemed too small for the two of them. She was overwhelmingly aware of him.

His eyes danced as she shifted further away from him, but he answered her seriously. "The Pactmaker has supplied your records to me. It is only fair that I do the same. These are my medical tests. I am completely healthy. I have been given my suppression shot this month, so pregnancy should not be a concern for you either. There are payment records from my employer, too, showing my ability to provide. There are statements from friends and family detailing my character. These are all records to let you know you are safe with me. That I am, what do humans usually say? A good guy."

"A prospective mate resume," she muttered. She knew the Pactmakers checked out everyone. Barely looking at the device, she put it aside. "Okay, I understand. You're wonderful. I'm sure you're kind to small kids and animals. But that doesn't mean I'm ready to just jump into bed with you. All these people know you, but I don't know you."

"You will." Moving the device from her side to the floor, he scooted over and leaned toward her. His eyes, those bright blue piercing eyes, were suddenly burning. "You chose Seduction. That means you will follow the rules of courtship according to that choice. We need to understand one another, *sherree*. Yesterday we kissed, mouth-to-mouth, tongue-to-tongue. Today we will do more of that. But today, you will allow me to run my hands over your body, to learn each curve. I will not remove your clothing."

His voice, which had turned husky, became firmer and more determined. "But, *sherree*, hear me well. I will do my best to take things as far as possible. I want you. I want to rock inside you and feel your sweet walls gripping me. I want to taste every inch of you, know what makes you tremble, what makes you wet."

A shiver went through Sharon followed by a wave of heat. He was seducing her with words, with mental images. It was brutal in its effectiveness. Licking her suddenly dry lips, she tried to form some response, but his gaze dropped to her lips and the words died in her throat. Her body was stiff with tension.

Reaching out one hand, he began running it along the edge of her blouse. Goosebumps followed in the wake of his fingers. His mouth was close to her ear as he said, "This garment is so thin. Already your breasts swell and your nipples harden. They ache for my touch, don't they? For my hands. For my mouth."

The moist warmth of his breath teased her ear as he leaned further down and began placing kisses along her throat. He continued kissing and talking as he worked his way down. "I would like to run my tongue around your nipples. I would play with them; make them ache for the sweet pressure of my mouth. Can you imagine how it will feel when I finally suck on them?" The mental picture of his mouth sucking on her breast nearly scalded her.

Kissing his way back up to her chin, his mouth moved to the corner of hers. As his hands moved from her neckline to the upper swells of her breasts, he whispered, "Easy..." She wasn't sure if he was talking to her or himself.

Sharon felt like she couldn't get enough air. His words and his touch were too much. She felt her chest rising and falling rapidly under his hands. She began to tremble as the excitement rushed through her. Already, she was growing wet, hot.

Running his tongue along her lips, he said, "Let me in."

Her trembling lips parted under firm pressure from his. The kiss was growing harder, hotter. Slanting his head, he took her deeper, thrusting along her tongue, running his tongue teasingly along her teeth and the inner edges of her lips. Then returning back inside, to stroke.

Her eyes closed and the muscles in her legs went lax. She began to duel with him, meeting each thrust with her own tongue, feeling the wet slide and unconsciously asking for more. With a moan, he gave her more.

Sharon felt one of his hands move down to her breast. He avoided the hard nipple, merely gripping lightly across the upper swell and then sliding around the side until he held her from underneath. As he began to shape her breast, kneading and pressing, she moaned and opened her mouth even wider. Their mouths met in a sexual feast.

She hardly noticed that her body had slipped downwards toward the arm of the couch. If she had looked down his body at that moment she might have seen the huge bulge of his aroused cock. But all she could feel or see was his mouth, his hands. She was drowning in a sea of sensation.

Lifting his mouth a fraction, he said softly, "I am going to touch those hard nipples now. You are aching for it, are you not?"

Sharon's answer was weak but understood. "Yes..."

Lifting his lips away from hers completely, he looked at her. Her mouth was swollen and wet. She opened her eyes. Those beautiful *mer* green eyes were dazed, the pupils dilated. Looking down, he saw the hard points of her nipples against the fabric. Bringing both his hands up, he covered her swollen breasts with them and felt those stiff nipples stabbing into his palms.

His cock, already hard, throbbed in time with his heartbeat. She was so responsive. He wanted to thrust inside her wet heat, to feel her close around his aching cock. He clung to his control.

Sharon gave a little cry as his hands finally covered her breasts. The contact of his palm against her nipples gave a little relief to her aching tips, but it was short lived. The ache continued to build. When he used his fingers and began playing with those twin points, she involuntarily arched her back, wanting more.

Twisting, lightly tugging, he played. Rough and gentle, by turns, his touch kept her surprised and restless. Looking into his face, she saw masculine satisfaction and hunger. For her. That look drew her almost as much as his touch.

As one of his hands began drifting downward onto her stomach, she felt that light brushing sensation in her mind again. Like the feel of his tongue lightly teasing her mouth before entrance, his mind touched hers, tempted. When she felt the brush again, she stiffened and said, "Wait!"

Lifting his hungry gaze to her again, he said, "No, *sherree*, I am within my rights." His hand continued over her stomach. Her legs tightened and she frantically drew them together in protest.

With a sigh, he placed a gentle kiss on her mouth. The hand and fingers at her breast never faltered, but the hand heading south paused. "Spread your legs for me now, Sharon. You have no choice in this. You chose yesterday when you took the Oath."

Her hands, hanging limply at her sides until now, came up in defense, grabbing the top of his. "I don't want this," she said desperately.

The hand under hers grabbed and then took her arms over her head. With one hand, he kept her pinned. She strained to get her hands free, but he was too strong. The hand at her breast began to move downward.

He said, a little less patiently, "That is a lie. Already your wetness shows through on the cloth. You made a vow, Sharon. Honor it or I will assume my vow to go in courtship stages is broken as well. Spread your legs for me," he demanded.

Sharon's heart was pounding in her ears. He was right. She did want him. She was throbbing, swollen and wet between her legs. She knew he meant what he said. Anger and passion were mixing inside her, making her arousal confusingly intense. She relaxed her legs, and with a look of resentment at his high-handedness, she slowly opened them.

His eyes were hard as they stared down into hers. "Wider."

She opened her legs wider and waited in trembling silence for his touch. When it finally came, she nearly arched off the couch. He ran his palm lightly over her mound. Just as he said, her wetness had soaked through the material making her feel as if it was skin on skin contact.

Looking into her eyes, he ran one finger along her lips, pausing briefly to tease her clitoris, then followed the line down to her opening. As that finger circled her opening, his thumb came back up to tease her clit with tiny strokes again and again. She arched up into his hand, but he merely continued the teasing pressure through the cloth.

She was burning up, wet and shaking. She'd felt passion before, but this kind of need was extreme and frightening. He seemed to know just where to touch and how. As he played and toyed with her, she grew wetter. The ache was intense. She needed more.

The slippery sounds of his fingers playing with her sweet sex pleased him. He made a little hum of approval in his throat. Her lower body was arched upwards in need. Her hips were unconsciously moving in an age-old rhythm against his hand. The temptation of her stiff nipples beckoned. Bending his head down, he found one hard nipple through the slippery material, took it into his mouth, and sucked.

Sharon heard a groaning sound and realized it had come from her. Her upper body arched, pressing her nipple even harder into the suction of his mouth. He pulled harder and then opened his mouth to lick around the aching tip. She was coming totally unglued. As he switched to the other nipple, laving it with his tongue and gently biting, then sucking, she whimpered and said, "Please…"

The fingers between her legs continued playing ruthlessly. She watched as he lifted his head from her aching breast, looking into her face. His eyes were heady-lidded, his mouth swollen and wet. He touched his tongue to the tip of her nipple and then said, "What do you want, *sherree*? Should I take this material from you and place my mouth on your breast? Or would you like me to touch you here…" one finger probed lightly inside her as far as the thin skirt and even thinner panties would allow, "with nothing to block me from giving you greater pleasure?"

Glancing down past his face to his body, she could see the hard outline of his arousal pressing against his pants. A tiny patch of wetness showed through the material near the top of his erection. Thinking about that hard bulge, she saw it flex against his pants. Just seeing it flex made her imagine his hard cock filling up that swollen, aching emptiness between her legs. She wanted that hard cock pressing inside her, filling her. She wanted him.

"It feels so good," she moaned as his hand continued to stroke. Her hands, still trapped in his large one, pushed against the pressure of his grip, but he held her still. Her very vulnerability excited them both.

The thumb against her clitoris pressed a little harder, then began circling the distended bud, sending bursts of pleasure outward with each touch. The tension in her body stretched tighter. His eyes continued to stare into hers as he watched her climb. "It can feel even better, *sherree*. Give in to it. Give in to me. Let go for me now."

Her hips were rising and falling against the pressure of his hand. She was on the edge, nearly desperate, half-blind with need. She felt her lower body tensing and tightening.

"Come for me, *sherree*. You are so wet. Give yourself to me." With those words, he pressed hard.

Sharon came apart under his hand. She closed her eyes as wave after wave of pleasure went through her. Caught in the grip of her climax, she couldn't do anything, think anything. There was only the pulsing pleasure of her body and the feel of his rough skin against her slick flesh through the cloth.

When she again became aware of herself, she could barely breathe from the overwhelming sensation of release. Her whole body was limp and flushed. She felt drained and shattered. Opening her eyes, she saw his face. He still looked intensely aroused, but mixed with the arousal was approval. He looked pleased.

Suddenly realizing just how wildly she'd been thrashing, how loudly she'd moaned, she felt shy. She tried to look away, but the hand between her legs came up to gently hold her face in place. The light musky scent of her arousal drifted to her from his fingers. She felt her face flush even more.

Liken smiled and placed a gentle kiss on her mouth. The hand holding her arms in place relaxed, and she brought her hands to her sides.

Liken's hungry gaze burned into her. He cleared his throat, his voice emerging husky and deep. "That was so beautiful, *sherree*. You are so beautiful."

She brought her hands to his chest and began scooting a little away from him. Now that her head was clearing, she suddenly wondered if he would push her further. She wanted him, but was afraid he would assume she'd fall in with *all* of his plans if she went further.

She also felt shaky and overwhelmed. She had never experienced anything like what had just occurred. The vulnerability was frightening. She had been pretty out of control.

He had made her that way. Suddenly, she just wanted to get away from him for a while. She wanted to feel back in control. Would he let her go?

Liken knew she wasn't ready for a complete merging. As much as his throbbing cock would have liked her to be, she wasn't ready to continue. Her climax had nearly sent him over, too. He was too close to the edge and she was too inexperienced to proceed.

Sharon held her breath as he seemed to make up his mind. She knew if he truly pressed her, she was too vulnerable to say no. They both knew it.

Bringing his fingers from the side of her face, he brought them to his mouth. He ran his tongue along them slowly, watching her face, savoring the taste of her. Her heart seemed to stop.

He stood up from the couch as if in pain, and slowly moved away from her. A few steps away, he paused and quietly said, "You taste like my happiness." He stared at her a moment longer in silent hunger, then turned and slowly made his way out of the room.

Sharon felt her heart resume beating. Lying on the couch, still reeling, she could only wonder. He made her vulnerable. She had lost control, yet he had been able to walk away. Maybe he cared enough about her to leave unsatisfied. Or maybe he wasn't as vulnerable to her as she was to him. She didn't know.

She only knew that when she left this place, she would want him for the rest of her life. Her body was aching for his touch. Her emotions weren't too far behind. She didn't see a lot of happy endings ahead. Somebody was going to get hurt.

Sitting up and glancing toward the empty doorway she whispered sadly, "That's funny. You taste like heartache to me."

Chapter Five

Sharon retreated to her bedroom and a change of clothes. She wanted to explore the house, but the need to avoid Liken overrode her curiosity. She would be here for weeks. Right now, she concentrated on getting herself together.

From his point of view, she was sure it seemed simple. He could have sex with her for the next three weeks. At the end of that time, he could go to Earth, get pledged to her, then come back home. The next day, he could go to work just as he had before she'd entered his life. He wouldn't be leaving his home, his friends, and his job.

If he could stay on Earth, she might consider pledging with him. She knew it wasn't possible, though. Shimerian men visited Earth frequently, but couldn't remain more than three weeks at a time. Their bodies couldn't adjust. If they remained longer, they began to grow ill. Within a week after the onset of illness, they risked death if they didn't return to their own atmosphere. A lot of them came to Earth for a vacation, but no one stayed.

Another problem was their dominating ways and old world attitudes. Shimerian males were fiercely competitive. Given the lack of females, it was understandable. They were extremely dominant, too. Even Liken, who seemed gentle and patient a lot of the time, seemed to think subduing her sexually was the answer to any challenge from her. It might be exciting, but it was annoying, too. He was bigger and stronger, more sexually experienced. Any physical altercation could have only one result. She was too vulnerable to his attractions to think otherwise.

The thing that bothered her the most was the Shimerian viewpoint on love. To Shimerian males, love was not an important issue. Pledge relationships were based on sexual compatibility and mutual respect, even friendship.

She knew that she couldn't stay with Liken without falling in love with him. She couldn't be intimate with him day after day, living with him, talking to him, without falling for him along the way. That knowledge deep inside herself was one of the reasons he scared her so badly.

If she could just accept what was happening as a good time, "interplanetary nookie" as she had joked with Kate, then it might be different. But something inside her responded to him emotionally.

She didn't like it. She had been right when she'd laid eyes on him. He was a heartbreaker. Sitting on the bed, lost in her thoughts, she almost didn't hear him when the door slid open and he stuck his head in the doorway.

"Sharon, we are due to meet with my brother for midmeal. Are you ready to go?" He took in the turmoil on her face and wisely kept his tone neutral.

She could sit on the bed all day brooding, but it wasn't going to solve anything. She stood up and walked toward him. "Sure," she sighed. "Let's go." Following on his heels, she trailed behind him through the house and out the sliding front door. When they got outside, she stopped in wonder.

"It's beautiful here," she said in surprise as her surroundings struck her. She had been asleep the night before when he brought her in. Looking around, she saw a row of dwellings, side by side in the pink glow of the day. Again, the bricklike material was glowing like the office buildings had been the night before. Most were box-like in shape, without windows.

However, the facades of the dwellings had wonderful carvings decorating them. They depicted landscapes of lush vegetation. The glow seemed to make them more alive, more beautiful.

Most of the dwellings had plants growing around the buildings. The large leaves were a light yellow, but with flowers of red and delicate pink. There were black walkways leading to the entrance of each building. She would have expected grass yards around the walkways, but instead there was a lush carpeting of some blanketing foliage. It had tiny pink flowers in contrast to the creamy white of the dense leaves. It was strange, but also strangely beautiful.

Liken smiled, pleased with her appreciation of his home. "Thank you, *sherree*. It is like this always. The temperature rarely varies. We do not have the seasons here as you have on Earth."

He began to walk with her along the black central walkway between the two rows of dwellings. He took her hand in his, but she pulled it back after only a few seconds and pointed out a nearby plant. He did not reach for her hand again. As they walked, she asked questions about the different plants and dwelling carvings. He answered her questions easily, although he did shrug with laughing ignorance when she asked for the names of some of the flowers.

They passed several couples strolling hand in hand, most of them Shimerian males with Earth females. The couples were distantly friendly, calling out greetings as they passed. She could tell that they knew Liken and by their admiring glances could tell that he was well liked. He avoided lengthy introductions by keeping them moving, responding in a friendly manner that didn't encourage further conversation.

When they were alone again, she continued to pepper him with eager questions. As they talked, she lost some of her guardedness and began to relax with him. When Liken casually took her hand in his this time, she merely smiled and kept talking.

He was surprised at the simple pleasure he took in her company. Her enthusiasm and curiosity were a delight. She had a bright, inquisitive mind. As he answered her questions, he found himself charmed.

Sharon had a sudden thought. "Where are we going? I mean, I know you said lunch with your brother, but are we eating at his house? Does he live near here?" Tilting her head up at him, her hand still trustingly in his, she asked, "Do we have to go through a portal?" Her enthusiasm waned a little. She wasn't eager to travel through another portal.

He shook his head. "This city is called Glowen'da. We live close to the city center. There is a public eatery there where we will meet my brother. He lives in Karten'sha. It is a quick trip through the western portal. Knowing your love for portals, I asked him to meet us here today." His gaze was teasing.

She smiled in relief. "I know portals are commonplace here, but I'd like to get used to them gradually if you don't mind. Walking into that blackness feels like stepping off a cliff and hoping there's something to catch you below. You probably don't think twice about it anymore, but it's a little eerie to me."

Tugging her hand, he pulled her close and gave her a hug. "I know there is a lot of change for you, *sherree*. Just remember that I am here at your side." Giving her one last squeeze, he released her and pointed toward a group of buildings a couple of blocks away. "There is the eatery. It is called *Jerlanks* ."

The building looked much like the surrounding office buildings. Much larger than private dwellings, each building had a carving on the outside that effectively demonstrated its function. *Jerlanks* had a large carving of people eating and drinking, some heads tossed back with laughter, like a large party was occurring within its walls.

Walking faster now, they reached the building in very little time. As they entered through the archway, Sharon saw a large dining area filled with square tables. Looking around the room, she was struck by the large number of males present. There were about ten women, all with male companions. The women were all wearing thin outfits similar to hers. The rest of the tables, maybe twenty-five or thirty, were crowded three or four to a table with men.

As she and Liken paused to scan the room, a noticeable hush descended. Feeling as if every eye in the room was on them, she hoped Liken located his brother fast. She was extremely conscious of male eyes lingering on the prominent thrust of her nipples beneath the blouse. As a man stood at one of the back tables and motioned to them, she followed Liken in relief. Conversation again resumed around them as they threaded their way through the tables.

Approaching Liken's brother, she noticed immediately that he was the good-looking guy who had given Kate a hard time. Liken nodded his head at the man. He smiled even as his voice comfortably teased, "Sharon, my brother, Tair. Do not let him charm you." His voice filled with pride as he introduced them more formally. "Tair, this is my pactmate, Sharon." Gesturing toward Tair, he said, "*Sherree*, you remember Tair. He was present at our Oath ceremony."

It was easy to believe they were brothers. Both had the same powerful build, although Tair was a little leaner. His dark hair was longer than Liken's hair, with more curl to it. The arrogant stance and charisma were identical, though. Duel heartbreakers, she decided. She gave him the beginnings of a shy smile.

Smiling warmly in response, Tair took her hand in his and said, "Welcome, Sharon. It is a pleasure to meet my future link. Liken doesn't deserve you, but he was ever lucky."

Sharon smiled back helplessly. She had no idea what he meant by link, but he really was charming. "It's nice to meet you, too. Although you're really jumping the gun since we only took the oath yesterday." She added quickly, "We still have three weeks to decide if we're compatible."

Tair arched a questioning eyebrow in Liken's direction at her comment, and a silent message passed between the two men. "Ahhh. My apologies. Apparently my brother has not worked his magic on you yet." His eyes were amused.

When Liken lightly hit his arm, the amusement only grew. "Please sit with me." With an easy gallantry that reminded her of Liken, Tair pulled out a chair and motioned for her to sit.

Taking a seat to his left as he gestured, she saw Liken sit down in one beside her. They were each sitting on one side of the square table. She felt dwarfed between the two men.

Looking over at Tair, she said quite innocently, "You must be the one with magic. I don't think I've ever seen anyone leave Kate speechless before. She's used to getting her way. I was impressed at the oath yesterday."

Tair laughed. "Well, I can believe she would be a worthy challenge to any opponent at any game. She was quite fierce in her protection of you."

Suddenly swamped with missing her friend, Sharon's smile dimmed. "Yes, she is. She's a very loyal friend." Images of the good and bad times she had shared with Kate flashed through her mind. She wished fiercely that she could see her friend and tell her what had happened so far.

Sensing her longing, Tair placed his hand over hers. He sought to reassure her, although he couldn't quite contain a secretive smile at the knowledge that the two friends would be together sooner than either of them could imagine. "Sharon, you will always have her friendship. You will be together with her again. You have my oath."

Shrugging off her sudden mood, she attempted to lighten the tone of the conversation. With a brisk nod of her head, she said, "Of course. It's only three weeks. I'm just used to having her around to try to arrange my life. Kate has very definite ideas on making your own happiness."

Her smile widening into a grin, she said, "she just happens to think she knows the best way for everyone to go about it." Her grin slowly turned into a chuckle.

Tair's eyes were dark with appreciation. "Yes, I believe she does. That confidence is very apparent. I doubt she gets surprised very often."

Sharon laughed. "The horrible part is she's usually right. Of course, it was her bright idea that got me into this, uh...situation...in the first place." The memory of a much younger Kate urging her to sign passed through her mind. With a shake of her head at their youthful naiveté, she glanced toward Liken.

Liken was smiling. "So I have Kate to thank for my good fortune. For that I owe her much. Perhaps she will be rewarded in the future for her good deed." He shot a sidelong glance at Tair.

Tair's eyes held a promise. "I have no doubt she will."

At that moment a man appeared, asking if they were ready to state their selections. Sharon gave Liken a questioning look. He said to her, "If it pleases you, I will select for you. I know you are not yet familiar with the foods here."

He was certainly being careful about appearing domineering. Giving an assenting nod, Sharon listened as he ordered. Nothing was familiar, but she hoped for the best.

After the waiter disappeared, Liken turned to Sharon. "Forgive me, *sherree*, but I need to ask Tair about something."

He turned to Tair. "What is happening with Bek?"

As Tair filled him in, Sharon realized they were discussing one of his work cases. Tair must be a cop, too, from the way he talked. As the waiter brought them their food, conversation around the table turned to lighter topics.

Tair asked how she had enjoyed her time on Shimeria thus far. Fighting off a vivid memory of their activities on the couch that morning, Sharon felt her cheeks warm. Her enthusiastic response to his caresses still mortified her. Making a polite response, she avoided Liken's knowing gaze.

Quickly, Sharon began complimenting the food. As they told her the name of each dish, she asked questions and spoke enthusiastically of the beauty of the neighborhood. Both men made an effort to keep her entertained and at ease. Many times, masculine heads turned at the sound of her laughter during the meal.

Lunch passed quickly. Tair finally said regretfully, "I have enjoyed this time much, but I cannot stay longer. I must report back to my command." His signaling nod brought the waiter immediately. The waiter took his ID card and disappeared into the other room. Coming back almost immediately, he handed the card back to Tair with polite thanks. Tair stood and gave a little bow toward the two of them. "Please stay and enjoy. I have paid for all of us."

Liken made a noise of protest, but Tair overruled him. "It is my right as link of the oath couple." Offering a slap to Liken's shoulder, he said, "Guard her well, brother. Else some sneaky male might steal this delight." With a wink at Sharon, he left.

Liken's smile was rueful as he heard Sharon laugh. "Charm in abundance, I know. Should I worry he has swayed you with his tricks?" His eyes were teasing.

"Maybe. He's pretty smooth." Her smile was flirtatious. "Not jealous of big brother, are you?" she asked with false innocence.

He shook his head. "He might make you laugh, *sherree*, but you are mine in the end. Besides, that surface charm covers steel. He can be very ruthless. He took great pains to set you at ease. I appreciated it. I trust my brother."

His eyes took on a hard gleam as they swept the restaurant. His voice matched his eyes as he said quietly, "I am not so tolerant of others." At his look and words, several of the men who had been eyeing Sharon quickly turned away.

Sharon was surprised to hear the conversation around her dip and then pick up volume again. Then she remembered the Shimerian hearing. A little part of her perked up at his jealousy. He was publicly stating his claim. His heart might not be vulnerable, but he was feeling possessive. It was a start. If he could feel jealousy, those feelings could deepen over time. Love might be possible.

Feeling a little lighter, she asked, "What do we do now?" Almost immediately she realized she would probably get some embarrassing answer.

Although his eyes gleamed, he merely said courteously, "I thought I would show you the city. "

She nodded her assent eagerly. Going back to the house would put them in intimate territory. She wasn't ready to tangle with him again.

Of course, she knew that she couldn't put it off indefinitely.

Chapter Six

They explored Glowen'da for the rest of the day. As they walked around the city, Sharon realized the similarities to Earth. The contact and constant flow of travelers between the two planets were slowly blending the cultures. Although the landscape was alien, there was a familiarity she felt as she walked and asked questions.

She was surprised as well by how much she and Liken had in common. They had both lost their parents at a young age. They both enjoyed reading and similar types of music. As they went from place to place, there was a strange sense of comfort between them. Liken surprised her with his enthusiasm. He seemed to be having a good time just being with her, seeing things through her eyes. It was flattering.

Inevitably, after a time, Liken turned them toward home. Sharon's feet and legs were beginning to feel the effects of an afternoon spent walking. When they reached the house, she felt her earlier tension begin to return. Turning quickly toward the bedroom, she said, "I'll just rest a while."

Liken stopped her with a hand on her arm. "You can rest in here, *sherree*."

She looked away from him. Her gaze alighted on the couch and she immediately took a step back. "I don't think so." Their conversation after the Oath ceremony, when he said he could repeat any intimacy, flashed through her head.

Pulling her into his arms, he said, "I had hoped we made progress this afternoon. Why do you still fear me?"

She looked into his face. He seemed honestly perplexed. "I'm not afraid of you. I just think we should take things slowly, that's all." In fact, she was hoping they could put off any form of intimacy for several days...or more. She needed time.

46

A dawning understanding passed over his face. "I think I see. You do not fear me. You fear yourself."

"Don't be ridiculous." She felt the first stirrings of anger.

"Very well, then. You fear your response to me." He sounded understanding, but his face was hardening. He was growing frustrated with her.

Sharon said, "I don't want to fight. I just want you to leave me alone for awhile." It was time to put more distance between them, if she could.

"This I will not do." His voice was firm. "You are trying to retreat. You hide from me but more…you hide from yourself. You want me just as much as I want you. You are bound to honor your oath. This is our knowing period. What we do is expected."

" *I didn't expect it, okay?* " Her voice was rising. "I'm tired of you throwing duty in my face. I know what I vowed. Theoretically, I guess just skipping off planet and having sex with a strange alien guy is supposed to be easy. But it's not. I'm not casual. The two guys I was with before may not have been heroes, but they were decent guys that I cared about. You want me to just get naked and have sex with you like it's easy. It's not. I've never been with someone like you. You make me feel…" her voice faltered. Sharon suddenly realized that she was afraid of how he made her feel.

"Out of control? Hot? Overwhelmed?" he suggested huskily.

Sharon paused at his words, and thinking quickly, nodded. "Okay fine. All of those things." She didn't like where this discussion was going.

"Is that so bad, *sherree*? The attraction between us is intense. It is our fortune. You say you do not like feeling out of control, but I know sexually, it makes you hot. I know seeing you that way makes me hot. You may not be comfortable and safe like in your controlled world, but you like what I say to you. You like what I do to you. I would wager that right now you are wet from my words. Perhaps you need to learn that there is no harm in giving up control. That you are safe with me."

He was right, but she didn't like admitting it. She was wet from his words. She blushed, knowing her tightened nipples were obvious against the thin barrier of her top. There was no way he could fail to notice her obvious arousal. Her body was betraying her.

Liken could see and sense how affected she was by his words and presence. He reached out and ran his hands along the sides of her body in one slow stroke. Sharon tried to move away, but he merely picked her up and carried her to the couch. Coming down on top of her, he again pinioned her hands as he had earlier.

Peering into her face, his voice brooked no argument. "I will not take you tonight. I will bring you to peak with my hands and my mouth on this couch until we grow hungry. We will eat the evemeal with you in my lap, my hands on your body. Then we will return to this couch. You will come for me, *sherree*. You will ache and come and ache for more."

She swallowed roughly.

"You will get used to this hunger between us. Your comfort with me will be assured. But know this, tomorrow there will be no clothing between us. You will not hide behind the safety of your inhibitions. I am a Shimerian male. We are highly sexual, dominant beings. I will not pretend otherwise. To truly know me, you must be willing to know yourself."

Somewhat angrily, his mouth came down on hers.

His hard kiss gradually gentled into teasing caresses. As she responded with less reluctance and more enthusiasm, he left no part of her untouched. The feel of his hands and mouth through the thin barrier of her clothes was overwhelming.

The next hours were unbelievable. He was relentless. Using his hands and mouth, he brought her to climax after climax. As he had promised, he never removed her clothes. Even sitting at the table, eating, one hand always roamed her body. Leaning back against his chest, she accepted bites of food as she arched into the fingers tweaking her nipple or gliding between her legs.

Later, back on the couch, her body grew exhausted. When he finally sat up and moved away from her, she felt like there wasn't a nerve on her body that hadn't been stroked. She was swollen, her breasts tender. Between her legs, she throbbed and felt a pulsing awareness of him with every beat of her heart.

Looking into his harsh countenance, she marveled at his control. He hadn't lost it once. It was frightening. His face was lined with the costs of his effort, but he had certainly made his point.

Early on, her defenses had toppled. She had eagerly sought his caresses, even encouraged them. He had given her pleasure after pleasure, but always stopped short of removing her clothing. He had a deeply ingrained sense of honor. He hadn't misused her or gone back on his word.

She couldn't pretend to herself any longer. She did know a lot about this man. She did want him. She couldn't fight both him and herself any longer.

Getting up on shaky legs, she faced him. "I'm going to sleep now. You've made your point. I want you. I'm not really afraid of you." She felt vulnerable, exposed. "We'll sleep together tomorrow. But you might think about this: sex isn't enough to tie me to you permanently. I may go to my grave wanting you, but I'll be buried on Earth. I'm not going to get lost in you and your world. I'm entitled to my own dreams."

He looked genuinely shocked. "I don't want to take everything from you, Sharon. I want to build a life together with you. If a life on Earth was possible, I would be there with you."

She looked skeptical. "Easily said, when you'll never have to do it. It's so easy for you. You get everything you want." She gave him a level look and then left the room.

He watched as she left, his body screaming for release, his emotions in turmoil. Liken felt like howling. He dropped his head into his hands. The only thing he truly wanted was *her* .

In the quiet of the room he was temporarily using as a sleep chamber, the night progressed and the activity of the previous hours kept playing through his mind to torment him. He remembered her softness, her response to his caresses, and the way her body would get wet at his touch.

That night Liken got very little sleep. Besides the aching frustration of his body, his thoughts restlessly turned the situation with Sharon over and over. She was resentful of leaving her homeworld and her own plans. She felt fearful of her vulnerability to him. Perhaps the best way to lessen that fear was to demonstrate to her that she had power over him as well. That wouldn't be any problem.

He sighed. Only someone with her level of inexperience could have missed the effect she had on him. His cock felt painful with the need to go to her and show her immediately.

Another problem was her need for control, for not letting go. She didn't like to lose control, didn't like to be open and vulnerable. Well, she was fighting a losing battle. She was wrong in not realizing sex could form a level of intimacy more powerful than a hundred of her Earth "dates." She was so powerful in her vulnerability and so totally unaware of it.

She was so beautiful and honest in her responses. It reached him on an emotional level that he had never experienced with any previous partners. Because she was so reluctant to share herself, it merely made the sharing more poignant, more special.

He felt powerful when he drew a response from her, it was true. But at the same time, he felt helplessly drawn to her. He wanted her more than he had wanted any other woman physically. Mentally, he wanted to know her thoughts, to see the world from her viewpoint. Emotionally, he wanted to bring joy to her life and watch those eyes light from within with happiness. He was well and truly mired in her. There could be no going back at this point.

He turned onto his back and stared at the ceiling. He had to find a way to make her want to stay. With a grimace he faced his next thought. He had been very careful with her thus far. Once they began having sex, the urge to merge telepathically would grow stronger. He would eventually lose control.

If she worried about being lost in him now, he could imagine her reaction to that. She would be horrified and panic. If she rejected him during the merge, he could hurt her terribly. He had to initiate her carefully.

When they did merge, she could leave him at a later time. The loss of immediate mental intimacy would be incredibly painful for him. He was risking a lot more than she seemed to think. He had to find a way to bind her to him heart, mind, and soul.

He sighed. Easy for him, she had said. Right.

* * * * *

Sharon spent a restless night tossing and turning in her bed. She could hear Liken's movements in the other bedroom. The house was so quiet that she could hear the rustle of the sheets as he turned one way and then another. She tensed a couple of times as she heard him get up from the bed and pace the room.

She knew he could by rights come into her room and begin touching her again. Her body, exhausted and swollen, still ached with the knowledge of what he would do to her. Yet, each time, he returned to bed without entering her room. She was relieved. Mostly.

She thought about why he hadn't just finished things between them tonight. He wanted her to get used to him sexually. She couldn't help but wonder why he was being so careful. He could have pushed her into more. She was helpless in her attraction to him. There was more to his caution than he was telling her. She felt sure of it.

He was an alien. Granted, he appeared to have the same equipment as any Earth male. Why the caution? Wasn't sex the same? She thought about the two times she'd felt his mind brush against hers. She didn't like the thought that he might enter her mind the way he would enter her body. She had avoided asking him about the mind thing because it was too scary.

There had been too many things happening in too short a time. She felt overwhelmed. She hadn't wanted to deal with even one more surprise-especially the thought of him inside her head. Would he be able to read all her thoughts? Her secrets? Would he be able to do it anytime or just during sex? What could he do? She felt like running away from him as far and as fast as she could. Her heartbeat pounding in her ears, she struggled to calm down and reason things out.

Liken's sudden appearance in the doorway at that moment nearly scared her to death. She gave a muffled shriek and stared at him in alarm.

"Sharon, what is frightening you?" he asked gently as he came into the room and sat down on the edge of the bed. He was dressed only in a pair of loose black pants, tied at the top with a small white cord. His chest, large and muscular, gleamed in the dim light as the lights suddenly became a little brighter.

"Did you do that?" she asked in surprise.

"What?" he seemed confused by her question.

"The lights. How did you make them brighter? Where are they?" She kept looking around the room for some kind of light source.

He seemed to be choosing his words carefully. "Yes. I did make it brighter in here. I will show you how another time. You are very anxious. What is wrong?" His voice was soothing.

It was strange. Since he had entered the room, she had been feeling calmer. She didn't know if it was his presence or the interruption from her disturbing thoughts. She needed to get a grip. Whatever the mind thing was, she couldn't just freak out about it and have a heart attack. She needed to know more about it. Maybe it wasn't what she thought at all.

She needed to approach this logically and get more information. Liken reached out and gently brushed her hair off her forehead. Looking at his face etched with concern, she decided now was as good a time as any.

"Liken, what is that mind thing you do?" Her eyes bravely held his as she braced for the worst.

His face carefully went blank. "This is what has you so fearful?" He had hoped to avoid the explanation until after their merge.

"Well, yes. I mean, I started thinking about tomorrow. About us being together…" her voice grew a little fainter. "What's going to happen? Will you be inside me? Inside my head?"

Liken could see even in the dim light her cheeks were flushed. She was embarrassed, but still wanting answers. He felt an unexpected wave of tenderness go through him. How to explain without scaring her to death? "*Sherree*, you don't have to be fearful. When our bodies join, our minds will join as well. It is a wonderful thing, a beautiful thing."

She sat up a little, carefully keeping the sheet around her. "Okay, but what does that mean? Is it just for a moment? I mean, am I going to have you in my head all the time after that?"

She looked very unhappy at the thought. "Not exactly. It's a little hard to explain. I would rather show you than try to describe it." He was aroused at the mere idea of it. He was trying to hide his growing arousal from her, but it was impossible to hide the hardness pressing outward from his pants.

Pinned by his heavy-lidded gaze, Sharon felt uneasy. He wasn't really answering her. "What's the big secret? Why won't you tell me?"

Liken didn't want to lie to her, but he couldn't tell her either. For a fleeting second he wished she had picked Challenge or Capture. He could have merged with her immediately without her consent. It would have been shocking and painful for her, but effective.

The impulse to possess her was strong and the talk of merging was making him hot. Reminding himself that Sharon would not be Sharon if she had picked one of the other options, he decided to give her a small preview without revealing everything. It might lesson her fear. Provided he could stay in control enough to withdraw in time. *Time...*

Suddenly he realized it was past halfeve. In fact, his time restriction was up. He could take her now. Looking into her face he realized she was growing angry at his evasion. She had no idea that they could now move to the last stage. Perhaps that could work to his advantage.

He moved his body closer to hers on the bed. Something must have shown in his face because Sharon suddenly gave a violent pull on her sheets. It sent him tumbling to the floor.

He ended up sprawled on his butt, eyes wide in shock. It was a contest as to which of them was more surprised. Her hand flew to her mouth and her eyes were huge.

Jumping out of bed, she was careful to wrap the sheet around her body quickly. Backing toward the door, she let out a nervous little giggle before she could stop herself. "I really didn't mean to do that. It's just...you had that look you get right before you pounce on me. I was just going to grab the sheet and get out of bed..." Her voice was shaky with suppressed laughter.

"You think thrusting me to the floor is funny, do you?" His voice was fierce, but she could see a gleam of amusement in his eyes. He stood up with fluid grace and began stalking toward her slowly.

"No, not really." She tried not to laugh, but he had looked so shocked. It was the first time she had ever had him at a disadvantage and it felt good. "I can't help it if you're clumsy, you know..." She continued to back down the hallway. Looking around wildly, she turned around quickly and made a sudden break for the kitchen.

Giving a mock growl, he caught her quickly and swung her into his arms. Laughing, he managed to keep hold of her while she wiggled and squirmed. Looking into her laughing eyes and flushed face, he had never wanted her more. His expression changed to open desire.

Sharon stopped squirming as she instantly became aware of her position. Looking down, she realized the sheet had become loosened and was dangerously close to falling off. With a quick grab, she managed to keep from losing it altogether. Clutching it to her, she looked up into his face.

In his eyes was a naked hunger that took her breath away. Swallowing past the sudden lump in her throat, she said, "I think you should put me down now."

His arms tightened. Suddenly moving toward her bedroom, he agreed. "Yes, I think I should."

When he reached the bed, he gently put her down on her back, and then followed her. Covering her body with his own, he kept most of his weight on his elbows as he gazed into her face.

Sharon began to tremble. "It's time, isn't it? We're not going to stop this time." Her eyes searched his face, although she already knew the answer.

Shifting his weight to one side, his body no longer looming over her, he moved the other arm across her until his hand gently closed on hers. Her fingers were white where they gripped the sheet. "No, *sherree*. We're not going to stop this time..." His voice was husky with need.

He began prying her fingers from the death grip on the sheet. Unconsciously responding to the need in his tone, she began to relax her grip. When she let go, he took her hand and slowly brought it to his mouth. Gently kissing her fingers, his mouth moved to the palm of her hand. She felt the moist heat of his mouth on the sensitive center of her hand as he gently licked then sucked. She felt a wave of heat all the way to her toes. Her trembling increased.

Feeling her body tremble, he released her hand and began gently stroking her hair. "*Sherree*, I know you are afraid of the merging." He hesitated. "We will go slowly. We will do this thing together." Again, he searched for words. "I have not merged before either. I know what I have been told. But that is not the same as doing it. My mind will touch yours, just as my body touches yours. I will go slowly, but there will come a point when I lose control. You will feel but a brief pain, a flash, like a piercing headache. And then there will be only pleasure for both of us."

He waited for her response. The ache to possess her was like a living thing inside him.

She raised a trembling hand to his face. "Okay." Her eyes were tear-bright as she put a shaky smile on her face. "We'll try this together. I can handle a little headache."

At the gentle touch of her hand on his face, he shuddered. He was so proud of her he could barely breathe. "*Sherree*, I need you to trust me in this. When the time comes, I am asking you not to turn away or fight me. It will be frightening, but please trust that it will be all right in the end. I will not let anything bad happen to you. You know that, do you not?" The promise in his voice eased her as nothing else could.

Her eyes were full of dawning wonder. "I do know that." This big, fierce man was practically vibrating from her touch on his face. He wanted her very badly, but he was trying very hard to reassure her. He didn't just want her. He wanted her willing. He wanted her to trust him.

This wasn't just sex. Until this moment, she had felt completely helpless in her attraction to him. Now, she suddenly understood that he was just as helpless in his attraction to her. It was quite a revelation. Somehow, it made her feel stronger, more powerful. She had felt off balance and overwhelmed since he had suddenly appeared. Now, for the first time since that moment, she understood that maybe he had felt just as off balance.

She had been trying to cope with sudden changes, but he had been trying to figure out how to make that coping easier for her. She still felt nervous, but a lot of her fear vanished. He was doing the best that he could, just as she was. Moving her hand from his face to behind his head, she began to pull him toward her. When she felt his breath on her mouth, she whispered, "I trust you, Liken."

With a little moan, he took her mouth. The kiss was fierce, his mouth hard and demanding. Thrusting his tongue between her lips, he swept inside, enjoying the sweet taste of her. When her tongue began to duel with his, his control, already sketchy, slipped. He moved his hand from her hair and swept it to the edge of the sheet to pull it down. Hearing her low gasp, he suddenly paused and pulled back. "I am sorry, *sherree*." His breath was coming in pants. "I want you so much..." With effort, he pulled himself back under control.

Her lips were swollen and she looked dazed. With more tenderness, he returned to her mouth and began gentle, biting little kisses. He moved his mouth across her face to her ear, and then slowly down the side of her neck. His hand, at the top of the sheet, began to inch it down. When at last it was down to her waist, he pulled back a little to look at her.

Sharon opened her eyes. He had stopped the drugging kisses to the side of her neck. She froze as she realized the sheet was now down by her waist. His face was pulled tight, his eyes nearly black with wanting. His gaze moved over her breasts like a physical touch. She could feel her nipples hardening almost painfully.

With a little sound of approval, he moved his head down and began to suck. With a loud moan, she arched into his mouth. Pulling back a little, he began running his tongue around and around the hardened nipple. "You are so beautiful...so responsive..."

He switched to the other breast and began licking and sucking it. "I want them hard and red from my mouth..." His hand moved back to her abandoned breast and began massaging. Sharon shuddered with the pleasure of it. "You feel so good to me, *sherree*..." His mouth continued to tease and torment her breast.

His fingers on the other breast began to focus on her nipple. He gently rolled and pulled. Sharon could not hold back another moan. He quickly switched breasts. Licking, sucking, even gently biting, his mouth was driving her out of her mind. She brought both hands to the back of his head and pressed him even closer.

With a pleased chuckle, he complied, growing rougher, more demanding. "That's it...you are feeling it now, are you not?" She was twisting underneath him, trying to get closer. "I think I will keep these nipples hard and wanting all the time. You are very sensitive. I plan to discover how sensitive..."

Her hips were rising and falling. He was still on his side, half bent over her. He caught the edge of the sheet in his hand as her hips rolled upward and pulled it quickly past her waist. Pulling back from her breast, he looked down at what he had revealed.

She was incredible. Those full breasts tapered to a small waist then rounded to generous hips. The dark triangle of hair between her long legs was glinting with moisture. He felt his mouth water.

With a little groan, he moved so that his upper body was between her legs. She raised up a little on her elbows to look down at him. Holding her gaze, he began placing light kisses on her stomach around her navel. She looked dazed, as if she was in a trance. The musky smell of her sex lured him downward. Still holding her gaze, he licked down her stomach to just above her curls. Her head went back and her entire body shuddered.

Placing light kisses into her curls, he kept his gaze on her face. Blowing gently into her soft hair, he said firmly, "Look at me." She lifted her head slowly as if it was heavily weighted. Green eyes locked with blue as he said, "Watch me taste you..."

With that, he swept his tongue in one long glide from her clitoris downward. Probing her opening, he pushed his tongue into her as far as it would go, and then journeyed back to circle her clit. He began to gently lap, reveling in her taste, her scent. He moaned low in his throat and the vibration nearly sent Sharon over the edge.

Her body had been reduced to sheer sensation. The feel of his hands as they massaged and tormented her breasts, the feel of his mouth and tongue between her legs, were all too much. She was hot, her body aching. She couldn't seem to get enough air. He was eating her alive.

She was wetter than she'd ever been in her life. She could feel that slick wetness dripping down. She could see his head moving between her legs. As he gently sucked on her clitoris, his demanding gaze held her captive. One hand moved from her breast. There was a sudden pressure inside her sex as one long finger probed. She felt herself tightening, the tension building. She wanted his hardness between her legs, filling her up. She wanted his cock plunging into her. She muttered, "Please..."

He moved back from her to stand up. Still lying on her elbows, she watched him as he untied the top of his pants and pulled them down, stepping out of them. He wore nothing underneath. He stood back up, already moving to get back on the bed.

"Wait!" At her word, he froze in surprise. Licking her lips without realizing just how provocative the sight was to Liken, she said huskily, "I want to see you."

With a visible nod in relief, he walked to the head of the bed. Turning her body toward him, she took a slow inventory. He was magnificent. The hard, sculpted muscles of his chest gave way to a narrow waist and lean hips.

His cock thrust upward proudly toward his stomach. It was larger than the ones she had seen before. Just the sight of it made her mouth go dry. It was about eight inches long, with a large tip already nearly purple in color. As she looked, it gave a little jump, as if in recognition. With a start, her gaze leapt up to his face. He was watching her reaction closely. With a little smile of approval, she licked her lips. "Wow. You are amazing."

A broad grin spread across his face. Apparently, human male or alien male, they all wanted some sign of approval when their masculinity was on the line. His voice was deep and rough. "I am glad you think so, *sherree.*"

Her smile widened in response. Reaching out her hand slowly, she let one fingertip glide from the tip of his cock all the way to the base. When she reached the base, she encircled it with the rest of her hand. He was so large; she could barely put her fingers around him. His answering groan was so loud, she nearly let him go.

With lightning reflexes, he brought his hand over hers, holding it in place. His head was thrown back with his eyes tightly shut in pleasure. Sharon felt her body tense with wanting. He looked so hot. As his hand moved hers on his cock in slow up and down motions she watched the planes of his face grow harsher.

He looked powerful and vulnerable at the same time. His masculine beauty singed her senses. Feeling a shudder move through him, she felt powerful. She suddenly stopped the motion of her hand. "Look at me, "she demanded.

He opened his eyes abruptly. He looked wild, nearly out of control. She could see him visibly trying to grab hold of his discipline. Some devil within her wanted to push him right to the edge. To make him as out of control as he always made her.

Without warning, she leaned over and took as much of him into her mouth as she could. The feel of his hardness in her mouth was nearly indescribable. His skin was smooth and soft, although his cock was hard and huge in her mouth. She could actually feel him throb as she lightly stroked her tongue along his length.

Liken froze, every muscle in his body locking into place. He was totally focused on the moist heat of Sharon's mouth on his cock. It was unbelievable. Jerking his hand out from under hers, he brought both hands up to her head, trying to hold her in place. His knees felt weak and he could literally feel the blood drain from his face.

She disregarded his gesture and began to move her head up and down, her mouth moving almost the length of his cock, sucking. His heart seemed to stop in his chest. He could barely breath. His hands clenched fistfuls of her hair as she moved again and again carrying him closer to the edge. With a moan, he gave himself up to the pleasure and to her. He let her take him with her mouth until he knew he was in danger of coming.

Drawing on every ounce of discipline he possessed, he pulled her head back and away from his cock. When she raised glowing green eyes to his face in question, he stared down at her. With a muffled oath, he pushed her back on the bed and came over her, letting her feel the full weight of his body, the intensity of his need. Shifting underneath him, she felt his hard cock graze her sex and suddenly went still beneath him. Breathing heavily, he shifted his weight up onto his elbows and used his legs to push hers apart. Leaning down, he began kissing her frantically.

Sharon was overwhelmed. Liken's lower body was pressing into hers. His mouth was eating at hers like he was starving. She returned his kisses eagerly, wanting more, needing more of him. With a muffled moan into her mouth, he began to rub his cock against the outside of her sex. She was drowning in sensation. With an answering moan, she pressed her hips upward into his weight.

It took a second before she realized something else was happening as well. She could feel his mind pressing against hers. Even though he had done it before, it startled her enough to make her go still beneath him.

With a little moan, he breathed into her mouth, "Trust me, *sherree*...please-it will be so good..."

His hips pushed down against hers again, pantomiming the act they both craved. She pushed back, feeling bursts of pleasure at the friction of their bodies. He immediately adjusted his position so that the next time he pressed, his cock pressed at the entrance to her opening. She shook with desire and nerves. "I do want you..." She raised her hips.

His next thrust took him a little inside. He slowed his movement. "You are so tight. I will be careful..." With a gentle thrust, he moved further in. He could feel the tightness of her inner walls gently stretch to accommodate him.

Sharon felt his hardness filling her. She was stunned by what she felt. He was too big. She had to relax or it was going to be painful. She gasped and tried to ignore the pressing feeling of him in her head. She could feel the weight of his mind against hers like a tangible thing. It was scary. He seemed to be pushing into her body and into her mind at the same time. She was tensing up. She couldn't help it.

Liken slowed even further. His forehead was coated with sweat. He looked like he was in agony. "*Sherree*, stay with me... " His next thrust was firmer, making significant headway. He was nearly all the way inside her now.

She could see what his gentleness was costing him. With a deep breath, she consciously focused on relaxing her inner muscles. The press of his mind against hers had eased a little, which helped. The next thrust he went deeply, completely inside her. She gasped.

When he was in her to the hilt, they both stopped moving for a second. It was exquisite.

Sharon felt stretched and full. It was so incredible. For a moment she shut her eyes, just savoring the feel of him deep inside her. Then her eyes opened and locked on his in wonder.

Her look seemed to melt something inside him. His eyes lit and his mouth curved tenderly. Leaning down, he softly kissed her mouth. He began thrusting gently in and out of her.

Each thrust inward lit her on fire. She began to move with him. She wanted more. Eyes closing, head thrown back, she arched upward further, seeking the strength of his body. Her hips surged to meet his thrusts.

As if he had been waiting for that response, he arched his spine. His thrusts became harder, faster. With each thrust, she could feel his mind pressing harder against hers. His mind was probing at hers, just as his body was probing. Eyes opening in fear, she held his gaze as if her life depended upon it.

With a moan, he muttered, "Trust me. Please..."

At his plea, she felt something inside herself give. She did trust him. Suddenly, she felt a blinding pain in her head, as if someone had driven a spike through it. She screamed. "It hurts! Oh, god, it hurts!"

They both stopped moving. Tears sprang to her eyes, and she instinctively moved her hands up to her head. For a minute, all she could feel was the overwhelming pain. Then, gradually, she became aware of something else. Feelings, not her own, began to register. She could feel him in her mind like a wave. It was like he was moving through her. She could feel waves of concern and regret, but mixed with those was a sense of satisfaction and possession.

His voice was gruff with concern. "Are you all right?"

Feeling a little hysterical, she shook her head no. She couldn't speak.

"Just relax for minute, *sherree*. All will be well. You have my oath on it."

Sharon could feel and hear his sincerity. His actual words suddenly penetrated. Oath was probably an unfortunate word choice at that moment. *It was their stupid oath that had gotten her into this...whatever this was*, she thought angrily.

Reaching down to place a gentle kiss on her lips, Liken said, "Maybe so, *sherree*, but I am grateful for that oath. I am grateful for you."

With a start of surprise, she realized he had known what she was thinking. She immediately wondered if he could read her mind all the time now. She was horrified at the thought.

With a little smile, he said, "Not *all* the time, *sherree*. I will never completely leave you, but you will have some privacy. To do otherwise would be unhealthy for both of us. Ahhh, you still feel horrified. Do not fear this merging, Sharon. There are a great many benefits for me to show you." He gently thrust into her body. "Let me show you."

A strong wave of pleasure caught her by surprise. She was feeling not only her own pleasure, but his as well. As his thrusts grew stronger, she arched her body in response.

With a little moan, he said, "Yes, that is it."

His thrusts increased in tempo. As she rose up to meet him, she felt waves of pleasure surging back and forth between them. It was impossible to separate the two sensations. With a groan, she pushed against him harder, wanting more.

He rose up on his elbows, gaining leverage. He was really surging into her hard, pulling back, then surging forward to the hilt again and again. It felt so incredible that she could barely breathe.

Looking down into her face, Liken muttered, "Merging allows me to know how you feel when I do this..." He pushed into her hard on the downstroke and used his hips to pin hers.

She felt the pressure on her clitoris and cried out in surprise and pleasure. His answering groan was deep and husky. He kept stroking her like that again and again, making the pressure inside both of them build higher and higher.

Without realizing it, her hands were running from his shoulders down his back all the way to his hips. She grabbed onto his ass and held on, her nails biting into him. The tiny pinpricks of pain nearly sent him over the edge. He slammed into her harder. With a muttered oath, he grabbed one of her hands and pulled it over her head, then quickly did the same with the opposite hand. Holding both arms over her head, he kept pounding into her.

With ruthless precision, he never lost rhythm. They were both moaning now. Sweat turned their bodies slick. Driving into her, he stared down into her face. Between gasps of air, he said, "Go over...just give into it...no more control, *sherree*...only this..." He was rough, demanding, pushing her even harder.

All the tension building inside her seemed to tighten in that moment. With a scream, she let loose, feeling her body contract and then release over and over again. Waves of pleasure poured through her, sending her higher.

As her inner muscles milked him, he moaned loudly, still pumping. Her pleasure sent him right over the edge. With an even louder groan, he exploded, spewing into her. She could feel his warmth inside her as the waves of his pleasure suddenly hit her, too. She was blind with pleasure, deaf with it. For a moment, the two of them were locked together in shared pleasure, unsure who was feeling exactly what and not really caring. It was intense, unbelievable.

When the feelings began to fade, he seemed to suddenly realize he was leaning on her heavily. He carefully twisted to lie on his back, bringing her up against him. With her head on his chest, his hand rubbing her back, both of them focused on simply breathing. Eventually, the gasping sounds of their breaths ceased and the room grew quiet.

Sharon tried to make some sense out of what had just happened. It had been incredibly intense, unlike anything she had ever experienced. Sex was not like whatever this had been. This was something else.

Liken's voice broke the silence. "It was not sex, Sharon. It was merging. And it was incredible."

Sharon entire body went stiff. The hands on her back never faltered, just continued with their soothing motions. "I thought you wouldn't be able to read my mind all the time." Her voice held accusation as well as hurt. She rose up a little to see his face.

With a little grimace, he shook his head. "You misunderstood. I said you would have some privacy, *sherree*. It is not that I cannot read your mind all the time. It is more that I will not."

"Well, stop then." She was getting freaked out. "Wait a minute...you can do this anytime, even if I'm not in the same room with you? Even if..."

His voice was patient. "Yes, even if you go back to Earth. I would like to remind you, though, that you will not be going back to Earth. Do you honestly think we are not compatible after this?" His eyes were beginning to glitter with anger.

He was angry, but underneath that, he was worried about losing her. Sharon realized she could feel his emotions quite clearly. She didn't have any trouble separating what he was feeling from what she was feeling. There was some distance now. It was different than it had been when they were having sex, more clearly defined. Hmmm. He could read her mind, but she could read his emotions. That might prove interesting.

"I didn't say we weren't compatible sexually. But there's more to a relationship than sex." Her mouth turned up at the corners in a sleepy little smile. "Even if it is great sex."

Going along with her lighter tone for the moment, Liken consciously relaxed his shoulders. "Of course." His voice held lazy male satisfaction. "Great sex, friendship, great sex, respect, great sex, liking, and then, of course, there is great sex. I did mention that one, did I not?" His smile was teasing.

She shook her head in mock surprise. "I believe that's the first I've heard of it. And to think I held the belief that men are shallow creatures with no clue about what's important in a relationship." Her eyes were lit with laughter, but her lids were falling. She was trying to stay awake, but it was a losing battle.

With great tenderness his hand moved from her shoulder to the back of her head. "I think I do not have the energy left for this debate nor do you." With a gentle push, he moved her head back onto his chest. "You are exhausted, *sherree*. Let us rest now. Tomorrow is soon enough to discuss male flaws."

Unconsciously rubbing her cheek against his chest, she relaxed into the gentle feel of his hands moving soothingly over her back. She let out a little sigh. "Liken..."

Her voice was so soft he would not have heard her without his extraordinary hearing. "Yes?"

"It was beautiful, wasn't it?" Her voice faded a little with each word. Her lids closed as she drifted off.

Reaching down to place a soft kiss on her head, he whispered, "Yes, *sherree*, it was beautiful."

He lay there in the dim room seeing images of Sharon in his mind. Sharon standing across from him as they made their oath. Sharon staring at the portal, her eyes wide with fear and courage. Sharon at the table eating, biting into the yellow *rerha* fruit, her grimace comical as she quickly put it back onto her plate. Sharon coming apart in his arms, in his bed.

With a sigh of his own, he reduced the room to darkness, and ignored the renewing ache in his body. The merging had been beautiful. But it was not just her physical beauty and their passion that had made it so incredible. It was her inner beauty as they joined that had brought such joy. He would never grow tired of experiencing the wonder of her.

They were going to be very happy together. She could not leave him. He would do whatever he must to make sure of it. Her comment about males being shallow echoed in his mind.

His last thought before sleep claimed him rang with determination. He might be shallow, but stupid he was not. He would find a way to keep her.

Chapter Seven

The next morning, Sharon hesitated in the doorway of the kitchen area. Liken had his back to her. He was once again dressed in black, although he was barefoot. He was reaching into an oblong recessed area, gathering fruit from inside, and then placing them in a bowl. There was a panel with buttons to the left. When he had gathered enough, he pressed one of the buttons and a small section of the wall slid back in place.

The Shimerian version of refrigeration or food transport, she guessed. She waited for him to turn as she gathered her composure. What exactly were the Shimerian rules of behavior for the morning after? She pasted a polite smile on her face and decided she could bluff her way through it. She was calm. She was sophisticated. He turned and spotted her in the doorway. She was in trouble.

She felt heat climb into her cheeks. "Do you ever wear anything but black?" The words all ran together and her voice was too high. She cringed inwardly. She hadn't meant to sound critical.

His eyes glinted with some unnamed thought. He said, "It denotes my profession. Only guardians are allowed to wear black." His voice teased her gently as he added, "Should we talk of footwear next or would you come greet me properly?"

Feeling foolish, she walked over and gave him a quick kiss on the lips. She kept the bowl between them and moved back too quickly for him to grab her. Walking back toward the table, she could see it was already set. There were beautiful flowers of some kind resting in a vase in the center. There were cups by each plate and a pitcher next to the flowers.

Her voice was very serious in an attempt to remain composed. She didn't want him to realize how deeply nervous she was feeling. "Can I help with anything?"

She looked like she was facing an angry death squad instead of her lover. He responded with equal gravity, although he felt like laughing. The urge to tease her was almost irresistible. "No, but I appreciate your offer of assistance. I am merely placing this bowl on the table and we will be ready."

She sat down in the seat before he could assist her and watched him put the bowl on the table. She scooted her chair into place and placed a small cloth from the table into her lap. He sat down across from her. With a little nod of his head, he gestured to the bowl. "Please take whatever you desire."

Her gaze flew to his face, but his tone was innocent. Deciding to give him the benefit of the doubt, she studied the fruit. Immediately she noticed there were no bitter yellow ones. Picking up a purple and red one that she remembered was pretty tasty, she took a bite. It was strangely salty for a fruit, but pleasant.

Again in that same overly innocent tone, he said, "It is indeed fortunate that you enjoy salty flavors." His eyes were devilish.

She choked. "Okay. Enough. I haven't had breakfast yet. I'm not up to mind reading and double entendres. I've had that bloodbath of a shower, but I need caffeine. What are the odds that you have coffee?" She wasn't annoyed but his teasing wasn't helping her frayed nerves.

He smiled. "I am sorry, but we do not have coffee." He gestured to the opaque cup in front of her. "We do have *ykanze* juice. It is very refreshing."

She peered suspiciously at the dark green liquid in the cup. "It looks like cough medicine." When he laughed, she took a cautious sip. It was surprising good. The liquid was hot and a little spicy. It tasted somewhat like a Bloody Mary. She felt the heat as it made its way to her stomach. "Is it alcoholic?"

He shook his head. "No, it is not fermented. It is also not addictive, although many claim it unthinkable to begin the day without it."

"I like it." Her voice reflected her surprise. "It's different, but it's good."

He looked as if he wanted to tease her again. At her discouraging look, he merely shrugged and began eating. The two of them ate in companionable silence for a while. She concentrated on her food in a conscious effort to avoid thinking too hard. When she finished, she looked up to find him watching her. "What?" she said, a little apprehensively.

"I am merely enjoying the sight of you this day, *sherree*." His gaze roamed her body with possessive satisfaction. "I have fantasized about you for so long. It is still a wonder to have you here."

Straightening in her seat, she decided it was time to take control of the situation before sex clouded things. With as much firmness as she could muster, she said, "We need to talk."

He winced. She guessed those words struck fear into the heart of any man, regardless of home planet. With a resigned shrug, he nodded his head. Sharon was relieved at his agreement. It was time to get some answers. She had been avoiding some things and he had deliberately distracted her about others. That was going to change. She was a librarian. Information was knowledge. Knowledge was power. Where to begin?

She remembered his comment at the portal. It had been nagging at her since that time. "What did you mean when you said you knew about me a year ago?" She wiped her face with the cloth from her lap.

"I found you telepathically a year ago." Liken paused, searching for the best way to make her understand. "You would have experienced it as a kind of daydream. I had been reaching out to you since my twentieth year and then suddenly, you were there. My mind brushed yours."

"How old are you?" What if Shimerians aged differently? She hadn't thought to ask about it until now. He could be much older or younger than her, she thought.

"I am the equivalent of thirty-four Earth years." He answered her unspoken thought. "Earth years and Shimerian years are roughly the same. I was thirty-three when I found you."

She thought about that for a minute. "Why did you wait?" She quickly tried to correct that. "I mean, not that I'm complaining or anything. I'm curious."

His gaze were steady on hers. "You were not ready, Sharon. I knew the adjustments you would have to make would be very hard. I wanted to give you time. Time to yourself. When I connected with you, I saw your image of your future."

When she merely continued to stare at him in confusion, he elaborated. "You think of yourself as very ordinary. You are cautious by nature. You value safety and control. The future you envisioned was very comfortable—your job at the library, a few good friends, a very ordinary man who would love you, one or two children. Nothing extraordinary. No trips to foreign planets. No alien pactmates. Nothing too different from the safe life you were leading. You did not want adventure, Sharon. You did not want disruption and challenge and a new culture. In short, you did not want a life with me." His voice held no hint of hurt, merely stated the facts.

She let out a breath in protest. "Okay. Thanks for making me sound like the dullest woman on Earth. If you were so convinced that I didn't want a life with you, then why wait a year and then summon me to oath? I don't get it."

He considered her words. "I waited to give you as much time as I could in that safe life. I want you to be happy, Sharon. You may not admit it now, but that safe life you were leading was growing boring."

She thought it over. She had been growing restless of late. Over the last couple of years, she had begun to wonder what was missing in her orderly life. She had felt a kind of wistfulness for something more. She had never managed to figure out exactly what *more* entailed, but she had been conscious of it. However, that didn't mean she had been yearning for adventure on quite this scale. "What if I had married one of those ordinary men, huh?" Her tone was challenging.

His look was fierce. "You would not have pledged with another man after we connected. Our destiny was decided in that moment."

"So, what does that mean? You thought you'd give me time to grow bored? And then rescue me from my idiotic little life, is that it?" She was getting angry. Could he be any more insulting?

"I am not trying to insult you. I am merely explaining. You needed time to see that the path you were taking would not make you happy. You needed time to yourself so that you could adjust to all of the changes later." He was losing patience. She was trying to distance the two of them.

She could feel his irritation. It was strange to be so closely attuned to someone, even when arguing. She wasn't sure what to make of it. She tried for a placating tone. "I don't want to fight. I'm just not sure I like you being the one to make that kind of a decision about my life. I make my own decisions."

He challenged bluntly, "Would you have wished for me to claim you a year ago?"

She considered the question honestly. "No, I guess you're right. I probably would have been even more freaked out then than I am now."

Her agreement calmed him. "I was aiming for your happiness then, *sherree*. As I aim for it now."

With a little nod, she acknowledged his words. "I appreciate that. I believe you mean it. I just don't like the feeling that you were waiting in the background, calling all the shots."

He looked a little puzzled at the statement. Then understanding seemed to hit. "I see. I understand, but it was the correct thing to do at the time."

"Okay. Let's put that aside for a minute. What do you mean you connected with me a year ago?" Could he have known about her for a year without her being aware of it? The thought unsettled her. Just how much did he know about her?

Liken sensed her growing unease and decided a full explanation might help her. "Perhaps I should explain some other things first. Shimerian males, from the time they begin school, learn Shimerian and Earth cultures. Our studies included Earth languages, customs, ideas. It was a preparation for our future. At the same time, we learn how to focus our mental abilities."

Her attention was caught. She interrupted. "What exactly are those abilities?"

Liken chose his words carefully. "Some of it is difficult to explain. We can harness mental energy and convert it to other types of energy. In that way, I was able to control the light mechanism this morning. I confess, however, that I do not have much of what you would call telekinetic ability. Also, we are able to reach out with our minds and touch the minds of others. We can all shield against others to a certain degree, but it varies according to individual abilities. For instance, I am a high degree shielder, but I am even better at probing."

She could attest to that. Memories of him thrusting into her last night swamped her. The thought brought a blush to her face.

His expression reflected his amusement at her thoughts. "By probing I mean getting information from another. It is very helpful in my profession. When I need to question someone, even if they are uncooperative, I am able to get the information I need." He was not boasting. He was considered to be one of the best probers in his section.

She could see how that would be a huge advantage with a suspect. So much for the right to remain silent. "Your English is very good. Have you used probing to help with that?"

He looked pleased with her compliment. "Yes. The schooling we received was effective, but a lot of Earth expressions are very confusing. Your slang is quite colorful. Probing has been very helpful in understanding it."

She considered his words. "Of course, to be exposed to slang... Have you been to Earth before?" She didn't know why she found the idea so surprising.

"Yes, of course. I have been to Earth many times. To many of your different countries. You have a great variety of cultures. It is quite amazing." He smiled at the thought of his visits to Earth. They had been quite educational and highly entertaining.

"Wow." She suddenly realized something that should have been obvious. She knew from last night that he was a very experienced lover. There weren't many unattached Shimerian women. So he must have been having sex with...

He raised his eyebrows. "I have found your people to be very friendly. Earth females in particular seem to find Shimerian travelers quite exotic. Although I was never able to stay long, I developed many...friendships...during my stays on your world."

The emphasis nearly made her snort. She'd bet on it. She had seen Shimerian males before, of course. Although she personally had never had much contact with them, she had never paid much attention in the past. Other than their good looks and larger size, most of them pretty much blended in with the surrounding culture. Just ordinary travelers touring the city or out having a good time. Probably, she conceded to herself, too big and powerful looking for her to want to cross paths with them much either.

Looking back, she realized none of them seemed to be lacking in female companionship. She suddenly pictured Liken out having a good time with some other woman. She frowned. His past was none of her business she told herself firmly. For that matter, after the knowing period, it was no concern of hers if he slept with someone else. Right? Her heart gave a pang at the thought.

He looked pleased. "There is no need for jealousy, *sherree*. I want only to be with you now. We are merged."

"Stop doing that!" she said sharply. "Stay out of my head. You said I could have some privacy. It's not right for you to just march into my thoughts and read them like today's newspaper."

This was the part of the discussion he had hoped to avoid. He knew it would put them in conflict, but he did not want dishonesty between them. "I cannot completely leave you, Sharon. Our minds have been merged." He tried to find a way to make her understand the truth of it.

She was indignant. "Oh, that's just great! Don't you have some control over this thing?"

He felt his patience strain at her tone. "Yes, I have some control. But a part of me is always with you. I can withdraw to a certain degree, but when you are agitated, as you are now, it is..."

He tried to think of a way she would understand. "It is like having the volume of a radio turned to the maximum level. You broadcast. I cannot help but listen. After a time, I will become better at blocking you, but it will be helpful when you become better at not broadcasting."

He was reading her every thought. This was not good. She needed to calm down. She could feel his growing impatience pressing against her in waves. She was in over her head. She should be coping with overdue fines or putting away books on their proper shelves. She was a librarian, for goodness sake. She liked order, and quiet, and calm. She was a reserved, quiet kind of person. This was all too...chaotic. Her life had turned inside out-alien planets, mind merging, incredible sex.

She let out a little breath. "All right. I'll try not to broadcast. You try to stay out as much as possible, okay? I don't like the idea of you snooping around in my mind, knowing every little thing..."

As she thought of the possibilities, she suddenly felt very vulnerable. He would be able to know everything. Not that she had a lot of dark secrets, but she was human, after all. She had things she would never tell another person. Things she wasn't particularly proud to share with someone else. Fantasies in the dark of the night she wouldn't even share with a sexual partner. The whole idea filled her with intense discomfort.

He looked apologetic, but there was heat in his eyes as well. "I am trying to respect your wishes, Sharon, but you are becoming even more upset. There should be no shame or embarrassment between us. I know your inner self. It is incredible to me that you can be so blind to your own beauty, both physical and inner."

Reaching across the table to take her hand, his voice became husky. "I would not use our bond against you, *sherree*. I do not wish to hurt you. Anything I have learned from our sharing will be used only for your pleasure and mine." His thumb was gently stroking her hand.

Her gaze slid from his and she tried to pull her hand from his grasp. She still felt incredibly exposed. He knew too much. She needed some space to come to terms with what he'd told her. With obvious reluctance, he let her pull away completely.

She promptly scooted as far back as her chair would allow. She tried to turn the subject to safer channels. She decided to go on the offensive. "I know you've been with other women before. You've had sex without merging. Why last night?" *And why me* she wanted to add, but didn't quite have the nerve.

"You are my pactmate, my future pledgemate." At her instinctive movement to disagree he flashed her a fierce look. "I could have had sex without merging with you, it is true. I tried to wait. The initial merge is somewhat painful and frightening to the female. Some choose to merge right after the Oath. I tried to be patient. I thought it might be easier when you knew me better. I also waited as long as I could out of prudence. You were not happy with the Oath. I thought you might have even greater problems with the consequences of merging." His tone said he had been right.

"But you could have held off, right? I mean, this merging business is permanent. Even after we go our separate ways, you'll still be lurking in the back of my mind!" The more she thought about it, the angrier she felt. Once again, he had taken a choice out of her hands. After knowing her for only two days, he had simply decided that the time was right and linked them together permanently.

His frustration pushed back at her. His face grew harsh. For a minute he stared at her in silence. Then, as if coming to some decision, he spoke. His voice was too controlled, almost cold. "I see I have been taking the wrong approach with you all this time. I thought easing you into our new life would be best. Now I think it is time for you to confront reality and accept that your life has changed permanently. There are things you do not know yet."

Angrily, she pushed her chair back and stood. "Oh, now is the time for me to face reality, huh?" Her voice was sarcastic. "In what other ways are you planning to disrupt my life? Let's see…you could take me from my home and my friends and my job? Oh yeah," Her resentment was making her chest tight. "You've already done that. How about you invade my privacy by reading my innermost thoughts? Oh, that's right. You've done that, too."

Her voice broke and she had to swallow. Her tone softened. "I think I've faced plenty of your reality, thanks very much. I don't care what other surprises are around the corner. I've had enough of your reality."

Still seated, he looked up at her. Very softly he said, "Sit down." His tone demanded complete obedience.

When she didn't immediately respond, but continued to stare at him, he said, "You claim I have been making your choices for you. You do not wish to be treated as a child with no say in its future. Sit down and I will explain what choices you have at this time."

She could tell that he was out of patience. She could feel his anger like a living thing in the room. Holding his gaze, she carefully sat back down in her chair. "Fine. Explain."

"How many pactmates do you think file incompatible?" he asked in a conversational tone completely at odds with his expression.

She was caught off guard by the question and tone. "I don't know. I've heard that there aren't many, but I really don't know." She couldn't remember any statistics if she had ever even learned them.

"Not many." He nodded his head. His hard gaze still on her face, he continued. "One could say not many. More accurately, one should say none. There has never been an incompatible filing."

In total shock, she wondered whether he was telling the truth. "That doesn't make sense. Somewhere along the way, there had to have been some." She couldn't keep the disbelief out of her voice.

"No, Sharon, there have not been any. When a Shimerian male connects with his mate, it is not some kind of accident. He has been searching for a particular female, one that matches him mind and body. Why he is able to find her at a certain time and not before, that is a mystery. By the number of unattached males still seeking mates, you can understand that many spend years waiting and searching."

His whole body leaned forward as he said sincerely, "No one understands why it happens when it happens. But the truth is, once he connects with her, he recognizes his mate. There can be no other. Because his mind has touched hers, she unconsciously knows he is out there. She does not know his name or who he is, but the idea of that mate is there. She knows there is someone just for her. She cannot settle for less."

He watched as the anger drained from her face. "You understand what I am saying because you have felt it yourself."

Ignoring the building confusion in her expression, he continued. "We are mated in a way that cannot be denied. Our merging was inevitable. Our lives are intertwined and will never be separate again. You may fight against it or refuse to acknowledge it, but it will not change what will happen. It is convenient that you were on the register. If you had not been registered, I would have found you and taken you. It would have been more difficult, but I would have gotten you here in the end. We are meant to be together. You can fight me, but you cannot fight yourself or the rightness of our mating."

They sat there in silence as she digested his words. His anger was cooling, but there was a new hardness to his resolve.

In a subdued tone, she said, "I don't know what to think anymore. I can't seem to get my feet under me before you pull out the rug again." She rubbed a weary hand across her forehead. She looked into his eyes. "You're saying neither of us had a choice. That our coming together was cosmic destiny or something." Her eyes seemed to be begging him to help her understand.

His expression eased a little. "Cosmic destiny? Perhaps." Maybe she was truly beginning to accept. He knew she did not completely believe, but it was a beginning. It was time to show her their compatibility before she tried to distance herself again.

Standing up, he held out his hand. "Come, Sharon. We have talked as you requested. There is no need to spoil the entire suntime with weighty matters."

When she did not put her hand in his immediately, he walked around the table and took her by the arm. She stood up, but pulled free from his grasp quickly. Her action wasn't intended to insult, but he felt that way.

"Enough! Still you pull away. It is always the same. You run from me. You run from yourself. No more." With a tug, he pulled her into his arms.

She pushed back from him as much as she could in protest. "I'm not running!" She didn't want to prove him right so she forced herself to be still. "I'm thinking about what you've said."

"We are through with this talk," he muttered just before his mouth closed over hers. His kiss was demanding, giving her no choice but to respond. Under the hard pressure of his lips, her mouth opened and he thrust his tongue greedily inside. With a little moan, he pulled her tightly against him.

Her body remembered the wee hours of the night, even if her mind had been trying to block the memories. With a groan of her own, she pressed closer, enjoying the feel of his hard body. The kiss continued, steadily growing hotter, wetter. Her arms moved up his chest.

With an impatient noise, he reached under her bottom, pulling her up so that his hardness pressed into the notch between her thighs. Drowning in sensation, she wrapped her legs around his waist. His cock pushed against the heated softness of her sex, and they both stilled in pure enjoyment.

Then, with determination, he began walking down the hallway. Each step was pure sensual torture. By the time they reached the bedroom, he felt as if his cock was going to burst before he could get inside her. Sitting down on the bed, he placed her standing in front of him.

As she looked down into his face, she realized there was no point in trying to resist him. She could fight him, but she couldn't fight what he made her feel. With her surrender came another realization. This would be no patient, gentle union. His eyes were black with desire. His hands were rough as he pulled her blouse over her head and tossed it to the floor. He leaned forward immediately. His hungry mouth latched on to an aching nipple and he sucked it hard into his mouth.

Her mind shut down completely. She groaned and arched her back, feeling the delicious pull, wanting more. Her hands went to the back of his head and held him there. For the next minute he greedily sucked, pausing only to lick or gently bite. His hands roamed from her back to her hips covered only by a thin skirt and panties. He began kneading, flexing his fingers into her soft flesh.

He switched to her other breast, giving it the same attention. She was burning up from the wet heat of his mouth and tongue. With a little whimper, she shifted her weight from one leg to the other, conscious of the aching heat between her thighs. She felt overwhelmed with pleasure, out of control with need. Her hands were equally rough as she reached down and pulled his shirt over his head.

The muscular strength of his chest gleamed. She ran her hands over it, pausing to tease the flat nubs of his nipples. The answering jump of flexing muscles under her hands indicated his pleasure at her touch. She started to climb onto his lap.

Before she could get on top of him, he pushed her back. She paused in confusion. With a pained grin, he shook his head, stood up, and bent to remove his pants. In response, she reached down and quickly removed her skirt and panties.

Feeling his hungry gaze on her as he sat back down, she felt self-conscious suddenly. Holding the panties and skirt in her hand, she straightened. Gathering her courage, she looked into his face.

What she saw there surprised her. There was desire and approval, but more than that, there was need. He looked nearly as out of control as she felt. With more confidence, she threw the clothing to the floor and stood there proudly in front of him.

His gaze roamed her body, from her hair to her toes in a near physical caress. His obvious admiration made her feel powerful. He wanted her badly. He had wanted her for over a year. Swallowing past the dryness in her throat, she said, "I want you right now."

Heavy lidded, his gaze returned to her face. "Then take me, *sherree*." He reached out and helped her straddle his waist. Her knees were over his thighs, her breasts even with his mouth. Reaching down, she found his hard cock and ran her hand up and down it in a fisted motion.

He dug his hands into the sheets. His head went back and she licked the sweaty line of his throat. Balancing so that his cock was at the very edge of her entrance, she paused. His hands came to her hips.

With a shake of her head, she said, "No, I'm taking you, remember?" She was going to be in control this time around.

His head came forward and glazed eyes met hers. "This time, *sherree*. This time." Reaching a hand forward to toy with her clitoris, he said, "But I can induce you to hurry."

With a muffled moan, she slid down onto his cock halfway, before control reasserted. She used her hand and to push his hand away from her. Placing her palms on his shoulders, she levered her body back up. Staring into his face, she sank back down, slowly, inch-by-inch. Then she pulled back up with that same slow movement.

Feeling heat suffuse her body, she realized quickly that in torturing him, she was torturing herself. With each movement upward, his hard flesh rasped against the sensitive nerves of her inner muscles. As she slid back down, the pleasure flared, his hard cock filling the empty ache.

He let her control the pace, feel her own power, and satisfy her own need. This was a fantasy of hers that he had known would be delicious torment. He knew it was only a matter of time until his control broke. Her movements were growing faster. As her tight sex squeezed his aching cock, he felt the pressure building at the base of his spine.

Like the too-tight stretch of a rubber band, his control broke. He said in a hard voice, "No more."

His hands came around her like steel bands and his fingers dug into her hips. He began lifting her up and then pushing her down as he arched upward inside her.

Her nails dug into his shoulders as she lost control of her motions. He leaned forward as far as he could and began licking her nipples, teasing those hard points as if he had never tasted anything so sweet.

Between his mouth at her breast and the hard stroke of his cock, Sharon lost control. She blindly followed his guiding hands, any thought lost in a haze of need. She could only feel the rise and fall of her own body. Her focus narrowed down to the building pressure of her throbbing sex. She felt the tension gathering, her body tightening in anticipation of the coming pleasure. With a frustrated whimper, she breathed, "I'm going to come..."

She was taken by complete surprise when Liken thrust fully into her mind. He filled her head, his pleasure mingling and then multiplying her own. Screaming his name, she clung helplessly as the tension in her body broke. The pulsing contractions of her body went on and on as wave after wave of release flooded her senses.

She heard his strangled moan as her orgasm pushed him over the last edge of control. He erupted inside her, pouring into her, his entire body shaking in release. His hands on her hips were bruising, but she was barely aware of the pain. Her head fell limply on his shoulder, her entire body relaxed and heavy with exhaustion. She couldn't move. She didn't even want to move. They remained in that position for several minutes.

Finally, she lifted her head back off his shoulder and pulled back to see his face, unaware of the sensual picture she made at that moment. Her hair was a tousled mess, her face rosy and sweaty from exertion. Her eyes were glowing with satisfaction as she smiled and said, "So maybe there are some advantages to merging."

With a sense of surprise, Liken realized he wanted her all over again. Within minutes of the most powerful orgasm of his life, he was already beginning to harden inside her. As her eyes widened in shock, he wrapped a hand in her tousled hair and began pulling her head forward for a kiss. Shaking his head in mock disagreement, his lips curved as he said, "You will have to prove it to me, *sherree.*"

She answered his mock serious tone. "Well, if I must, I must. I am ever obedient."

He couldn't contain a snort of disbelief at that statement. His quiet, docile little librarian was incredibly strong-willed.

Pressing her mouth to his, she teasingly nipped his bottom lip and then gave it a conciliatory lick. She was enjoying their play.

Catching the back of her head more firmly, he spoke against her lips. "Obedient you are not...but I can be patient for a time." He grinned widely and watched as fire began to fill her eyes. To prevent her from answering, he began to actively kiss her. As the tone of the kiss began to change from playful to hungry, any response flew from her mind.

Many hours later they emerged from the bedroom motivated by the need for food. They were both passion-drunk and nearly reeling, but their faces were mirrors of happy satisfaction. Issues like destined pledgemates, incompatibility filings, and obedience were pushed away in exploration of their mutual pleasure in each other. For a brief time.

Chapter Eight

For the rest of the week, Sharon tried to keep an open mind. She wasn't sure that she believed the whole destined mate theory, but she was willing to give it a chance. Her attraction to Liken was more powerful than anything she could ever have imagined. Maybe they could love each other. She didn't like the idea of leaving Earth, but she decided to consider what living on Shimeria could mean. Maybe they could be happy together. Liken had taken great pains to show her the advantages of a life on Shimeria with him.

Each day he took her on explorations of his home world. They went to museums, restaurants, and even shopping. The "commerce centers" as he called shops were especially fun. Her face heated and she felt the warmth of desire wash over her as she remembered that trip. It had started out innocently enough when he asked if she would enjoy some shopping. They had wandered into a commerce center in the business district. Walking into the feminine shop, she thought he looked out-of-place and adorable as he seriously considered the women's clothes.

The shop had a range of colors and sizes, but the outfits were pretty similar to the ones she wore. Like most shops on Earth, the clothing hung from racks. Sharon spied a female clerk toward the back of the shop and was surprised to note that she was human. She was tall and thin, with her blonde hair pulled back into a classic bun. The female clerk came forward, eyeing him appreciatively. "May I assist you, *Isshalee*? "

Sharon bristled a little at her tone and look, but Liken appeared not to notice. He answered her seriously. "My pactmate would like to purchase some garments. It must be something special, to match her beauty."

Reluctantly turning her attention to Sharon, the clerk studied her thoughtfully for a moment. "I am sure that we can find something for you, *Isshal* ." Walking over to a rack filled with outfits, she drew out a halter of shimmering blue, with a very short skirt and panties to match. "I believe this will compliment your eyes and fair complexion quite well."

Sharon studied the length doubtfully. "I don't know. It looks a little short." It certainly didn't look like something a librarian would wear on Earth.

Liken laughed. "I believe it will look incredible on you, *sherree*. Why don't you try it on?" He wanted to see her expression when she saw herself in the outfit. Even more than her expression, he wanted to see her long legs and full breasts in that little shirt and short skirt.

Nodding uncertainly, Sharon agreed. She was trying all kinds of new things these days. She might as well go with the flow. Following the clerk into a back area of the shop, she saw that there were a series of buttons along the wall about every six feet. As the clerk pushed one, the section slid back to reveal a dressing room.

Sharon walked in and turned to get the outfit from the clerk. She was stunned to find Liken right behind her, holding the outfit. He walked through and the section slid shut behind him. She asked, "What are you doing in here?"

Liken lifted a brow. He thought it was obvious. "I'm here to watch you try on the outfit, *sherree*."

She watched him place the clothes on a hook in one wall and then sit in a chair in the far right corner. There were no mirrors to be seen. This planet was bizarre. "You mean they don't have mirrors here? I'm just supposed to rely on your opinion?"

He laughed. Pressing a button on the wall next to the chair, Liken waited for her reaction. Her astonished expression as the hologram emerged was priceless.

Sharon was staring at a three-dimensional hologram of herself. As she moved, the image moved with her, reflecting her actions. It was very lifelike, looking real enough to give her the feeling that there were three of them in the room, although two of them looked exactly alike. She cautiously moved around the room, trying to figure out where the hologram would end. As she reached Liken's chair, the image faded abruptly. She exclaimed, "That is so weird. It's so real!"

He laughed again. "Indeed it is. As you can see, we have no need for mirrors. You can see for yourself using the hologram how the clothing looks."

Sharon realized he expected her to change in front of him. He had already seen every part of her naked, she reminded herself. There was no reason to be awkward about it. Resolutely, she pulled her blouse over her head and heard Liken's breath catch in his throat.

Gaze jumping to his, she saw the raw desire heat his gaze immediately. He looked at her breasts, and she felt her nipples tighten in a tingling rush of response. Embarrassment be damned, she decided. He was looking at her like he couldn't get enough of the sight. Holding the blouse in one hand, she walked toward him and handed it to him.

He took it automatically and set it on the floor beside him, although his gaze moved to her face. She knew what that look meant. She was not having sex in a dressing room. She stepped away from him and reached for her skirt, conscious of his gaze on her. Still, it might be fun to tease him a little. She felt her own blood heat at the thought.

Liken watched as Sharon turned her back to him and began to slide the skirt over her hips, slowly. Did she have any idea how crazy she was making him? He read her thoughts, finding them a jumble of conflicting needs, desires, and ideas. He couldn't sort them out. When she turned around, he saw the triumph and feminine power in her expression and decided she knew exactly how he felt.

He smiled in appreciation and settled back in the chair to enjoy the game. Pasting a calm expression on his face, he tried to appear disinterested. He shifted in the chair as his hard cock throbbed in direct dispute of his efforts.

Sharon wasn't fooled. She searched his face as she walked toward him clad only in panties, a pair of slender sandals, and a smile. She could feel the pleasant hum of arousal coursing through her. She could feel his gaze roam her body from her head to her toes, lingering on her face, breasts, and those tiny panties.

She was getting to him. Tossing the skirt, she stepped back again and reached for one of the bows holding the sides of her panties together. His gaze followed her hand and she saw him swallow.

Abruptly moving her hand away from the panties, she turned her back to him and bent over. She had to clear her throat once, before her husky voice would emerge. "I'd better take off the shoes. They don't match the new outfit." Her position hid her knowing smile.

Liken clinched the arms of the chair until his knuckles grew white. She was giving him an excellent view of her round ass, enticingly curved under the small panties. He wanted to stand up, rip the panties off, and plunge his cock into her wet heat from behind. She was going to get the fuck of her life if she kept playing with him like this.

Having removed her sandals, Sharon stood up and turned to face Liken again. Her gaze went from his hungry face to his whitened knuckles on the arms of the chairs. He was barely in control. There was something so arousing about undressing in front of a fully clothed man, watching your every move.

She began to imagine what it would be like if they actually had sex now in the dressing room. She looked at the bulging cock tenting his pants and felt wet with the idea of having him inside her. Some demon was driving her now. She was caught up in the game as much as he was, maybe more. She wanted to feel his hands and his mouth on her body.

Her breasts were aching, the nipples sensitive. Unconsciously, one hand came forward, lightly touching her mound through the panties and then moving from her stomach upward in a caressing motion, stopping at her breasts. When she rubbed one hard nipple, she realized suddenly what she was doing.

Jerking her hand back to her side, she tried to regain a little control. She would never have sex in a public place. It was highly inappropriate. Someone might see them or hear them. Even as she reminded herself of that fact, she felt her arousal grow. She wanted to make him crazy. She wanted to see if she could drive him past that phenomenal control.

Liken gave a strangled moan and shook his head as if clearing it. When he spoke, his voice was pure temptation. "You have forgotten that I am in your mind, *sherree*. Your fantasies are quite intriguing. I do not share your reservations. Don't you want to know what it would be like? Take the panties off for me and I will show you. I will touch and taste you exactly as you imagine. Take them off." His tone started as a sultry request and ended as an order.

She hesitated. Reaching down, she pulled one string and felt the knot come undone. His face grew harsher, a flush washing over his cheekbones. Swallowing past the lump in her throat and disregarding the inner voice whispering caution, she lightly tugged the second string and felt the panties fall to her feet.

Liken stared at the curly hair of her sex for one long moment. Abruptly standing up, he watched her eyes widen as his hands went to his pants. With rough movements, he shoved open the buttons until his straining cock sprung free. Pressing the button to activate the hologram, he stalked toward her.

Sharon felt a wave of apprehension. He looked savage. Seeing a sudden hologram of herself at that moment was a shock, even as the hologram changed to become both of them. He stalked around her until he was behind her, his hands coming up to grip her shoulders so that they faced the hologram together.

She saw an image of contrasts. Her fair skin, although flushed, looked pale in comparison to his darker complexion. His hands looked huge on her shoulders. Her eyes were heavy-lidded and dark. Her breasts were full with hardened nipples thrusting outward, as if begging for his touch.

He loomed behind her, his face etched in lines of aroused hunger. She watched with fascination as his masculine hands closed over her breasts and began to massage. She moaned at the sensation and leaned into his touch.

The woman in the hologram did the same. Liken spoke in a seductive whisper next to her ear. "It is like making love while watching another couple. Or maybe like another couple watching us as we make love."

Sharon shuddered at the arousing thought. He knew exactly how to make her crazy. This whole thing was crazy. She tried to regain some control.

She stepped back, but that brought her along the hard length of his body. She could feel his shirt and pants against her nakedness. She felt his cock press against her lower back and the top of her ass. She wanted him so much it was nearly painful.

Liken moved one hand to her sex and began caressing her heat. She was soaking wet. With a quiet hum of approval he played, teasing and circling her clit. He felt her weight sag against him. The couple in the hologram echoed their movements. It was all too much for him to withstand. He was tired of being patient.

Roughly turning her, he placed her back against the left wall. His mouth latched onto one nipple, sucking roughly. Sharon moaned and looked down at him, but then her eyes were drawn back to the hologram. She watched the man's cheeks cave in as he sucked, nearly swallowing the woman's breast. The answering pull on her own breast nearly burnt her alive.

Liken lifted her by the hips with her back to the wall and then paused with her above his cock. Lowering her, he felt her sultry heat swallow him. He slid into her wetness and sank to the hilt. As their bodies merged, he merged his mind with hers. Her legs came around him to cling to his waist.

He pulled out and then thrust into her again. Sharon's head fell back against the wall. He could hear the thoughts in her mind, feel their pleasure building with each stroke. He paused, still buried in her heat.

Leaning forward, he whispered, "Remember, *sherree*, you must be quiet. If you are not quiet, the clerk will hear you."

Sharon tensed at his words. She had forgotten her surroundings. They shouldn't be doing this here. She realized her hands were clinging to his shoulders, her fingers digging into the silky material, and tried to push against his shoulders. She began to protest softly, "Liken..."

Liken covered her mouth in a passionate kiss. When he raised his head, he began thrusting again. He leaned forward and whispered quietly, tauntingly, between thrusts, "You must not call out. Someone might hear. There may be others here, too. What if they discovered us fucking, *sherree*? How would you feel?"

She moaned and then tried to muffle the sound. He thrust harder, his cock slamming into her now. Still his voice, not quite steady, taunted in her ear, "Are you going to scream for me, *sherree*? When you come will you scream?"

She gritted her teeth as her body tightened. She felt his pleasure grow along with her own. The hard thrust of his length inside her, pumping hard, was pushing her toward release. She craved it. The impulse to cry out was overwhelming. She clamped her mouth shut and tried desperately to be quiet.

Liken felt his breath hitch and tried to suppress his own moan. She was so hot and tight around his aching cock. His words, meant to arouse her, were acting on him, too. He moved his legs forward to gain leverage and thrust harder.

Suddenly, they heard the voice of the clerk from one wall away. "Isshal, is the outfit to your liking?"

Liken never paused in his thrusts. He was not stopping even if the entire planet walked in at that moment. His muscles strained with the strength and depth of his thrusts.

Sharon, on the other hand, was nearly hysterical with arousal and fear. Her heart felt like it would pound right out of her chest. She was right on the edge of release, dying to go over, and terrified of being discovered.

The clerk's voice was closer, rising higher with curiosity. "Isshal, I asked if everything is to your liking?"

Liken growled in a low snarl, "Answer her."

Sharon whispered hoarsely, "Yes," and repeated it more strongly. Liken slammed into her and she turned her face away in a desperate bid for control. Her gaze landed on the hologram couple fucking wildly next to them. Her voice rose into a scream as she yelled, "YES!" Her orgasm exploded through her like the detonation of a bomb.

Liken let out a loud groan as he felt his own scalding release. He felt the pressure move from his spine and then outward as he came in an overwhelming flood of pleasure. He was mindless with the pure animalistic relief of it.

Eventually, his legs grew weak and he shifted, making sure he would not drop her. Dropping his sweaty forehead to Sharon's, he tried to find the strength to move. Sharon was in no better shape. There was a long moment of total silence.

The clerk said with some amusement, "I am glad you are pleased, Isshal. Take as much time with the outfit as you need. I can understand your enthusiasm. I will not bother you again."

They left the store with the new outfit, although Sharon never did try it on at the shop. Liken took care of the payment with his ID card. Sharon never quite looked the clerk in the eye again, although she thought the clerk sent one or two knowing smiles of understanding her way.

Neither Sharon nor Liken could stop smiling. When they were walking home, she found out the Shimerian term for a dressing room was a "trial booth." She had certainly tried something new. Trial booth, indeed.

Coming back to the present with a start, Sharon realized the memory of yesterday was enough to make her wet and aching. She could hear the sounds of Liken taking a shower. She knew she could join him in there, but they were getting ready for a trip to the local Earth library. She really wanted to see it, and Liken had looked so pleased with his little surprise when he announced their destination for today.

Willing her aching body to relax, she focused on how much she had learned this week about Liken and Shimerian culture. It was a strange and beautiful planet, similar to Earth in so many ways and yet so remarkable in its differences. The people she had met were friendly, although seeing so few women and so many men everywhere was startling at times. She had even seen some families with children, although most of the children were boys.

She knew Liken had been careful to shield her from the less pleasant aspects of Shimerian life. Although she had not seen any evidence of it, she knew they had crime because Liken and Tair were cops. A few times on the *shimvehi* she had seen angry-looking faces with exasperated commuter expressions, but there had been no outright violence.

She and Liken had gotten along very well. He was bad about arrogantly assuming he knew what was best for her, but she pointed it out to him quickly enough. There had been minor disagreements, but most of the week had been spent in getting to know each other and learning the little things about each other that only a lover can know.

Liken had discovered that she was scared of heights, secretly read erotic stories, and had incredibly ticklish feet. She had discovered that he loved his job, that he hated Earth television, and that he was a total sucker when it came to small children.

She had been amused to watch as a tiny girl, the daughter of one of his friends, begged him to give her a *delheza* ride. Liken had given her a helpless glance and then proceeded to place the girl on his back, running and hopping while making " *delheza*" noises. He looked ridiculous, but the little girl was laughing wildly.

When Sharon and Liken had left his friends, she had teased him a little about it, but he had merely given her a red-faced shrug, as if to say, "What could I do? She asked me." It was sweet. He could be so sweet.

Sighing, Sharon walked over to the couch and sat down. She could hear the red water turn off in the bathroom. She imagined his naked body emerging from the crimson shower. She was ready to either leave for the library or jump him in the bathroom. She wished he'd hurry up.

Sharon noticed his ID card lying on the couch next to her. Picking it up restlessly, she turned it over and over in her hand. The ID card brought her back to the memory of their shopping trip. Watching him hand over his ID card at the shop that day, Sharon had wondered later about the Shimerian monetary system. Liken explained that all transactions were recorded on his card. Later, he showed her the computer in his home where he transferred the information.

His ID card was similar to a debit card from what she could tell, although it also seemed to be a computer disk of some kind. His computer was linked to central computers maintained by the government. His paycheck was deposited in his account on his computer on certain dates. It was all paperless. The librarian in her admired the organization and efficiency of the system.

Liken appeared in the living room archway, interrupting her thoughts. He looked clean and energized. He was wearing the usual black, but he looked happy and boyishly excited. He really wanted this trip to the library to be a special treat for her. He grinned, looking pleased with himself, and said, "Are you ready, *sherree*? I know you are anxious to leave so I hurried."

Sharon laughed and nodded. She knew what he had been doing. "You know I am. Don't pretend you haven't been lurking in my head."

He laughed with her and corrected, "I do not *lurk* , *sherree*. I was merely enjoying your memories of our time together."

Crossing the room and extending a hand to her, he grinned shamelessly. "Although perhaps we should squeeze in a quick shopping trip between the library and meeting Tair."

She shook her head in mock reproof. He had been lobbying for another shopping trip since that day. "You have to be the only man in the universe who loves shopping."

Putting her hand in his, she let him pull her up from the couch and felt his arms come around her in a hug. Leaning back to look at his face, she said, "Of course we'll go shopping again." Her face went bright red. "Just not to that same shop."

He threw back his head and laughed. She was such a delightful mix of contradictions-sexy and passionate one moment, and then sweet and shy the next. Leaning down, he whispered into her ear, "As long as we go to a shop with a trial booth."

Sharon could feel heat spread through her at his words. She had been right when she first saw him. He was sex personified. He had only to look at her or say something to her and she melted like wax. She cleared her throat. "I believe we were headed to the library, right?"

Liken was experiencing his own surge of arousal at the thought of another shopping trip. Placing a quick kiss on her forehead and taking his ID card from her hand, he moved away from her and said, "We'd better go. The librarian, Gar, will not be happy if we are late. He is eager to give you a tour."

* * * * *

The library was a wonder. Walking inside the outer archway of the building, Sharon expected to smell the familiar scent of books. Instead, when they walked in, she saw row after row of disks. In the center of the room there were comfortable chairs in a large open space. Seated in the chairs were maybe thirty or so adolescent Shimerian males. They stared at her in apparent fascination until a warning look from Liken made them duck their heads to the notebooks in their hands. Liken took her by the arm and led her to a counter area.

The librarian was a much older male. He had silver hair and an air of quiet dignity. He looked up with a welcoming smile as they approached. Stepping out from behind the counter, he approached Liken.

Handing the man his ID card, Liken nodded his head respectfully and placed a palm on the man's shoulder. The man mirrored his movements, which Sharon knew was the Shimerian form of shaking hands. When they stepped back, Liken put his arm around Sharon and said with obvious pride, "Gar, I would like to introduce you to Sharon Glaston, my pactmate. Sharon, please meet Gar Deyzan'can, the head librarian here and an old friend."

Gar gave Sharon an admiring glance and a warm smile. His voice was strong in contrast to his frail body. "I am most pleased to welcome you, Sharon."

Sharon gave him an answering smile and said, "Thank you. I'm pleased to meet you and very excited to learn about Shimerian libraries."

Liken was quick to add, "Sharon was formerly a librarian on Earth. It is a real pleasure for her to meet her counterpart here." He knew that Gar was aware of that fact, but he wanted to remind him of their earlier conversation.

He was assuming that she would stay here on Shimeria. Sharon didn't appreciate his use of the words "former librarian", but she let it go for the moment. She was really interested in the library and didn't want to spark a disagreement with Liken right now.

Gar seemed to have caught something of the discord in her expression. He said, "It will be a pleasure to show you, Sharon. Let us start your tour." He walked quickly behind the counter and reached down. Pulling a flat notebook from a stack behind his desk, he showed Sharon how to operate the small reader. The entire front of the notebook was a display screen.

Walking over to a row of disks, he placed one in the side of the notebook. He then inserted Liken's ID card into a slot on the other side. With a little hum, the screen lit up and displayed the cover of "A Tale of Two Cities" by Charles Dickens. The words were in English. He handed her the reader.

Placing her finger to the option screen in the upper right hand corner, she learned how to flip from page to page and even how to choose which translation she wanted to read. The language options included Earth languages as well as Shimerian. She learned the disk contained all of Dickens's works, as well as a biography of the author and all literary criticism.

Gar gave a little sigh and told her, "You should have seen the lists of works and other information first, but someone has neglected to press the reset option to return to the main index. It can be frustrating."

Thinking of her own library, she gave him a look of sympathy and said, "I know what you mean. Back at my library, we can never seem to keep people from placing books back on the shelf incorrectly."

Liken saw the look of understanding pass between them and smiled. As Gar led Sharon on a tour of the building, explaining the organization and operation of the library, Liken trailed in their wake. Watching her expressive face, he could see her enthusiasm and love of books. Her curiosity and quiet sincerity charmed Gar just as it did anyone within her orbit. He could tell she was enjoying the outing tremendously. She was happy and he felt a swell of happiness himself that he had given her this experience.

Then, he felt a flash of guilt as he wondered if she knew he had an ulterior motive. He had already spoken with Gar about

Sharon working at the library, but had sworn the older man to secrecy. This was, in a way, an informal position interview. Seeing Gar and Sharon in such accord meant she could probably work there on some basis.

It was another step toward convincing her that she could be happy on Shimeria with him. Uneasily wondering if she would accuse him of managing her choices again if she knew, he hoped she would be too happy to examine his motives very closely.

At the end of the tour, Liken and Sharon paused at the main counter. Liken removed his ID card and handed the notebook back to Gar. Placing his hand on the older man's shoulder and nodding his head, he said, "Our thanks for your kind assistance, Gar. We enjoyed the tour very much."

Gar returned the gestures and said with a smile, "No thanks are necessary." He aimed a smiling look Sharon's way. "It is a pleasure to share the experience with a fellow lover of books. She is quite wonderful, Liken. Best get her pledged quickly."

Turning to Sharon, Gar said, "My thanks for your company. I hope I will see you again, Sharon."

Sharon gave him a bright smile. Gar was a knowledgeable and efficient librarian, and a charming man. She said warmly, "Your library is a marvel and I appreciate the tour. I enjoyed it so much. I'm hoping to see you again, too." She wasn't sure if she was staying on Shimeria or not, but now wasn't the time to worry about it.

With smiling faces, Liken and Sharon exited the building and began walking along the pathway outside. Placing her hand on his arm, Sharon looked up at Liken. "Thank you for today."

Looking into her shining eyes, Liken felt a fresh wave of guilt. Deliberately reminding himself that he would have brought her just to experience her enjoyment, he placed a gentle hand against her cheek. "You are welcome, *sherree*. It pleases me to see your happiness."

The look held for a moment as they stared at each other. Removing his hand from her cheek and grabbing hold of hers, he moved them forward. After a few steps, he looked down at her. His eyes held a teasing light. His smile widened into a grin and he wagged his eyebrows suggestively. "If you wish it, you can show me your gratitude later in private."

She laughed and swung their clasped hands as they walked. "Oh, how generous of you. Let's see...what could I possibly do?" She cast him a sideways look under her lashes. "I could cook dinner tonight."

He stopped and with a mock growl, shook his head. "I think you can do better than pushing the meal buttons on our transport machine. I had in mind a more intimate activity." The look he gave her was hot with desire.

She turned her head and made a great production of letting her gaze roam his body. Her expression was speculative. "I don't know...what could be more intimate?"

She appeared to be contemplating the question. Stepping closer and bringing her free hand to his chest, she brushed her body against his. "This could take some thought." She pulled her hand from his grasp and ran it teasingly down his chest to the top of his pants. "A great deal of thought." She could feel his cock start to harden.

He wrapped his arms around her and pulled her into the hard planes of his body. His eyes were dark with desire. "You are an intelligent woman, *sherree*. I have great confidence in you."

Abruptly breaking his hold, she danced away. Her face had flushed with desire as well, but her eyes were teasing. "Unfortunately, I can't think about it now. We are late for supper with Tair."

His look said she could expect retribution later. "Yes, teasing does tend to make one forget the time." He was secretly thrilled with her easy flirtation. She felt comfortable enough to tease him sexually.

With a mock sigh and a glance at the time device on his wrist, he said, "We will continue this later. Now, I am sorry to say, you are right. We will be late if we do not hurry."

With matching smiles, they hurried along the pathways leading to the eatery where Tair waited. When they entered the building where they had met him the last time, Sharon barely noticed the sudden hush and the fascinated stares. Looking around for Tair, she spotted him in the far right corner of the room. Smiling and waving, she headed for his table.

Weaving her way there with Liken behind her, she never saw Tair's sweeping look around the room. His predatory gaze froze his fellow diners in place until they looked quickly away from Sharon's form and focused on eating. The mental warning had been so brief and effective that Sharon reached the table completely unaware.

With a silent nod of acknowledgement for his assistance, Liken sank into a chair next to Sharon. In contrast to just a few seconds earlier, Tair's face had a gentle smile when he turned to Sharon. "You are looking quite beautiful, Sharon."

Smiling with obvious happiness, Sharon said. "Thank you, Tair. We went to the library today."

Tair frowned in mock astonishment. "So that is what has left you flushed and put a glow in your eyes?" He glanced over at Liken and shook his head in reproof. "We need to have a discussion, brother. "

Watching the blush climb into Sharon's cheeks, Liken said with a laugh. "I do not believe the library is solely responsible, Tair." He leaned toward her and gently nuzzled her cheek. "Sharon has found other things on Shimeria that are also highly enjoyable."

Sharon felt like her face was on fire. They were ganging up on her. She was in too good a mood to let them get to her. She felt sexy and happy and powerful. She was not going to give in to embarrassment at their teasing.

Clearing her throat, she decided to fight fire with fire. Placing her hand on Liken's thigh under the table, she watched his teasing grin begin to fade. She gently stroked the taut muscles in his thigh, her fingers heading up toward his crotch. Liken had turned to stone at the first touch of her hand.

Turning toward Tair, she leaned toward him and spoke in a throaty voice that spelled pure sex. "Oh, yes. I have found several activities to...arouse my...interests."

Tair seemed trapped in her heated gaze, his heart rate climbing at the sound of her husky voice. Deliberately moistening her lips, she smiled inwardly as both men stared in fascination. This femme fatale business was easier than she thought it would be.

Carefully straightening her shoulders as she leaned back in her chair, her breasts rose to prominent attention. Again, both men seemed unable to pull their gaze away. Feeling the power of her allure, she smiled and raised her free hand to lightly stroke her throat. "Are you guys really hot?" Her mind filled with naughty images, the fantasies making her pupils dilate.

Their eyes widened. Tair stared at her stroking hand and then dropped his eyes to her breasts. Her nipples hardened. Wetting his lips, he swallowed.

Liken was in no better shape. Her hand under the table reached its destination. His bulging arousal was pushing against his pants, flexing under her fingers. He made a strangled sound and quickly moved one hand to hold her in place. He was rock hard and throbbing.

In an innocent voice she exclaimed, "I think it's hot in here, don't you?" Deciding she had neatly turned the tables on them both, she looked around for a waiter. Catching his eye, she nodded toward their table. He walked toward them quickly.

The waiter gave her an efficient smile and asked, "How can I be of assistance? Have you decided on your choices?" His words forced their attention away from her.

Liken's grip on her hand relaxed and she took advantage of the moment to pull her hand back into her own lap. Tair sat back in his chair and visibly worked to regain his composure. She looked from one man to the other. Other than the dark awareness in their eyes, they looked pretty normal.

In a cool and natural voice, she said, "I think they could use something to cool off. What kind of refreshing beverage would you recommend?"

As she discussed the various choices with the waiter, Liken and Tair looked at each other. Tair's eyes were speculative as he spoke in their own language. "*That one is deceptive. She has more fire than she knows.* " He was still sweating a little from his reaction to her.

Liken's eyes were gleaming. Sharon was far bolder and passionate than most people realized, including herself. " *Yes, I know. She is incredible.* "

Tair shook his head in disbelief. " *A librarian. I thought she was the quiet one.*"

Liken laughed quietly. "*She sees herself that way. To be fair, I don't think she realized she was broadcasting her fantasies to the two of us. She is unaware of our link or the power of such images.*"

"*You haven't told her of linking? Or what it means?* " Tair was incredulous. He was shocked that Sharon was unaware of the coming link. It was natural to hide the knowledge from prospective Earth mates until after the pact to lesson any fear, but he could not believe Liken had not explained to Sharon about it before now.

Liken was exasperated. "*I am only just now getting her comfortable with merging, brother. She was sexually inexperienced. I'm not going to scare her to death.*" Sharon had been resistant to intimacy from the start. He had no doubt that she would react badly to the idea of linking. Human culture was so strange.

Tair conceded that point. "*I can understand. You don't have much time left, though. We must perform the linking tomorrow next. Shocking her at the last minute is not a good idea.*"

Liken grimaced. "*I know. I plan to tell her tonight. I thought after an enjoyable day and some time in your company, she might not be as shocked at the idea. You could play your part by staying non-threatening and charming.*" It was more of a reminder than a request.

Sharon spoke up at that moment, startling the two men. "Hey, guys, I hate to break up your little talk, but the waiter here needs to know what you want." She was curious about why they were speaking Shimerian suddenly.

When they turned identical charming smiles in her direction, she felt distinctly uneasy. What were they hiding? Although she had picked up a few Shimerian words and phrases, she had no idea what they had been saying. If she stayed on this planet, she would need to learn the language. Being in the dark about what they had been discussing was making her nervous.

When they each had given the waiter their choices for the meal, the waiter left for a back room. Silence fell between them. Liken and Tair could both sense her rising uneasiness. Hitting on something that would divert her attention and make her happy, Tair spoke quickly. "Sharon, I have good news for you."

His comment startled her. She couldn't imagine what he meant. "Good news for me?"

"Yes, I think it will make you very happy." With a glance toward Liken, he turned to face her fully. "Kate is my pactmate."

Her shock was easy to see. "What?!"

"I will be invoking the Oath after you return to take your pledge next week. You and Kate will not be separated." He waited for her look of happiness and relief. He had looked forward to seeing her reaction to this news for some time.

She began laughing, which caught the two men by surprise. As her laughter rose in volume and her shoulders began to shake, their puzzlement grew.

Tair, wondering if he should take insult, could make no sense of her reaction. "You find the thought amusing?"

"I find the thought hysterical," she choked out. "She's gonna kick your ass."

He looked thunderous in response.

Liken quickly cut in, "I am sure Sharon does not mean to insult you, brother." He shot a reprimanding look at Sharon.

She just rolled her eyes in response. She really hadn't meant to insult him. The comment wasn't directed at Tair's abilities as much as it was Kate's reaction. Bringing her laughter under control, she tried for a conciliatory tone. "I didn't mean to insult you, Tair. Really. No offense meant."

Tair's voice was stiff. "You do not know me very well, Sharon."

Sharon realized he was serious. He felt insulted, his pride injured. Feeling badly, she tried to explain, "No, I know that. I don't doubt you or your, uh, abilities. I have to point out, though, that I do know Kate. She's my best friend in the world so I can tell you the truth. Nobody walks on Kate. She can be a cast iron bitch if you try."

Tair's shoulders relaxed a little. "I know about her temper, Sharon." That temper was going to make things quite interesting between them. He smiled at the thought.

She leaned forward. "That's not really what I meant. Kate doesn't do submissive. Liken's domineering ways make me crazy and, believe me, I let him know about it. Kate, on the other hand, would've just killed him and been done with it. No need to compromise or explain. She might even be a little sorry afterward, but she'd get the job done. She'd never put up with Shimerian attitudes." She looked at Liken to see if he, at least, understood.

"Sharon, look at me." It was an order, given by Tair in a voice that was intense and compelling. He didn't sound like himself. She watched as Tair's face grew harsh. His eyes, which had looked gentle and charming in the past, took on a predatory hardness. His mouth held a touch of cruelty. "Do I look like I do not know how to get what I want?" The change in him was drastic to see.

"Tair?" Sharon said his name with a questioning note. She felt a pang of pure panic. The man sitting next to her had become a dangerous stranger. He stared at her in silence. She swallowed, "I get your point." She clasped her hands together in her lap and suddenly wondered if insulting him had been such a bright idea.

Liken's hand covered hers in her lap with a comforting warmth. Aiming a warning glance at Tair, he said, "My brother will make Kate very happy in the end, *sherree*. Do not worry."

Sharon wouldn't place any bets on that statement. She was relieved to see the waiter approaching the table. As he placed their dishes in front of each of them, they remained silent.

Even after he left, Sharon stayed silent, lost in her thoughts. She had no idea if she was staying on Shimeria, regardless of how well things had been going. The last week had been a kind of honeymoon period, but she knew there were bound to be conflicts ahead. She and Liken had spent most of their time in a sensual haze, not wanting anything to spoil the pleasure. They were both on their best behavior. It couldn't last indefinitely.

She wasn't sure if she would stay, so the thought of Kate becoming Tair's pactmate didn't bring a lot of comfort. If she stayed, Kate might still file incompatible. If Sharon filed incompatible, Kate might choose to stay. It was unlikely, but seeing Tair in a new light, she knew it was possible. Kate was used to calling all the shots with men. Sharon had always figured the right man for Kate would be one she couldn't walk all over. Maybe Tair was the right man. Or alien, in this case. Either way, the future was still uncertain.

"You are not eating, Sharon." Liken's voice broke into her thoughts. "Are you truly upset by Tair's news?"

Liken knew by her face that she was upset. He was trying to stay out of her thoughts more, since they were both adjusting to the intimacy. He knew it made her uncomfortable, particularly when she was upset.

Sharon made an effort to appear more relaxed. She took a quick bite of her food, but her turmoil made it tasteless. "Not at all. I'm fine." Her deadpan voice said just the opposite.

Tair felt guilty for ruining her mood. She had been radiant when she entered the eatery and sat down at the table. His voice held unmistakable remorse when he spoke. "I thought only to bring you happiness with my news. My apology to you, Sharon."

She looked into a face that had grown softer. His eyes sought to reassure her. She liked Tair, even trusted him to some degree because he was Liken's brother. He was trying to regain her earlier comfort with him. She wasn't fooled.

With serious eyes, she studied him. "Thank you, Tair, but the apology isn't necessary. What happens between you and Kate will be up to the two of you. I would like you both to be happy. If you end up happy together, that would be terrific."

She wanted to put them on an easier footing as well. With more enthusiasm than she felt, she picked up another square-shaped bite of mystery meat and popped it in her mouth. In an abrupt change of subject, she swallowed and said, "What exactly am I eating again? This is delicious." She picked up another bite and turned to Liken to answer her question.

He regarded her solemnly. "I am glad you find it so tasty, *sherree*. It is called *ufrantri* and is considered quite a delicacy."

He waited as she put the bite in her mouth and began to chew. "The literal translation would be yellow worm in your language I believe." Sharon choked a little as his words registered. Liken winked at Tair.

Worm? They were feeding her worm?! Sharon felt the moist meat in her mouth and nearly gagged. Should she swallow it or find some way to ditch it in her napkin? She was pretty sure it was bad table manners to throw up the main dish in a crowded restaurant. Even on weird Shimeria. She decided then and there that adventure sucked. Exotic cuisine. Yeah. Right.

Liken did not let her suffer for long. "Go ahead and swallow it, *sherree*. It is not really a worm. I said that was the literal translation. It is actually not a meat at all, but a tubular vegetable." He could not contain his laugh at the killing look she aimed his way.

Tair began laughing, too. "It is similar to your potato, Sharon, but longer in length and narrower." As she swallowed and continued to glare at both of them, they laughed harder.

Liken's voice was apologetic but his eyes sparkled with mirth. "I could not resist."

Reaching down, he picked up another square shaped bite. This one was brown. Holding it out to her, he said. "Come, *sherree*, where is your sense of adventure? I would not feed you something abhorrent, would I?"

Taking the brown thing in her hand, she examined it suspiciously. Her voice was dry. She said firmly, "I believe I prefer my adventure between the covers of a book."

"Not you, *sherree*. You are a woman of fire." His voice held a sultry warmth while his eyes dared her to put the bite in her mouth.

Sharon felt the heat climbing into her cheeks at his passionate reference. He was driving her crazy on purpose. She was sure of it.

"Oh, that's right. I'm a new woman these days. I think nothing of interplanetary travel. I seek out new life and new civilizations. I boldly go where..." She slapped her free hand against her forehead in mock surprise. "Whoops, that's not me. What was I thinking? I'm just the idiot who tastes whatever you give her."

She rolled her eyes. Pushing aside any thoughts on what it might be, she put the bite in her mouth. She was relieved to find it tasted pretty good.

Liken watched her with satisfaction. "An idiot? I think not. I would say you trust me, *sherree*. And that makes you very smart indeed."

"I trust you not to poison me at least, "she said with an exasperated smile. Her voice was light. She wasn't about to feed that colossal arrogance of his.

His gaze held hers. "Progress is still progress, however small." Both had forgotten Tair, who was listening to the exchange with great interest.

She shrugged and looked away. "Or maybe I just can't resist a dare."

She felt him lean toward her. His breath tickled her ear as he whispered, "We shall see, *sherree*. Soon. In that you can trust." To Sharon, the words sounded part promise, part threat. With Liken, it never paid to grow too complacent.

The rest of the meal went by uneventfully. They talked and laughed, enjoying themselves. When Liken and Sharon left the restaurant, she felt alive and happy in a way she couldn't remember. Pushing all thoughts of the coming decision from her mind, she basked in her newfound contentment with Liken. They made love that evening with tenderness and passion, both of them avoiding anything that might break their fragile sense of happiness and accord.

That profound sense of harmony made what happened next seem even more painful. Everything went straight to hell the next day. After a lovely evening with Liken and Tair and then a night of incredible pleasure in Liken's arms, Sharon had no clue the very next day that things were going to change in a heartbeat.

Or rather, things were going to change with one word.

Chapter Nine

"You want me to do *what* with your brother tomorrow?" Her voice was strangled with disbelief.

They were sitting in the living room after supper or "evemeal" as he called it. They were casually talking and the conversation had drifted to Tair. Leaning cozily against his side, listening to the mellow sounds drifting from the machine hidden in the wall to her right, Sharon had no clue he was about to toss a conversational grenade her way. She moved out of his arms and turned around to look at him.

He knew he looked like he was headed for a funeral. He had been dreading this conversation for so long. He winced and said, "I will explain..."

"Explain?" she interrupted. "Yeah, that would be good. Because I could have sworn you just told me I'm supposed to get it on with your brother!" Her voice was rising. Surely he hadn't meant what she thought he meant.

He looked confused. He was familiar with most human slang, but her words made no sense. "I'm not sure of your meaning."

"Let me clarify then. Did you just tell me that you're going to try to force me to have sex with Tair?" Her gaze locked on his face, hoping for some sign of disagreement.

His expression cleared. He looked appalled. "That is not what I said." Slowly enunciating his words, he said, "You will be linking with my brother."

Now it was her turn to look confused. "I don't understand."

Liken took a deep breath as he gathered his patience for the battle ahead. He should have told her last night as he had planned, but he had procrastinated, not wanting to disrupt their harmony. He could no longer wait.

"These are dangerous times, Sharon. Believe me, I see that as a guardian every day. I have protected you from harm so far, but I will not always be with you. You are linked with me through our merging, but Shimerian law and custom require at least one other link. If you were in distress, I would know it and come to your aid. The second link with a close friend or family member is to ensure that someone else is available as well."

She cautiously nodded her head. "I can understand the theory, but I'm not merging with Tair."

His eyes went hard. "No, you will not *merge* with Tair."

"What do you mean by linking then?" She was calming down. He wasn't talking about her having sex with Tair. Maybe this wasn't as bad as she thought.

"He will link to you mentally. Think of it as a pathway from your mind to his."

"You mean he'll be in my head, too?" She was not having two guys traipsing around her thoughts whenever they wanted. Liken was bad enough.

"Not really, *sherree*. His mind will pierce the shield I have built for you and leave an opening for him like a doorway." His voice was reassuring. He was glad to see her calming.

She didn't really like the idea of a doorway in her head. "Can anybody walk in?"

"No, only Tair and, of course, me."

She mulled it over. "Can he walk in anytime he wants and just know what I'm thinking?"

Again, he answered in that reasonable tone. "He would only travel the link if you were in distress, *sherree*. Tair is trustworthy. He will not spy on your private thoughts. He will hear when you broadcast loudly, but otherwise your thoughts are safe." They would be even safer when he taught her to broadcast less openly, but the process would take time.

She couldn't shake her unease. She liked Tair. She could even understand having a second hotline installed as a backup for emergencies. She didn't like the thought of giving anyone access to her mind. She didn't have any choice with Liken. It was too late. They were already merged. Linking with Tair, however, was still within her power to choose. Another thought occurred. "Why did you say tomorrow? Were you just suggesting we get it over with then?"

Liken's mouth firmed. "Tomorrow is the tenth day of our knowing period. Merging and linking must be complete by the end of that day. It is the law."

She looked indignant. "Screw the law."

He felt his temper begin to stir, but held it back. "Again, it is there for your protection, Sharon. Females on this planet are cherished and protected above all else."

"From what? This place is peaceful. It's not exactly a hotbed of crime. I don't understand what I'm supposed to be protected against!" She was trying to sort through the confusion.

In a careful voice he told her. "When we merged, I built a shield to protect you. It is not invincible. But when Tair layers his strength over mine, you will be safe from nearly anyone. There is evil on this planet, just as evil exists on your own. The difference is that on my planet, an evil man can use his mind to cause harm. He can literally probe into the minds of others. If they fight him, he can cause a great deal of damage. When I probe someone who is unwilling, I do it with great skill and care. I do not cause harm. I care whether I hurt or kill someone."

His mouth was grim. "You cannot even imagine what occurs when a criminal attempts a merge on an unwilling female. She will fight him because it is instinctive. When I merged with you, as a human you had absolutely no defenses. You were not able to struggle and I was careful to cause no damage. Now that I have put defenses in place for you by building a shield, for someone to try to force a merge..."

His voice trailed off as if he didn't even want to contemplate it. "It would take a lot to break my shielding. If it broke, you might survive, but the damage would be terrible. By adding Tair's shielding to mine, we increase the odds that it would never happen."

He paused, drew a deep breath, and continued. "I would see you protected to the greatest degree possible. Adding Tair's shielding to mine is necessary, *sherree*."

Sharon nodded her head in understanding, but she wasn't completely sure that it was really necessary. This mental shielding business was bizarre.

To make sure she understood his point, he gave her an example. "What if I put a piece of cloth over a peach? I could take a needle and it would take only a pinprick through the cloth to get to the peach."

Holding her gaze, he willed her to take his next words seriously. "Now what if I take a metal bowl and place it over that same peach? It would take a sharp hammer and considerable force to punch through the metal. But if the hammer punched through, you know what would happen to the peach."

She looked sick. "I see what you mean." There was no missing that imagery. "So between you and Tair, nobody's gonna get through."

He hoped she was right. "There are no guarantees, *sherree*. Tair and I are both very strong shielders. It would be nearly impossible. I cannot lie and tell you it could not happen. I can only say that we would probably all three die in such a case."

His words struck right into her heart. He would protect her with his life. Tair would protect her with his life. Her chest tightened with the thought. In a desperate attempt to lighten the moment, she blurted out, "Who says guys can't commit?"

He let out a startled laugh. For a moment there, he had been mortally afraid she was going to cry or something equally as terrifying. With tremendous relief, he said, "Indeed, we poor males are often judged most unfairly." He winked.

She laughed too. Regaining her composure, she became serious again. "All right, I'll link with Tair. What exactly do we need to do tomorrow?"

He was past the first obstacle but he knew her agreement was not secure. Bracing himself for the explosion, he said calmly, "At the point of your orgasm, while we are merged, he will link with you." He waited in silence for her to work it out.

Her brow wrinkled in confusion. "That's bizarre. Why the point of orgasm?" She still hadn't considered the rest of his statement.

"At the point of orgasm, *sherree*, you are most vulnerable. You are out of control, unable to think. Your senses and the power of our minds merging will overwhelm you. There is no chance you will try to fight him."

"Couldn't he just link with me in my sleep?" she suggested hopefully. It seemed more logical and less bizarre.

"I cannot merge with you when you are sleeping without sleeping myself. Tair will need my help to get past my shielding. Besides, you might awaken and try to fight him." The tension of waiting was killing him.

"But how will he know the exact point of orgasm?" A sudden thought crossed her mind but she couldn't believe it.

Very calmly, speaking softly, Liken said. "Because he will be with us."

Her eyes widened and she shook her head in automatic denial. "With us?!" Her heart began pounded and she felt lightheaded. "What do you mean with us?!"

"He will be in the room with us. Once I have merged with you, he will be touching you. He will wait and then link with you when you come." His voice was firm. The expected explosion occurred immediately.

" *No way*! I can't believe this! I can't believe you would even go along with this!" Her voice began to get shrill. "One minute you tell me you and Tair would die trying to protect me. The next minute you casually announce that the three of us…"

Her voice broke and tears were a burning pressure behind her eyes. She jumped up from the couch and turned her back on him. Staring at the wall, she tried to regain some control.

Liken felt his chest tighten at the anguish in her voice. He opened his mouth to speak, but she seemed to sense it and held her hand up. It was as if by throwing her hand up, she could ward off his words.

He sucked in a breath and let it out slowly. He couldn't handle the thought of reducing her to tears. He waited for her to speak.

After a minute, her shoulders straightened and she turned to face him again. Her eyes were dry chips of ice, but her voice was even colder. "I'm not fucking your brother." Each word was spaced with emphasis.

The welling emotion in Liken's chest turned to fury in an instant. "I did not ask you to fuck my brother."

Her voice was like a bullet. "Then what do you mean he'll be there during sex. How will he be touching me?" Crushing cynicism filled her tone.

His voice was harsh. "Most of the time he will be across the room. After I merge with you, he will press his body along yours."

" *No* . I won't be any part of this." She spoke resolutely. "I'll take my chances. No link." She started pacing, her movements echoing her inner agitation.

Liken stood up and towered over her, stopping her in mid-stride. Any last bit of patience he had was gone. "You will do it. Tair will build you a better shield."

"He can build a better mousetrap if he wants to," she shot back, "but he's not doing it in my head."

He grabbed her arms and glared down at her. "There will be no sex between you since that is your will. But body contact is necessary." He felt like shaking her, but didn't.

She raised a rebellious face upward. "Oh right." Her voice was sharp enough to cut glass. "He'll just be watching us and rubbing against me while we fuck. I don't know why I thought that was sexual."

His jaw was so tight it would probably lock permanently. "Enough. You will do as you are told." His tone was final.

She gave a laugh of disbelief. "That's it? I'll do as I'm told?!" She thought that maybe her head would blow off from sheer temper. "Listen, big guy, you merged with the wrong gal. I'm not a child you can order around."

His voice was ruthless. "You will obey me in this. It is for your protection."

The tension was thick enough to cut with a knife. "I won't obey you in anything, but especially not this. What are you going to do tomorrow, rape me?" Her voice turned ugly. "Will Tair watch that too?"

110

He abruptly turned loose of her. His voice was colder than she'd ever heard it. "I am done with this. I will be back later when you have regained your reason."

He turned and headed for the door. Hitting the button nearly hard enough to leave an impression in the wall, he strode past the sliding door and turned back. His voice was mocking. "Your trust is quite touching, Sharon. Your resourcefulness is impressive as well. You have found yet another way to run."

He leaned wearily against the doorway. Bitterness was carved into his face. "You forget-I know your fantasies. I was at the table with Tair last night when certain images ran through your mind. You grew wet at the thought. Deny it to me if you must, but be honest with yourself. The thought of my brother in the room with us scares you, but you are not as outraged as you pretend."

He stared at her for a minute, but she made no response. He turned and walked down the pathway. The door slid shut in his wake.

His words struck her like a blow. Sinking to the ground, she tried to calm down. As she wrapped her arms around herself in unconscious comfort, she felt numb with grief. Hurt was a living thing in her chest.

He didn't love her. You couldn't have love without respect. He thought she would obey him like a child. She could only gasp in outrage. He thought it was okay for Tair to be with them.

It was at that moment she realized she could feel his hurt and anger pressing upon hers. It was flowing between them, a benefit of merging, causing magnified grief. Wiping a hand across her face wearily, she wondered how things could have gone so wrong so fast.

Cosmic Destiny. It sucked.

Chapter Ten

Tair opened the door of his home to find a seething Liken on his doorstep. He spoke in Shimerian. "*Enter, brother. I could feel your anger raging at me all the way from your dwelling.*"

Liken walked past him and Tair pushed the button, sliding the door into place. Turning around, he leaned against it and watched his brother storm into the living room. Walking to a button on the wall, Liken pressed it and removed a bottle of *lerj*. Bringing it to his mouth, he took a healthy swallow.

Tair winced. The potency of the alcoholic drink was well known. He could attest to it himself. Liken must have scorched his insides with that big of a swallow.

Moving to join his brother in the living room, he sat down on the couch. Liken paced with the bottle still in his hand. In the voice of someone trying to sooth a wild animal, Tair said, "*Liken, you and Sharon are both broadcasting at an alarming level.*" He rubbed his hand across his aching forehead.

Liken really looked at his brother for the first time. There were lines of stress in Tair's face and there was dull pain in his eyes. Knowing his own face looked worse, he felt guilty nonetheless. "*My apologies, Tair.*" He made a visible effort to calm down.

"*You and Sharon are building the hurt and anger between you, Liken. You need to pull back from her for a time. It is dangerous.*" Tair hated to see his brother in such shape. The voice of reason was definitely needed here.

With a nod of assent, Liken worked on withdrawing and blocking Sharon as much as he could. He could not sever himself from her completely but he could block her out for a time. They both needed it. He knew Tair was right.

Tair gave him a tired smile of approval. *"I am glad you see reason. You need to put your emotions aside, brother, and begin thinking instead."*

Liken felt another wave of anger move through him, but he focused on getting it under control. *"I suppose you know what was said."*

Tair's voice was wry. *"I could not help knowing. It was practically an assault."* He felt sorry for both of them. The angry words and feelings from their argument made him feel raw and unhappy.

Liken felt guilty again. *"We had no right to so abuse you, Tair. I can only say that we are newly merged and we will learn better control with time. Again, my apologies."*

Tair waived them aside. *"There is no need, Liken. I am much more concerned with what has happened. Why is she so resistant?"* He couldn't understand why Sharon would be so against such a natural thing.

Liken knew Sharon very well, perhaps even better than she knew herself. *"There are many reasons. She is afraid, uncomfortable with her growing sexuality. She doesn't completely trust me. She was raised in a culture very different from our own. She viewed you being in the room as a desire on my part to share her. It doesn't reconcile with her idea of love."*

Tair shook his head. *"Those are all things that can be handled with reassurances and patience. We are a very sexual culture, but possessive as well. You need to get her to understand that my linking with her is not a betrayal. It is customary. As a matter of fact, it is necessary. She judges it as an infidelity and assumes you do not care for her. You must show her she is wrong."*

Liken collapsed into the chair across from Tair and took another swig from the bottle. *"Easily said, brother. How can I make her understand? I tried reasoning, I tried ordering, and still she refuses to trust me. She pulls back from me."*

He slouched down and laid his head on the back of the chair. *"She fights me for every inch of progress. I think I can hold her and then she slides out of my arms and runs from me again. It is maddening."*

"*So it is just your pride aching.*" Tair's voice was suspiciously smooth.

"*Of course.* " Liken's voice was firm, but he was rubbing his hand over his chest unconsciously. "*She is merely a woman, pactmate or no. I grow sick of rejection.*"

Nodding in agreement, Tair gave him a half smile. "*So do not worry, brother. In a few days, you can file incompatible. You will never see her again. The portal to Earth is always open. There are many females there besides her. Not another pactmate for you like her, but there will be females who are not so impossible.*"

Liken's head came up. He heard the goading tone in his brother's voice but ignored it. His voice rose as he agreed, "*That is right! I do not need this chaos. Who needs her?*"

Tair sat waiting silently. It wouldn't be long, he was sure. The room was quiet until the silence was broken by Liken's sigh. His voice full of misery, Liken said, "*I do. She is mine and I am not giving her up.*"

Tair sat forward and grinned. "*Okay, brother. Then you will keep her.*" His face turned serious as he said, "*What you have tried has not worked. It is time to stop trying and start doing. You have never backed down from a challenge before.*"

Liken set the bottle down and leaned forward with new resolution. "*You are right. Tonight she is through running from me. What cannot be taken with gentle patience can still be held by force.*"

He felt a new sense of calm and purpose. Sharon was at home weeping in anguish, he was sure. He would go to her and make things right. Then, he would force her to face herself and her relationship with him.

Opening his block with her, Liken went completely still. Both men felt the blood in their veins turn to ice. Jumping to their feet, they headed in a panic for the front door.

Sharon was not at home. And she certainly wasn't crying.

Chapter Eleven

Sharon was at the eatery. She had grown tired of sitting on the living room floor after Liken left. After about a half-hour in absolute misery she felt a sudden emptiness. Without being sure how she knew, she could tell Liken had withdrawn from her nearly completely. She should have been happy to have him out of her head. Instead, she felt a sense of loneliness that only added to her hurt.

Finally, she stood up with renewed purpose. With each step around the room, her hurt became swallowed by anger. How dare he order her around and expect her to wait for his return like a child? She was a grown woman. She had come to this planet, had mind-blowing sex with a near stranger, gotten laid in a dressing room, and eaten exotic food. She wasn't some sweet helpless young thing too scared to leave the house.

She was tired of just reacting to whatever he did next. It was time to take charge. Past time. He had hurt her, but she wasn't going to sit around and whine about it. The thought of possible danger crossed her mind. She was connected to the big idiot if she ran into mind trouble. Anything else she could handle herself. She needed to get away from *his* house. She was going out. To hell with him.

Leaving the house, she walked angrily for a while, not really caring of the direction. She was oblivious to her glittering skin or the beautiful glow of the buildings in the silvery moonlight. She didn't see anyone else until she was nearly in front of the eatery.

There were Shimerian males coming out and a few going in. Their dark features reminded her of Liken and she moved forward with resolution. She was not a prisoner, waiting for her jailer to give her permission to leave the house and have a night out.

Walking through the archway, she searched the room until she spotted an empty table. Around her, a dozen Shimerian men paused with their drinks halfway to their mouths. Another handful nearly choked as they watched her cross the room. There was complete silence.

Sharon was angry enough not to care. Sitting down at the empty table, she sent a sweeping glare around the room. Just great. More men. Like she wasn't sick to death of them already. And where were the damn women on this planet tonight? It was testosterone hell.

A waiter she recognized from her previous visits appeared at the table after nearly running across the room. She looked up at him with a grim parody of a smile. "Bring me something alcoholic and put it on that idiot Liken's account. You remember me, don't you?"

He flashed her a cautious smile. "Of course, Isshal." He seemed ruffled. "But I don't understand...alcoholic?" The word was unfamiliar but his shock at seeing a lone unescorted female in the eatery at this hour was enough to cause greater confusion.

She searched for another word to explain. "Fermented. You know, a beer. Hell, a shot of tequila might be better."

He must have understood what she meant because he nodded and hurried into the back. Sharon glanced around the room again, noticing conversations in low tones being carried on around the room. At least they weren't staring at her like an exotic animal escaped from the zoo anymore.

Her thoughts turned inward as she thought about the ugly scene with Liken. The more she tried to push it away, the more their angry words echoed in her head. She was trying to stay angry. Angry was a lot better than hurt.

The waiter came back with a small bowl and set it down in front of her. She looked down at it in surprise. It looked like cream of wheat or something. She couldn't believe it. She was too shocked to say anything as he nodded and scurried away.

She felt defeated. Her shoulders slumped. Nothing on this planet made any sense. She muttered to herself, "Ask for a beer and they bring me baby cereal. I hate this place. I feel like an idiot. What am I saying? Men are idiots."

She felt a big body drop gracefully into the chair across from her. Lifting her gaze from the bowl, her mouth dropped open in shock. In the chair across from her sat possibly the most gorgeous guy she'd ever seen. He had a face like a dark angel. His black hair fell in soft waves just ending at the top of massive shoulders. He could have dropped down from heaven if it weren't for his eyes. They were dark brown, nearly black and the hardness in them said he'd seen hell.

His lips curved upward in a smile that never reached those eyes. "Even idiots have their uses, *sherree*, wouldn't you agree?"

The sound of him calling her by the same endearment Liken used caused her heart to clutch. "What does *sherree* mean?" Yet another question she should have asked long ago.

He looked amused by her question. He spoke in English with just a touch of an accent. "It is an endearment that doesn't really translate well. I guess the closest English word would be baby."

Anger washed through her all the way down to her toes. "It figures. He treats me like a child. I should have guessed he's been calling me one."

His smile widened. His voice was like chocolate, soothing and wickedly tempting at the same time. "I cannot imagine any man treating you like a child."

She blushed. She stammered out a reply as her heart beat against her ribs. "I didn't mean..." There wasn't anything to say that wouldn't mortify her even worse.

He was openly grinning now and it transformed his face. He looked like a mischievous little boy. "I presume you are speaking of your missing pactmate?"

She was startled. "Why would you assume I have a pactmate? And why would you assume he's missing? I could just be out on the town by myself to relax after a hard day at the office. Besides, I could be pledged."

He shook his head. "You are unescorted. You are too beautiful to be unclaimed. And you are from Earth. Yet, you are still here alone. That means there is an unhappy pactmate somewhere close by." His voice was persuasive. "Tell me his name. Perhaps I will not mind fighting him for a woman such as you."

That scared her a little. She wasn't the type of woman that men brawled over. She wouldn't mind kicking Liken's ass, but she didn't want him actually fighting some other guy. Especially not someone like this guy. They would hurt each other for sure.

She needed to get rid of him. With a little shrug, she said, "Does it matter? Look, I just came here for a beer. I've got one idiot male and I don't really need another one, okay?" Sharon looked away, hoping he would take the hint and leave her alone.

His voice was firm. "What is your name? And his? I will not leave until I know." Turning and staring into those dark eyes, she knew he wasn't going to let the matter drop. And he wasn't going to leave either.

"I'm Sharon Glaston. My pactmate is Liken da'Kamon." Just saying Liken's name made her eyes burn and her chest tighten. Suddenly, she felt despondent again. She looked away or she would have seen his obvious surprise.

When she had a little more control, she turned to face him and saw him eyeing her speculatively. His grin was back. "So, Liken is the idiot causing you such distress."

Her eyebrows rose. "You know him?"

He said easily, "We have met. What has he done to make you so unhappy, Sharon?"

She wasn't sure she wanted to tell him. He seemed nice, but there were those hard eyes.

He saw her indecision. With a nod, he gestured the waiter over. Speaking in Shimerian, he had a conversation with the waiter, who then went to the back. Focusing on Sharon again, he flashed her a friendly, easygoing smile. "I am Jadik Listan'dy. I will buy you that beer."

She smiled because she couldn't help it. "That would be great. Thanks, Jadik." For the next half-hour, they kept up a friendly conversation. Sharon was on her second beer at that point, so she was feeling much more relaxed. Jadik seemed a lot less dangerous now. His light question caught her by surprise. "Are you linked with Tair?"

He said it so naturally that she answered without thought. "No and I'm not going to. He can go to hell." Her voice changed from friendly to angry as thoughts of her earlier conversation with Liken came to mind.

His eyebrows lifted. "I would have thought... They are brothers, after all. Who has Liken picked then?" He seemed genuinely surprised.

Sharon smiled grimly and said, "Oh, he picked Tair all right. But it's not going to happen."

Jadik stared at her a minute. Finally he asked in a neutral voice, "You object to Tair?"

She gave an exasperated sigh. "No, I like Tair just fine. That doesn't mean I want to link with him." How could she make yet another male understand that she didn't want to link with anyone?

His face turned serious. "You must link with someone, Sharon. It is for your own protection." He paused, then continued, "And it is the law."

Sharon's expression closed up. "I don't need this lecture from you, too."

Jadik studied her curiously for a minute like he couldn't figure her out. "Why would you object to linking?"

Her face turned red. "Look, it may be normal on this planet, but I'm not *from* here, okay? I don't do threesomes." His brows climbed higher. She mumbled a little and then finished with, "Hey, I'm a librarian," as if that explained everything.

Jadik laughed. He was really enjoying her. Too bad Liken was her match. "Sharon, I think what you have here is a cultural misunderstanding."

He sobered. "Linking must be done at orgasm, there is no other way. The participants must be touching. The more contact the better. Again, there is no other way. But, it is perfectly natural. There will be touching, but it will go only as far as the three parties decide."

She flashed him a skeptical look. "And how far is that?"

He grinned. "That will be up to the three of you. Whatever happens, I cannot see you doing something you do not want. Not the woman who burst through the door into this place and demanded a drink. I would say you will be fine."

She flushed and looked uneasy. "I don't know. I don't like the idea of it."

He leaned forward and his grin grew even broader. "Don't you?"

Her face was on fire. She shook her head in denial. He laughed softly and reached across the table to catch her hand. Rubbing his thumb gently across her palm, he said softly, "Maybe I should ask Liken to let me substitute for Tair."

Her gaze flew to his face in panic. He was only kidding, she was pretty sure. Her pulse was pounding so hard he could probably feel it. "I don't think that's a good idea." She pulled on her hand, but he didn't release it.

"Why don't I ask them both? They should be here any moment now." As he said the last word, Liken and Tair came through the front door.

Sharon saw them in the doorway as their gaze landed on her. She didn't need to be connected to anyone to know that they were both furious. She yanked her hand from Jadik's grip and gave him a blistering look. "How did you call them?"

He shrugged innocently and gave her a mock wounded look. He said, "Tair is my best friend," as if that explained everything.

Her glare grew hotter. She felt furious and ridiculously betrayed. "It figures! Idiots tend to stick together!"

He threw back his head and laughed. Liken and Tair reached the table and stood on each side of her. Reaching down, Liken pulled her from the chair and pinned her against his side.

She got out, "Get lost!" before Liken silenced her with a deadly, "Not one word."

She wasn't about to get into a big scene here at the restaurant with him. She, at least, could show some dignity. She would have plenty to say when they got home. She gave a curt nod. She couldn't resist saying one more word. "Fine."

Liken turned from her and said, "My thanks, Jadik. You have displayed true friendship this night."

Jadik nodded. "No thanks necessary. She is a treasure worth guarding." He turned to Tair. "I will see you soon, friend." Tair nodded and added his thanks.

Walking over to Sharon, Jadik placed a hand under her chin and raised her fuming gaze to his. "Welcome to Shimeria, Sharon Glaston. May you find pleasure," his eyes glinted, "and great happiness here." Pressing a light kiss to her mouth, he turned and joined some other men at another table.

She stood there in shock. He had kissed her casually as if he had every right. This planet was crazy. Liken began walking toward the door, pulling her along by the arm. Tair followed in their wake.

When they got outside, Sharon opened her mouth to speak. Liken stopped walking and leaned down to press a hard, tongue-thrusting kiss to her mouth. The kiss went on for a full five minutes. She tried to pull away, but that only made him jerk her hard into his body. The punishing invasion finally stopped. His voice brooked no argument. "What must be said, will be said in our home."

They stared at one another. Tair stood off to one side, patiently waiting. Sharon gave a nod of assent. The three of them started walking toward home-in silence.

Chapter Twelve

When they arrived at Liken's house, by unspoken agreement they moved into the living room. Immediately, Sharon pulled away from Liken's grasp and moved to the far side of the room, putting as much distance as possible between them. Tair turned to Liken and said, "I am glad she is safe, brother. I will leave you now."

Liken put a hand on Tair's arm. "Wait, Tair. I need you to stay."

Sharon's eyes grew wide. "Why does he need to stay for our fight?"

The two men stared at each other for a moment. Tair nodded his agreement and moved to sit on the couch. Sharon looked from one to the other as some understanding passed between the two men.

Liken said with utter calm. "You risked your safety tonight, *sherree*. There will be no fight."

She had a bad feeling about all this. She tried a placating tone. "I wasn't in any danger. Nothing happened."

Liken started walking toward her. "No, we were fortunate indeed."

He was trying to intimidate her and she wasn't going to let him get away with it. "I'm not afraid of you."

He sighed. They were less than a foot apart. "I know what you are afraid of, *sherree*. It is time you faced some of your fears." He pulled her to him and wrapped his arms around her.

She stared up into his face. It was determined with no hint of tenderness. He bent and placed his mouth over hers before she could respond.

His lips were firm and demanding. She kept her lips pressed tightly together and tried to keep her mind clear. Moving one hand to her jaw, he exerted gentle pressure. "Open your mouth, *sherree*. Now." His voice was deepening with desire.

Her mouth parted under the pressure of his hand on her jaw. He swept his tongue inside her moist warmth, thrusting deeply. She groaned and tried to put some distance between them with her hands against his chest. He removed his hand from her jaw and wrapped both arms around her, pulling her against his hard body. The kiss was overwhelming and intense. He wasn't asking for a response. He was demanding one with every thrust.

She could feel the heat spreading through her body. Her hands dropped from his chest and fisted at her sides. Her nipples tightened into hard peaks. He pressed her breasts harder into his chest in response. With a small moan, she began kissing him back. The angry words and deep hurt from their fight faded into the background of her mind as her senses took command. No matter what had been said, she hadn't stopped wanting him. He was like a fever in her blood.

Suddenly Liken tore his mouth from hers and abruptly turned her so that she was facing Tair. He was still sitting on the couch, watching the two of them with heated eyes. Under his stare, her thin blouse and skirt felt like little protection. She took a step backwards, which only brought her against Liken's hard body. He wrapped an arm around her waist instantly to hold her in place. She could feel the hard bulge of his aroused cock pressing into her lower back. She couldn't move.

Liken used his free hand to sweep her hair to one side and began nibbling on her neck. He gently bit and then licked along the sensitive nerves of her throat. Pausing near her ear, he said, "Does it matter so much, *sherree*, that he is watching us?" Her mouth went dry.

He continued his gentle assault on her throat. He tightened the arm holding her waist as his other hand lightly rubbed her stomach. She could feel the heat of his hand through the thin silk of her blouse like a burning brand. Her stomach muscles tightened in response. Her breathing sped up as she tried to squeeze more air into her lungs.

Liken's hand began climbing until it reached the underside of her left breast and paused. Sharon's body went stiff with tension.

He nipped her neck a little harder. It didn't hurt, but it surprised her.

He covered her breast with his hand and gave it a gentle squeeze. His thumb began slowly circling the tight point of her nipple. The pleasure ran from her nipple in a line to her sex. She was swollen and wet. She couldn't stop the shudder that went through her. She closed her eyes.

Tair said huskily, "Open your eyes, Sharon." She was startled enough by his voice to do what he said. She saw him stand up and move toward them, his bulging arousal obvious against the front of his pants.

She felt a wave of fear, closely followed by a wave of arousal so strong her knees went weak. She leaned more heavily against Liken. Tair stopped in front of her and raised a gentle hand to caress her cheek. "Trust us, Sharon. It will go no further than you wish. The linking must be done."

Sharon could almost physically feel the arousal push away her fear. With a shaky voice, she said, "Okay." She could feel the relief in both men.

Liken gently turned her toward him. His eyes were tender, his happiness washing over her in waves. With a smile he said, "I think we'd be more comfortable on the couch."

She nodded her agreement. Liken walked to the couch and sat down. Tair followed him and sat in the chair across from the couch. She walked over to join them, wondering what would happen next.

Liken unbuttoned his shirt. As always, the sight stole the air from her. He was so beautiful. Her hands itched to feel those rippling muscles in his chest. He was reading her thoughts now because his lids lowered and he said, "You know I love to feel your hands on my chest, *sherree.*"

She smiled and sat down beside him. Running her hands over him, she could feel the tension in his muscles under her fingers. She toyed with his nipples and without thinking leaned over to lick circles around one. His hand came up behind her head, tangling in her hair. He leaned into her mouth and hands with a groan. She pressed open-mouthed kisses over his chest, using her tongue to tease and taste the salty tang of his skin. He couldn't stand it for long.

With amazing speed he lifted her and brought her over his lap until she was straddling his thighs. She could feel the hard press of his cock as it strained against her through their clothes. She put her hands on his shoulders for balance and their mouths met in a long drugging kiss.

Tair's eyes burned into her back. It felt wicked and sexy. Her passion raised another notch.

Liken moved his hands up under her skirt, finding the strings of her panties. His mouth devoured hers in a searing kiss. She felt an almost imperceptible tug and then the front and back of the panties fell away. Taking the silk in his right hand, he gently pulled them out from under her.

She was completely covered by her loose skirt, but she felt exposed. Pushing down, she rubbed against his hardness. She knew he could feel her wetness through his pants, but she didn't care. It felt so good.

He arched upward to push harder against her. It brought a moan from both of them. He grabbed her hips and pulled her down onto him as he pushed up. They rocked together for a moment, simply enjoying the sensation. Liken moved his rough hands upward, warming her back with long strokes.

His hands pulled her blouse from underneath her skirt. She shuddered when she felt his hands touch the smooth skin of her naked back. She felt the heated breath of his mouth over her right nipple as he took it into his mouth and sucked. The thin silk of her blouse wasn't much of a barrier as it grew wet. She arched into his mouth, silently begging for more.

He sucked harder as his hands on her back pulled her blouse up. As she felt it rise, she pulled away and lifted her arms over her head. Once the material cleared her head, she saw him toss it by her panties on the other side of the couch. He transferred his mouth to her left breast and began licking it in teasing circles, hungry eyes watching her face.

She knew Tair was watching them, that he could see her naked back. But the pleasure she was feeling pushed all thoughts of Tair to the back of her mind. She was completely lost in Liken.

With a tortured groan, Liken pulled away from her after a few moments. Her nipples were red and wet from his mouth. She ached to have his cock inside her without the barrier of their clothes. She lifted up and pressed her hand against his arousal. "I want you." She barely recognized the husky voice as her own.

Liken moved one hand to his side and pushed a hidden button through its hole. Pulling back the fabric in the opposite direction, he then released another button on the inside. He pulled back that flap and his cock sprang into view. Sharon was impressed. "Pretty nifty."

She smiled and wrapped her fingers around him with one hand. Stroking him slowly, she watched as his face tightened with pleasure. The velvety skin of his cock felt good in her hand. He was fully erect, hard as stone. She pumped him, watching moisture bead at the tip.

He stopped her with his hand. "I must stay in control, *sherree*," he said tightly.

Lifting her up by the hips, he sat her down slowly on his erection. When he was in her to the hilt, she gave a little whimper of approval. She was full and aching with the need to move. Her hands moved to his shoulders as she lifted up. He guided her, keeping her rhythm slow and steady. Sweat beaded on his brow from his concentration. She would lift up until his cock nearly came out of her and then sink down hard. Losing herself in the pleasure, she didn't see Liken nod past her shoulder.

Tair's hands stroked her back. She went rigid with surprise. They all stopped moving. Sharon could feel Liken's cock flex inside her. He was buried to the hilt. Her gaze sought Liken's, finding only tenderness and reassurance. She took a deep breath and let it out. She leaned forward and placed a tentative kiss to Liken's mouth.

He responded and his hands on her waist began moving her again. Tair stroked her naked back, placing wet kisses along her spine. She caught fire and her skin flushed all over. The pounding of Liken's cock stroking inside her increased as their pace quickened. She was on the edge of orgasm.

Feeling the tension in her body, both men stopped and pulled back. She gritted her teeth in frustration. "Why?" She demanded an answer from Liken.

He gave her an apologetic look and lifted her completely off him. She stood there looking down at him in surprise. "What's wrong?"

Liken said quietly, "Everything is right, *sherree*, you just need to turn around."

Tair kissing and touching her back was one thing. She wasn't sure she was ready for him to see her naked breasts. She wasn't totally against the idea, she just felt nervous. Liken smiled. "It will be okay."

She squared her shoulders. Being honest with herself, she acknowledged that she was lost in the pull of her own sexuality. If she didn't want to turn around, nothing Liken said could have convinced her.

She turned around in a rush, deciding she would do it like ripping off a Band-Aid. Her gaze fell to Tair. He was sitting on the floor in front of her, looking up. His eyes darkened as he looked at her breasts. They were swollen, her red nipples jutting out from Liken's attention.

Tair raised his gaze to hers and slowly began unbuttoning his shirt. She felt Liken's hands grab her waist and position her nearly sitting in his lap facing away from him. Pushing up her skirt, he gently lowered her aching sex down onto his cock from behind. He filled her fully, stretching her inner walls, and the intense pleasure sent her climbing back toward orgasm in a hurry.

With a moan, she threw her head back, savoring the sensation of his cock deep inside her again. He began to move her up and down in an ever-increasing rhythm. Still holding her gaze, Tair slid his shirt off his shoulders. *They were both built like gods* was all she could think.

With a half smile, Tair moved forward and put a gentle hand low on her stomach over her skirt. Her stomach muscles contracted and she moaned in response. Encouraged, he drew up onto his knees and placed his hands above Liken's on her waist. The pressure was building inside her. Liken's hands fell away and then came under her arms to close over her breasts. He began to toy with her nipples.

Her hands came up and clung to Tair's shoulders in surprise as Tair's hands on her waist moved her up and down. He leaned forward and licked a path from her shoulder up the side of her neck. She felt Liken lean forward until he was nearly touching his chest to her back. Suddenly, he merged with her. She could feel the weight of his pleasure building on top of her own.

Tair's nibbling kisses moved south from her throat to the tip of one breast. Liken's hand pushed her breast upward toward Tair's tongue. Tair licked the nipple in one slow circle and then sucked it into his mouth. Looking down at him sucking on her nipple, she gave a loud moan. She couldn't take much more. They were making her crazy with need.

Liken drove his hips upward hard, just as Tair pushed her downward with equal strength. Then they both paused. With a cry, Sharon felt her body begin to pulse. Pleasure radiated in waves from her sex. She was burning from the inside out, blind and deaf to anything but the sensation of fulfillment and relief. The tension left her body in a great pouring rush.

She never even felt Tair's hands leave her waist as he wrapped his arms around her. He released her breast and moved upward. Pressing his naked chest against hers, he held her as closely as he could. Liken's hands slid to her back, making soothing motions. Gritting his teeth in frustration, Liken's face was a strained mask as he concentrated hard.

Tair put his forehead against hers and probed carefully. He had to be accurate, forceful, and quick. Sharon felt a sharp pain in her head, but it was over before she could really react. In less than a minute, both men's shoulders relaxed.

In his relief, Liken's concentration wavered and his control slipped away. He let out one long moan as his cock spurted and pulsed, sending liquid warmth inside Sharon's gripping sex. Sharon was still merged with Liken so his release sent her over the edge again.

Tair's arms tightened around her in shock. His own orgasm caught him by surprise-he hadn't come in that manner since he was a boy. They all remained motionless except for the shudders racking their bodies. The room was utterly silent except for the sounds of their ragged breathing.

Tair was the first to move. Rocking back, he sat down on the floor. With easy movements he gathered his shirt and put it back on. Sharon opened her eyes as Liken's arms came around her and squeezed gently. She felt amazingly relaxed. She ought to feel weird or guilty somehow, but she couldn't work up any concern. She felt good. There was no doubt about it.

Smiling, she levered herself off of Liken and moved to sit next to him on the couch. She grabbed her blouse and pulled it over her head. She was still wearing her skirt. She didn't bother with the panties. Liken refastened his pants. She felt his arm come around her and she put her head against his shoulder. As they all recovered, her mind began to process what had just occurred.

She had just had a sexual encounter of sorts with two men at the same time. It wasn't really a threesome in the literal sense, but she wasn't totally sure of the definition of threesome either. Deciding to think about it some other time, her thoughts drifted. Liken had given her incredible pleasure and Tair had been sexy and strangely sweet. She was so glad that it had been Tair who had linked with her and not someone else. Even Jadik.

Liken and Tair exclaimed in unison, "Jadik?!"

She glanced from one to the other in surprise. "What?"

As the name registered, she said firmly. "Both of you get out of my head right now."

Tair looked apologetic, but his voice was wry. "I will leave you as soon as my control is better, Sharon. My apologies."

He stood up. Before his shirt fell over it, Sharon noticed for the first time the large wet spot on the crotch area of his pants. Her face bloomed with color. Giving her a satisfied, lazy smile, Tair sat down in the chair across from them.

Liken's voice rumbled in her ear. "Your reference to Jadik and linking took us by surprise, *sherree*." There was a pause and then he smiled. "You had an interesting conversation with him at the eatery, did you not?"

Sharon rolled her eyes. "It takes a special kind of arrogance to just pluck something out of a person's head if you want to know what she's thinking."

Liken grinned. "I did not hear you complaining very hard earlier when we strove to please you. Did you hear any complaints, Tair?" he laughingly asked.

Tair laughed. "I think I will be going now. Sharon, your thoughts are growing louder."

Sharon laughed. They were arrogant, but she wasn't really getting angry. She felt too satisfied. The three of them stood up and walked toward the front door.

Pausing in front of the doorway, Liken reached out and gave Tair a quick hug. When Tair looked surprised, Liken said seriously, "My thanks to you, brother. We are fortunate to have your help."

Tair shrugged. "You would do the same." He turned to Sharon.

She wasn't sure if she should hug him or not. It was awkward. He solved her problem by pulling her into his arms and leaning his face close to hers. One hand cradled the back of her head and he brought his lips down to her mouth.

When she realized he meant to kiss her, she expected a brief, casual goodbye kiss. The heat of the kiss shocked her as his mobile mouth took her by storm. She responded without thought even when his tongue thrust against hers. He pulled back and smiled. She was dazed and breathless again. She couldn't think of a single thing to say.

He gave a husky laugh. "Welcome to Shimeria, Sharon. I am honored to be your link."

She said weakly, "Thanks." This planet was one surprise after another.

Liken and Tair both laughed. Tair walked through the doorway and headed into the silvery night. Liken pressed the button and the wall slid soundlessly shut.

Putting his arm back around her shoulders, Liken began walking Sharon toward the bedroom. His voice was still amused as he said, "Relax, *sherree*. The linking relationship is not complicated. Tair will kiss you, but only in greeting, and it will never go further than that. It is a harmless thing, a benefit for providing protection."

A horrifying thought struck her. "Are you and Tair linked? How did you..."

He couldn't help it. She looked so repulsed. He laughed. "Yes, Sharon, but two Shimerian males do not link in the way you just did with Tair. We simply drop our shields and establish a mutual link. It requires a great deal of trust."

So, the weird linking relationship was because she was female and not a Shimerian male. She and Tair were linked and that meant they had a kind of casually intimate relationship. Liken wasn't jealous at all. She wasn't sure how she felt about that.

Liken and Tair made it seem so natural. Sexuality on Shimeria was very different. Even Jadik had kissed her and that was okay. But Liken had seemed jealous when other males paid her too much attention, like in the eatery. Could things get any more confusing?

When they reached their bedroom, she sank down on the bed. She wasn't going to think about the bizarre customs of Shimeria. She'd sort it all out tomorrow. She wasn't going to worry about it tonight.

Liken sat down beside her and bent down for a kiss. His mouth paused over hers as he whispered, "There will be no worrying, *sherree*. You will experience only pleasure this eve."

And true to his word, he spent the rest of the night proving it.

Chapter Thirteen

The next morning Sharon murmured sleepy objections when Liken gently shook her shoulder. She was exhausted. She heard a low chuckle next to her ear.

Liken said, "*Sherree*, I know you are too tired for loveplay. Please open your eyes for a moment."

Her lids felt like lead weights as she gradually came awake and opened her eyes. He was sitting on the edge of the bed, smiling down at her. She smiled back and said, "Good morning."

His smile broadened. "Indeed it is." He placed a soft kiss on her mouth. Drawing back, he looked regretful. "I am sorry to wake you, Sharon, but I must leave for a time. A few matters at my workplace require immediate attention. It was unexpected. I am sorry but it is something I must handle."

"An emergency?" she asked, still half asleep.

"No emergency. Just a few details that cannot wait until after our knowing period." His voice was filled with regret.

She nodded her understanding. Her sleepy brain was beginning to function. "It's no problem. I'll just drop by the library or something." A thought struck her. "Liken, can I ask you to do something for me today?"

He nodded before she even finished her question. "What is it, *sherree*?"

Memories of yesterday were beginning to swirl in her head. The lovemaking and the fighting. She needed some time alone to process them. She needed some space. She needed him out of her head, but she didn't want to disturb their fragile peace. She raised unconsciously pleading eyes to his face.

His eyes turned tender and he gave a half laugh. "When you look at me with those eyes, *sherree*, you can have whatever you want."

Sharon said carefully, "I don't want to hurt your feelings, but I've got a lot to think about today. A lot has happened in the last ten days. I really need some time to myself, okay? I mean, I don't want to be self-conscious, worrying about you randomly tuning into my thoughts."

He sighed. "I understand, but I do not scan your thoughts for entertainment, Sharon. It is the way of my people. It is a special closeness that lovers share. I wish you would become more comfortable with it."

She said softly, "Maybe I will if I have some time to sort it through. I don't know."

He nodded. "I will withdraw and block you if that is your wish. At least for today. You have my oath."

Sharon knew that if he gave his word, he would abide by it. His emotions told her that he wanted to keep contact, but would do as she asked-for today, anyway. She gave him a smile of gratitude and said softly, "Thanks... It means a lot to me."

He leaned down and kissed her slowly. It was a sweetly searching kiss, strangely different from any other they had shared. They lingered, mouths seeming to convey things they couldn't put into words. When they slowly pulled apart, they stared at each other silently for a moment.

Finally, Liken cleared his throat. "I will return before evemeal, *sherree*, perhaps sooner. Enjoy this day." His hand caressed her face and then he turned and left the room. She could hear the front door sliding closed a moment later.

She sat up and moved to the edge of the bed. Standing, she walked to the far side of the room. Pressing a button on the wall, she stared at a hologram of herself. Like the one at the shop, it served as a mirror. It was nice to have one at home, although she was still growing used to it. More than once, she had been startled by the three-dimensional depiction of herself. It was like having an identical twin mirroring her every move.

Today, the image greeting her didn't look like her twin. She was staring at a stranger. The woman facing her looked nothing like the Sharon Glaston she knew. Her dark hair was tumbled around a face with glowing eyes and swollen lips. Her nude body had small red marks from a night of passion. She looked rumpled and strangely sexy. The passionate creature staring back at her looked powerfully female and mysterious.

Sharon backed away and sat down hard on the bed. Her image stayed in her mind. She was that woman. Maybe she had always been that woman and it had taken Liken to make her see it. He had ripped her out of her safe little world and stripped away that protective outer shell that she presented to everyone around her.

She had always thought of herself as a cautious woman who was content to lead a rather routine life. She was everyone's dependable friend, the person who could be counted on to be reasonable. Other people led lives of messy emotion. She was the one that could be relied upon to help them clean up the mess.

She was stable and structured and even a little boring in some ways. No surprises, no real passion, and no real pain. But underneath all that lived a woman who could rage and fight and hurt like anyone else. A woman who could be passionate and difficult and not at all reasonable. A woman who could love deeply.

Sharon's head dropped to her hands. There, that was the crux of it. People who loved deeply risked being hurt deeply. And in the last ten days, she had fallen passionately, deeply, foolishly in love with Liken. There was nothing cautious or reasonable about it. It was utterly ridiculous. It made absolutely no sense, but it was undeniable.

He made her feel out of control. He challenged her and seduced her and pushed her at every turn. It was frightening, but she had never felt so alive in her life. He was arrogant and domineering at times. He could be sweetly tender and giving. Physically, he was a fantasy male come to life.

Sometimes, he understood her better than she understood herself. At other times, she wondered if he knew her at all. All she knew was that the last ten days had been the most incredible, happiest, most confusing days of her life. And she didn't want it to end. She wanted to spend the rest of her life loving and fighting with Liken.

She thought of the library on Earth, her job, her friends. She knew she could get a job on Shimeria, probably even at the local Earth library with Gar. Her heart twisted in her chest at the thought of being separated from Kate. More than anything right now she wished Kate were here so that she could talk to her and tell her how she felt. Of course, if Tair had his way, Kate might be living here, too. She cheered at that thought.

The bottom line, though, wasn't whether she should give up her old life or not. The bottom line was whether she had the guts to step out on a very high limb. She would have to start a new life on an alien planet with a man she loved-a man who might or might not love her back.

She thought sometimes he did love her. When he looked at her with such melting tenderness, she could almost believe it. But, at other times, she felt like a possession he had claimed and wouldn't give up. He had tried very hard to make her happy, but she wasn't sure if it was to make her stay or if he loved her enough to want to see her happy.

She had felt his affection and happiness run through her many times. She could make him happy in the long run. She was almost sure of it. They could have a good life together. Did she have the guts to try?

Sharon felt her heart pound at the thought. She had come to a strange planet. She had slept with an alien and eaten weird food. She had yelled and cussed and been completely unreasonable at times. She had two men with a doorway into her head, and a near threesome under her belt. Did she have the guts to grab her own happiness? Hell, yes she did!

Her head came up and a huge smile filled her face. The old Sharon would have stayed sitting on the bed half the day, listing all of the reasons why it was a bad idea to let emotion rule. The new Sharon stood up and headed for the bathroom. She was going to see Liken and tell him she was staying. She was going to risk everything and tell him she loved him.

Her confident steps faltered as she thought of his reaction. What if he stared at her blankly, or worse, uneasily thanked her in response? Well, then, she'd just have to kill him.

She strode into the bathroom like a soldier headed off to battle. Kate would have applauded.

Chapter Fourteen

An hour later, having eaten and showered, she headed out the front door dressed in a shimmering blue blouse and skirt. It was the outfit they had purchased during their shopping trip. She didn't care if the outfit was more revealing than anything she had ever worn on Earth. Besides, she knew it was the most flattering thing she owned. Her hair was gleaming around her shoulders and she felt ready to take on the world.

She had seen Liken's office a few days ago. On one of their trips into town, he had taken her by and given her a tour of the place. His coworkers had been curious about her, but unfailingly gracious and charming. Their respect and affection for Liken had been apparent.

Sharon had considered waiting until he returned home from the office in the afternoon, but had decided against it. She had made her decision and was eager to forge ahead. Besides, being impulsive for a change wasn't a bad thing. Liken's work hadn't sounded critical, merely something minor that couldn't be put off. She would surprise him with her visit and give him a good reason to rush home.

Entering the building where he worked, she began walking toward his office in the back. A few people smiled and greeted her, but she answered them with brief, friendly responses and kept walking. She couldn't wait to see Liken. She reached the doorway of his office and felt her entire body turn rigid with disbelief.

Liken was embracing a petite redhead. His mouth was moving over hers with gentle hunger and she was responding with enthusiasm. She could feel his tenderness for the woman run through her in one long wave. Sharon's mind blanked. A pain so sharp it felt fatal hit her in the chest. Disillusionment and agony cut her to the bone. When she could draw a breath, the words tumbled out from her mind to her mouth without a second in between.

"You cheating bastard." Her voice was actually soft, but his head came up with a snap. She must have screamed it in her mind because he winced in pain and brought a hand to his head. He looked shocked to see her. The redhead turned in surprise. Sharon's face was without an ounce of color. Her voice shook as she said, "I thought I would surprise you by showing up. I guess I did."

Liken took a step toward her, but she threw up her hand in response. He spoke her name, "Sharon..." but that was all he had time to get out before she spoke again.

"So you had to go into the office today, huh?" She looked at the redhead, who was beginning to frown in confusion. She said flatly, "I'm his pactmate." The woman's eyes widened.

Sharon felt a welcoming numbness spread through her, overcoming the pain. Liken said firmly, "Sharon, you must listen to me..."

She cut him off. "No, I don't need to listen." Looking at the redhead, she said, "You're welcome to the faithless asshole. Enjoy him while you can." She looked back at Liken. "You can go to hell." With fragile dignity, she turned and started walking away quickly.

She heard the woman say "Liken?" in a throaty, questioning voice. His voice murmured in response.

She sped up. Reaching the doorway of the building, she started to run. She could hear his voice behind her yelling, "Sharon, wait!" but she didn't stop. She kept running, taking side paths at random, one after another, wanting only to escape.

She ran until her legs ached and her vision was too blurred to see where she was going. She finally stopped and looked around. She was in the park area. Walking to a tree with huge red leaves, she sat down under it and drew her knees to her chest. She took gasping breaths and stared blindly ahead. She couldn't even cry. The shock and pain were so deep that her chest hurt, but her eyes remained dry. She sat in rigid silence, totally unaware of her surroundings.

Her mind raced in frantic circles as she strove to block the image of Liken and the redhead from her mind. He had feelings for that woman. That kiss was not platonic. It had been passionate. And she had been on her way to tell him...

The first edge of anger shot through her. And he had been... He was a bastard, plain and simple.

Her nostrils flared. Fuck risking and destiny, and most especially fuck that cheating Liken.

Chapter Fifteen

Liken was sitting in his office alone when Tair appeared in the doorway. Leaning back in the chair, he said wearily in English, "Hello, brother."

Tair leaned negligently against the frame. "Hello, brother?" he echoed. "Is that all you wish to say?"

Liken arched an eyebrow. "What is it you expect me to say?"

Tair shook his head and walked across the office, dropping into the chair across from Liken. "I do not know. It seems so mundane when your pactmate has been screaming in my head."

Looking at Liken closely, his eyes widened. "You, however, are conveniently blocking her and are left unaffected."

Liken laughed, although it sounded hollow. "Unaffected? You are wrong. Nonetheless, I am blocking her because I gave oath that I would not scan her thoughts this day."

His brother was an idiot. Tair gave him an amazed look. "Why would you do such a thing?"

"She wanted privacy to sort out her thinking, she said." Liken sounded as if the weight of the world pressed him from all sides.

Tair gave a snort. What a mess. "Well, I believe she needs to do a great deal more sorting now. She believes you have betrayed her with Elana."

Liken felt the pain of it strike home. "I know." He kept seeing her face in his mind. When he had looked at her, the agony and distrust on her face had struck him like a blow. He had stood there in shock unable to move or to think. In that moment he had believed she was lost to him forever. She would never trust him enough to stay.

He could bind her to him sexually. He could physically keep her with him. But he could not force her to love him or trust him. She had to give it freely. He felt helpless and confused.

140

When they had taken the oath, he arrogantly thought he could make her want to stay. He was a Shimerian warrior, a guardian, used to righting wrongs and winning. She was a woman, physically smaller and weaker. She was inexperienced sexually and would be easily seduced. She would give up her old life and make a life with him on Shimeria. He would make her want him and want this life.

Now those thoughts seemed foolish and amazingly selfish. He couldn't force her to love him or trust him. She would not stay without those things. The realization was devastating and humbling.

Tair sighed. This pactmate business was trickier than it had seemed. He asked, "What are you going to do?"

Liken shrugged. "I will give her time and then we shall see." He couldn't seem to get the look on her face out of his mind.

It was Tair's turn to lift an eyebrow. "She is hurting, thinking the worst. Do you not care?"

Liken's glare would have knocked a lesser man than Tair from his seat. "She brings pain to herself with her own distrust. I will explain later."

Tair knew his brother enough to comprehend the real hurt underneath that anger. He said quietly, "I think your own wounds prevent you from seeking to heal hers."

The accusation was pure truth and Liken couldn't deny it. "True enough. I am angry. She should have asked for an explanation instead of assuming the worst."

Tair laughed. His voice rang with skepticism, "As you would have done if you had found her kissing an unknown male?"

Liken felt instant rage at the mere thought. "I would not have left without demanding answers."

Tair made a mock sound of sudden discovery and said, "Ahhhh. So you were doubly wounded. That dignified exit was lowering, was it?"

Liken looked and sounded defeated as he said, "She was so controlled. No woman who loves a man could have acted in that manner."

Tair's face was sympathetic, but his eyes were amused. "Why would you care? She does not have to love you to stay and be pledged. She is but a woman."

Liken's voice was just short of a yell. "I love her! Are you satisfied? Will you cease this endless prodding?"

She was beautiful and frustrating and intelligent and stupid. She made him angry, she made him laugh, and she made him ache with sweet pleasure. She was perfect and riddled with faults and everything in between. He would love her until his dying breath, and probably beyond it. It infuriated him. She infuriated him.

Tair laughed, not unkindly. "At last. I was about to lose all hope for you, brother. Now, let us see if we can get past those wounds to the truth. Why would she hurt so much if she had no love for you?"

The words pierced Liken's emotions and cleared his mind. "Why, indeed?" His heart lifted. She had to love him to react so strongly.

He felt another wave of pain at the thought of her distrust. "She may love me, but she does not trust me. I think she does not even trust herself."

Tair sighed. "True enough. I am out of questions and answers, brother. Would you like me to find her and bring her to you?" As their link, he was responsible for her protection, but volunteering was really more of an impulse to help.

Liken shook his head. "No. It seems now I am the one who must sort through his thoughts. She will come home when she is ready. She is much stronger and more passionate than she thinks. She will demand answers. I have no doubt. Would you just watch over her until then? Make sure she is all right?"

"Of course," Tair replied. He hated to think that Liken and Sharon might not work their problems out. They were perfect for each other, even if they didn't seem to understand it yet. He asked, "And will your answers persuade her to stay? Will she trust you?"

Liken stared at his brother. "I guess that is one question only time will answer." At the moment, the thought was not encouraging.

Chapter Sixteen

Sharon sat under the tree for quite some time. Several hours passed as thoughts swirled like a storm in her head. Eventually, the pain settled like an aching weight in her chest but her mind had cleared somewhat.

She couldn't reconcile Liken lying to her and making love with another woman while committed to her. He had been honest with her in the past, although not always forthright. She would have bet her life that he was a faithful, honorable man. In a way, she had bet her life. Her new life.

It didn't make sense. Fury filled her. Since she'd stepped onto this planet, a lot of things hadn't made sense. It had been one surprise after another. She had found herself and risked everything and been crushed in the end. Well, she could crawl back into her shell and never come out. Or she could get back up, and face him and demand a few answers. If she turned messy, and emotional, and ugly, then he would just have to deal with it. He had broken her heart, but she would survive it.

She wasn't going back to the person she had been before him. She wasn't running from anyone or anything ever again. Being cautious and reasonable might produce a safe and comfortable life, but she wanted more than safety. She deserved more. And she would have it. Even without Liken.

Her eyes focused on her surroundings for the first time. She recognized where she was and felt a quick pang of relief that she was in the park and could find her way home. She stood up. Tair stepped out from the shadows of a huge tree to her right. She was startled. "How long have you been there?"

He shrugged in response. His face was a remote mask. "I will escort you home."

"I don't need an escort." Her voice was sharper than she meant it to be. "I know the way."

He stared at her with a coolness that was chilling. "Nonetheless, I will walk with you."

She had no idea what he was thinking or feeling. He seemed distant and unapproachable. Now it was her turn to shrug. "Fine."

They turned and began walking. When he remained silent beside her, she angled her head up at him and frowned. She was the injured party here. "What's your problem?"

Again, he leveled her with that chilling gaze. He remained silent. She said coolly, "Whatever." She would deal with Tair after she dealt with Liken. She was saving all her energy for the confrontation with Liken.

They walked in silence until they reached the pathway to the house. As they approached the doorway, Tair paused and put a hand on her arm. She stopped and turned to face him with a questioning glance. He searched her face and then said with cool precision, "You never greeted me. You will do so now."

"What?" She was totally confused.

He smiled grimly. "I am your link. You never greeted me, Sharon."

Her eyes widened in response and her mouth fell open a little in surprise. He wanted her to kiss him? Now?

His mouth came down on hers ruthlessly before she had a chance to respond. He thrust his tongue past her parted lips and explored her mouth like he owned it. Her hands came up to his chest to reflexively push him away. He merely wrapped his arms around her tightly and continued the punishing kiss.

She realized that her heart hadn't been carved out of her chest. It was beating frantically. She could feel treacherous arousal begin to spread through her body. Without conscious thought, her lips and tongue began a dance of response. She wanted him, but only in a physical sense. She didn't love him. He wasn't Liken. Just the thought of Liken and the pain in her chest ached like a dull tooth. The kiss gentled, and finally, he lifted his head. "You will remember this."

She was totally confused again. "What?" Did he mean remember him after she left for Earth?

His smile was wicked and the warmth had come back into his eyes. This was the Tair she remembered well, not the cold, cruel man from the eatery. "Goodbye, Sharon." He walked away from her in the direction of town.

Sharon stood there, feeling perplexed. Mentally throwing up her hands, she turned and walked to the front door. She hit the button and it slipped open in immediate response. She braced herself and walked in.

Walking into the living room, she saw Liken casually sitting on the sofa. He looked up at her and raised an eyebrow as she strode to the center of the room. He didn't look upset. He looked perfectly calm.

How could he look so normal when she was dying inside? It was the last insult to her battered heart. Her voice could have cut glass. "I am going to discuss this morning with you. While we do it, you are keeping your hands to yourself. When we're done here, you're packing a few things and staying somewhere else. With Tair or with your girlfriend, I really don't care. But you are not touching me again. On the twenty-first, we'll go back and file incompatible. I deserve better than a faithless liar."

His face never changed. They might have been discussing the weather. It pushed her fury up a notch.

With infuriating calm, he said, "You want to discuss this morning. What is there to say?"

His voice was soft, so even-tempered, and she could not feel a trace of emotion coming from him. She could feel the dam holding her temper spring several leaks. "I'm your pactmate. How could you be with someone else? You may not love me, but you should have had enough respect for me to..."

He cut her off. "You want to talk of love and respect?" He gave a cynical laugh. "Perhaps we should begin by speaking of trust."

Her voice rose. "Maybe we should. I trusted you, you bastard!"

Suddenly, she realized Liken was not as calm as she had assumed. He was sitting on the sofa, but the hand resting on the arm was gripping it so hard his knuckles were white. It was the only warning she had of his real state before he burst into motion.

He sprang from the couch and grabbed her by the arms. She looked up into his face and saw pure fury. He shouted, "You know nothing of trust!"

She felt the dam burst open and white-hot fury broke free. "I know you were kissing that redhead and enjoying it! I know you have feelings for her! I know I feel like a fool and it's your fault! I know you're an asshole! Take your hands off of me!"

His face went white. "I will touch you whenever I like. I will do whatever I like! I am your pactmate!"

"And she's your lover!" The accusation rang in the silence of the room.

He shook her until her teeth rattled, then abruptly let her go. Taking a step back, he said flatly, "I am her link."

The words took a moment to register. As he stared at her in furious silence, she echoed, "Her link?"

He gave one swift nod. "Yes, her link. Her name is Elana and she has been pledged to my friend, Revka, for over three years now."

"But you love her...and you were kissing her..." Her anger was fading into confusion.

He told her grimly, "I do not love her, at least not in the sense you mean. I am her link. I care for her as Tair cares for you."

Suddenly, the little scene with Tair outside the house took on a new meaning. His words ran through her mind again. "I am your link. You did not greet me. Remember this..."

"Are you saying she was greeting you, that you've never had sex with her?" She couldn't keep the doubt from her voice.

He looked exasperated. "Yes, she was greeting me. As for sex with her, it was on one occasion during the initial link."

When Sharon would have responded, he lifted an eyebrow and said, "Not everyone is as uncomfortable with the thought of a threesome. The linking process is different depending on the participants."

Sharon felt the color rise in her face. Her heart picked up speed as she suddenly focused on something he said earlier. "You don't love her."

She nearly sagged with relief. He wasn't in love with the redhead. The truth in his voice had been obvious. She believed him.

She thought of Liken's lack of jealousy regarding her actions with Tair. Shimerian culture was very different from Earth. The linking partners shared intimacy but it was not considered a threat or a betrayal. She felt the last of her anger die. Embarrassment and sorrow rose up in its place.

"I'm sorry. I didn't know." She felt guilty as she considered what had happened from Liken's point of view. She hadn't trusted him, hadn't even let him explain. Her hurt and anger had been too great.

He nodded stiffly. "You could not know. You did not wait for an explanation."

The accusation in his voice was easy to hear, but she could feel anger radiating from him without it. Underneath the anger was a layer of hurt. She had hurt him. She was surprised at how much her distrust had hurt him.

She stepped forward and placed a tentative hand on his chest. "Liken, I really am sorry. I couldn't think. I was just so hurt and angry." She thought she detected a slight relaxation of his tense shoulders at the sincerity in her voice.

He sighed, and his face lost some of its grimness. "You have no cause for jealousy, Sharon." He sounded tired now. "Why were you at the office today?"

Sharon swallowed. Here was the tough part. Her emotions felt raw. She had been on a roller coaster of feeling today, and she was worn out by the experience. "I wanted to talk to you." She wasn't going to chicken out, but she needed a moment to work up her nerve. His hurt was proof he loved her, at least a little. She had to take the risk and be honest.

He continued to stare at her in silence. Sharon tilted her head back further to get a better look at his eyes. He looked impatient. Taking a deep breath, she let it out in a rush. "I came to the office because I wanted to tell you that I love you. I want to stay. I'll pledge with you."

He looked like she had hit him on the head with a shovel. When he continued to stare at her, dumbfounded, she felt her nerves leap. "I mean, if you want me to stay. I…"

He wrapped his arms around her and squeezed the rest of her words right out of her. His voice boomed next to her ear. "How could you think I would not want you to stay?"

The pressure in her chest lightened. He really wanted her to stay. He hadn't said he loved her, but it was a beginning. She leaned back and peered up at him. "I'm sorry, but I've been so confused. When I saw you kissing her, I just…"

He gave her a hard look. "Yes, I know what you thought." Some of the warmth left his face. "Yet, as always, you were so very controlled. You did not stay and demand answers. You did not make a scene. You might have lost your precious control."

The accusation hurt. "You have no idea how I felt…"

"No, I do not. How could I? You left." His hands came up to her shoulders. She could feel a new tension in him. "Tell me, *sherree*, what would happen if you gave up that control of yours. Why does it frighten you so much? Would it be so terrible?"

Unease spread through her body. Where was he going with his comments? "I don't know."

He shook his head. "I think you do. I think you cannot trust enough to give that much of yourself. You say you love me, but do you trust me enough to truly lose all control with me? To show me yourself?"

He was scaring her, but she was honest enough to admit he could be right. The safe thing to do would be to take a step back from him and end this discussion now. She wasn't going to do it. She was through playing it safe. "I don't know, but I'll try."

His smile held a cruel edge. She knew he wasn't going to make it easy for her, not when she had hurt him so badly this morning. "Then we shall see."

Liken turned from her, not wanting her to see the hope on his face. Would she really give him her trust? Thoughts of her dark fantasies flashed through his mind. Walking across the room, he sat down on the couch. "Remove your clothing. Now." His voice was firm, as if he expected some resistance.

She felt a shimmer of nerves. To her embarrassment, she could feel a growing arousal at his tone. He was going to try to take control and dominate her sexually, she knew. It went against her every feminist principle, but the thought didn't stop the warmth spreading through her. She wanted him. Even more, she wanted him like this.

Taking a deep breath, she brought her hands to her blouse and drew it over her head. She tossed it to the floor. She could feel his heated gaze watching her every movement. Her nipples tightened under his gaze. She bent down and hurriedly began to take off the skirt.

His voice was cool and distant, a direct contrast to the heat in his eyes. "Turn around. Take it off slowly."

She turned around and began sliding the skirt over her hips. She was left only in her skimpy panties, facing away from him. She turned around to see his face.

"I did not tell you to turn around, *sherree*, did I?" He sounded angry.

She shook her head. "I just wanted…"

His smile made her nerves jump again. "I know what you want. I have been inside that mind of yours, remember? You have quite an interesting fantasy life. I believe it is time for us to explore some of those dark little secrets." He motioned her forward. "Come to me."

As she walked across the room, she was acutely aware of her exposed body. At the mention of her fantasies, a dark thrill had gone through her. She could feel herself blushing. Stopping in front of him, she waited for his next move.

"So willing, *sherree*. I am impressed." His voice was faintly mocking. He grew serious again. "Lay facedown across my lap."

No, she wasn't going to do it. She could feel the moistness between her thighs and was mortified. She was not going to lie across his lap. Would he really spank her because she had turned around? Or because of her distrust this morning? Shame warred with arousal. She shook her head.

His eyes were as hard as his voice. "Do it."

Cheeks burning, she shook her head. "No."

Reaching out roughly, he pulled her downward until she collapsed on his lap. Squirming, she tried to break free, but he was too strong. Eventually, she found herself draped across his lap, staring down at the floor. She protested. "This is ridiculous. Let me up. What do you think you're doing? Are you crazy?"

The hard pressure of his hand on her back kept her down. His other hand came down with a light tap on her ass. "Be still."

She was shocked. He'd actually done it. She went still from surprise.

She heard his low chuckle. "Very good, *sherree*." He raised his hand and delivered another couple of smacks. He wasn't hurting her, but she felt her bottom begin to grow warm. With a sense of embarrassment, she felt the wetness between her legs grow, too. She squirmed.

The hand on her back grew heavier as he kept her in place. "You still think you have some choice, I see. Perhaps I should make myself clearer." She felt a tug on each side of her panties as he released the strings. Cool air brushed against the warm cheeks of her bottom as he lifted the back of the panties away. She was exposed.

She felt his rough hand lightly caress one pink cheek. Suddenly, he moved his hand up and he began lightly spanking her again. The minor sting of his hand was nothing compared to the heat blooming inside her. She couldn't understand it. She was trembling with excitement and nerves.

Suddenly, he stopped. His hand lightly traced her bottom. His voice sounded husky, but it was still firm. "At this moment, you are wondering what I will do to you. What you will let me do to you."

His hand moved lower and he trailed one finger along the wetness of her thighs. "You are so wet." Her body tensed as he lazily drew that finger upward toward her sex. He teased her swollen lips and then probed gently inside. With a moan, she went limp.

"That's it, *sherree*. I can feel your walls clinging to me. Tighten around my finger." He brought the rest of his fingers under her and began circling her clit. It was exquisite torture. She felt him pressing and playing with her. The finger inside her began moving in and out. She let out a whimper of need. It felt so good, but she wanted his hard cock in place of his finger.

Bringing her head up and turning, she could see his hard cock straining within his pants. "I want you inside me."

He withdrew his finger from inside her and trailed it along her swollen lips again. "Do you?" His finger left a trail of wetness in its wake as it slowly climbed upward between the cheeks of her bottom. Reaching the tight bud of her ass, he lightly touched the knot of nerves. "Where?"

Oh no. She was not into anal sex. No way. Her body tensed instinctively. She made a strangled sound of protest.

He laughed. "Nervous, *sherree*? I am in control here, remember? You have no control. I can fuck you any way I like." He continued to tickle that tight ring of nerves with light strokes of his wet finger.

Her sudden twisting motion away from him nearly sent her sprawling to the floor. She landed on her knees and began to stand up. Her panties fell away, and she was naked, standing in front of him.

Like lightning, he grabbed her hips and brought her forward to his mouth. Her knees went weak as she felt the stroking heat of his tongue across her clit. She closed her eyes and her head went back. It was too much. He sucked and circled, and probed delicately until she was moaning with the pleasure. Suddenly, the incredible sensations stopped. She opened her eyes.

Liken stood and looked at her with the eyes of a hungry predator. She took an instinctive step backward in surprise. He smiled. He took a step forward and then grabbed her. His movements were rough, but the hands on her arms were gentle as he turned her and walked her around to the back of the chair. Pushing her facedown over the back of it, he put one hand on her back to hold her down.

The rustle of his clothing as he unbuttoned his pants was the only sound in the room. With no other warning, his hard cock thrust into her aching sex. He began pumping in and out of her roughly. She felt her whole body catch fire. She began to push her hips back against him to meet his strokes. He brought one hand down into stinging contact with her bottom. His voice was firm. "No."

She stopped in surprise, but let out a moan of protest. He brought one hand forward and began to toy with her right nipple. His rhythm remained ruthlessly steady even when he said softly, "You will not come until I allow it."

The tug on her nipple was a passionate torment. She ached with it. She was growing frustrated at the slow rhythm of his thrusts. She arched her back to take him deeper. She wanted more, damn it.

He knew what she wanted, but he was the one in control. He had the nerve to laugh. "No, *sherree*."

She felt another stinging tap. Anger was beginning to mix with need. "Faster. Go faster and deeper." She wasn't sure if it was a demand or a plea.

He responded by slowing and gentling his thrusts. "Ask me nicely and I will consider it." His mocking tone deliberately provoked her.

She could feel her temper straining and struggled to rein it in. "Go to hell. I don't want this anymore. Let me up!"

He thrust his cock all the way into her, in one hard thrust. Buried to the hilt, he brought his fingers from her nipple down to her sex. He found her clit and began teasing it. "What is wrong, *sherree*? Will you beg me to continue or to stop?" His mocking tone said he knew she wouldn't ask him to stop.

She wanted to demand that he stop immediately, but he was filling her and pressing against her clit with such skill. "Bastard."

He laughed again. "Your language is deteriorating, Sharon." He gave her a couple of hard, deep thrusts in reward.

She moaned and pushed against him, fighting for each stroke of his cock. The war waged for some time. She was getting desperate for release. Frustration, passion, and anger were raging inside her. Each time she grew close, he would pull back and then change rhythms. It was maddening.

She spat angry words in between strokes. "You're driving me crazy. Cut it out! I mean it. You fucking tease."

His only response was another slap to her bottom as he continued the torment. His hand on her hip moved and he trailed one finger between the cheeks of her bottom. Drawing moisture from below, he circled her tight bud with teasing strokes.

She went hot and then cold. He wouldn't. She had no sooner thought it, then she felt a gentle probing pressure as his finger dipped inside slightly. It was foreign and scary, and she was ashamed to admit, exciting. It didn't hurt, but she felt the last shred of her control snap away. She let out a scream of sheer frustration.

As if he had been waiting for that sound, he merged with her in one hard push. The feel of his pleasure mixing with hers sent her right to the edge. She was terrified he would stop. "Don't stop."

His voice was dark with need. "Ask me to fuck you harder." It was an order.

"Please fuck me harder." Need was clawing at her. She was completely out of control.

"Swear you'll never leave." He ruthlessly pounded his cock into her sex.

"I swear it." She almost screamed the words.

"You're mine. I can do anything, have anything I want." His thrusts became faster and she was moaning over and over.

"Yes, anything…"

He spoke through gritted teeth, "Then come for me." His finger on her clit pressed inward as he arched his spine to add strength to his thrusts.

Her scream echoed loudly as she shattered into a million pieces. Her lower body clenched and pulsed around his cock and his still embedded finger. With a loud groan, he lost control and found his own release.

He fell forward and leaned against her back, his big body covering hers. His hands came around her to gently stroke her breasts.

Sharon lay beneath Liken, too exhausted to move. She felt hollow inside, as if someone had come in and swept everything away. It was strangely peaceful. She felt totally vulnerable and exposed in a way that had nothing to do with her body's nakedness. She loved Liken and needed him and had no defenses against it.

She felt tears on her face and realized with a sniff that she was crying. She had lost all control, acted like an animal, and the world hadn't ended. Liken was still holding her, pressing gentle kisses to the side of her neck. She felt his feelings run through her. His tenderness, his warmth, and his love wrapped around her. Realizing he did love her brought on a flood of fresh tears.

Liken grew aware that Sharon was crying beneath him. He quickly rose up and turned her over with concern. Tears were streaming down her face. Looking horrified, he picked her up in his arms and carried her to the couch. "Sharon, did I hurt you?"

She shook her head and tried to say no, but only sobbing sounds came out. She ducked her head into his chest and wept.

Liken wrapped gentle arms around her and tried to understand. He was relieved he hadn't hurt her, but he couldn't understand why she was crying. Sharon never cried. She had come to his planet and confronted massive changes without shedding one tear. Now, suddenly, she was sobbing as if her heart was broken. He thought about scanning her thoughts, but remembered his promise.

With dismay, he wondered if he had pushed her too far too fast. Rubbing her back as she sobbed in his arms, he ached at the sight and sound of her tears. He whispered, "*Sherree*, please...you are killing me with your tears...I am sorry... Please tell me what has hurt you. I love you. I cannot bear to see you hurting." His words of comfort continued, in both Shimerian and English, but Sharon was too shattered to respond.

Finally, she pulled away from his chest and tried to get herself under control. She felt free suddenly. She knew she was naked in the arms of a nearly fully clothed man. Her hair was a tangled mess, and her face was splotchy with tears. Her nose was running and she looked horrible.

Gone was the cautious, tidy, undemanding Sharon. The end result wasn't as pretty maybe, but it was honest. Her life was in shambles, but she had found herself and someone who loved her in the midst of total chaos. It was everything she had avoided, and at the same time, everything she had secretly wanted. "I love you, too. It's okay. You didn't hurt me. I just feel relieved and overwhelmed."

He had been in her mind for nearly two weeks and he still could not understand her. She was a mystery to him, one he hoped to spend his life solving. "I do not understand. You are crying in relief?" It made no sense.

Sharon gave him a shaky smile. "I'm fine."

He shook his head. "I think you are still hurting because of this morning. I am sorry I did not come after you and explain about Elana."

"No, really. I do understand. And I'm sorry I didn't trust you enough to ask for explanations. I had gotten my nerve up to risk telling you about my feelings and seeing you with her just shocked and destroyed me."

He pressed a gentle kiss to her mouth. "*Sherree*, there are things in our cultures that are vastly different. I know that there are adjustments we both will have to make. I have been arrogant in thinking all the adjustments would be yours. We will work together to solve any problems that arise. If the kissing makes you unhappy, I do not understand it but out of respect I will not do it." It was said as a promise.

Sharon placed a hand to his cheek. "We love each other. We trust each other. We can face whatever we have to face together."

Liken's arms tightened. "I am so fortunate to have found you, *sherree*. I want a life with you and children. I want to make you happy."

Sharon's smile was blinding. "I wouldn't mind a few little Likens myself. And you do make me happy."

Their mouths met in a kiss of wonder and love. When at last they pulled apart, Sharon dropped her hand and began unbuttoning Liken's shirt. With a playful grin, she said, "Now, let's talk about this tendency you have to dominate me in bed."

He let out a satisfied laugh. "I am a Shimerian male, am I not? Do not pretend you dislike it, *sherree*. I know otherwise. I know all kinds of interesting, dark fantasies you ache to explore. Would you like to discuss them?"

She felt heat rise to her cheeks as she finished the last of the buttons. Spreading his shirt, she leaned forward and swirled her tongue around one of his nipples. She could feel his big body tense. Her husky voice dripped satisfaction as she said, "Nope, I believe it's my turn for a little revenge."

She placed teasing kisses in a steady downward path. Peeking up at him through her lashes, she watched his eyes darken with arousal. She paused and unbuttoned his pants. He went completely still under her hands. "You'll have to adjust..."

Liken watched the dark curtain of her hair lower over his lap. When her mouth closed over his aching cock, he couldn't stifle his moan. He could feel the blood leaving his head and heading south.

Bringing his hands to tangle in her hair, he arched upward helplessly. He had one last thought before his mind went completely blank. She was a librarian, for goodness sake, and she had conquered a warrior.

Chapter Seventeen

On the twenty-first day after her departure from Earth, Sharon, Liken, and Tair stood on the Shimerian side of the portal. They were waiting in line to transport back to Earth for the pledging ceremony. Tair glanced over his shoulder at the pactmates. Sharon was dressed in her pledge clothing. Her shimmering white halter was thin, and showed off her full breasts beautifully. Her white skirt stopped at mid-thigh calling attention to those wonderful legs. She certainly did not resemble any librarian Tair had ever seen.

Liken was in black, but his boots shone and he was wearing some expensive scent Tair could not identify. Tair studied the couple with great satisfaction. Sharon looked radiant and Liken could barely keep his eyes off of her. They were obviously happy. Sharon turned to him suddenly and said, "Tair, we need to talk." Her voice was serious.

Both men shuddered in instinctive dread at her words. Liken shot him a look of sympathy. Tair couldn't imagine what he had done. He couldn't keep the defensive note from his voice. "What is it, Sharon? Perhaps another time would be better to have this discussion?"

She wasn't being put off. "No, I don't think so. When are you planning to make Kate your pactmate?" It had been on her mind for some time.

The line moved forward. There was only one person ahead of them now. Tair shrugged and said, "She will be at your pledging today, will she not? It is an ideal time."

His casual gesture belied the depth of his real feelings. He was anxious to claim his pactmate. After seeing Liken and Sharon together, especially this last week, he was eager to start his life with Kate.

Sharon nodded slowly. "Well, yes. But, don't you think I should talk to her first? Maybe explain a few things about Shimeria? It might smooth the way." *It might prevent major warfare* she wanted to say.

Tair smiled. "No. Absolutely not. She will learn as you did."

Sharon couldn't contain her doubt. Since she liked Tair and loved Kate like a sister, she wanted to spare both of them some of the pain and confusion she and Liken had gone through in the last few weeks. "She's a lot more...ummm...explosive than I am, Tair. I don't think her knowing period will be as easy as mine."

Tair laughed. "I am relying on it." He stepped through the portal and was gone.

Sharon turned to Liken, who was watching with an incredulous look on his face. "What?"

"Easy? Your knowing period was easy?" Sheer amazement permeated his voice.

She laughed. "Compared to Kate, believe me, I was easy."

Liken placed a hard kiss on her mouth. "Maybe they will be fortunate and find love as we have." Her eyes softened and he placed a tender hand on her cheek n response. She heard people in line behind them shifting restlessly. She turned and walked forward.

Grinning shamelessly, Liken waited until she was about to enter the portal. His voice echoed in the large room. "If not, a little interplanetary nookie won't kill them." The others in the line around them heard his words and laughed along with him.

Sharon couldn't help it. Men were always so sure of themselves. She laughed. "No, but Kate might." She was still laughing as she stepped into the portal and disappeared.

As he stepped through the portal on her heels, Liken thought about his soon-to-be pledgemate. He was very grateful she had agreed to make a life with him. His sweet librarian was beautiful, intelligent, and a fiery dream come to life. She was walking, talking love personified. She meant everything to him.

But, obviously, she did not know Tair. He felt the grin on his face grow wider. Sharon was going to be surprised again.

Of course, not as surprised as Kate...

The Switch

Diane Whiteside

Acknowledgments

My deepest thanks go to…

Eric, for answering endless questions about the Rangers,

Karen, for making sure that Beth walked smoothly in the ways of both Japan and America,

Louise, for describing Tiffany's illness so well, and

Delores, who quickly told me how Sean got out of the Army when I was running hard to meet a deadline.

You've been marvelous friends and I couldn't have written Sean and Beth's story without you.

Chapter One
Seattle
November 2001
Monday, 4 PM

Beth stood on the street corner, waiting for the light to change. Her Savile Row black suit shed Seattle's rain as easily as the London weather of its makers. It also set her apart from the other pedestrians in their serviceable jackets and jeans.

Beth tossed off any envy for their comfort. She'd worn suits for too many years in gatherings where status was measured by one's tailor. This suit was more formal than most, especially with the black silk shirt, black hose and black pumps. It was also perfectly appropriate for hosting a luncheon meeting with Japanese bankers. Somehow, being a Treasury bureaucrat and conversing easily in English and Japanese was easier in decorous clothing.

But her beloved black and gold scarf nestled against her throat, reminding her of other occasions when a woman could wear a formal black suit and be considered all the more female for it. Events that sometimes began in public but always ended in private, with both herself and her lover well-satisfied. Her mouth quirked at the thought, remembering how boneless a sated man could look when he was finally permitted to climax at the end of a long evening's play.

The light changed and she crossed, following the other walkers' lead in dodging the puddles. This neighborhood was old and eclectic, only recently returned to prosperity. Its streets were solid but would probably betray their age later that evening by collecting rivers and lakes, instead of trickles and puddles, from the promised heavy rain.

Beth checked the street number of the closest store and strode briskly on. Two blocks past the dungeon and half-way down the block were the directions. A bookstore just down the street from a professional BDSM dungeon definitely sounded like an escape from work.

The dungeon had a good reputation in the scene but that didn't matter at the moment. She'd rather visit a bookstore than look for partners in Seattle's BDSM scene.

Time was precious now, especially for a brief reprieve from the conference. She had spent weeks preparing for its intense discussions on East Asia's banking systems, fiscal stability, and more. But even her absorption in those demanding plans had paled against the events of September 11th; not surprising, given the funerals she had attended afterwards.

A shop ahead drew her, with its spill of bright light across the sidewalk under a festively striped canopy. If nothing else, she could check street numbers in comfort before making one last dash to the bookstore she sought.

A few steps more and she read the store's name: The Wise Old Owl. A fat orange tomcat slumbered under its emblem of a gilded owl.

Travel books offered a sunny escape in the front windows. The bright colors of children's books offered another kind of vacation for tired parents. White walls and blonde wood bookcases reflected the light and bright colors, welcoming the casual visitor. The store was quiet now and seemed empty of customers as it awaited the evening rush.

Beth smiled at the sight and walked in. She'd found her diversion.

The doorbell rang softly, announcing her arrival.

Beth quickly fastened her black umbrella, being careful not to shake any water off onto the books. Her gaze studied the store looking for clues to the books she wanted.

The clerk spoke from behind the counter in front and she glanced over at him. Gary, according to his name badge, was 20-something, slender and very fit with a full head of dark hair above a goatee. He was also more formally dressed than she'd expected for this neighborhood in a shirt and tie. But the store advertised old-fashioned service with its modern selection, so perhaps he dressed for the more traditional aspects.

"Good evening, ma'am. Can I help you find anything?" he offered.

"I'm looking for some erotica. Can you help me?" Beth answered bluntly, not willing to waste time.

"Oh yes, that's right at the back. Any particular kind?" he asked as he headed down the center aisle to show her the way.

"Heterosexual erotica, please," she answered, satisfied with his easy response to what could be an embarrassing request.

Gary went straight to the back wall and turned right at the row of bookcases leaning against it.

"We've got that right here on this shelf. Anything else?"

Beth looked where he indicated. Interesting titles offered themselves from less than half of the shelf. The rest of the bookcase seemed full of titles from other genres, mostly critical studies of literary classics. She sighed.

"Non-fiction sexuality?" she questioned.

"Just to your left, across the aisle."

Beth glanced over and saw some more possibilities.

"Gay erotica too please, if you've got it. And perhaps a little lesbian?" she questioned, hoping for a wider selection.

"Oh, that will be in the bookcases right in front of this one. You'll see the gay erotica first and then the lesbian," he replied casually.

"Thanks," Beth responded as she started looking more closely at the heterosexual titles. They were primarily well known series from major publishers. Beth snarled to herself: if she saw one more volume of letters to the editor of a famous magazine, she'd probably scream. She'd come to this eccentric neighborhood to escape the familiar, not to revisit clichés.

Beth paused, hearing a voice rumble through the wall. The man must be on just the other side, given how easily she heard him.

"No, I'm not interested in their offer, Tim. Business may be slow but I'm not going to accept an offer of less than half its appraised value. They'll have to do a lot better than that, if they want to beat out the other bidders."

Beth smiled at the controlled growl under the words, sounding as ferocious as a weapons buyer in a bazaar. He showed more discipline and force than many of the currency traders she'd worked with in Manhattan. Her fingers stroked a book of couples' erotic fantasies, while she enjoyed the deep music of his voice.

"I'll call Phillips tomorrow and tell him. That everything?... Have a good time at the game." A click signaled the call's end.

Beth sighed, unconsciously regretting the lost voice. Her hand lingered on the book for a second longer before she moved along the shelf. She picked up the latest volume of a favorite series and considered its list of contributors.

A door to the back opened and a man came through it. Beth blinked, startled, and saw a big blond Viking walk in. He stood well over six feet, more than tall enough to make her five feet, nine inches seem petite. He was built of all bone and muscle, moving with the same unselfconscious ease as a leopard. A jagged white scar etched his right forearm from wrist to elbow, half-hidden under a gloss of bright hair.

The blue flannel shirt above his jeans and work boots emphasized his blue eyes and his strong arms under the rolled up sleeves. He wore a serviceable watch on his right wrist and a narrow black metal bracelet on his left, bearing a single line of text. Perhaps he was selling his truck, given clothes like that.

His hair offered the only counterpoint to the lumberjack image: it was cut high and tight to his skull, leaving a thick golden pelt at the top of his head with white skin on the sides and back. That combination of dense silky hair with sculptured bone and tendons promised unique sensations to the lucky lady who found his head between her legs.

He looked down at her, as he closed the door quietly. From this close, his eyes were the same deep, vivid blue as the Hope diamond. Their gaze met and locked.

He stared at her, his eyes darkening with surprise and interest.

Her gut twisted with lust and her breath caught with a barely audible gasp. Her hand instinctively started to rise, eager for contact.

"Was everything the way you wanted it, Sean?" asked the clerk, coming to meet the newcomer.

Sean froze and then shrugged as he turned to face Gary.

"Yes, the apartment's really clean, Gary. You and your lady did a great job on that after you moved out. How's business, anyway?"

"Doing good. Slightly better than last year, actually."

The two men grinned at each other, in perfect harmony over a victory, and moved back towards the front of the store.

Dear heavens, Sean looked just as irresistible from behind, with broad shoulders rising above a hard, narrow masculine ass. Old memories stirred, of Scotsmen dancing in their kilts when one of their own came home safe from war in the South Atlantic. Strong bodies sweating and men's eyes gleaming with joy as they held their ladies. Herself at ten years old, watching quietly.

Beth moved to the other side of the aisle. Non-fiction offered a wider selection than heterosexual erotica, plus a better look at him.

The two men paused to chat in front of the movies section, with posters gleaming behind them. A young boy with black spectacles and a thunderbolt scar flew out of the sky over Gary's head, an image of scholarly intensity echoed in the living man.

But Sean's hand rested on a stark red and black book, its cover shouting "Black Hawk Down." A warrior's book obviously, next to a man who looked fit to carry a sword in battle.

Beth frowned, shrugging off the temptation to follow him, and returned to browsing. Sean was very interesting but real-life offered more pitfalls than fiction. She'd come into this store to find a fantasy to go to bed with. Surely books were the better choice, their paper and ink men far safer than flesh and blood. She could begin the real hunt after returning home, where friends could help find a good mate.

The front door slammed open, its bell falling into an urgent jangle. Beth glanced up and caught sight of the newcomer in the mirror over the back door.

The girl was too thin, her eyes looking like dark pools in her stretched white face, while her sweatshirt and jeans left trails of water on the carpet. She was shaking as she wrapped her arms around herself, staring around the room. Was the rain why she looked so distressed or was there something else? Beth found it difficult to judge, given the distortions of the mirror's curved glass.

Gary and Sean had stopped talking when the door opened. Their gaze met in perfect understanding before Gary went to the girl. Sean considered the store's windows, sweeping every foot of sidewalk beyond with his glance. Then he moved to the other side of the book display, where he was closer to Gary and enjoyed clear passage down the center aisle to the front door.

Was he covering Gary's back?

Beth turned to see more directly, rather than through the mirror.

"Can I help you, ma'am?" Gary's voice was softer, even more polite than his greeting to Beth. The girl visibly gulped hard before she looked at him.

Beth cursed under her breath as she saw the blood trickling down the girl's face. Probably not a bad injury, given the small amount of blood, but it still needed to be attended to. She took a step forward, instinctively planning to help.

A roar of wind and traffic noises announced someone else. A young man burst in, looking like a rabid bulldog with his protruding eyes and clenched jaw. He pushed back his sweatshirt's soaked hood and stabbed the trembling girl with one quick glare.

"Damnit, Shelby, why the hell did you come in here?" A few quick steps brought him to the girl. He didn't hesitate when he brushed against a display, sending books to the floor.

Shelby stammered something that might have been words and shrank towards Gary, who moved up next to her.

The young man cursed and reached for her. "Come on, Shelby! You know better than to run away. Just cut the crap and come with me."

"Perhaps you should ask the young lady what she wants to do." Sean's voice was very calm as he came forward.

The kid jerked around to face Sean, breaking his concentration on Shelby.

"Don't be stupid, man. Shelby's my bitch and she knows she can't leave. Just get outta my face and we'll be out of here."

"The young lady," Sean said slowly, with the slightest emphasis on the noun, "may have another idea."

"Doesn't matter if she does. She's coming with me." The kid started to grab Shelby and Sean shifted, blocking the attempt.

"Damnit!" The kid's hand moved and silver blossomed in his fist. He lunged towards Sean with the knife.

Sean's hands came up as he pivoted smoothly.

The kid yelped an instant later, just before metal clattered against a bookcase and dropped to the floor. Sean held the kid easily, one arm tight against his back. The kid twisted wildly and yelped again before standing still.

"Let me go!"

"Not yet. The young lady's wishes have yet to be considered. What do you want me to do with him, Miss Shelby?" Sean's voice was as unhurried as if he discussed dinner plans, instead of an attacker's disposal. Beth's eyes widened at the quiet mastery in his deep voice.

The girl's eyes were enormous as she stared at her rescuer. "I don't want any trouble," she began and stopped. She tried again. "Can you just tell Tony to leave, or something? So I don't have to see him again?"

"Are you sure, ma'am? He might come after you if the police don't lock him up."

"I've got someplace safe to go. And, and, I don't want to talk to the cops. They'd just cause more trouble for me. So would you please get him out of here?" Shelby seemed on the verge of tears.

"Yes, ma'am, if you're quite certain that's what you want."

Shelby nodded jerkily.

Sean marched the kid towards the front. Shelby stayed silent, watching them leave.

Just before they reached the door, the kid halted and tried to turn around.

"My knife! Give me back my knife!"

"No. Just be glad you're leaving here with your skin intact."

The kid struggled furiously but Sean quickly brought him under control.

Sean spoke again, his steady voice given more emphasis by the boy's anger. Beth shivered at its cold promise.

"Remember one thing, kid. The deal's off if you hurt the young lady. You do that and I'm coming after you. Got that?"

Beth watched the kid's face shift from a youthful sneer to terror as he absorbed Sean's promise. He swallowed hard before answering.

"Yeah, I understand," he mumbled, before adding a surprising "Sir."

"Good. Now go."

"Yes, sir."

The kid opened the front door quickly and was running before he reached the next store. Sean watched him go and then turned back into the bookstore, his face relaxed and thoughtful. The orange tomcat in the window rolled and stretched, leaving one paw lifted into the air in an impolite salute.

"How would you like a cup of coffee and some dry clothes?" Gary offered the girl. Shelby eyed him suspiciously.

"It's okay, Shelby. His fiancée owns the clothing store across the street. You can change there and make a phone call while you drink some coffee."

Shelby visibly relaxed at Sean's explanation. Beth smiled; she understood agreeing to any suggestions couched in a deep purr, especially when uttered by the man who'd just saved you.

"Okay," Shelby decided shakily. "I've got money though, enough to pay for whatever I need."

"Of course you do," Gary agreed soothingly. "Let's go see what Shannon can find. Would you handle the store until I get back, Sean? I'll send one of Shannon's clerks over if I'll be gone long."

"No problem. I'll just do some browsing while I wait."

Gary snorted and fetched an umbrella from behind the counter. He guided Shelby across the street, picking his way through the puddles and sheltering her as solicitously as if she were a queen.

Beth watched Shelby's growing comfort with a smile. A real-life drama had ended happily, unlike many. A strong man had freed a girl, hopefully forever, from another's greedy clutches. Beth wished briefly she'd had that sort of protection from her avaricious fiancé. But she'd ended the engagement herself and paid the price.

She sighed and returned to the books' safety.

Beth exhausted the non-fiction books in a few minutes and headed for the gay and lesbian fiction. She followed the bookcases' labels, moving deeper into the narrow path between them like an archaeologist following a tunnel into a buried city. Ethnic fiction, Jewish fiction, African-American fiction, all glided past without receiving a second glance. The bookcases jogged to the right and she froze.

The big Viking stood there, calmly reading a book. Beth took a deep breath and considered what to do next. Did he want to strike up an acquaintance? Did she? She quietly took her place in front of the bookcase next to him and waited, hoping he'd act on the interest he'd shown earlier.

Beth quickly realized that the gay erotica section was entirely at her disposal, since Sean was standing in front of the lesbian erotica section. His book's cover, which he held just below the level of her eyes, was an elegant but explicit work of art celebrating the joys of women pleasuring each other.

Beth smiled to herself: who was she to complain when she enjoyed artwork emphasizing the male body? And that was a very nice male body only a step away from her too. Too good to be easily ignored, especially since he wasn't wearing a wedding ring.

The lack of a ring was hardly an infallible signal of availability, any more than its presence always meant monogamy. On the other hand, its absence did offer an opening.

"Congratulations on rescuing that girl," she offered quietly, looking up at Sean over a year's best anthology which featured a cover more remarkable for blandness than titillation.

Sean blinked and stared at her, clearly startled.

"Uh, yeah, Gary did a great job, getting Shelby over to Shannon's place. I'm sure she's already warm and dry by now."

Only years of high-stakes trading, where a twinge of emotion could cost millions, kept Beth from dropping her jaw. Didn't Sean realize that she was complimenting him? Or was he just uninterested in talking to her?

"Yes, Gary was very efficient, wasn't he?" she responded and tried to think of something to say that could only be seen as mentioning Sean.

Sean smiled and nodded at her commonplace response, coughed briefly and went back to his book.

Beth frowned briefly and then followed his example. Reading seemed like a more promising option than conversation. A minute's study convinced her that the anthology was as boring as its cover and she shoved it back into place, easing her frustration.

Then Beth began to seriously browse the books, enjoying the latest from favorite publishers and authors and discovering new works. She picked out a volume, studied the cover (very nice leather harness on that stud, thank you), before reading the back blurb. The man on the cover looked uncomfortable, as if he had challenged the photographer to make a good picture.

Of course, Sean would probably look better in that harness than the cover model did, given his advantage in height and broad shoulders. Or maybe scarf bondage would suit him better, offering such a marvelous contrast with his intense masculinity.

A moment later, she was skimming the words inside, looking for images to savor and enjoying the texture of pages as they slid under her fingers. She put the book back, regretting its total lack of plot, and her elbow brushed Sean.

"Oops! Sorry about that." She drew away slightly and he smiled down at her.

"No problem," he said easily.

He didn't stammer when she touched him first. That opened some interesting possibilities.

Beth and Sean slowly worked their way through the shelves, enjoying a companionable silence as they studied covers and turned pages. The scarf caressed Beth's throat like a living being. Her varying positions as they took books from different shelves allowed her to see him from different angles, especially if she took care to never look directly. Her enjoyment of the more blatant artwork was increased by her sidelong glances at him. Images from the books were overlaid by visions of Sean, hot and naked and thrashing. The only sounds were the soft rustle of turning pages and their breathing, with an occasional whisper of clothing.

"Could you please fetch me *The Oy of Sex* ?" Beth asked, her voice husky in the quiet. "It's on the top shelf, to your right..."

Sean handed it to Beth, just as she reached up to take it from him. Their hands brushed on the book's elegant binding and lingered. Beth slid her hand over his, enjoying his warm strength, and took hold of the book next to his fingers. Her nipples rubbed uncomfortably against the lace restraining them.

Sean stared down at her and then smiled slowly. He hummed quietly when he went back to his books. Beth wondered exactly what he was thinking. He had a splendid bulge behind his jeans' zipper.

"Excuse me," Sean murmured.

Beth glanced up, startled out of her fantasies, just as he reached around her to push a teetering book back onto its shelf. Her movement brought her next to him, her shoulder lodged against his chest. She felt his arm encircle her shoulders and she waited, eager for his next move. She tossed her head back to clear a lock from her face and flinched when the movement ended with a jerk.

"Just stand still, ma'am. You've got your hair caught between the bookcases," Sean soothed her. He put his book down on a shelf and then gently freed her hair, while his other arm never left her shoulders.

Beth watched him, poised and willing, her mouth half-open as she hoped he would come closer. To her delight, he bent his head to hers very slowly. Her eyes closed in anticipation as she felt his breath on her cheek.

"Sean?" Gary's voice broke the silence just as Sean's lips touched hers.

Sean froze and then straightened up. Beth silently rehearsed some unflattering Japanese descriptions of Gary's ancestry.

"Back here, Gary," he answered. "It's been quiet since you left." He stepped away from Beth so Gary could see him between the bookcases. She was fiercely glad of his voice's hoarseness.

"Okay," Gary responded. "Thanks."

Sean returned to the erotica section but didn't come close to Beth again.

Piqued, she considered her options. A quick check of her watch told her that something needed to happen soon, before she had to return to the conference. She turned and headed out of the aisle, back towards the bookstore's front.

A small smile played her mouth when she heard Sean's sigh at her departure.

"Did you find everything you wanted?" asked Gary as Beth came up to the counter.

"Almost," she said, remembering that big book on the edge of the gay erotica. "Actually, I was looking for *The Male Nude* by David Leddick. Do you have it?"

"Oh yes, it's at the bottom of the bookcase at the end of the gay erotica. Right next to the lesbian erotica."

Beth thanked him and retraced her steps. Was Sean listening?

Just as she got there, a masculine arm came up from the floor towards her, with a book resting in the big palm.

"Is this what you're looking for, ma'am?" Sean offered.

"Yes thank you, that's exactly what I was looking for." Her hand glided over his as she took the book.

"I could have bought it over the Internet but I really wanted to touch it first, you know?" she remarked, trying to sound innocent. "Some of these are just so cheap that they're not nice at all to handle. I really prefer something that feels good in your hand, especially when you're going to spend some time with it."

She came to a stop, hoping that he'd hear the hidden meaning. Her focus lifted slowly from his chest to his face. His eyes were heavy-lidded as he looked down at her and he smiled slowly.

"Is there anything else you'd like to see, ma'am?" He answered her double entendre with one of his own.

"I'd like a look at you," she said honestly, too caught up in the moment's electricity to remember her wariness of relationships.

Sean stared at her and didn't move, clearly uncertain as to what he should do next.

Beth shook her head at him and chuckled softly. Then she looked him over deliberately, lingering on his mouth before surveying the rest of his lean body. He was breathing hard and shaking slightly by the time she finished. But he hadn't tried to leave.

Beth took his elbow and took him out of the store to the back, where they found themselves in a narrow hallway. He unlocked an inconspicuous door and held it open for her to go ahead of him.

Beth found herself in a small room that seemed to be as much storeroom as office. Sean put his books down on the desk then took up position under the high windows and watched her, his arms folded across his chest. Rain fell from the roofline outside, casting a curtain of sound around the room. She put her books down next to his and turned to face him.

Sean's response was fast and strong. He took command and kissed her like a starving man. His hand tightened on the nape of her neck, holding her head against any effort to move away. Beth responded willingly, startled by his intensity and his skill.

His tongue probed her mouth, twining around her tongue before exploring the various shapes and textures available to him.

His cock blazed against her like an iron bar fresh from the furnace, restrained only by his jeans and her suit.

Beth felt his self-control slipping away and tried to think.

Sean's hands slid down her back, pulling her closer to him. His knee pushed but couldn't separate her legs, given her skirt's tightness. He pushed again and Beth gasped, self-preservation starting to re-emerge. Thought was difficult, as her year's celibacy demanded relief from this man. Now.

He yanked at her skirt, growling into her mouth. Wool ripped like a gunshot.

Beth jumped and Sean stopped kissing her immediately.

"Back off, big guy!" Beth snarled. His hands fell away from her and he stepped back. One step, two steps, then the wall brought him up short. He braced himself against it, like a soldier summoned for discipline.

She looked down to see a three-inch tear rising up the skirt's side seam, showing her leg as an evening gown would.

Anger bubbled up in her, followed by silent giggles. He'd ruined her suit but she'd made herself available. She hadn't been this clumsy in an embrace since high school. Two adults, grappling in a storeroom like teenagers. She clamped down hard on the giggles and began to think. A private room, a gorgeous guy who was waiting for her next move. The situation had possibilities.

"I'm sorry, ma'am," he began, looking appalled. "I apologize for ruining your skirt. I'll replace..."

"You clumsy jerk. What the hell made you think you could maul me? Is that what I invited you back here for?" Beth growled, coming so close to him that she could see individual eyelashes.

"No, ma'am." Sean shook his head, his face frozen. He was definitely standing at attention.

She frowned at him, contemplating what to do next. It was time for her to take control.

He watched her warily. Something in her softened at the caution in his eyes. How long had it been since he'd held a lover, for him to kiss her that hard? Who had rejected him, for him to be that ignorant of a woman's interest?

"Apology accepted, Sean. Now then, this encounter is about what I want, not you. We'll deal with your pleasure after you satisfy me. Any problems with that?"

"No, ma'am." He frowned, clearly trying to think what to do next. Beth smiled to herself and pondered how best to surprise him. It was time to play and hopefully fan that spark into a flame. She tamped down the voice that said it was too easy to find magic with this stranger.

"Now, you're going to keep your hands to yourself while I study you. Understand?"

"Yes, of course." He was bewildered. And enticing.

"Do you have any idea how beautiful you are?" she asked.

"What? I'm not..."

She stopped his denial with a raised finger.

"When I want to hear your voice, I'll tell you. Got that?"

He managed to nod.

"By the way, I'm Beth."

He nodded a greeting.

Beth stepped back a pace and brazenly looked him over, feeling the spark between them growing.

"I like your taste in clothing. The blue flannel shirt matches your eyes. Step away from the wall so I can see all of you," she growled. He promptly obeyed with a martial snap. Beth filed the implications away for later use.

She strolled around him, tracing his shoulders with her fingers. His head swiveled to follow her but he remained otherwise motionless.

She rested both hands on his chest when she stopped in front of him.

"So soft too. It rests against you like a lover. A girl could be jealous of its closeness," she teased and he choked. Good; she'd managed to shock him so much he couldn't find a conventional response.

"You are marvelously sensitive, Sean!" Beth chuckled, watching the color surge into his face. She caressed his cheek and he blushed more. His arousal pushed his jeans against her wool skirt. She bit down on her lust, while still following the electricity between them. She couldn't build a fire if she lost control now.

"Show me more, Sean. More of you, the flesh and blood man. Not a frozen image, caught in black and white between a book's covers. Show me what that lucky shirt is touching," she purred.

"Beth, please," Sean hesitated.

"Did I say you could speak?" Beth snapped and smiled approval when he shook his head. "Now show yourself to me, Sean. You know I can't harm you."

Sean's fingers fumbled but he managed to unbutton his shirt. He took it off slowly, more because of nerves than art. Beth watched him, pleased at her ability to stay disciplined but scared by the threat he offered. He was so incredibly tempting.

Finally, he managed to drop the shirt onto the desk behind him and stood to face her again. He wore no under-shirt and his bare chest and back gleamed under the room's single lamp. He was long and lean, beautifully muscled but elegant. He had an animal's economic grace of powerful function, rather than a man-made mass of muscle hiding the body's true potential. He was magnificently furred in shades of gold. A thick mat of golden fur, which darkened as it formed a narrow trail downwards, covered his chest.

He breathed raggedly but watched her steadily, without any attempt to hide himself or stop her.

Beth covered his nipples gently with her palms, enjoying their hard spikes. His hands lifted and she glared at him. They fell back without touching her. His nostrils flared as he drew a shuddering breath.

Beth rested her forehead lightly against him, testing if he'd push her again. Sean swallowed hard and trembled but didn't budge. He smelled of sweat and hunger. He wouldn't move until she gave him permission.

Heat rolled through her body, from where it had simmered deep inside. Her silk panties were suddenly very damp, as her core melted under his blue eyes. She wanted far more from him than the prickle of his hair between her fingers. But caution still sounded in her ears, matched by the need to see his pleasure. Somehow, ensuring that this starving man found joy was more important than any physical satisfaction for herself.

"Unzip your pants," she demanded, her voice harsh with its burden of lust.

He promptly complied, then slowly fanned his fingers to spread his jeans. His engorged cock gleamed hot and red, the color of life, against the white skin of his groin. It was uncut and thick against the dense fur, entirely natural. She doubted her hand could wrap completely around it at the base, just below his foreskin's beautiful ruffled cowl.

She had seen a great many cocks, both aroused and quiescent. She'd played with some and been intimate with a handful. But she'd seen very few like his that made her start thinking of stallions. Big studs, not polite riding horses. A Lipizzaner perhaps, or an Andalusian.

Her tongue crept out to briefly caress her lips.

Beth swallowed hard and considered his entire body, staring at the magnificent male caught in full living color before her. His appearance was much more exciting than the black-and-white photos of pretty boys in the book on the desk, much more interesting than any other man she'd ever seen. Her body trembled and she jerked it back under her leash.

Sean's eyes darkened as he watched. His mouth curved in a hard smile as he waited for the next order, barely breathing.

"Touch yourself," came her hoarse demand.

Sean curled a hand around his cock and began to stroke it slowly, watching the way her eyes followed his every move. His thumb traveled over the head in a curling touch and then his fingers slowly pulled on his shaft, lengthening it even more.

Beth sighed as the single frozen image of a strong man became a flow of pictures, all colorful, all arousing. She was very hot, her throat dripping with sweat under her scarf.

"Drop your pants and show me your balls."

Sean pushed his jeans down over his hips to his knees and openly displayed all of himself to her. Dear heavens, his balls more than matched his magnificent cock. She put her fist to her mouth to stifle a whimper as she watched him.

His fingers traveled lightly over his balls, outlining them. He stroked them a little more, cupping them in his palm. His eyes caught hers. He wordlessly questioned her approval. Beth's eyes blazed back at him. Couldn't he tell how much she liked watching him?

"Damn you, go on," she hissed.

His smile blazed in startled triumph, that of a man who had set a woman trembling by simply allowing her to see him. He growled, low and deep in his throat like a tiger that scented his mate. Then he began to stroke his cock again, deepening and quickening the contact. His mouth tightened a bit when his rough hand snagged on the sensitive skin.

Beth moved abruptly and pulled the scarf from her neck.

"Use this."

She tossed the scarf at him and Sean caught it. He ran the scarf through his hand, stretching it out to its full length. It was soft and yet very strong against him, lying over his palm in invitation. It caught slightly on his calluses and yet pressed delicately against the edge of his hand. His breathing deepened.

Sean slid the scarf behind his sac, obviously savoring the feeling as it caressed the sensitive skin. The scarf outlined his arousal and lifted it closer to Beth. He pulled it delicately back and forth, then between his balls to separate them. A few more strokes and then he swept the scarf around his balls, covering them in a silken fretwork.

Beth purred at the contrast between the scarf's gold and black, his deep red cock, and his groin's white skin.

Then he moved the scarf up his cock and began to stroke, curving the silk around, moving it back and forth, up and down. Her body throbbed in unison with the scarf's dance.

His hand moved faster and faster, until gold seemed to be pouring over his groin. His face contorted in ecstasy at the sensation, still watching her fascination with his movements. A deep bellow tore from his throat as an orgasm took him and he poured his seed into the gold.

Climax blazed through Beth at the sight, as fierce and unexpected as a shooting star. She bit down hard on her hand to stay silent but staggered trying to stay upright.

Sean's eyes slowly opened and he looked at her.

Beth was shaking after her own release. A thin trickle of blood ran down her hand from where she'd bitten her knuckle. She tried to catch her breath.

An electronic ring cut through their silence and Beth jumped. She looked around and grabbed her purse off the desk, fumbling to stop the cell phone.

"Damn, not another one of Holly's so-called emergencies," she cursed, rapidly pressing buttons that seemed all too small at the moment. "Yes," she snapped, bringing the phone up to her ear. The answering voice bewildered her. "Mr. Griffith?"

Beth took a deep breath and tried to think. Why was her office's director calling?

"Yes, of course I remember that meeting in September," she assured him. Her eyes glanced over to see Sean slowly sliding his jeans back up his hips. She swallowed and yanked her attention back to the voice in her ear.

"Yes, I'd be honored to represent Treasury...Tomorrow morning at eight is fine. No, it won't conflict with the conference..."

Sean finished fastening his jeans and looked at the wet scarf in his hand. Hot color blazed across his cheekbones. Beth followed his eyes to the scarf and lust pooled again between her legs. Somehow she kept talking, hoping that she made sense.

"Can you get me directions to the FBI offices? Thanks...Certainly I'll let you know what happens. Good night."

Beth snapped the phone shut. Finally she had an opportunity to get involved in the hunt for terrorists. But all she really wanted to do was put her hands on Sean again.

"I'll have this cleaned for you. When can I give it back to you?" Sean asked.

"There's a reception tonight to kick off the conference so I couldn't get back here until ten or so." Hunger echoed in her words.

Sean brightened at the promise of another encounter.

"Just come back here as soon as you're done. I'll be waiting."

"Are you sure the bookstore will be open? The neighborhood is a little rough."

"I'm the landlord so it'll be open," Sean smiled at her.

"Okay." Landlord? He looked like a janitor.

"If you can't make it, call me at this number." She handed him a business card, which he took without taking his eyes from hers. He fumbled in his back pocket and managed to produce a business card that she accepted wordlessly.

Beth finished gathering up her books and stepped towards the door before coming to a stop in front of him. She reached up her hand and gently ran her finger across his mouth. He stroked her finger with the tip of his tongue.

"Save the scarf for then, hunh?" she suggested softly. He smiled down at her.

"Anything you say, ma'am. Anything at all."

Chapter Two
Monday, 5 PM

Sean sagged back onto the desk an instant after the door closed behind Beth. The bravado that had kept him standing after that incredible rush disappeared with the sound of her departing feet.

Had it been a dream?

He looked at the card in his hand. Two lines of script showed: Elizabeth Nakamura and a Washington, DC phone number. A single rose lay at the bottom, etched in gold and complete with thorns.

He smiled wryly. Fair warning, but he'd risk thorns any day for a rose like her. What games did she want to play when she handed out a card like that? His cock stirred eagerly at the thought.

He'd jacked off as assiduously as any other Ranger during his time in the Army. He'd collected more than his share of memorable jacks along the way from those solitary exercises: the Panama Jack, the Gulf Jack, the Somalia Jack, the C-17 Jack, and more. But none of those compared to jacking off while she observed, then realizing that she'd climaxed from watching him.

Of course, it had been a long time since he'd been with a woman in any fashion. Twelve years since he and Tiffany agreed they shouldn't sleep together, given the discomfort from her second stroke. To tell the truth, staying out of Tiffany's bed hadn't changed much in his life except for killing any hope that she'd come to enjoy sex.

But Beth had blown all the old memories out of his mind. Thankfully, she hadn't been put off by his clumsy behavior. He shook his head, remembering how he'd fumbled the ball in the bookstore. Then he'd heard her voice again, seducing him into the backroom.

Not that he needed much encouragement. It had been so easy to follow her lead, measuring the electricity rising between them by the heat in his cock and the fire in her eyes.

"Thanks, Adam," he whispered to his friend's ghost. Adam had left his family's real estate business, including this building, to Sean, shrugging off assurances that he'd live for years to come. "I've tried to keep my word to you; guess you just threw in a new twist."

Live for both of us, Adam had demanded on that last evening. *If anything happens to me, you live for both of us.* He'd died the next afternoon, shot down by a Somali mob.

"What's his status?" The voice crackled again in Sean's memories. There was a long pause, filled with other desperate voices over the radio, before the answer came.

"KIA." Killed in Action. Silence. All the other Rangers listening in had carefully not looked at Sean, giving him time to regain his composure. Then he chivvied them into motion; there was a lot of work to be done to get their remaining brethren home safely. He'd been fiercely glad to go out with the rescue convoy.

He looked at the scarf, crumpled up in his hand, before lifting it to his nose. His musk was there but so was a spicy sweetness, evoking womanhood. More woman than he'd ever hoped to encounter. And she'd cared about him and his comfort, enough to give him the clothes off her back. That act alone made Beth totally different from Mrs. Wolcott and her demands on his high school ignorance.

He closed his eyes and breathed deeply, dragging her scent in and memorizing it.

Beth. Female. Treasury, working with the FBI. Dangerous lady. A skillful, experienced, successful leader, as his cock would gladly attest. Hopefully, he'd see what lay under that proper black suit tonight.

He laughed when his phone rang. At least this interruption had waited until Beth left. A quick flip of his wrist and Caller ID told him who sought him.

"Yeah, Mike," he answered.

"Hi, Dad. Mrs. Hemmings just called to say that she'll be here in twenty minutes to see the furniture."

"I'll be home by then. If she gets there first, just show her the guest room."

"No problem, Dad."

"Mike." He hesitated.

"Yeah, Dad?"

"You got any problem selling your mother's old bedroom furniture?"

"Nah, it just reminds me of how she was so trapped in it at the end. I'd rather remember her in other ways, like how she taught me to cook."

"Okay, Mike, if you're sure." Sean let his voice trail off, inviting Mike to say more if he needed to.

"Oh, I'm positive. It's time for us both to clean house and move on. Me to West Point, God willing. And you to, well, something all your own." Mike was very calm, as he usually was on this subject. But he'd always been older than his years.

Sean flinched slightly, not as much as the other times when Mike mentioned the coming changes. Still, he'd rather hunt Scuds in Iraq again, than enter the dating game for the first time. Tiffany's pregnancy had yanked him into matrimony before he'd ever seriously looked for a lover.

"Hey, you'll get in," Sean managed to reply, trying to deflect the conversation.

"If not, then I'll enlist." Sean could almost hear Mike's verbal shrug.

"We've talked about this before, Mike," Sean snorted. "College first, then the Army."

"And I've said this before. Army will pay for college, while I'm in. One way or another, I'm in the Army next fall."

"Mike…"

"There're things to be done, Dad. And all I've ever wanted was to be Army."

"Yeah," Sean conceded the last point. Time to end this subject for the moment. "I'll be home in ten. See ya."

Sean closed the phone. Was it easier to think about Mike's departure with a woman's silks in his hand?

He pulled his pickup to a stop in back of his small house and ran inside, leaving the scarf on the truck's seat. He could see Mike in the kitchen, talking to Deirdre Hemmings while he stirred a simmering pot. Sean stooped to greet Dudley with an ear rub. Dudley was too old now to jump up in welcome, as his Golden Retriever warmth demanded and was delighted when his humans came to him.

"Hello, Deirdre, Mike."

"Hi, Dad."

"Hello, Sean," Deirdre responded. She was a good-looking blonde a few years older than Sean, still wearing scrubs from her nursing job. Her daughter Carol, Mike's girlfriend, would look just like her in another twenty years. "Mike makes a spectacular spaghetti sauce. I wish I cooked the way he does."

"It's just the way Mom taught me," Mike shrugged.

"Good thing too," Sean agreed. "I can manage microwaves and heating MREs; nothing else. Can I get you anything, Deirdre?"

"No, thank you. I just wanted to run over and see the furniture before Tracy gets home from ballet class."

"Why don't we go up and look at it then?" Sean suggested.

Moments later, they were upstairs in the tiny guest room hidden under the eaves. The white and gilt furniture gleamed in the filtered light from the skylights. He'd had the additional windows installed when an old Army buddy, now a Delta Force operator, came to visit. Rick loved to sleep under the stars and Sean didn't want him to feel confined. At least, no more cramped than that bed made anyone over six feet feel.

Deirdre stopped in the doorway, staring at the bedroom suite.

"Wow," she managed, moving forward to finger the lace canopy. "It's gorgeous, Sean. Tracy will love it."

"Good. I can drop the set off at your house on Friday morning, if Dave can help me unload it. It's all solid wood."

"Oh yes, he'll be there. It's the perfect present for Tracy's tenth birthday. I just can't believe you'd have anything like this in your house. How did you find it?"

"Tiffany bought it while I was in AIT," he answered, referring to his time in Infantry Advanced Individual Training. Fourteen weeks of high summer in Georgia, enduring days with a heat index over one hundred fifteen degrees, while the Army made him into an infantryman. And Tiffany tried to find something she liked about being a military wife. "I refinished it like this after Mike was born so it was just the way she wanted."

"Were the bedspread and canopy hers too? The pink ruffles and lace canopy are lovely but they don't look like you."

"She picked them out on her last birthday. But the mattress and springs are new since Tiffany's death. It was cheaper to replace them than get them cleaned, after she'd been bedridden for so long. They're seven years old but they've only been lightly used."

Deirdre nodded, still stroking the pink brocade.

"Tiffany must have loved this, even when she was sick. A double bed will be huge for Tracy but you must have folded up like a pretzel to fit."

Sean's mouth twisted. Pretzel was a good description for the times he hadn't just hung his feet over the end. Tiffany's petite frame had fit neatly.

He wondered what Beth would look like in this bed and laughed silently at himself. He doubted he'd notice the furniture if Beth was undressed.

"That must be why Mike says he remembers you sleeping on the floor in his room so often when he was a kid," Deirdre mused.

So Mike remembered that? Well, Sean had done it often enough. The floor had felt like heaven after training or field exercises. It had also been blessedly free of Tiffany's whining.

"Can I have the bedspread and canopy? Tracy's such a frilly girl, unlike Carol, that she'll probably like it."

Sean roused himself, glad to move on.

"Sure, we won't use it. I'll get it cleaned and bring it on Friday too."

"Thanks. We'll be glad to pay for the cleaning."

"Don't worry about it. That's just part of taking the bed."

Sean hesitated for a minute. Carol and her mother were very pragmatic but Tracy had seemed more fanciful on the few occasions they'd spoken.

"Something else, Deirdre."

Deirdre looked back at him, poised to start downstairs.

"Tiffany always wanted a daughter, a little blonde princess to giggle and shop with. She'd be glad Tracy has the bed. And tell Tracy that Tiffany didn't die in this bed. The aneurysm broke while she was at the doctor's office and she died in the hospital."

Deirdre patted him on the arm.

"Thanks, Sean. I'm sure she wouldn't have worried about Tiffany's ghost but now, she can just think happy thoughts about this bed."

Sean nodded and stayed silent, glad that somebody had happy thoughts about this bed. He saw Deirdre out and went back into the kitchen, where he grabbed a beer. Tiffany's last traces would be out of the house on Friday, except for a few photos, all but two in Mike's room.

"When's dinner?"

"Give you five minutes and then I'll start the noodles, okay?" Mike answered, his husky frame barely fitting into the tiny kitchen.

"Great," Sean answered and headed down the hall. *All busted condoms should produce results like Mike*, he thought, not for the first time.

He automatically shifted his shoulders to avoid brushing the family photos on the wall, which Mike had hung when they moved in. He paused to straighten a favorite, remembering his family's beginning.

He'd been back in that small Dakota town for Christmas, his first leave from West Point. He'd partied hard with Tiffany, both talking about their plans; general for him and movie star for Tiffany.

Later they'd gone to a back bedroom, clumsy with inexperience and alcohol. He could still hear Tiffany's hysteria when the condom broke and his promise to stand by her and the baby, if there was one.

He'd gained a family that night but Tiffany had lost hers. Her father had thrown her out when he learned she was pregnant and had never seen his grandson.

Their wedding picture hung on this wall: Tiffany in black, her pregnancy as blatant as her tear stains, and him in his sergeant's uniform, hours after being released from West Point.

Mike's birth picture held center place, with Tiffany's usual anger and resentment briefly washed away by the miracle of birth. He'd been exhausted and ecstatic when holding his son, after being snatched out of the field during AIT for the birth. It was the happiest time he'd ever known with Tiffany, two weeks before the first stroke hit her and slightly paralyzed her face and right leg.

She had avoided cameras after that.

It had been the first of eight strokes, although so many people had spoken to her about changing her behavior. Sean had tried everything he could think of to get her to stop drinking, stop smoking, eat better, and try to live long enough to see Mike grow up.

But Tiffany had continued to do what she found easiest, while hiding the traces as much as possible. Teaching Mike to cook had helped her eating habits, the only real change she ever made.

There were more pictures of Mike, taken whenever Sean made it home on a birthday or holiday; they were usually outdoors-hiking, camping, fishing, or hunting - with Dudley always laughing happily at the camera. It was still surprising that Mike had chosen those memories for this wall, rather than school pictures.

And there was Mike's eleventh birthday, the last picture of the three of them together. It centered on Mike proudly showing off his black belt in karate, grinning from ear to ear. Sean had carefully looked him over, making sure that every pleat was precisely placed in the white cotton and the black silk belt perfectly tied. Then Mike had demanded to inspect his father's turnout, checking every detail against an old manual that he'd managed to squirrel away.

So there was the master sergeant's uniform, three chevrons and three rockers on his left sleeve. Four hash marks on Sean's left cuff, for his twelve years of enlisted service. Black beret with his Ranger battalion badge. The Ranger tab and scroll on his left shoulder, with the scroll again on his right shoulder and its memories of Panama. Silver Star and a Bronze Star with oak leaf, including a V for Valor. A Purple Heart, thanks to the Gulf War. Four rows of ribbons in all over his left breast, plus those unit citations above his right pocket.

Combat Infantry badge above his gleaming Master parachutist wings, complete with a gold star for that nasty combat jump into Panama. Pathfinder and Expert Marksmanship badges, sitting side by side on the flap of his left pocket.

Sean had stood at attention and kept a poker face while Mike approved the placement of every element with a ruler. Then he'd helped Tiffany into the photographer's armchair and taken her walker beyond the camera's relentless memory.

The picture showed Tiffany in her favorite sky-blue dress, her makeup as much art as anything in the photographer's portfolio. She'd practiced her expression and her posture in front of a mirror, hiding the effects of eleven years of strokes, pain, and careless living on her once fairy-tale prettiness.

The most recent photo showed Mike in his football uniform, poised to throw the football. It hung next to the picture of Sean's grandfather in his Ranger uniform, standing among the prisoners of war that he'd rescued in the Philippines.

Sean touched the realigned picture with a gentle finger.

"I met a lady today, Mom. I'm going to see her again. I think you'd like her," he whispered.

His mother smiled back at him, caught by the camera, three weeks before a drunk driver mowed her down and left Sean alone in the world.

He took the stairs two at a time, whistling.

Sean quickly stripped beside his big waterbed and got into the hot shower, still whistling. He washed himself automatically, reliving his earlier encounter in Gary's bookstore.

Who'd have thought to find a beauty like that among dusty books? She looked both exotic and familiar with those high cheekbones under the enormous dark eyes. Her hair was a hood of living black silk framing her face and protecting her vulnerable long neck. Her red mouth was the most carnal invitation he'd ever seen, especially when it closed around her fist as she watched him come. She'd smelled like some spicy new temptation from the Orient when he'd stood next to her, pretending to look at books. She was tall enough that he wouldn't worry about hurting her if they lay together. Her curves were rich, promising to fill his hands.

And the look on her face when he dropped his pants...

He fondled his cock as he remembered that slow trickle of crimson running down her hand while her chocolate-brown eyes devoured him.

A moment later he was very hard as he imagined the same lady, now a priestess in scarlet silk with hair pinned up to bare her neck, ordering him to perform for her. Trails of water slid over him, silken as a woman's hair, as he stroked himself, responding to the priestess' detailed instructions. He imagined the lady's mouth wrapped around his cock, drinking him down.

He closed his eyes and fought back the rising pressure in his balls, intent on building his fantasy for as long as possible. He imagined her long fingers cupping his balls, squeezing them slowly as the tension built into painful demand. He swore, imagining how her white teeth would delicately scrape his shaft. He gave himself over to his imagination, finally shuddering when the priestess' finger probed his ass and demanded his climax. He groaned as white jets splashed the tiled wall.

Sean opened his eyes and sighed, enjoying a harder-edged satisfaction than he usually took from his hand.

Still, fantasies were great but usually remained just that: fantasy, not real life. Maybe she really would come back tonight. If she did, he'd do a lot to make this fantasy live as long as possible.

Mike couldn't know about it, of course. Kids needed to believe in fidelity, not one-night stands.

He got dressed quickly and carried his blue sweater. Months ago, Mike's girlfriend Carol had said that Sean was too hot for women to resist in anything that color. He'd avoided wearing it since but now he needed all the ammunition he could get. If Beth liked him in blue, he'd wear it.

Mike's eyes widened when he saw the sweater that Sean dropped on the table by the door. He glanced at his father's face but quickly went back to serving dinner.

"What's in that box, Mike?" Sean asked as he sat down to dinner.

"Jenny's mom, Mrs. Davison, dropped it off. She made some chocolate truffles and thought we might like some. There's also some of Ms. Anderson's apple pie."

Sean flinched at the mention of the women who kept chasing him. He'd never given them any encouragement.

"I'll take the candy and pie to the women's shelter tomorrow," Sean decided. The ladies there always liked sweets.

They talked about Mike's science project during the rest of meal, stopping only when a horn blew from in front. Mike jumped up and started clearing dishes rapidly. Dudley came to his feet carefully, tail wagging as he begged for an opportunity to investigate the visitor in person.

"Go on, Mike. I'll finish that. Try not to stay up too late tonight at Sam's house."

"Sure, Dad. I'll take Dudley with me too, okay? You know he likes playing with Sam's collie."

Dudley's tail wagged faster at the mention of his name. Sean looked down into the pleading brown eyes and chuckled.

"Fine. You two have fun and I'll find something to do on my own."

Mike grabbed his coat and bag then came back to the table, reaching into his pocket. A small packet hit the table and Mike stepped back.

"In case you need a few extra."

Sean looked down at the table then laughed out loud at the box of condoms lying there. So the young master was helping out the old man. Well, he couldn't remember the last time he'd bought any and hopefully they'd be useful.

He hugged Mike briefly and then lightly pushed him out the door. He had dishes to wash and preparations to make.

Sean arrived at the PTSA meeting a few minutes early and took a seat in the front on the aisle.

Linda Davison showed up a few minutes late, announced by her usual cloud of stale cigarette smoke. She stood next to Sean and pointed at the chair beside him, ignoring Pete Andrews' opening remarks. Sean groaned inside but came to his feet, trying not to disturb the people around them more than necessary.

He returned to his seat but shifted as far towards the aisle as he could, trying not to touch or smell the woman. She was dressed in her favorite outfit, which emphasized three different shades of green. Four shades if you counted the corrosion on her watchband. The combination reminded Sean of the Florida swamps he'd first met in Ranger School.

Linda pushed her foot against Sean's and he smelled her sour perfume. He shifted away but she followed, rubbing her leg against his. Sean stared straight ahead, looking forward for once to standing up before a crowd.

The meeting was as boring as ever, with the usual speakers rambling on about the usual subjects. Thankfully, Pete introduced him soon and he gave his standard treasurer's account, wincing at Linda's enthusiastic applause. Who did she think she was impressing, clapping for a routine talk about money?

He sat down next to Pete afterwards. Unfortunately, Linda stood up a few minutes later to talk about the upcoming school play and found a seat beside Sean afterwards. She leaned over to whisper to him as soon as the next speaker began. Mercifully, Deirdre hissed at Linda from the row behind to be silent.

He made two more reports, talking about the annual ski trip and repairing the school's ornate façade, glad he'd written the reports in advance. The time spent addressing the meeting was unusually welcome, as it gave him time to breathe some clean air away from Linda. Then he returned to his seat, ready for the meeting's open discussion portion.

Sean's mind slid to his approaching encounter with Beth and he began to review his preparations, barely listening to the long-winded talk about fund raising. Nobody mentioned anything that he needed to answer as treasurer. He wondered what Beth would want to do; his body promptly, and enthusiastically, responded. He shifted slightly in his chair to ease the tightness of his pants.

Linda Davison glanced at him and he went very still to avoid further notice. He shifted the financial report on his lap, hoping to hide the swelling behind his fly. He tried to focus on something messy, like cleaning up the school's usual burden of graffiti, to soften his arousal but failed.

His pants kept getting tighter, as he thought about the coming rendezvous, until his zipper bit into him. He bit down hard on the inside of his lip. He forced himself to relive that Florida swamp, remembering every detail of its mud and water moccasins and damnit stumps. He reviewed every type of poisonous snake found in that Florida swamp, all the details that he'd memorized as a Ranger instructor. But even thoughts of those dangerous snakes or the tree stumps, waiting below the water for an exhausted hiker, couldn't calm his unruly body.

Heat stayed coiled in his gut, even as the pain built in his cock.

His arousal finally disappeared when Mrs. Davison leaned over to whisper a question about the school's sewers. One whiff of her hair almost erased the memory of Beth's perfume.

Even so, it seemed forever until the meeting ended. Linda Davison immediately started talking to him and he concentrated warily on her words.

"Did you have a good meal tonight, Sean?" she cooed. Sean managed not to cringe at her breath's reek.

"Yes, thank you. Mike made spaghetti. His mother's recipe, which we both enjoy." He smiled to himself, when her eyes flashed at the mention of another woman, and kept talking. "Thanks for the candy. I'll take it to the women's shelter tomorrow as a treat for those ladies."

Linda's mouth opened and shut. Unfortunately, she found an alternate tack.

"Perhaps you'd like to come over to my house now," she cooed.

Sean's eyes narrowed slightly at her tone.

"I've got some more chocolate that you could taste, just to make sure those poor ladies would enjoy it. We could have some wine too and tell each other all about the good times and the bad."

Sean stiffened and began running excuses through his head. Linda kept talking, oblivious to his withdrawal.

"I've just had the most dreadful weekend. The toilet in my bathroom keeps running all the time," she whined. "I'm sure you could help me with it. And, afterwards, we could get to know each other better." She walked her fingers up his arm. He reshuffled his papers, forcing her hand to drop.

"Have you called a plumber?" Sean refused to think of how many times she had mentioned her toilets to him.

"Well, no, I haven't. I wasn't sure what to say." Her voice trailed off, inviting Sean to step in.

"Just tell him what you said to me, Linda."

Linda's eyes narrowed and she started to say something else, determined to get his assistance. Mercifully, Deirdre Hemmings cut in then, her eyes laughing at him over Linda's head.

"Linda, aren't you one of the chaperones for Thursday's Drama Club field trip?"

Linda stuttered, caught by the reference to hers and her daughter's obsession, then turned to Deirdre, losing contact with him.

"Why, yes, I am, Deirdre. Did you have any questions?"

Sean escaped swiftly, grateful to Deirdre for covering his retreat, and fled the school without making even the slightest promise to Linda of future contact.

He parked his pickup behind the bookstore and ran upstairs to Gary's old apartment, a furnished one-bedroom directly over the store. A few minutes' work and Sean had the scene set for seduction: dim lights, candles, wine. A quick check showed a variety of coffees in case the lady wanted something non-alcoholic.

Then he scattered some of his favorite books of erotica around the living room and bedroom: *Exit to Eden, Venus in Furs* , the *Beauty* trilogy, and others. Hopefully the same things would turn Beth on and she'd take the hint.

Mrs. Wolcott wouldn't have given a damn about the books. She swore that she only did what felt right, whether it was a demand for oral sex or to lay a belt on her husband's ass. He'd caught them at it from time to time when he was a hired hand, seen Mr. Wolcott iron-hard under his wife's punishing hand just before he exploded into a climax.

She'd told Sean the same thing on the Saturday night she spent with him as a graduation present. He'd enjoyed his hours with Mrs. Wolcott but he knew there'd only be that one time. He'd departed that small town for West Point the next day, finished with high school and intent on his future.

He'd never talked about it. But sometimes he allowed himself to remember. How alive he had felt, more intensely than at any time except in combat. Or with Beth just today.

Beth was so different from Mrs. Wolcott that she seemed a dream come to life. He'd dreamed so many times of having a woman watch him, while he jacked off. She'd cared about his comfort, too.

He trusted her, at least enough to suggest going further. That rich voice of hers had led him on so smoothly that he hoped she knew more, especially of things mentioned in his books and videos.

The books looked unfamiliar when seen in the open air, not engulfed in his hand or locked in a cabinet, hidden from Tiffany's shouted prejudices or Mike's youthful curiosity.

Old fears rose to haunt him but he set them aside fiercely. He'd do whatever felt good, as long as everyone was pleased and not harmed. And Mike didn't find out, of course.

A glance at the clock showed that there was still time left before her arrival and Sean sat down in the bedroom to refresh his dreams. Seconds later, he lost himself in his favorite scene in *The*

Claiming of Sleeping Beauty. His cock strengthened under the intimate words but he refused to touch it, simply enjoying the ache as he waited for his flesh and blood lady.

He lifted his head when the wind blew a gust of rain hard against the roof. The clock caught his eye and he cursed at the time. He dropped the book on the bed and ran outside to wait.

Chapter Three
Monday, 9 PM

Beth kept a polite mask on her face and continued chatting about predicted price fluctuations for Singapore dollars and Malaysian ringgits, as she covertly watched Akiro Ono observe her. Another ten minutes and she'd leave for the bookstore, to hunt more of the excitement Sean brought. An adrenaline rush that only the living could feel.

Pressured as these meetings were, they were still only low-level discussions to prepare for the time when the true decision makers would come to an agreement. Beth had been abruptly assigned to help arrange this conference after the new Administration decided to pay more attention, albeit "informally" and "privately," to concerns over the Japanese banks' debt portfolios and possible impact on the Japanese economy.

It was disconcerting to see the most senior Japanese banker present hover where he could snatch a few words with her. She'd dodged him earlier, letting Ed Johnson spout the necessary formalities. Akiro had obviously waited until only a few people remained at the opening reception. Most of the attendees had left for smaller, more informal gatherings, to renew old connections before beginning the real discussions tomorrow.

Who was he looking at: the Treasury bureaucrat, with colleagues that could help or hinder his bank, or the Western female, too ugly to be welcome in his family? The countess, his sister-in-law, had described Beth as too tall, too fat, mouth too wide, and a voice too deep for a woman. The marquise, Beth's Grandmother, had judged Beth "not enticing enough" in a voice colder than an Antarctic ice flow, during the confrontation with Catriona Nakamura.

She snapped her mind away from past humiliation. Both families had been right about one thing: she was far too Western to settle into a Japanese marriage, to a Japanese man and enacted according to Japanese customs.

But why was Akiro so eager to see her? For her connections now or because of their clans' history? She could think of multiple reasons why he would want to talk to the woman who'd been his nephew's fiancé. He wouldn't create a scene, not here. But things could still get very nasty.

Professor Hiroki Nakamura could probably make some guesses about Akiro Ono's intentions. But Beth hadn't spoken more than formalities to her father since that dreadful day in Tokyo. He'd been mute while her grandmother and mother dueled over the broken engagement. Her mother had shot torrents of scalding vehemence in Beth's defense, while her grandmother had parried and finally thrust with icy words that cut as deep as a glacier's crevasses.

Both women's words had hurt but not as much as her beloved father's silence. Her Japanese blood understood the need not to attack the family head in public, no matter how disastrously grandmother had been proven wrong. Her Scots blood hungered for warmth and reassurance from her favorite parent. Beth still couldn't forget that he hadn't wrapped his support around her in front of his mother.

Beth eased out of the conversation and watched the two bankers depart for the hotel's bar to further dissect currency, a safe conversational topic before tomorrow's talk of debt restructuring. Akiro approached and she greeted him formally, her words soft and her spine stiff as she bowed the smallest amount consonant with propriety.

"Good evening, Mr. Ono. It is an honor to see you here."

"Greetings, Miss Nakamura." His answering bow was lower than required. "I am delighted to be here and have this opportunity to speak to you in person."

She nodded politely and waited.

"It is a pleasure seeing old acquaintances, is it not, in unfamiliar places? But then, travel can take anyone to enlivening experiences."

What on earth was he leading up to?

"Indeed, the contrast of old and new can be fascinating to see," Beth responded courteously.

"Exactly." Akiro smiled in genuine relief, which baffled her. "A good parent should ensure that his child has the broadest education possible, which travel helps provide. My brother, for example, has just sent his son Genichi to Algeria."

Genichi? The pampered youngest son in an Islamic part of Africa? Beth blinked, trying to imagine how her ex-fiancé would behave far from Tokyo's nightlife. "An ancient country with connections to both East and West."

"Precisely." Akiro beamed at her but controlled himself quickly. "Your grandmother recommended the broadening effects of travel and my brother thought Algeria offered the greatest potential for learning. Indeed, he insisted that Genichi spend all his time there except when he is at home in Japan."

Beth nodded and bit down on the inside of her lip, trying not to snicker. Where on earth would Genichi find in Algeria the lavish lifestyle he demanded? What would he do for nightclubs? Shopping? Or gossip? Who would pay compliments to his wardrobe? And Algeria had been engaged in a civil war, although there hadn't been much talk of that recently.

"The count and the marquise are famous for their wisdom. I'm sure Algeria has much to offer the studious mind," Beth answered piously, invoking the aristocratic pasts of Akiro's family and her own.

"Quite so," Akiro agreed heartily. "My son Daisuke plans to study at Berkeley, under your esteemed father, next year. It is our hope that his sojourn will result in many blessings, including warmer ties between our kin."

Beth's eyes widened briefly. The two families had feuded for years, exacerbated when her father had ignored the unspoken assumption that he would marry an Ono daughter, and chosen Catriona McKenna, daughter of a British naval officer and granddaughter of an Orkney fisherman, instead. As balance, Beth's grandmother Keiko had strongly encouraged the engagement to Genichi and been furious when Beth ended it, no matter how great Genichi's insult to the Nakamura family. For

Daisuke Ono to become Professor Nakamura's protégé meant that both clans seriously wanted to end the dispute.

"I will pray for many such blessings for both our families," Beth answered in all sincerity. She roused herself from contemplating the implications of this news to offer an olive branch of her own. "Have you spoken much to Mr. Johnson yet? His wife is an ardent fancier of antique roses and he might be interested in your gardens."

"I had the honor of meeting him but we didn't discuss roses." Akiro brightened, pleased at the personal information about the most senior American bureaucrat present. Such touches were the essence of Japanese relationships, where business negotiations depended on the link between the individuals involved.

"He is over by the fireplace. He had some spectacular red roses in his office last week, that you might have heard of."

"Gallica roses perhaps?" Akiro eagerly half-turned towards Ed Johnson but recovered quickly. Beth smiled at him.

"Let me take you over to him. I'm sure he'd be delighted to talk roses with you." She rested her hand on Akiro's arm and headed for the fireplace. Ed quizzed her silently and she nodded fractionally. He finished talking to Eli Rosenbluth and smiled at Akiro and Beth.

"Ed, did you know that Mr. Ono raises some of the most famous roses in Japan? My grandmother says that he grows many of Empress Josephine's roses."

"Really? Which ones?"

Beth smiled and removed herself from their company, glad that the two gentlemen were doing well with each other but personally disinterested in flower gardens at the moment.

She glanced at the mantel clock, a stunning example of Art Deco in the restored hotel. It was past time to leave and she reviewed her options, strolling down the hall towards the lobby and the stairs up to her suite.

Should she spend time with Sean? Risky in many ways because she didn't know him and none of her friends in the scene had recommended him, as they had for every partner since Dennis. She wished once again that she'd listened to her friends about Genichi, instead of her Tokyo relatives extolling the advantages of a suitable marriage, with its bonus of ending the old antagonisms.

What would Dennis say about Sean? Dennis had been friend and teacher, as well as one-time lover and sometime master. He'd had an excellent eye for men, as befitted a bisexual male dominant. But his wisdom had been silenced forever on September eleventh.

She swallowed to erase the tastes of grief and fear in her mouth, to find the familiar nerves over a new encounter. Could she and Sean gratify each other, especially if he truly enjoyed submitting? It was always unpredictable, trying to guess exactly what and how best to please a new partner. And what if she wanted more of him than one night? That was a more frightening thought than pondering tonight's events.

Beth pulled Sean's business card out of her purse, for one last consideration. See him again or not?

She turned the little bit of pasteboard over in her fingers, considering what it said about him. Sean E. Lindstrom, President. Hepburn & Sons, Inc. Black letters below gave an address and phone numbers. The card was as clean and direct as the man himself. Did it smell of him?

A wet draft snatched it out of her fingers and slammed it to the floor.

"Here, let me get that," a man's voice rumbled.

"Thank you, Dave."

Dave Hemmings plucked the card up neatly, matching the tidiness of everything else about the Secret Service agent. He'd been brought in after September to handle security for this meeting and had rapidly calmed everyone's fears. His average height and ordinary features could readily disappear into a crowd, his presence marked only by his physical fitness and grace.

"Thinking of buying some real estate here in Seattle?" he asked.

"No, not at all. I met him in a bookstore this afternoon," Beth answered.

"The Wise Old Owl? Gary's bookstore?"

"Yes; how did you know?" Beth accepted the card back.

"Master Sergeant Sean Lindstrom was one of my instructors in Ranger School. He served with Gary in the Mog. Somalia," he explained at Beth's unspoken query.

Beth stepped sideways against the wall to allow latecomers access to the elevator. He moved with her so that they were in a small nook, under an ornately gilded wall-sconce. She kept her attention on Dave, willing him to keep talking.

"I didn't serve with him because I was never assigned to the Regiment. But people talked about him, called him a legend." Dave paused, looking back in time. "Silver Star from Panama, Bronze Star for Valor from the Gulf."

Dave nodded confirmation at Beth's surprise over the awards.

"There were a lot of stories about him but he'd never tell them. Especially jokes about how he could sleep anywhere, no matter what was going on." Dave's mouth twitched in remembrance. His radio hummed briefly and he came alert, then relaxed at the routine conversation. He started talking again, more briskly this time. "Sean spent his entire career as a Ranger, except for some time in the Old Guard just before he got out. That was after the Mog, where his best friend died." He crossed himself at the memory.

Panic's edge retreated from Beth, as she absorbed Dave's admiration of Sean.

"Married?" she asked cautiously, shifting to a subject of immediate concern to her.

"Widower."

Dave didn't add anything to the bald declaration, seemingly lost in memories. Beth remembered Sean's ignorance of his attractions and managed not to curse a dead woman.

"I'm meeting him tonight. Do you have any recommendations?" She kept the question open-ended, allowing Dave to discuss the subjects he felt important. Being Dave, he caught the implications.

"You can trust him, Beth. My daughter's dating his son and I'm not worried about her. Well, not too worried," he amended.

"But Sean is the man I'd ask to look after my wife and family, if I thought my time had come."

"Thank you." Fear became a memory, able to reappear but not soon.

"Just one other thing."

Beth cocked her head at Dave's hesitation.

"My wife Deirdre said that Sean's girlfriend would be the luckiest woman in Seattle."

Beth blinked, then blushed at Dave's grin. "Thank you, Dave, for your confidence. I'd better be going now, if I'm going to get there on time."

Beth ran upstairs to grab her coat, free to enjoy the night's potential. Playing with Sean had advantages, because she could walk away easily afterwards without worrying about any commitment. She wanted to feel the overwhelming rush of physical pleasure, nothing more, as her body relearned its most basic purpose in a man's arms.

She knew they could both enjoy themselves, given communication and trust. Tomorrow and its fears would have to look after themselves.

Beth relived their previous encounter as she drove towards the bookstore, remembering every word said and every movement either of them had made, as she looked for clues on how to proceed tonight. Sean had followed her instructions promptly, emphasizing her control of the situation.

She sighed softly, relishing the memory of how powerful she'd felt. Tonight's brief encounter could be a pleasant release from both the stresses of her job and the memories of her conservative behavior during her engagement.

Beth had always followed Genichi's smallest suggestions during their courtship and engagement, as befitted a proper Japanese woman being courted by a desirable Japanese man. She had felt the need to avoid any hint of aggressive Western femininity, given her half-Scots ancestry. Nevertheless even behavior that her Japanese grandmother would have praised hadn't prevented Genichi from publicly humiliating her.

She'd been in an important meeting at the American embassy in Tokyo that morning, planning to accompany Genichi to meet her parents and grandmother for lunch. When the formal meeting ended early, she took some of the participants back to her office to continue talking. They'd walked in to find Genichi in flagranté delicto with the office secretary on Beth's desk.

Beth could still hear the secretary's hysteria, when she climaxed at the same time she saw the audience. She could still see the Japanese bankers' faces as they avoided looking directly at Genichi, with his bony ass pumping below his French silk shirt.

She'd dropped her engagement ring on the floor and walked out, to face her family's upheaval and the world's gossip. She'd gone willingly back to Washington, glad to find fewer whispers.

She pulled herself away from the old memory; it was past time to move on.

She heard Dennis' voice in that last phone call from his burning office at the World Trade Center on September eleventh. *Live for both of us,* he'd demanded. *Make the most of being alive, for both of us. Find that one man who'll suit you and build a future.*

She'd promised Dennis that she would, while the tears ran silently down her face. Her office had been a silent refuge against the upheaval in the hallways beyond, as her coworkers first tried to absorb the news from New York and the Pentagon, then left in a tumbling hurry when the evacuation order came. She'd been too calm on the subway that day, as she plotted how to get involved in the hunt for Dennis' killers.

She had felt blazingly alive for the first time since then, when Sean had displayed himself behind that quiet bookstore. And now she could do more with him.

A big blond Westerner, gifted with a knack for submission, to play with for a few hours. Dennis would surely have approved.

The rain was coming down hard when Beth reached the corner across the bookstore, driven by a strong wind that blew rain into her face. Her hair was plastered to her skin by the time she reached Sean but her shoes were only slightly damp, thanks to some careful puddle dodging. He immediately caught her by the elbow and whipped her into the bookstore where water fell off her coat with soft plops on the floor.

Beth smiled ruefully up at him, conscious of the mascara blurred and running down her face. This was not how she had planned to meet a potential lover.

"You look wet to the skin, Beth. Why don't you come someplace where you can get warm and dry?" he offered.

"Thank you, Sean. That sounds lovely."

Beth found herself moments later in the small apartment above the bookstore, tidy and clean with candles casting a soft light and a gas fireplace burning brightly.

"Do you live here?"

"No, it's a rental property. Vacant at the moment." Beth nodded and looked around more closely. An old-fashioned cuckoo clock hung above the mantel and a store's neon light pulsed against the curtains, its red glow emphasizing a couple of books laid out on the small table. She started to remember the books' plots but turned her attention back to Sean as he spoke.

"Let me take that wet coat of yours. There's a bedroom and bathroom through there where you can freshen up. Would you like some coffee or maybe something stronger? You must be cold after that drenching."

"Thank you, I'd like some coffee. Decaf if you have it," Beth accepted and turned down the hallway. She caught his reflection in a framed poster's glass, as he avidly watched her departing back. Strength slid into her hunger for him. She kept her eyes straight ahead, not revealing that she'd caught the revealing look.

Beth closed the bedroom door and quickly found the bathroom. A brief search revealed a hair dryer and she set to work repairing the weather's attacks on her person. Unfortunately, her hair and makeup had taken the worst of it.

Still, a few minutes saw her hair acceptable again. And her purse provided the ingredients needed to rebuild her appearance, with a quick gloss of mascara and lipstick. A simpler look than she normally wore to play with a man but hopefully still effective.

An open book on the bed caught her eye, as she left the bathroom. She picked it up curiously and her eyebrows went up as she read how the Queen spanked Prince Alexi.

A moment's reflection brought the realization that the books in the living room were also stories of men being dominated by women. Further thought convinced her that the books must be Sean's and their presence must be planned.

He was cruising for a lover, telling her what he hoped for. No pressure on her, just an open door for her to walk through, if she chose to.

Beth began to consider possible responses to Sean's strong hints.

Chastity? Hardly. They both knew that this evening would end in the bedroom.

A vanilla evening, with pleasure for both while ignoring the books' suggestions? The safest course, but lacking the heart-pounding rapture of a well-played scene.

Sean had trusted her enough to risk humiliation by exposing his inner wishes. He couldn't be an experienced player, given his clumsiness at the bookstore. He could probably taste his nerves right now.

Years of practice knit themselves in Beth's backbone as Sean's fantasies hummed in her blood. She could show him a good time, taking the responsibility for their joint pleasure by dominating him. He wouldn't have to worry about a thing, which was possibly best for his inexperience.

Oh, the delights of introducing him to sexual play during a power exchange. Beth's eyes slitted as she purred at the possibilities, enjoying the throb of arousal beating in her throat.

The riskiest course but she'd take it. After all, if it didn't work with Sean, then she hadn't lost a relationship that mattered. She'd never dominated a stranger before, only men that she already knew were comfortable at submitting to a woman. Dominating a man was tricky, especially given the intense connection necessary to read his unspoken responses quickly and accurately.

She took a deep breath and focused her energies on feeling confident and strong and sensual. Her little black dress, fresh from the runways of Milan, and her pearl earrings were the epitome of classic feminine power, especially when combined with high heels and black stockings. Her body was emphasized by the sleek style, although only a small amount of décolletage showed.

Beth opened the door into the living room. Sean's head came up and he watched her from his post by the window.

"How do you want your coffee, Beth?" His voice came out in a clumsy rasp.

"Coffee can wait." Beth waved a dismissive hand. "Care to have some fun first, handsome?"

"Of course." His eyes were very wide and he licked his lower lip nervously.

She strolled across the room to him, enjoying how his eyes watched every movement. She looked him over slowly, taking in every detail of his appearance from the golden hair crowning his head to the leather boots on his big feet. Her eyes lingered longest on the growing bulge behind his fly and Sean's breathing faltered. Her eyes traveled slowly back up to his face and she smiled slowly, lasciviously at the open lust on his face.

She walked her fingers delicately up his right hand, enjoying the contrast between their hands. Hers were beautifully manicured, with nails only lightly frosted, while his bore signs of recent hard work. She caught his hand up and traced the lifeline in his palm. The gentle, repetitive caress eased his breathing into a rhythmic pattern.

Then she glided her hand up his arm to his shoulder, feeling the long lines of muscle under his brilliantly colored ski sweater. A cashmere or alpaca sweater would have been nice, soft enough to let her feel more of the muscle and bone underneath the wool. His eyelids grew heavy as he watched her face.

Beth stepped in closer to him and traced his jaw with a single fingertip. Such a strong face with eyes set under level brows, a straight blade of a nose, a slash of a mouth. The upper lip was tightly controlled above the more sensual lower lip, ready for laughter before cynicism.

"Were you in the military?" she asked. Only this moment mattered, not what anyone else said.

"I was a Ranger for eleven years."

"Did you wear a helmet?" She traced his temple back to his ear, finding the faint prickle of freshly shaved skin.

"Yes, ma'am." His heavy eyes watched her, questions kept back.

"How far down did the helmet come on your forehead?"

He marked the line with the edge of his hand.

"On the sides of your face?"

He showed her with both hands. She caught his wrists, keeping the frame around his eyes and mouth.

"Viking," she breathed, recognizing him from pictures in museums and old textbooks. He blinked in surprise but had the sense to stay still, letting the chemistry build between them.

"Viking," Beth said again and kissed him. She traced his lips with her tongue, exploring their shape and strength, until his mouth opened under her gentle urging.

"Viking warrior," she breathed into his mouth, just before hers took possession of him. They kissed slowly, learning each other's tastes and textures, until she pulled back. His hand dropped from her waist while she continued to caress his cheek.

Sean took a deep breath and let his eyes close. She fondled his neck, enjoying the difference between his masculine strength and its innate vulnerability, laid bare by his severe hair cut.

Beth gradually remembered her self-discipline.

"Have you ever wanted to worship a woman, Sean?" she queried huskily.

"Yes. Hell, yes," he groaned.

"Care to try it here and now, with me?"

He nodded, a pulse pounding in his jaw. He was still frozen, outlined by the rippling neon light.

"Of course, as the goddess present, I get to say what I want and you get to do it. Can you manage that?"

"I can do whatever you say, Beth," he vowed, his eyes blazing blue fire.

"Good lad," she sighed. "I'd rather like to be worshipped tonight. Come over here and rub my feet."

Sean immediately obeyed, dropping at her feet and reverently lifting off first one shoe, then the other. He set the shoes aside carefully, neatly aligned by the end table, and cupped her left foot in his hand. He slowly ran his thumb from her big toe up to her ankle, stretching and relaxing her aching bones. Her feet ached badly tonight, thanks to the combination of an old diving injury and the cold wet weather. His big warm hands were the perfect antidote.

Beth purred happily as he carefully rubbed her left foot and then her right. It was surprising that he followed her order so easily. This must truly have been his fantasy, although obeying orders of any type might be easier for a military man. But his enthusiasm relaxed her and she felt more and more like an irresistible woman.

"Enough, Sean," she directed when both feet felt relaxed and happy to face new adventures.

Sean sat back on his heels slowly and looked up at her, his eyes slightly glazed. His chest rose and fell raggedly, above the fat ridge in his trousers.

"Now take off your sweater and shirt. Fold them and set them aside so I can see your bare chest."

Her tone allowed for no argument and he showed no hesitation. He pulled his sweater over his head, then quickly stripped off his shirt, settling them as neatly as she'd demanded. He looked up at her again, waiting for her next instruction.

Beth studied Sean where he knelt, displaying the upper half of his body for her. The bright hair on his head formed a thick pelt, snatched back from curling by the short cut. Its gold was echoed by the dense mat of hair on his strong chest, hiding the small male nipples there, and the line of darker gold that led down to his waistband. Veins showed clearly under the milk white skin and emphasized hard muscles. Beth doubted that she could get both hands around one of his upper arms. And those beautiful forearms of his, with the elegant tracery of veins under the gilding of hair, were tempting beyond belief.

She walked slowly around him, studying every detail of his exposed torso. His back was burnished by a light sprinkling of hair, just enough to lend shading to the lines of muscle. He trembled when she ran a finger down his spine, cherishing the silky skin and delicate hairs there.

Beth swallowed hard, fighting the temptation to simply grab him, and moved to the sofa, dropping her purse on the floor next to her seat. A few details needed to be discussed before yielding to mutual hunger.

"I'll take that decaf now, Sean." She managed to keep lust out of her voice. "Black, please. Have some yourself, if you like. We need to talk about a few things before going further."

Sean gulped and stood up. He fixed drinks for both of them and brought them out. Beth accepted the mug and sipped it slowly, watching him.

"Did you bring the scarf?" Beth asked.

Sean nodded and fetched the black and gold trifle from his coat pocket. Beth ran it slowly over her hand, feeling the changed texture where his semen had soaked in. She ran her thumb slowly over one particularly sticky spot. She lifted it to her nose and sniffed it, enjoying the scent of masculine musk.

Sean's breath stopped in a faint gasp.

Then she set the scarf down in her lap and took another sip of coffee. Beth indicated the seat next to her and he sat down there, holding onto his mug as the one familiar thing in a changing world.

"Do you have a significant other?" she asked quietly, unwilling to mention Dave Hemmings' words. "I was engaged a year ago but broke it off."

"No, I'm a single parent; my wife died six years ago." Sean hesitated a moment before going on. "I've got an eighteen-year old son and I haven't had time to get involved with anyone since then."

It was a solid reason for his clumsiness. She did wonder what Seattle women had been thinking of, to let him stay celibate.

"I don't have any diseases that I know of." Beth said quietly, steeling herself for her first discussion of this touchy subject since Genichi. "However, I broke off my engagement because I caught my fiancé with another woman. I've been tested regularly since then for diseases that he might have given me, always with negative results."

She blinked at the violent look crossing Sean's face, following very quickly after his first relief. It seemed as if he could commit murder when he heard of Genichi's infidelity.

"I don't want you to have any reminders of Genichi, okay? So let's say the rule is not to exchange any fluids, just to keep things on the safe side. Agreed?" Beth recommended. She watched Sean absorb the implications and smiled when he nodded hard.

Beth's tension faded in his confidence's bright light and she let herself take another taste of his willingness. She ran her fingertip lightly over the back of his hand, feeling the prickle of hair. She began to lightly trace patterns, exploring the hard calluses and small scars. Her fingers then glided slowly up his right arm over the old scar.

"Purple Heart?" she asked softly.

"Training accident," he dismissed.

Something that big hadn't earned a medal?

"Do you have a purple heart?" she whispered, sliding the black metal bracelet around his wrist. Her eyes prickled at its remembrance of a friend named Adam and she quickly looked further to the living flesh underneath. She admired the branching vein, gleaming blue under the gilded hair and twisting over the muscle.

"Yeah. This bullet wound here, on my thigh." He showed her with his free hand. She touched it carefully, recognizing its closeness to his hip and the vital organs resting there. His hand dropped back to his side, opening and closing slowly like his other hand.

"Hospital time for it?"

"Couple of months," he shrugged, rejecting the opportunity to brag.

"Brave samurai," she murmured in Japanese. His eyes flickered but he didn't speak as she continued her delicate exploration onto his chest.

Her finger traced a pectoral muscle to its crowning areole and his eyes closed slowly. Beth caressed his nipples and chest, savoring the varying textures. Her hand spread flat, fingers sliding into his fur as her palm absorbed his heat. He shuddered and his breathing stopped, then slowly recovered as her hand stayed still.

"What form of service to a woman are you best at, Sean?"

Sean blinked and then looked at her. His eyes were very blue and very dazed. There was a long pause before he answered.

"Going down on a woman, ma'am." Beth swallowed hard at the thought, feeling her belly clench with lust. Time to shift things into a higher gear.

"Stand up and take your boots and socks off. Place them with the others, socks folded."

Sean obeyed quickly, eagerness blazing from every jerky movement.

"Now get rid of your pants." Sean dropped his trousers and set them aside neatly. His cock was visibly throbbing.

"Give me your wrists." Sean immediately held out his hands to her. A few quick loops saw the scarf wrapped around his wrists. He could have freed himself in an instant but he didn't try. He simply stood still, his hands turning slowly as he watched the silk grip him.

Beth retrieved a small shopping bag from her purse and dumped its contents onto the table next to her. Thank heavens for the stores in this eclectic neighborhood.

Sean's stunned eyes focused on a variety of condoms and dams, their diverse functions and sizes hopefully recognizable to him. He shook his head once, as if clearing his thoughts, and looked at her face. His enthusiasm still shone, softened now by trust in her judgment.

"Begin serving me, Viking," Beth said hoarsely, her own craving increasing to match Sean's blatant hunger.

Sean dropped to his knees before her. His slow caresses of her legs were followed by gentle laving as his mouth explored her. Beth slid her hands into his hair and savored every sensation. Her knees fell open and he murmured wordlessly as he explored higher, sliding her skirt away. He followed muscle to the vulnerable hollow behind her knee. He licked and sucked first one hidden pulse point, then the other knee. Trails of fire ran up to her core from every touch. The scarf echoed his movements with delicate silken caresses against her legs.

Beth laid her head back, moaning encouragement, and slid her hips forward on the sofa. He worked higher, growling with pleasure when his tongue slid under the edge of her silk stockings. She groaned when he nipped her bare skin lightly, then licked it sweetly to ease the small pain. He sighed in a tone so deep it almost rumbled, when he finally slid aside her briefs' black silk and found her melting center, every fold already gleaming with dew for him.

"Sean."

He snarled but stopped before his mouth reached her there.

"What did you forget?"

He blinked at her, confused.

"What did we agree to do, to protect each other?"

Comprehension flashed over his face. He cursed softly and turned to retrieve a dam from the heap on the table, then hesitated at the wide selection.

"Think now, Sean. What color do you think would be best? Remember they're flavored, if that makes a difference."

"Flavored?"

"Oh yes, darling. Vanilla or perhaps a fruit scent, to add an accent to my taste."

He grabbed for one as the last syllable glided into the room. And he fumbled when he opened the packet, releasing the scent of vanilla and cinnamon.

"Good lad," Beth cooed and leaned back for him, her eyes dancing as she watched his clumsy placement of the dam over her nether lips. "Careful now. They're very thin so you can feel everything. Everything, do you understand, darling?"

She stretched and purred when his tongue found her again. It slid leisurely along her folds, learning her outlines and developing a rhythm that pleased her. Backwards and forwards his tongue traveled to a regular beat that built a matching tattoo in her veins. Her body tightened and flowed wet for him, like a mountain spring under the warmth of a May sky.

Then he turned his attention to her clit, circling and lapping until it rose proud and strong for him. Beth gasped when he hummed his enjoyment, making her flesh vibrate in delight. Sean was incredibly good at this, his lips soft and flexible while his tongue was capable of surprising strength.

Beth clasped his head, eager for more contact, her voice husky as she sighed her pleasure. She caressed him, enjoying the primal connection to his muscle and bone and letting her hands telling him when to repeat or move on, when to go lighter or harder, where to go next.

She eased into her orgasm slowly, savoring every ripple of pleasure that rolled through her body.

When Sean tried to pull away afterwards, her hands tightened on his neck pulling him back into her

"More," she demanded simply.

He obeyed, just as simply. Her stockings were discarded at some point and later her briefs. Beth paid little heed to those details, being far more interested in how he used first one finger, then others deep within her. Only the moment's rapture mattered now as she rode the long, deep waves. Her hands and legs stayed in touch with Sean and his tension.

He varied his strokes, using a varied pattern that drove her wild when she realized he was writing her name with his tongue. Then he changed his rhythm until she could no longer guess when he would touch her next, whether sooner or later. She dissolved into another climax, her breath sobbing in a plea to him for more.

Time to finish now, while she still had enough stamina to attend to him.

"Enough."

The word hung in the quiet room. Sean hesitated for a moment and then stopped.

Beth dragged herself back from near unconsciousness and watched him as he sat up slowly, his face wet from the many orgasms he'd given her. She lay quietly against the sofa, too weak to move while savoring the aftershocks. She could have stayed there forever, enjoying the efforts of his hands and mouth between her legs, the feel of his hair.

She saw Sean step away and closed her eyes.

Then a washcloth began to clean her up. She swallowed hard as emotion caught her unawares. No man had ever cherished her like that, pleasuring her and then easing her down afterwards, unless she'd given him a direct order. Amazing that Sean did so, especially when he'd had no satisfaction himself.

A small door shot open and the cuckoo popped out to begin whistling midnight.

Chapter Four
Tuesday, Midnight

Sean knelt on the floor in front of Beth, fighting himself for control of his arousal. He needed to grab her and pull her down on the floor under him. Fantasies crowded into him, frantic to come to life with a willing woman. Tasting her and driving her into rapture had been marvelous. He had felt so alive and powerful when her body moved in response to his urging.

But long years of military discipline, learned in the harshest surroundings, restrained him now and kept him obedient to her leader's voice. So far the rewards of obedience had been better than any fantasy: the smell and taste of her, the shockwaves rippling through her under his mouth and hands. Heedless of such niceties, his body now demanded completion for itself. Just when he thought he had to reach for her, her voice broke the silence.

"Stand up and take two steps back." He rose immediately, still facing her, his hands in front of him held together by her scarf. He had retied it when he washed up and it clung to him, still wet from when he pleasured her.

His fully erect cock throbbed with life. It seemed to leap when he saw her eyes on it. Her voice caught him again, before conscious thought could return.

"Turn around slowly." Sean rotated, intensely aware of every change in her breathing as she studied him. His skin seemed to burn under her gaze. He growled softly as he grew even more aroused.

Beth stood up and walked over to him. He shuddered when she touched his back but began to moan as she lightly caressed him. Her hand traveled up over his shoulder and then down his chest as she walked around him to stand in front of him. Both hands began to play with his pectoral muscles then his nipples, evoking groans from him. Her mouth enjoyed one nipple, nipping and licking, lingering over the taste and texture. His hands clenched in the scarf. Where had she learned exactly how to drive him mad?

Just when he thought he couldn't stand it any longer, she shifted to the other nipple. He closed his eyes, totally lost in sensation as she worked first one nipple, then the other harder and harder. Her hands drifted lower but never stroked him where he was hardest.

"Spread your legs. Wider. Yes, that's good."

Beth broke off suddenly and walked away to the table, where she studied the scattered safe sex supplies.

"Extra sensation? Yes, you'd probably like those little ribs rubbing you when I start licking." she mused. "Extra large, of course. Colored? No, I don't think so. I'd like to see your natural skin tones."

His mind struggled back to life, fighting to process the implications.

Beth's eyes danced at his expression.

"Flavored, perhaps?" she offered.

He choked but turned it into a strangled cough.

"Like the sound of that? Okay, flavored it is. We'll go with the classic: mint."

He'd shopped for sex accessories and toys before; considered the merits of cock rings, tit clamps, vibrators, butt plugs, and more. He'd bought, played with them in private, locked the ones he liked best in the cabinet under his bed, and discreetly disposed of the others. He'd considered himself an experienced shopper. But he'd never shopped for condoms, never studied their advantages and disadvantages, since he'd left Tiffany's bed and the need for protection behind him.

His jaw fell open when she came back and dropped to her knees in front of him. She studied him closely for a long time and his lungs forgot to fill.

She leaned forward and blew a single, soft warm breath that rippled the clear liquid dripping slowly down his cock. His knees buckled but he locked them fiercely. He would remain standing, somehow, while a woman's mouth touched him intimately for the first time.

Her hands were quick and deft as she sheathed him, then leaned back to study her work. He couldn't think, couldn't move, couldn't breathe. She was so unbearably skillful with that condom.

She kissed his groin where it gleamed white behind his deep red cock. Her hands cupped his balls, his blond curls wrapping around her elegant fingers as she studied him.

"Beautiful," she murmured and puffed on them gently. His hips quivered as her mouth and hands danced with him. Her scarlet mouth closed around him, looking just like his fantasy.

Then she went to work, humming with pleasure against his inflamed skin. She explored every fold in his foreskin, teasing out every nerve ending until he begged for mercy. Then her tongue dealt long strokes that glided up and over then down his aching cock, delicate flicks against the sensitive point under the glans, rich swirls around his tight balls. She cherished each of his balls in her mouth until he was sobbing, overwhelmed by an electricity that he couldn't resist.

Beth cupped his ass, guiding his response until his hips thrust in rhythm with her expert touch. Her black hair tangled with his blond thatch, intimate and startling. His world narrowed to the feel of her mouth, driving his need to completion, until he was more desperate than he'd ever been in his life.

She straightened up and shook her hair free, allowing him a clear view of her movements. Her tongue delicately outlined the slit at the uppermost tip of his cock, then began to swirl around and around, lower and lower. Her breathing shifted as her tongue swept over him, devouring him like hard candy. Her mouth prowled down his cock and took him entirely into her.

He gasped at the sight, his pulse pounding deep within his balls. Words broke free from deep within.

"Beth! Damnit, Beth, please. I beg you, you've got to…"

His breath broke as her throat gripped him.

"Fuck," he groaned. "Oh, fuck."

Her finger circled his asshole and then pressed hard.

"Yes!" he shouted. "Fuck, yes!" His orgasm burst, every wave thundering through him from the base of his spine, through his entire body, tearing out of his balls and bursting through his cock. She worked him greedily, her hands and throat muscles combining to drain every drop out of him into the condom.

Sean collapsed on the sofa as his legs gave out on him, panting hard. His eyes closed, unable to accept any further stimulation.

A few moments later he felt a hot wet washcloth tenderly cover his genitals. He whispered his gratitude as she gently took care of him.

Beth sat down beside him and wrapped her arms around him, stroking his hair and crooning softly. He buried his face against her shoulder and held on to her, still shaken by the intensity of his climax. She'd even cleaned up the used condom, as he'd tidied up the dams.

"Let's go lie down, darling. Come on." Beth urged him to his feet and into the bedroom. He collapsed on the bed, still dazed, and she tucked him up under the covers. His hand shot out and caught her wrist.

"Stay. Please stay just a little while longer," Sean pleaded, not caring how he sounded. He needed every minute he could get with her.

Beth hesitated then nodded. "Let me get out of my dress."

"You can put on my shirt if you'd like," Sean offered. She patted his shoulder gently and he closed his eyes.

A few minutes later, the bed gave under Beth's weight as she got in on the far side. He immediately turned to her and pulled her into his arms, delighted at her nudity. He cradled her, breathing in her scent, while trying to rebuild his sanity.

Minutes passed while his breathing returned to normal, echoing the steady rhythm of her heart as her breasts rose and fell against him. She traced an idle circle on his back, while her satin-smooth leg rested between his.

Sean tried to stay awake, even as his sated body relaxed against her satin skin, so he'd have more to remember later. She was so close to him that he felt the breath moving through her body and into his, until their chests rose and fell in unison.

"Do you dream about being spanked by a woman, Sean?" Her voice was a soothing thread in the sheltering dark.

"Yes," he said hesitantly, trying to find words. Beth rubbed his back, silently urging him on. "After my mother was killed, I lived with foster families until I went to West Point. One lady spanked me. I don't even remember why; could have been any number of things. But I do remember how hard I was while she did it and how good it felt when I jacked myself off afterwards."

The words came easier now; Beth hadn't shrieked curses at him for perverted thoughts.

"I was a pretty wild kid until Coach straightened me out, reminded me of my mother and grandfather's teaching. He wanted me to stay on the wrestling team and go to college. My last year in high school, he got me a job at the Wolcott place, the biggest ranch in town. Mr. Wolcott was quite a man. He had a world championship buckle for bull riding, and a Bronze Star as a Marine in Vietnam."

He fell silent, remembering that spread in the Dakota Badlands and the big man who dominated it and the small town nearby. Beth leaned her head against his arm and watched him quietly, her brown eyes soft and curious. "What happened then?"

"One afternoon early on, I was cleaning out an old tool shed by the house when I saw Mrs. Wolcott and Mr. Wolcott..." Sean stopped, startled by the surge of lust that welled up at the memory. Beth rubbed his nipple then flicked it. He blushed at the reminder that she liked his stories and his arousal.

"Uh, Mrs. Wolcott was applying a leather belt to Mr. Wolcott's butt. Lots of blows, lots of force. His ass was red as flame and his cock was rigid enough to dig a well with. Then she made him lie down on the kitchen floor and she rode him like he was a wild bronc."

"Go on," Beth murmured and began to delicately lick his nipple, keeping it erect but not urgent.

"I'd been with girls before but not much. I'd certainly never seen anything like that. Christ, I damn near came in my pants just from watching. After that, I started spying on them. I can still see her taking his quirt to his back or her fancy high-heeled shoes, if he didn't lick her just the way she liked. They played games like that a lot."

Beth dragged her teeth lightly over him and he croaked the next words.

"He enjoyed it as much or more than she did, judging by the look of his cock."

Beth's tongue circled him, as she eased off just a bit.

"I studied and memorized what they did, so I could remember it later. Matters went like that all of my senior year and through graduation. They enjoyed themselves while I spied on them, then played it back in my dreams."

"Then what?" Sean pulled his few remaining brains back from the feeling of her suckling slowly and happily on him.

"Finally came the Saturday night before I left for West Point. My friends gave me a goodbye party but I didn't stay very late. I went back to the Wolcott ranch to look around for the last time. That's when Mrs. Wolcott spoke to me."

"What did she say, Sean? Please tell me the rest," Beth urged softly. She watched him from luminous, eager eyes, while still caressing him with one hand. Still interested, still sexual, still unoffended.

Sean shrugged and went on, biting back fear. He'd said this much so he might as well finish. Maybe she wouldn't turn away afterwards.

"She knew that I'd been watching and she wanted to give me a special goodbye present: spend the rest of the night with me, playing the same games she did with her husband. I tried to say no but she countered every argument I had. Her husband was in Fargo and wouldn't be back until Monday. Hell, he'd even told her to do it!"

Sean shook his head, still unable to really believe that a man would tell his wife to fool around with somebody else.

"None of the hands ever came near the main house for chores so nobody would know. And I agreed.

"We played games that night until my ass was so sore that I couldn't easily sit down for days, and riding the bus out of town was hell. She taught me a lot about how to pleasure a woman with my hands and mouth, punishing me hard when I didn't do things just right. It was every dream I'd had and more. And I loved it and I don't regret any damn bit."

He looked into Beth's eyes fiercely, willing her to believe the next part. "I didn't come once though. At least, not inside her cunt. That would have been adultery."

"I believe you, Sean, and I'm glad that you had such a good time. Plus...you're so sexy when you think about past pleasures," Beth purred, sliding a little closer somehow. "Did you ever see her again?"

"No, the last time I went there was the following Christmas and the Wolcotts always wintered in Arizona. Tiffany and I, we partied together some and the condom broke. She got pregnant, her family threw her out. We never went back after we married."

Sean brooded over the past, seeing Mrs. Wolcott's serviceable white bra above her tight jeans, that wide leather belt gliding through her hands. Beth traced his jaw with a finger and the old memory vanished.

"I had a lover too that I'll always remember," Beth offered. He looked down at her, startled and curious to hear what she wanted to reveal.

"I went to Harvard for my MBA, a long way from home and any of my former boyfriends. I went to an alumni reception one Saturday night, just to meet people. I saw Dennis there, talking to a professor that intimidated me to death. But that professor was trying hard to impress Dennis! I was fascinated and kept watching. When Dennis left, he asked me to come with him and I said yes. I was in his bed within an hour."

"Did you like him?" Sean tried not to let too much jealousy into his voice.

"Dennis? Yes, very much. We had a wild affair for the next year before things cooled down, to mostly friendship. Then he started really teaching me, although he'd taught me a lot before. First, he taught me how to submit, which was sweet. And then he taught me how to dominate a man, which I loved." She held her breath while she waited for his reaction.

"So he's the one who taught you how to lead, like you did today?" Sean supposed he should be thankful to this unknown man.

"He taught me most of what I know. He introduced me to people, other Doms and subs who could also teach me. I've been involved in the SM scene for about eight years now." Her voice died away.

"Do you still see him?"

Beth looked him straight in the eyes.

"He died on September eleventh. His office was at the World Trade Center above where the plane hit. He called me to say goodbye, when he knew he wouldn't make it out."

"Oh damn, I'm sorry, baby! I shouldn't have made you think of that. Please forgive me."

"It's okay, Sean. I've got to learn how to talk about him."

Still, she buried her face against him, her shoulders shaking slightly.

Sean caressed her head, letting the silky strands fall through his fingers. He hated bringing grief into anyone else's life. Slowly the silence became more comfortable.

"Fantasies, Sean? Care to talk about fantasies?"

"Sure thing, Beth." He tried to think of one that might interest her.

"In the Army, I used to dream about being a soldier in a fantasy world, full of swords and dragons. Captured by Amazons," he went on more strongly when Beth smiled up at him. "And then tested to see if I was good enough to serve the Goddess' priestesses." His voice trailed away as he tried to phrase another story to make it acceptable to a strong woman like her.

Beth broke the silence after a few minutes.

"I've got fantasies too, Sean. I think a lot about spending a weekend with a man who'll do anything and everything I want. I can imagine so many things to do with such a man."

Sean's arms tightened around her. "Oh yes!" he breathed against her hair. His cock twitched slightly against her hip and subsided slowly. Sean cuddled her closer and remembered the fool who had humiliated her. It would be a privilege to show her what cherishing really met.

"I've fantasized about being a Frenchwoman, interrogated by a Resistance leader for collaborating with the Germans. Questioned fiercely. And sensually." She sighed at the vision, then went on. Sean shivered at the thought of her, tied up but still spitting defiance.

"And sometimes I dream about being overpowered by a barbarian, just slamming into me. Forcing me...and yet always knowing that he wouldn't really harm me."

Her voice was very soft as she made the last confession. He kissed the top of her head.

"It'd be an honor to carry out a fantasy of yours, Beth. Maybe take some time and do it up right," Sean murmured.

Beth licked his chest in response. "Time? Perhaps a weekend's worth of fantasy, Sean?"

"Oh, yeah," he rumbled, his body warming to the possibility. A few days' adventures with Beth? "Yeah, I could spend a weekend with you easily."

He kissed her cheek, before finding his way to her mouth and a long, sweet kiss. Finally, he lifted his head.

"Think about it, sweetheart," he suggested. "Two of us, alone for a couple of days, making some memories to take back to the real world? I'm game, if you are."

Beth caressed his cheek, her smile a quiet glow in the dark room. "I'll think about it, Sean."

She relaxed silently back into his arms and he settled her more closely against him, relishing how easily she curved against his body. The only sound was the clock in the other room, its regular beat marking each minute. He fell asleep, thinking about barbarians and Amazons, Beth's soft hair teasing his throat.

"Wake up, Sean. I've got to leave in a few minutes but we need to talk first."

Beth held a coffee mug under Sean's nose. His eyes opened and he was immediately alert, hearing the cuckoo whistle from the front room. Every detail of the previous night ran through his mind and coalesced into the realization that she was still here with him. A glance at the bedside clock told him how little time she had left before that meeting with the FBI.

He relaxed and sat up, instinctively pulling the sheet up over his lap to cover his hard-on. Beth put the mug into his hand and then sat down next to him. Fully dressed, damnit.

The rain whispered against the windows, quieter than the beat of his heart.

"Yes, I'd like to take you up on your offer of a weekend. As you knew I would," she teased gently. A small grin tried to form on his mouth but he kept his eyes fixed on her.

"So, next weekend? From Friday night until Sunday night."

It wasn't really a question but Sean nodded slowly anyway. Mike would be spending that time with the Hemmings' relatives in Portland. Dudley had an invitation too, earned by his shameless fondness for Mike's girlfriend.

"Do you have any limits of what you will or will not do, Sean?"

"No, ma'am. I'll do anything you want." Being with her was unpredictable but ecstatic. He knew a weekend with her was the best offer he'd ever had from a woman or would ever get, no matter what she intended.

"The excitement for you will be what I want?"

"Oh yes, ma'am, that's exactly right." His cock throbbed at the thought of her pleasure.

"Physical limitations," Beth considered. "I broke my foot during a diving meet but it's healed now. Still, I don't like to stand for long in very high heels. Do you have any?"

Sean shook his head immediately. "No, ma'am. I've got no problems at all since the doc said my back was healed. I still work out as I did in the Army so I'm up to whatever you want."

Beth's eyes sparkled at his eagerness. "I do yoga every day, Sean, plus swim and hike regularly. So don't worry about me." She paused for a moment before going on.

"Don't agree so easily, Sean. You have to do some other things before Friday."

Sean's gaze flashed up, caught by her tone.

"I want you to write down at least one of your most submissive fantasies and one of your most dominant fantasies. You have to give me the complete story, everything that happens and how much you're turned on. Step by step."

Sean gulped at the thought. Write down every detail? Beth chuckled wickedly.

"Just leave the packet for me at my hotel before Thursday night. I've written the address down in the kitchen." She kissed his shoulder, then nipped him lightly. "And fair is fair. I'll do the same and send it to your office. Double-wrapped envelope, to protect your privacy."

Sean blinked at the idea of seeing her fantasies on paper, something outside any of his previous sexual experiences or imaginings.

"Now, you're a generous lover but we both need a little more reality than just saying whatever you want, plus writing a couple of fantasies. So, have you ever heard of a list of things that you can say yes, no, or maybe to? Things like oral sex, bondage, spanking, whatever."

Sean thought hard, considering some of the non-fiction books locked in his bedroom. "Are you talking about a negotiation checklist? I've seen something like that in several of my books and I've read them on-line too."

"Excellent. Fill one out, including every activity that you can think of. Also be sure to write down all your needs and desires, what you must have and what you hope to have happen if you're going to be sexually satisfied this weekend. No guarantees of exactly what will happen, of course, since I choose what goes on."

"Okay," Sean answered slowly. She wanted him to write up that sort of thing? Just so she could be sure he'd be happy? But how could he talk about something that he'd always kept so private?

"I also left a jazz club's name in the kitchen. Meet me there on Friday night, ten pm. You'll be back there forty-eight hours later, on Sunday night. Park your car where it'll be safe for the entire weekend. Bring only the clothes you stand up in and the scarf, which must be clean. Got that?"

"Yes, ma'am," he agreed promptly, fascinated by her operations plan.

"Preparations," she mused, before snapping out her requirements. "No alcohol or other mind-altering drugs for at least twenty-four hours before Friday night. In addition, and this is not negotiable, no orgasms for any reason whatsoever for twenty-four hours in advance."

Sean's jaw dropped open.

"Do you agree?" she demanded.

"Yes, ma'am." He shut his mouth.

Beth searched his eyes for a minute and then nodded. She went on briskly.

"You'll also need a manicure, pedicure and facial. The facial must occur no later than Thursday. No hair removal except a maintenance hair cut."

Sean nodded, storing away the instructions. A facial? Why did she want him to do that? Men don't need fancy skin treatments, surely. Or maybe they do in her world. Full comprehension would come later, especially after his cock stopped doing the thinking. It stood at full attention right now, more than ready to charge into any battle she commanded.

"Repeat what you're supposed to do."

"Report on Friday night, at twenty-two hundred hours in a sober condition, to the address given. Bring the scarf provided but no other clothing except the street clothes being worn. Complete a manicure, pedicure and facial no later than Thursday, plus routine hair cut."

"Very good." A small smile curved her mouth. "What are your clothes and shoe sizes?"

Sean rattled them off.

"Any questions?"

"No, ma'am," he replied promptly.

"Good. I'll see you Friday night then, Sean."

Beth leaned forward and kissed him on the mouth. Sean quickly put his coffee cup on the nightstand and kissed her back. They both gave themselves up to the embrace until Beth finally stopped it and sat up. Sean watched her, enjoying the sight of her swollen mouth and heavy-lidded eyes.

"Now be sure to show my friend a good time," she whispered in his ear and her hand squeezed his cock hard and fast. Sean choked and jumped, only to chuckle reluctantly at her grin.

Sean leaned back with a sigh as the front door closed, sliding the sheet back to fondle himself. The events of the previous evening had astonished him but plans for the coming weekend surprised him even more. He had considered weekend rendezvous before, especially after Mike started going away on trips with his friends, but this was very different. He didn't have to plan anything, unlike the offers other ladies had hinted at. He would be free to enjoy himself and her.

He looked down at his cock, rearing red-hot and urgent against his belly. She'd welcomed it as her friend. He shook his head at how comfortable she was with his privates.

A good time? He remembered one of his most familiar fantasies.

The guardsmen were at their usual afternoon's sword practice, their intensity only slightly increased by knowledge that the queen was in residence and possibly watching them from the tower above. She was a hard mistress who demanded the utmost from them and they worked hard to satisfy her. Her implacable standards had been confirmed by battlefield victories time and time again. Now men came from miles around to serve her but only the best survived to serve in her personal guard.

Today was a different day from most. Every man on the terrace knew that the queen had tossed her latest page out of her quarters before dawn, complaining that he was a boy who knew nothing of how to please a woman. No matter that the lad was four and twenty and a prince of the neighboring country.

The guardsmen had seen more than one man stagger from the queen's rooms. They also knew that, in this mood, she'd hunt the castle for a man to satiate her and they all wanted to be that man.

Sean fought hard against the other two guardsmen, practicing the strokes and counters needed to face a pair of attackers. A final flurry saw them on their knees, offering their swords in surrender. He waved them away and leaned on his sword, while he caught his breath. Sweat pooled under his padded leather vest and breeches. There was still time for one more bout before sundown.

"Sergeant!" shouted the chamberlain. Sean bowed in response and waited.

"The Queen commands your presence. Come with me." The chamberlain pivoted and strutted off, his rich silk robes swaying. Sean tossed his practice sword to his second-in-command and followed, his boot heels very loud in the sudden silence. The other guardsmen stood aside for them, their faces changing from sudden comprehension to envy.

The chamberlain led him down a long corridor inside the palace. Sean kept his face controlled, trying not to show the wild hope that built in him with every step.

Two eunuchs sprang to open the heavy doors at the corridor's end. Sean's leather breeches were suddenly too tight as he passed through the doors into the famous rooms beyond. He had heard whispers of these quarters but never thought to see them.

"Well, Sergeant? Do you have any objections to what follows? You do realize what is about to occur." The chamberlain's shoe tapped impatiently. "Her Majesty demands nothing less than absolute willingness."

"No, sir. That is, yes, sir, I am entirely willing to serve my queen in this manner, as in any other." Sean's throat was tight but he got the words out. He tried not to watch the queen's chief eunuch, waiting just beyond the self-important chamberlain. Tonio had served her since she came to the throne as a girl and knew more of her secrets than anyone still living.

"Quite right. Tonio, please forgive my haste in fetching the sergeant here. I'm afraid there wasn't time to wash him."

"Of course, sir. We'll make sure that he is very thoroughly cleansed before he goes upstairs. We cannot let anything else upset our mistress."

Merciful goddess, he was truly going to see the queen. Would he be permitted to view her naked body?

"Get undressed, sergeant, and put everything in that chest. We've a great deal to accomplish before sundown."

Sean stripped to the skin, stored his belongings as instructed, and followed the stout little eunuch into the next room. It was tiled in crisp patterns of black and white that highlighted the line of spigots along one wall and the ceiling above. An enormous tub held pride of place in the center. His sweaty, stained body felt clumsy and out of place in a washroom designed to show any speck of dirt. Two enormous, ebony-black eunuchs awaited, dressed only in black leather aprons.

"Scrub him well, boys," Tonio snapped, his embroidered silk sleeve falling back as he shook a finger in emphasis. "A triple dose, rather than the single dose we gave yesterday's pretty boy."

The eunuchs saw him through two cold showers and a hot bath, until he would have sworn that no dirt dared linger under their suspicious eyes. Then they made him crouch over a curved pole that held his ass in the air for all to see. They filled his backside three times with warm water from a greased hose, never allowing him to fight the intrusion before they drained it out. In fact, Tonio lectured him at great length throughout on the importance of being clean throughout his body, given the queen's fondness for riding men's arses.

Sean considered the eunuchs' restraints on him and Tonio's lecture rather superfluous, given the hardness of his cock during the process. Like every other man in the guardhouse, he'd heard stories of the queen's delight in utilizing every portion of a man's anatomy. Like most, he'd trained his ass in hopes of one day experiencing those likings and his arousal reflected his anticipation.

They oiled his entire body and shaved every hair not present when he left his mother's womb. When he was as clean and smooth as a new sword, they showered and bathed him again. Finally, they covered him again with the same scented oil until he gleamed like a marble statue. The oil was probably an aphrodisiac, given their caution in handling it.

Tonio led him into the last room, where mirrors caught his reflection from every wall and soft carpets hid any sound. His eyes widened when he saw the golden jewelry Tonio brought out for him. The cock ring was a gilded leather strip, adorned with sparkling diamonds. There was a golden phallus to match, its jeweled handle cunningly carved to permit passage of a leather strap. He needed several minutes of slow, deep breaths before he could shelter that immense phallus inside his ass. Its pressure sent a surge of blood through his pelvis and beyond, making the cock ring bite harshly into him.

"Excellent," Tonio praised. "Smaller than her usual choice but still large enough to prepare you."

Sean shivered at the possibilities.

Then they harnessed him in gilded leather, straps running between his legs to hold the cock ring and phallus steady by anchoring them to the wide belt around his waist. More leather crossed his shoulders and chest, accenting his muscles and leaving his nipples available. They promptly responded by tightening and Tonio clucked approvingly. Jeweled collar, cuffs, armbands and soft boots completed the set. A sprinkling of gold dust on his shoulders, chest, cock and balls accentuated his straining excitement. The entire outfit was an eroticized version of a smith's attire when working the forge.

Tonio wrapped a crimson velvet cloak around him and took him upstairs through a secret passage. His cock felt huge against the restraining leather as the velvet caressed it with every step. They emerged in the queen's bedroom and Sean looked around eagerly.

"He's ready," Tonio announced as his eyes swept the room.

"Not now, you dolt!" the chamberlain snapped at Sean. "There's no time to gawk. Get on the bed at once!"

Sean's mouth dried when he saw the huge bed. It was stoutly built of the kingdom's finest iron and had four pillars, one arising at each corner. A torch burned from each pillar, lighting the bed like a stage for one of the queen's favorite pageants. Crimson velvet spilled to the floor on all sides in a blazing sweep of color that almost distracted him from the golden straps falling from every side and pillar.

Tonio snatched the cloak off Sean, who climbed up on the bed then spread his arms and legs as directed. The chamberlain and Tonio quickly strapped his wrists, ankles, neck, and waist to the bed, leaving him virtually immobile. They departed silently and hastily, leaving him alone to face his mistress.

Sean looked up and saw a stranger in the gilded mirror cunningly mounted on the ceiling. Body opened wide for any touch, eyes and mouth heavy with passion, cock begging for use. He was caught in a gilded spider web, awaiting his queen.

She came in silently and he saw her first in the mirror. She wore a long, white robe that gave away few of her secrets. Her black hair spilled over her shoulders and she studied him for a long time from hooded eyes. Then her eyes raised and she scorched him with a single glance of lust.

"Your Majesty," he croaked, all poise gone. She smiled at him and his blood ran cold. Or was it hot under so much hunger?

"Have you waited very long, sergeant? You seem eager."

"Years," he growled. Her laughter rang through the room.

"Such a long time, sergeant!" she mocked. "Still, I think we can find a use for such patience." She ran her hand down the closest pillar and up the strap to his wrist, checking the tension. He trembled but managed not to jerk against the bonds.

"Well placed; tight enough to hold you fast and enough slack that you can last for hours. I shall have to compliment Tonio."

Hours like this? He prayed for the strength to satisfy her.

She checked every strap that held him. Then she explored every outstretched limb until he was quivering.

"Please, Your Majesty," he began, too aroused and frustrated to maintain his usual silence. "I beg of you..."

"So you have a voice! Splendid. I was beginning to wonder if you could utter sounds that entice as much as your body."

Sean tried to make sense of her words. She wanted him to talk?

"Sing again for me, my stallion. Your voice belongs to me as much as your arousal." Her hands slid up the inside of his thigh until they cupped his balls.

"Please!" he choked, jerking against the bonds.

Her thumbs circled his balls, lifting and separating the fragile eggs in their pouch.

"Oh please, fuck me, please..." The words poured out of him.

"Excellent," she purred. She left his balls and he cursed loudly. Her hands came back to him in a sweep from his shoulders to his waist before returning to his chest. She played with his nipples until he thrashed wildly, promising anything if she'd only do something!

She disappeared and he looked for her wildly. He couldn't find her in the darkness beyond the torches and he prayed loudly to all the gods he knew for her return. Then her hands covered his eyes and he thanked the gods for her.

She kissed his mouth, sweet and long. Their tongues coupled together as he silently promised her a greater coupling with his loins.

She took her hands away and he saw her climb naked onto the bed above him. She knelt over his head and smiled wickedly when his body strained towards her.

"Curb yourself, my stallion. Show me what your tongue can do for my nether lips. A woman likes to be well pleasured before she rides a mount like you."

"Gladly!" he vowed. Then thought fled when she lowered herself and his face slid into her folds like a ship entering port. She rubbed herself restlessly over him and his mouth and tongue went eagerly to work. He licked, sucked and nipped at any part of her that came within reach. But he enjoyed it just as much when she used his features, especially his nose and chin, exactly as she pleased.

He exulted the first time she came, her thighs tightening around his head as the sweet ripples rocked her. He snarled in triumph when she rose over him again and sought more attention from his greedy mouth.

Still, he lay shaking with his eyes shut when she finally rose from him.

"Your Majesty, I beg of you," he pleaded.

His cock was only slightly less willing than it had been. His blood burned in his veins and his seed clamored in his loins, fighting to escape the leather bonds. He didn't know and didn't much care whether it was because of her or the aphrodisiacs they'd soaked him in. He simply knew that he needed her now as he'd never needed another woman. And that he would need her just as much for hours yet to come, if not the rest of his life.

"Sing for me again, my stallion. Let me hear the sweet sounds of your hunger."

She squeezed his cock hard and he jerked, nearly breaking one of the straps that held his belt.

"Please fuck me now, damnit!"

She leaned over him and pressed her hand down his belly from navel to his cock.

"I beg of you, fuck me! Oh merciful goddess, fuck, oh, fuck..."

She took him slowly, agonizingly slowly, into her womb. His voice died away at the feel of her hot sheathe around him.

"You are too quiet, my stallion. Sing for me again."

"Fuck, please fuck me, fuck, fuck, fuck..."

He chanted his hunger, slowly at first then faster and faster as she rode him, matching the speed of his words to her tempo. His voice grew louder and louder when she squeezed him as she rode. Everything he was or had ever been centered on the woman above him.

"Sean! Come with me!"

He exploded into his orgasm at the sound of his name, pumping his seed into her as fast as her greedy womb could strip it from him. Her matching orgasm throbbed around him and he screamed himself hoarse.

It seemed a long time before she stirred on his chest, although his body still shuddered. He watched the warm female body mantling him shift, as she turned her head to look into his eyes. Chocolate brown eyes met blue eyes confidently.

"I think that I have finally found a splendid stallion, sergeant. One good for more than a few hours. Days at least, but perhaps weeks or months. Even years if the goddess grants. Do you agree, sergeant?"

"Hell yes, Your Majesty," he growled. Then his head fell back to the bed as she began to explore the pulse under his jaw. Somehow, he was still semi-hard above the cock ring.

Sean took a handful of sheet and began to wipe his chest dry.

Friday night seemed like a long time away.

Chapter Five
Tuesday, 6 PM

Beth entered her suite with a sigh of relief at escaping the conference's pressures, if only for a few minutes. Her phone's message light was flashing, of course. Still, the modern recreation of 1920's opulence embraced her warmly. Twentieth century luxury and twenty-first century security, as Dave Hemmings always reminded everyone on the planning committee. They'd been lucky to reserve this hotel after September changed everyone's ideas of risk.

She picked up the phone and started checking her messages, stretching her back as she did so. The hotel staff notified her that a courier had delivered an envelope for her at noon; they'd deliver it to her room immediately, of course.

Beth drew the envelope closer to her as she deleted the voice message. A local doctor's office? A minute later, a doctor's note dropped into her hand, politely informing "To whom this may concern" of Sean Lindstrom's excellent health and cleanliness in regards to all private social matters. She smiled fondly at Sean's thoroughness and checked again for any other correspondence. He had delayed recording his internal needs, while rushing to provide a doctor's blessing for his exterior.

She pulled out her Palm Pilot and scribbled a note to ask her doctor to send a similar seal of approval to Sean. She quickly changed some items on her checklist from "maybe" to "yes," given Sean's attention to detail and his partner's well-being. She'd look over the checklist again after tonight's banquet, when she finished writing her fantasies. A few more taps locked the Palm against prying eyes.

She kicked off her conservative gray shoes, which went so well with her suit, and checked messages on her cell phone. High-heeled shoes but not tall enough to appear that sex was the only thing on her mind. Beautifully tailored, charcoal pinstripes but not so tight as to look as if getting back into Sean's bed was her first priority.

The first message, of course, was from Holly, better known as the Wicked Witch of DC to her subordinates' families. Five minutes later, and three replays, Beth decided that Holly had at least one more thankless chore lined up for Beth's return to Washington. She hadn't said which project so there was probably a mountain of useless tasks, all designed to make Holly shine before her superiors. At least she'd told Beth to rest and take some time off before coming back to the office.

The second message was from Mr. Griffith, asking Beth to call him at his home that evening. She scribbled down the number and dialed it immediately.

"Mr. Griffith?…Yes, this is Beth Nakamura."

His deep voice boomed in her ear, evoking an image of the man himself. A decade on Wall Street and twenty years of government service had polished but not erased the All-American linebacker from Alabama.

After a brief homage to social niceties, he dived into a detailed review of that morning's meeting among the law enforcement agencies, discussing the joint task force's plans thoroughly enough to hold her attention. It was her first chance to talk to him alone and Beth reveled in the opportunity to stretch her mind with currency movements, the game she knew best.

Next she enjoyed hearing his analysis of the various agencies' approaches to removing the terrorists' money, glad to finally be at least this close to hunting the enemies.

Finally, the conversation started winding down and Beth double-checked the clock. She still had some time to write before changing her clothes.

"Are you interested in becoming more involved in this effort, Beth?"

Beth's heart skipped a beat but she kept her voice steady for the least revealing answer.

"Very much so, sir. It's important work, both for the country and personally. I gave the task force my contact information and I've already answered another question for them."

"Hoped you'd feel that way. It always helps when there's something useful to do after seeing your friends pass over."

Beth murmured an agreement, eager to start on something beyond grieving. Her body felt intensely alive and yet her mind was crystal clear, rapidly sorting through that morning's meeting for clues to Griffith's question.

"Well, just keep doing what you can out there. Maybe I can shake something loose on this end."

"Glad to, sir." The phone went silent as Griffith hung up.

Beth put the phone down very carefully and quietly. Then she pumped her fist in the air, hissing "Yes!" in triumph. Finally, she was getting the chance to do something. Another sliver of the cold that had gripped her cracked and fell away.

She paced the room for a few minutes, her mind whirling in excitement. She quickly stripped down to her silk underthings, then happily ran through a handful of yoga exercises. Relaxed and focused afterwards, she sat down to write, eager to let loose some of the energy boiling up inside.

She took some deep breaths, gathering herself to focus on him and the fantasy. She wondered what Sean was doing now: writing perhaps? Or pleasuring himself? Hell, just thinking about that man pleasured her. Then she picked up the pen and began to write, letting her instincts drive the submissive fantasy she had promised him.

Beth waited for her knight on the steps to the great tower, beside but slightly behind his lady mother with her eyes downcast as was proper. Excitement bubbled up inside her and she could hardly wait to be alone with him.

He rode in at the head of his guard, their horses' hooves stirring up the dust and sending the assembled crowd into a fury of welcome. Women cried, children shouted and dogs barked. His great white warhorse sidled but quickly steadied under his firm hand. A groom ran to hold its head and he swung down easily.

He came up the steps, sword swinging at his side and armor clanking, and she felt his eyes find her, while he stripped his gauntlets off. She gave him a small smile and waited modestly while he greeted his mother. Then he came to her at last. She began to bow but he caught her face in his hands, halting her public homage.

"Little dove," Sean murmured and kissed her on the mouth. Sweeter than honey but not for nearly long enough. His hands gripped her shoulders hard, just short of bruising her. She leaned closer, yearning for more. But he lifted his head finally and smiled down at her, a cruel satisfaction curling his hard mouth.

"I destroyed the scum who insulted you. The monks chant prayers for his soul now, and his brother vowed to build a chapel to Saint Elizabeth, your patron."

She smiled, a savage delight gleaming in her eyes. It was not Christian to hate an enemy or be so glad at his death. Still, she had not been a Christian until her knight married her and old habits died hard. If her knight had been injured while dealing with that creature, she would have ruined the foul beast herself.

He kissed her again, hard and fast, heedless of their watchers. She yielded quickly, embarrassed at enticing him. She should have remembered that he liked occasional ferocity in his lover.

"Soon, little dove," he promised. She blushed at making her eagerness so apparent and cast her gaze down again. He lifted her chin with a finger.

"Is my bath awaiting us?" he questioned softly. She glanced up, startled, and met his eyes. Color flooded her cheeks again at the look there and she nodded.

"Everything is ready, my lord. You need only bring yourself."

"Very soon, little dove," he vowed in a deep rumble. "Let me deal with a few matters first and then I shall come to you."

Those few matters took longer than she would have liked but less time than she expected. She changed into a silk robe from her own country and wrapped a silk obi around her waist, as was appropriate for a kimono. He loved seeing her with only a single layer of silk covering her skin.

Finally, she heard his booted feet and spurs on the stairs to her solar, the glorious sunny room that his mother had given them. She shrugged at hearing him talk to his squire. Much as she wanted him alone, she knew that she wasn't strong enough to disarm him herself.

She bowed a greeting and offered him a goblet of his favorite spiced wine. He sipped it while the young man worked silently to remove his armor. Beth waited and helped as she could, her eyes hungry for every glimpse of him. He never spoke of his injuries and she scanned the padded undergarments for any hints of damage. But everything was at it should be.

Beth took a deep whiff of his scent from the padded vest: leather and horse and the sharp tang of the oil used to keep his armor moving freely. It was so intensely masculine that it sent a bolt of lust through her body. She fought for breath and caught the smell of his sweat, underlaid by a hint of his musk. Fresh musk, as if his body stirred now in anticipation.

She glanced over to his lap and saw his wool breeches tented by his cock's pressure. He cleared his throat in a harsh rasp and her gaze flew to his face. She blushed again at the naked hunger there but didn't look away.

"Thank you, lad. Get yourself gone; it'll be tomorrow before I have need of you again," he barked, his eyes never leaving hers. Her eyelids half-veiled her expression at the reminder of their audience and she waited until the door closed behind his squire. She rather thought the young man would be quickly seeking a maid to ease his lust, judging by the evidence in those breeches.

Sean stood up and unlaced his breeches. She sighed at finally seeing the beloved cock again, rising in red-hot splendor against his beautiful body. Her hand itched to touch it but could not, without his permission. He pushed the breeches off and dropped them casually on the floor before walking over to the tub. He settled into it with barely a ripple, until the water rose past his waist, and sipped his wine again. Rose petals circled and then lapped softly against him.

Beth allowed no hint of her disappointment to show. It was not for her to choose the time or place when they would couple again. She envied the innocent petals for touching him.

She quietly tidied up the solar, placing his clothes where the maids would find them. She stole glances at him from under her eyelashes and trembled when she saw one big, scarred hand idly circling a nipple. He knew her fondness for the taste of him there, how much she loved the strong muscles of his chest leading to those little nubs, how much she adored urging them into jewels that echoed the strength of his great cock rearing up below. She whimpered, the merest hint of sound, when his fingers plucked and then released. Her body quivered like a tightly-drawn bowstring, above the wetness between her legs.

"What is your name, little dove?"

"My lord?" She spun around to face him, bewildered at the question. Was this the start of a new game? "It is Elizabeth, as you honored me by remembering the blessed saint. Or Beth sometimes, as it suits you."

"No, little dove. What is the one that you carried first? The name they gave you in that far-off country where you were born."

"Keiko, my lord." She slid her hands into her sleeves and gave him a deep bow. It evoked the customs of that distant land, with its snow-covered volcanoes standing fast against the raging ocean.

"Keiko," he drawled, pronouncing it correctly. He had learned how to say it years ago, in the Holy Land where he captured her from those he called Infidels. Her eyes closed at the sound of the harsh voice lingering over her name.

"Keiko," he said again, his voice deepening. "Did they teach you to remain so far from your master?"

"Of course not, my lord!" She came to his side quickly, hunger lancing her veins like wildfire.

"You still keep yourself at a distance, Keiko," Sean drawled, hot blue eyes measuring every one of the few inches between them before sweeping over her body. Answering heat crowded her body and her nipples lifted in salute to him. She hesitated, looking at the hot water surrounding him.

A big arm caught her and swept her over into the tub. She squeaked and caught his shoulders for balance. Then he slowly allowed her body to slide down over his, his knees coming up to support them both. Her silk robe floated up around them in the water. Her hands fluttered against him, uncertain whether to hold onto him or deal with the robe.

He laughed and her gaze flew to him. Then she giggled, a silvery sound like the sunbeams dancing overhead. He hugged her close and they laughed together.

"It is good to be home with my Keiko," he told her, his fingers stroking her high cheekbones. Her eyes slanted shut, almost purring at the caress. Surely he wouldn't deny himself much longer.

"Do you have skin to pleasure me, underneath the cloth, Keiko?" She giggled again at the question. Enough water had entered the silk that it was nearly transparent everywhere on her body.

"I believe so, my lord. Should we look to see?"

"Indeed, little dove."

Her fingers fumbled a bit but she managed to remove the obi and toss it onto the bench nearby. She'd carefully placed the bench there earlier, just in case her knight wanted to play in his bath. Not everything recovered gracefully from a soaking.

Her kimono still clung to her chest and she paused for a moment, enjoying the flush of arousal on his cheeks. Then she slowly slid one panel aside, baring a single breast.

Sean growled and pulled her close, his head diving down to seize her. She groaned at the heat of his mouth and her head fell back helplessly. He suckled her strongly and she arched against the intense pleasure, gasping and sobbing at the echoing tremors in her womb. His hand skillfully played her other breast and she twisted on his lap, frantic for completion.

"Sean, please! Oh master, I beg of you, finish me! Please, please…"

His free hand swept down her back and over her ass where it nestled against his hip. Beth rubbed against it eagerly, willing him to finally give her his cock. She could feel it like an iron bar direct from the furnace, cradled between her buttocks.

"Please fuck me," she groaned and lifted her hips to try to capture him. He gave her his hand instead, tracing her folds like a map he wished to learn. She wiggled against him, her fingers diggings into his shoulder. He took her other breast into his hot wet mouth, sucking her deep as if to take her entire body into him. Her hips tensed again and again, thrusting against his all too skillful fingers.

"Please," she groaned in Japanese, "please..."

His eyes blazed in triumph at the heathen words, using the language that she had avoided since she became a Christian. He rubbed her clit roughly in the stroke she loved and she fell into orgasm.

While she was still spasming, he lifted her half out of the water and brought her down onto his cock. She cried out in surprise and satisfaction at the fullness she finally felt deep within. Another orgasm claimed her, while his cock sank into her like a hot knife into butter.

He lifted her and dropped her again, using his arms' great strength to pound himself into her. She gasped and sobbed as her orgasm's pulses refused to fade and instead built stronger into her spine. She couldn't breathe when he circled his hips a little, just enough to send tremors through another portion of her channel. Water splashed in every direction and rose petals clung to skin well above the tub's walls.

He grunted, the sound barely recognizable as words. "Fuck, fuck, fuck..."

She tightened her muscles around him, desperate to claim everything possible from his impending climax. He swelled further inside her and pulsed, then went over the edge, howling like a lion as his body poured everything it could into her.

She shrieked again as his hot flood propelled her into a final climax, this one thundering through her body in rhythm with his cock's ecstatic throb.

Beth collapsed against him, her lungs heaving as she struggled for breath. At least she'd had the wit to place towels where they could catch the worst of the tub's overflow.

She'd tell him about the coming child later, when she could think more clearly.

Beth laid down the pen carefully, savoring the last ripples of orgasm that floated through her body. She'd definitely have to wash up before dressing for dinner.

She also needed to erase the last sentence. She had never shared that fantasy with a man and a casual affaire was no place to start.

Beth was calmer when she saw her room again late that night. The banquet had gone more smoothly than she'd expected, given that most of the real negotiations occurred then, under cover of fine wine and seemingly idle questions. She'd had to concentrate fiercely, an effort that left her both drained and exhilarated. They really were on track, an astonishing feat considering the number of major banks represented and the amount of money to be repaid.

She blinked at the flashing red light; it was too late for a call from the East Coast. Properly requested, the phone yielded a message from her brother Jason.

"Beth? Jason here. Hey, Dad gets home from Japan on Monday morning. The whole family's meeting him and Mom at the airport. Since you're out here on the Left Coast anyway, care to join us? Call me back when you get in, no matter when. Hugs."

Jason's message was entirely too casual. The hair prickled on the nape of Beth's neck. What did he really want?

A family gathering? She hadn't been home to Berkeley since last Christmas. Then all the grandchildren's antics had shielded her from too much conversation with anyone. Her parents hadn't pressed. Of course, Father had never needed to coax Beth to talk to him. And Mother? Well, Mother always had so much to say that she rarely waited for Beth to speak.

Beth stirred, driven to honesty with herself. She was the youngest of four children and her three brothers had a different relationship with their mother. They spoke fiercely together, never hesitating to argue with each other.

She was quieter, preferring to think and act rather than cast a cloud of words over a topic. She and her Father had always understood each other, with only a few words exchanged. But Mother and her brothers needed to blather a great deal.

While Beth could talk easily to Jason, closest to her in age, and relax with the other two boys, she had removed herself gradually from her mother's orbit, allowing her to be the sole center of attention. In kindergarten, they had gossiped together, at least as much as a mother and daughter could. The level of communication had faded to a warm courtesy by the time Beth graduated from Harvard.

Last Christmas, Beth's ears had still cringed at any reminder of her mother and grandmother's argument in Tokyo. Any sound of her mother's brisk voice, honed to a commanding bark by years as an obstetrical surgeon, had sent Beth flashing back to that dreadful day. Instinctively, Beth had retreated into her shell and shut the recurring pain out by not talking to her mother unless absolutely necessary.

Of course, everyone else had probably noticed that the relationship was even worse than before. So Jason's message must mean that he wanted to patch things up, a typically clumsy attempt at subtlety.

Need stirred in her, to be part of a family again, no matter how imperfect. Sudden death had claimed Dennis and too many others. She needed to be part of a circle again, safe and protected by past memories and future hopes.

Jason was her favorite brother. His new wife was carrying their first child, due to be born after New Year's. It would be good to see Father again, hopefully as friends. Maybe it wouldn't be too bad to spend a little time around Mother.

She picked up the phone and dialed Jason's number from memory. She had already been given a week's leave to take after the conference. She could spend as much as she chose in Berkeley.

Wednesday's sessions were rougher than Tuesday. Beth used an unscheduled break to send her fantasies and checklist to Sean. A quick phone call sent her doctor's note to Sean. The best news was a message that her friend Jennifer had checked into one of the upstairs suites.

Beth brightened and called immediately. Five minutes later, the two women were hugging and laughing. They looked almost like sisters: the same height, the same black hair, the same slanted brown eyes in an oval face. But Jenn came from a mixture of Vietnamese and African-American, rather than Beth's combination of Japanese and Scottish.

Finally, Jenn stepped back.

"Come on now, turn around and let me see you. Gotta make sure that none of your measurements have changed since we last met."

Beth obediently stepped away and poised, pivoting a quarter turn every time Jenn flapped her hand.

"Girlfriend, I swear that you just keep looking better and better. You're going to put all us old married women to shame. You been working out more?"

"Same old, same old as I did at Harvard. You remember," Beth shrugged. Jenn raised a skeptical eyebrow and went to the bar.

"Okay, I'm teaching yoga twice a week now. I still volunteer Saturdays at the hospice, giving massages. No big deal."

"And I'll bet you're still working out with weights, just to maintain your back for the next time you set a whip dancing." Jenn fixed a stern stare on Beth, who shrugged.

"So what if I do? It's good for my health too."

"Yeah right! And there's the daily yoga practice, and the three times a week swimming, and the hiking," Jenn snorted, handing Beth a glass of iced tea. "Relax. It's my own herbal tea, brewed just for you."

"Thanks." Beth sniffed appreciatively and then drank, letting the golden liquid flow down her throat. "How's Jarred and the boys?"

"How much time we got?"

"Two hours before the really big dinner."

"So we've got two hours to talk, while you look over what I've found."

"I'll need to dress for that dinner," Beth pointed out.

"Got that covered."

Beth raised an eyebrow.

"Beth, you told me that there's a man in your life that you wanted to look good for."

Beth choked on her tea. "That's not what I said!"

"Near enough as makes no difference," Jenn corrected her sternly. "What does he look like?"

Beth opened her mouth and closed it again. They'd been best friends since their first day at Harvard School of Business. If Jenn had reached that conclusion...

Beth took another swallow of tea. Still, the affaire was Sean was only for a week, making it excellent practice for a different relationship. Hopefully something permanent, back in Washington. But she could talk to Jenn about that later. Jenn knew everyone and loved playing matchmaker.

"Good girl," Jenn approved. "Now, tell me about this stud."

Beth frowned at Jenn but complied. Once Jenn had made up her mind, you might as well try to topple the Sphinx.

"Remember the British TV show you liked, the one about Spain during Napoleon's time? And the British officer who'd been a sergeant?"

"In that tight green uniform? Beth, that boy was fine!" Jenn whistled appreciatively. "Are you telling me you've found yourself a hot one like that?"

"Oh yes," Beth nodded, taking a deep draft of tea and trying to avoid saying more.

"Well, if you think a few nights with a man like that is going to be enough, you've got more willpower than I do!" Jenn laughed, then sobered when Beth said nothing further.

"Beth honey, just let me pass on some advice my grandmother gave me. There are just not that many good men out there. If you find a good one, then you'd better snatch him up quick before someone else does."

"He's interesting, Jenn, not perfect."

"Girlfriend, if you're waiting for perfect..." The words trailed off and she gave Beth a quick hug. "That's enough from me. You know I'll be there for you, no matter what happens. Now then,

I've got a lot of clothes for you to try on while we catch up. There's a couple of numbers that would do for a fancy dinner."

"You do like being a stylist." Beth fell upon the new topic with enthusiasm, glad to be free of discussing her intentions toward Sean. Odd feeling since she'd told always told Jenn everything about her boyfriends.

"Oh yes, best thing I could have done with that fancy Harvard degree. Lots of fun to be had, shopping with other folks' money. Now get out of those clothes, down to your thong, and let's start looking at what I brought."

"Okay, but you have to tell me about Jarred and the boys now." Beth kicked off her shoes and started peeling off layers.

"Jarred's doing fine. Likes being a prosecutor, which surprised me. I thought he loved the police so much that he'd hate changing."

"Well, he had to do desk work after the shooting, didn't he? So isn't prosecution better than pushing paper as a cop?"

"I wasn't sure he'd think so. Maybe he'd love the police so much that he had to hang around, even if it was behind a desk. But he's happy as can be now. His leg has almost returned to normal but he plans to stay where he is, even talking about becoming a judge one day."

"A judge? Well, maybe that's not surprising. Remember how he lectured us when we first met?" Beth shimmied into the black dress. Matte silk jersey soothed her as it clung to every line of her body.

"Do I? Lord, you'd have thought the man only believed in the missionary position, the way he carried on." Jenn rolled her eyes and tossed a pair of black sandals to Beth. Beth raised an eyebrow at the stiletto heels but obediently sat down to put them on.

"Not surprising, since he had just arrested us at a fetish club," Beth pointed out. She looked at the one shoe she'd managed to don and shook her head at Jenn. Jenn tossed another pair over without missing a beat.

"Then the man turns out to be one of the best submissive males you're ever going to find," Jenn laughed, watching the second pair go on.

"Closeted, of course." Beth stood up and checked her balance in the high heels; they were higher than anything she'd worn recently but better than the stilettos that Jenn favored. She'd still be shorter than Sean.

"Of course! A tiger to the world but a pussycat in the bedroom, until I say he can roar. He said to tell you thanks for the Vegas trip. Yup, he'll join me out there on Friday, after I'm done setting up for your big weekend," she answered Beth's unspoken question.

She studied Beth's appearance critically, waving her hand until Beth finished turning. "You like?"

"You know it's perfect for dining out. What next?"

"Your goddess outfit for the big scene in Vegas. Brought you several choices for that one."

"Okay." Beth pulled the dress over her head and took off the shoes at Jenn's nod. "How're the boys?"

"Growing like weeds, when they're not driving their daddy and me crazy. Your godson's the worst."

"Really?" Beth's voice was muffled by black lace, as she twisted the dress into place.

"Oh yes. Did the oatmeal in the VCR business three times already this week."

"I thought you only had two VCRs." Beth tugged the zipper into place and turned to face the mirror. Black lace, high necked and cap sleeves before it swept down her body to her knees, ending in just enough of a flared skirt to permit walking. Sheer black illusion silk backed it from her breasts down in a nod to propriety. She looked like a cross between an oriental goddess and a Venetian courtesan.

"Nice dress but not for that scene. I'll keep it though."

Jenn came up behind her to look.

"Had to replace the VCR in the family room twice in the same week." She frowned at Beth's reflection. "Of course, you'll keep it; don't I always know what suits you?"

"That's just because we've gone shopping together so often. I taught you everything you know."

"Yeah, right! But thanks for taking me on those overseas trips. I'd never have learned so much or made all those connections without you."

"Don't mention it; you've done as much for me." The two women hugged before Jenn pushed a handful of red silk at Beth.

"I've never tried that one on. My figure's just not as firm as yours. But if you're in half as good shape as you look, this should make your man's eyes pop out of his head."

"He's not my man."

"Still missing Dennis?" Jenn asked softly. Their eyes met in the mirror.

"Yes, but I'm not in love with Dennis. I'm not sure I ever was!"

Jenn waited, letting Beth talk it out.

"I loved him but I don't think I was ever 'in love with' him for more than five minutes, every year or so. Every time I started to fall, I'd get reminded that he was bisexual and he liked having more than one lover in his life. He loved them and cared for them all but I couldn't fit in that circle." She flinched, remembering how deep the gulf had been between their needs, no matter how much they cared for each other. "He used to tease me about being too monogamous for my own best interests."

"That's not true!"

"He was right, Jenn. I want a lot and I want it all in the same man. If I was willing to have more than one guy in my life, I'd have an easier time." Beth fastened the gold button holding up one shoulder.

"What about Bob then? You know he'd lay down and die for you."

"Bob's a great guy but he's always submissive. Okay, so he's only submissive in the bedroom but still! And he's not really much into sensation. I want more." Beth shook the finely pleated silk into position.

"Like what?" Jenn's tone was carefully neutral.

"I've had a lot of time to think, Jenn, so I can answer that now. I want a sensation slut, somebody who'll enjoy stretching his body's limits for sensory play."

"Of course you want heavy sensation; anyone who's seen you play would know that.

"And is good at role playing," Beth continued, nodding agreement with Jenn's comment. "Rougher stuff, like soldier and amazon, not schoolboy and nursemaid."

"Fair enough. That all?"

"You know it isn't. I want a switch, somebody who can make me want to submit to him too."

"You're asking a lot, girlfriend. Heaven knows there's hordes of submissive men and it was still hard to find my Jarred. But you're asking for a man who can take you, just as fiercely as you take him. And you want marriage too, not just frequent play dates." Jenn's tone was softer.

"I know. One in a million, especially after you add in all the standard relationship stuff like honorable, kind, good with children, funny…"

Jenn frowned and tweaked folds into place, achieving the appearance of an ancient goddess. "There's a fellow out there for you, I know it."

"I hope so and I plan to start hunting as soon as I get back to Washington in two weeks. Will you help me?"

"Of course!" Jenn hugged her. It was a few minutes before they looked at the red dress.

"Oh yes. In fact, hell yes!" Beth struck poses reminiscent of Classical Greece.

"You'll really get this guy's attention," Jenn said softly and handed her a pair of shoes. Beth glanced at her in the mirror and decided to change the subject.

"Dennis made me his heir, did you know?"

"I'd wondered about that. Here, try on this leather number, just for me."

"He left a lot to charity, plus quite a few items to various people. But the bulk came to me." Beth paused significantly. "Including his dungeon and almost all of its contents."

The effect was everything she could have wished.

"Everything? Good God, girlfriend, he had more toys than anyone else in New York! Even if he usually did stick to a handful of favorites."

"Lots and lots of toys," Beth agreed, trying to zip up the strapless dress.

"Whips and floggers and paddles and canes," Jenn began to make a list. "Nipple clamps and butt plugs and dildoes and cock rings and…"

"Keep going. You haven't even mentioned the equipment like the rack or the slings."

"The collection of whips alone, honey! He had some beauties, stuff that's not made anymore. That set of Jay Marston whips, that beautiful ruby red Jay Norman whip…"

"He did leave one of the Jay Marston whips to Steve." Beth stretched the leather smooth so she could finish zipping. "And that fabulous Mad Dog blacksnake went to Toby."

"Dennis sure knew his whips," Jenn sighed, stepping up to help fasten the dress. "Lovely things to go thud or sting against a man's behind, get him all hot and bothered and ready for love…"

"Lovely things," Beth agreed, tucking the zipper pull into place. She considered herself in the mirror. Jenn knelt so Beth could step into the matching shoes.

"He showed you how to use them all, didn't he?"

"Oh yes. He taught me very carefully until he was sure that I understood them and would handle them well. We always met at least twice a year, just to play with flogging." The leather dress hugged Beth like a lover, covering everything but hiding nothing. She looked both powerful and irresistible at once.

She lifted her arm experimentally, moving into position to bring a flogger down on a lover. The dress stayed with her, still concealing her nipples. "Oh yes, this one is perfect but not for this weekend."

"Maybe you should push him a bit, flash him some leather. Got a nice deerskin flogger with me that you could borrow. It's soft enough for a rookie."

"No, I don't think so. He's ex-Army, a Ranger."

"Wowee, girlfriend, sounds like you got a tiger lined up for you!"

"You've heard of Rangers?"

"Jarred's brother, the Green Beret? He was a Ranger first. Won't talk about what he does now but he'll tell you about those Rangers."

"Really?" Beth felt a bit hemmed in by testimonials for Sean.

"You might want to think about leather."

"No, he hasn't demanded it and I want to do something that he doesn't expect. I figure he'd know how to deal with pain and humiliation, thanks to the Army. So I'm going in a different direction."

Jenn laughed. "You could have a point about that Army training. Do you really think it'll work?"

Beth smiled, the cream-licking smirk of a well-fed cat.

"You should have seen him blush when I admired his flannel shirt."

"Wicked. You are just totally wicked."

The two women looked at each other, trying to keep their faces straight. Then laughter burst through and they fell together, shrieking.

Beth returned to the hotel just before midnight, thankful that the dinner was finally over. She wore one of Jenn's finds, a gold brocade dress reminiscent of Audrey Hepburn. It had a high waist, deep neckline and little cap sleeves above a straight skirt that hugged her curves. A slit in the back made it possible to walk and a matching stole kept it suitable for winter wear.

Dave Hemmings waved at her from his post by the fireplace and she smiled at him. Then her eyes widened as she recognized his companion. Sean was here in the hotel.

She came over quickly, her eyes alight with welcome.

"Hello, Dave, Sean."

"Hello, Beth," Sean drawled, his hand coming up to stroke her arm briefly. She shivered at the touch. "I was just dropping off that packet for you, when I ran into Dave here."

"Really?" Only a more interminable dinner than usual, or an overwhelming attraction to this man, could account for such an inane reply.

"Good to see you made it back safe, Beth," Dave broke in. "I see that Tyler is back now and I'd better go talk to him. Night."

"Good night," Sean and Beth echoed. They stayed still after Dave left until more people came back into the lobby, shaking Beth into awareness of where they were.

"Would you like coffee or something, Sean? It's a nasty wind out there."

"Sure, that'd be good." He fell into place beside her.

Beth hesitated when she saw the number of people in the hotel bar. "Would you like to come up to my room? It's a suite and I can make coffee there."

"Whatever you want."

Beth turned to face him, considering the implications of her offer and his response. A day and a half since she'd last seen him but her body was as hungry as if it had been months.

"Actually, I've been thinking about something strong and hot and masculine. I can make coffee if you'd prefer, but I'd rather start with the other."

His blue eyes gleamed. "As I said, ma'am. Whatever you want will be fine with me."

He was silent in the elevator, avoiding contact with the other passengers by moving to the back. Beth sidled closer until she was leaning against him. His arm came around her waist, low enough that the others wouldn't see. She purred very quietly at his heat surrounding her, rising from the strength of his body and his breath in her hair.

He nuzzled her neck while she tried to open the door to her room. She thought about mentioning the security cameras overhead, then decided to focus on the door. She wanted to be filled by that big cock of his, as they hadn't done before. And she really preferred Sean naked in the bed for that, rather than a quickie in the hall.

Finally the door opened and they stumbled in, only to kiss passionately just inside. "Oh yes," she murmured, dropping her purse so she could lock her arms around his neck. "Oh yes."

Beth abandoned herself to the kiss, enjoying the lips and tongue that worked her mouth so thoroughly. His hands stroked her ass, in perfect rhythm with his mouth. She wrapped a leg around his hip, opening herself.

He shuddered at the increased intimacy and squeezed her. She moaned encouragement and pressed even closer.

"Beth, honey. Beth."

She opened her eyes at the hoarse croak and tried to think.

"I've got condoms in the nightstand," she offered.

"It's not that." His hand rubbed the underside of her lifted leg, then let it down slowly as she pulled herself together.

"If you're not saying no...and I don't think you are, given this," she wriggled her hips against him, enjoying the hard ridge behind his zipper. "Then what is it?"

"I want to make love to you. But I'd like to take my time at it. Get to know you and what you like."

Beth cocked her head, caught by his tone of voice.

"Have you ever done that before? Explored a woman?"

Color rose, bright and hot in his cheeks, but his eyes stayed locked with hers.

"No, Beth, I haven't."

She could be his first, the one who showed him what pleasures could be found in a woman's body. It was the sexiest thing anyone had ever said to her. Her body coalesced into a surge of longing.

"Yes," she croaked, then tried again. "Yes, of course, you can, my darling. Where do you want me?"

He considered the options, surveying the dining table, the sofa and the bedroom beyond. She thought wryly that his night vision must be excellent, since the only light came from a small lamp in the distant bathroom.

"On the bed will be good. I'll turn the lights on too, if I may."

"Certainly." She dropped her stole on the table and took up position by the bed. He turned on the lamps and the overhead light, leaving the sitting room in the darkness. Anyone on the bed would be fully exposed, yet isolated from the world beyond.

Beth had seen games staged at great expense for SM parties that left her far less excited than his simple arrangements. Moisture gathered under the gold brocade gown, leaving her both powerful and yielding at the same time.

He shrugged out of his heavy jacket, her eyes hungrily following every movement. He emptied his pockets carefully, setting the contents on the dresser.

He caught her watching him in the mirror and shrugged. "I don't want to lose anything and mess up your bed."

"That's all right." Why did such little gestures echo through her blood to her bones until she couldn't talk?

"Do you want to take your clothes off?"

"Sean..." His name was a hoarse cough. She tried again. "This time is for you. Tell me what you want and I'll do it."

He stared at her, startled. Understanding lit his eyes, followed by a bright blaze of delight. The thread snapped into place between them. When he spoke, it wasn't what she expected.

"Are those diamonds in your ears?"

"Yes, and around my wrists."

"I've always wanted a woman wearing nothing but diamonds."

Hot color swept over her breasts. They tightened and ached against the lace bra. His lips curved to show just a hint of white teeth. She trembled slightly but waited.

"Take the dress off."

She slid first one shoulder then the other free, moving as slowly as she could. She arched her back to reach the zipper and heard him hiss. His face was impassive when she looked at him but she still exulted in her effect on him.

Finally, the dress fell to the floor and she stepped free of it.

"The bra next."

The black lace of her pushup bra lent itself to even more delay. But eventually it too reached the floor.

"Thong now."

She shimmied out of it, timing her moves to the harsh sounds of his breathing. Now she wore only stockings and heels, plus the diamonds.

"Sit down on the bed."

He hooked a chair and sat down before her.

"Lean back, honey. On your elbows so you can watch too. And give me your foot."

She lifted one foot to his knee. He studied the handmade Italian shoe closely and then took it off, moving at a speed that made her efforts look like a Grand Prix race. He rubbed her foot and she purred; eyes slitting as she enjoyed the touch. She also confirmed that he had a foot fetish.

When he had reduced that foot and its attached limb to something resembling a warm puddle, he spoke again.

"Other foot, honey."

She opened one eye to look at him when he stopped. Both legs were relaxed now and totally sensitized to his touch. They lolled open, allowing him clear sight of her folds and the dew covering them. She was hot and wet and bothered, more than willing and ready for his next move.

"Now watch me take off the stockings."

She obeyed, enjoying how his thumb found the sensitive point behind her knee. She liked feeling his rough hand there, without the silk to hide even the slightest contact. Her eyes tried to close, so she could focus more on his fingers, but she managed to keep them open. He had ordered her to do so, after all.

He stroked the inside of her thighs, unerringly returning to the same spots that he'd mapped once before with his mouth.

"Lie down, honey, and show me your breasts."

She blinked at him, then obeyed reluctantly. Her hands slowly circled her breasts, then followed the delicate white veins to her areolas. She cupped and lifted her breasts out to him, rubbing her thumbs over her nipples and trying desperately to entice him closer.

He sat quite still and watched her.

Beth bit her lip and started again. This time, she half-closed her eyes and acted simply to please herself. The movements came more easily and her breasts responded eagerly, swelling and rising into her touch. She moaned and closed her eyes, arching her back to let her nipples push against her palms. She twisted and tugged one fat pink bud, gasping at the hot surge that flooded her body.

Suddenly Sean leaned forward and covered her breasts with his big hands, stopping her movement. Her eyes flashed open to stare at him.

"Take your hands away," he growled. She obeyed, running her tongue over her lower lip in anticipation.

He stayed still, simply encasing her with the rough warmth of his skin. Beth took a deep breath and tried to make her chest move against those tormenting hands. His mouth twitched but he didn't shift a muscle. She rocked her torso back and forth, trying to get the sensations she craved.

"Freeze," he snapped and she did so, startled by his tone of voice.

"Please, Sean," she begged, feeling the wetness gliding down her thighs. "Please!"

"Are you hungry, pretty lady?" he asked, his voice deepening. "Do you want me to handle your tits?"

"Yes!"

"Maybe..." he drawled. Beth whimpered but waited for him.

"Pretty lady," he said again. Then he finally handled her. He traced veins and muscles, mapped nerves until she wriggled, desperate for release.

"Please, Sean! Please, I need more! Ohmygawd," she gasped as he finally took her into his mouth. Her head fell back and she clutched him closer, until his body half-covered hers.

He grunted something but never broke contact with his mouth. Something in her bones noted that he was a fast learner, as his early awkwardness soon fell to a focused certainty. Maybe he was just a good observer.

"Sean!" she yelped at the first nip. He stopped immediately. "Damn you, Sean, more!"

She yanked at his head and he chuckled, only to start using lips and tongue and teeth to drive her wild. She writhed under him, pleading for more. He gave it to her with his hand, shoving three fingers inside to vault her into climax.

She started to come down from the peak, gasping for breath. But his hand never stopped. He kept thrusting into her, riding her without mercy until she begged again for more. Then he moved to the other breast and repeated the process until she shattered again.

She sucked in a deep breath when his hand covered her navel. His head lifted and he watched intently as she shivered under his light touch.

"Here too?"

"Oh yes, Sean. It's... not... called... my center...Ohgawd...for nothing." She tried to breathe as her body fluttered and tightened under his explorations. His finger circled, then probed into her navel.

What would happen when his mouth found her navel? Two more orgasms, the second when his big fingers found a new spot deep inside her. Stars burst behind her eyes and she arched off the bed when he repeated his attack on her G-spot.

She would have stretched like a well-fed cat if she'd had any remaining energy, when he finally lifted his head. He didn't touch her and she tried to open her eyes.

"Sean?"

"Roll over now."

Beth's eyes widened at the command in his voice. She wouldn't be able to guide him with her hands then, only respond to whatever he chose to do. She would have to totally yield and he knew it. But he demanded her consent first.

Hunger that she'd thought more than satisfied rushed back into her.

Chapter Six
Thursday, 1 AM

Sean looked down at the woman sprawled below him, her chest heaving and her brown eyes wide as she considered his order. Then she gathered herself together with a visible effort and turned onto her stomach, exposing her beautiful backside to him. She turned her head towards him and hummed at the look on his face.

Damn, but she was the most gorgeous creature he'd ever seen. Strong shoulders and back, narrow waist leading to the flared hips, long legs above those elegant feet. His mouth went dry for the rich globes of her buttocks. Diamonds gleamed at her ears and wrists against the ivory silk of her skin.

His dangerous lady, laying herself down for his pleasure.

He started at her neck, leaning over to touch her as delicately as possible. She shivered at the contact, telling him wordlessly that she liked this. He grew bolder in his explorations, exploring points that his readings had mentioned and following the clues of her body's response. She moaned and writhed, her eyes closing in primal anticipation.

He nipped her shoulder, remembering that she had enjoyed roughness elsewhere. She jerked and sighed, relapsing into shudders as he eased the mark with his tongue.

"You are so damn good at this," she gasped, her voice barely recognizable. He growled his success and nipped her again. Soon she was trembling under him as much as she ever did for caresses to her breasts.

He worked his way down her back and over her sweet ass. He hesitated there: would she permit this lust of his? If she refused, he'd honor that, of course. Still, he slipped his hand between her legs and encouraged her craving, without permitting release.

When she was almost incoherent under him, he spread her buttocks to see what was hidden in the cleft. Hell, her asshole was small and sweetly puckered. What would it be like to ride it? Better not to try that so soon.

Still, he snatched a dam and lube from the pile he'd dropped on the nightstand and covered her asshole. Then he kissed down from her spine, waiting for any objection.

"Sean! Oh yes, how did you know?" Her hips bucked back at him and twitched restlessly under his hands' pressure. He snarled in triumph and went to work in earnest, using his fingertip to tantalize her clit while his mouth thoroughly enjoyed all the sensitive points around her asshole.

She came under his encouragement, sobbing something in Japanese as her pelvis tried to grind itself onto him.

He rolled her onto her back afterwards, shivering slightly at how boneless she felt. She yawned and stretched lightly, then looked up at him. Her chocolate brown eyes blinked like a Siamese cat waking up on a sunny day, pleased with life now but willing to find more fun.

He had taken Beth to this level of sexual fulfillment but she was still ready to go further. This time was for him, she had said, but she looked as if she'd enjoy just as much as he did.

Even Mrs. Wolcott had never hunted for this much excitement.

"What next, darling?"

He smiled tightly at the lust shining in her voice. His cock couldn't wait for many more options. Maybe she was ready now to take him inside her. At least she wasn't afraid of his cock's size.

"I want to come inside you, honey."

Her eyes leaped. To his shock, she gushed wet against his hand where it rested between her legs.

"Oh yes, that's what I want," she agreed hoarsely.

"We'll go slow, honey."

She chuckled and shook her head at him. "You don't have to, on my account. You've made me more than ready for that big cock of yours."

"Damn, honey," he breathed. His fingers circled and pressed against her. She wriggled against him, opening herself up to him, as he stroked and played. Two fingers, then three glided into her. She moaned happily as her hips rocked against his hand.

Four fingers fit into her, stretching her wide. Beth groaned, blatantly enjoying being fucked by his hand.

Sean stood up and stripped with more urgency than art. Beth watched him, her fingers twitching on her thighs.

"Play with yourself, honey. Keep that fire burning for me while I get undressed for you."

He cursed under his breath when she obeyed. Years of watching videos couldn't compare to seeing a woman fondle herself at his request. He managed to grab a condom from the new stash in his wallet and fumbled it over his cock. He needed to practice looking good at this but she didn't seem to mind.

Finally, he knelt between her legs. He leaned forward to kiss her so she wouldn't be too frightened. She touched his shoulder before he came close.

"Do you want to watch, Sean?"

He blinked.

"See yourself enter me? Fucking me?"

"Hell, yes," he rumbled.

She spread her legs wide. He didn't need a second invitation before he took his cock in his hand and guided it carefully into her. She took him sweetly, her breathing deepening as her body flexed around him.

Sean took a deep breath and kept pushing in.

"More, darling, " she sighed, watching their joining as avidly as he did.

"Fuck," he growled at the sight. "Oh fuck," he growled again as still more disappeared. Then only the last inch was left in sight.

"Give me everything, darling," she said clearly.

He stared at her, startled.

"All of you, Sean. I can take you." She shifted under him, lifting her hips and wriggling slightly. His cock disappeared into her until their hair kissed and she smiled like Mona Lisa. She stretched, settling herself more firmly around him. Her eyes half-closed and her muscles squeezed his cock in welcome.

He made a sound that his primate ancestors would have understood. She was the first woman to take the full length of his cock.

"Fuck me hard, darling."

He snarled again and his control broke. His body lunged into action, hammering her. She would be bruised in the morning, maybe unable to walk, and he didn't care. He needed this woman now, needed this ride with an intensity he had never felt before.

And Beth responded to his urgency, throwing her hips up at him and grabbing his cock deep inside her. He grunted and growled, snarling sounds without words or tone, as lust boiled up within him. He rubbed her clit hard, snarling at her to hurry.

He drove their bodies up to the pinnacle as if it was a fortress to be stormed, then hurled himself into his climax like a victory. His entire body shook with the effects, leaving him half-blind and shuddering in the aftermath.

He managed a single half-coherent thought: had she finished? Then he felt her orgasm's echoes dying away throughout her body. He took a deep breath and fell asleep immediately, still inside and on top of her.

* * * * *

Sean yawned as he watched the coffee pot brewing the caffeine he needed. Her phone had rung far too early in the morning for his body. Maybe he was just getting old; he'd lasted longer without sleep during Ranger School. Still, he sure as hell hadn't this kind of fun then.

They'd said quick goodbyes after she ended the call. Now he only had to wait until tomorrow night to see her again. And get the ridiculous facial, manicure and pedicure over with before then. She'd reminded him of that step, although he hadn't forgotten and would have carried out that requirement. Orders were orders, no matter how silly they felt.

Sean stopped at Crissy's spa that morning to see if she could help him. They'd met in the Army, where she'd been a helicopter crew chief, and he'd helped her start up this business. Now, she ran one of the most successful day spas in the Pacific Northwest at this remodeled bungalow overlooking Lake Washington.

"Good to see you, Sean! What can I do for you?"

"I, ah, wanted to get some work done and I hoped that you could tell me where to go."

"Sure. If I've got an answer, I'll give it. Shoot."

"I need to get a facial, manicure and pedicure and I have to do it today." He looked straight at her, daring her to make a comment about his request.

Crissy blinked, then became all business. He remembered her briskness from the Gulf, where she'd been a five-foot bundle of energy that terrified most of the men she met.

"You'll do that here, Sean. Think I'll let you go anyplace else?" He was grateful that she didn't fuss over him.

"I don't want to bother you or take away from your regular customers..."

"Don't worry about that. We've had a couple of cancellations so there's slots to spare."

"Okay." He took a deep breath now that he was committed to this craziness.

"How much time do you have?"

"I've got the day open. Some meetings cancelled for me too. So whenever you can fit me in."

"Then you'll spend the whole day here and we'll get you out in time for dinner. Relax; we provide lunch."

"What? How the hell can a guy spend the entire day here?" The listening receptionist gave a strangled laugh, which she quickly turned into a cough.

"The gentleman's day package has hydrotherapy including an underwater massage, a full body polish, sports massage, cleansing facial, pedicure and manicure, scalp treatment, and a haircut. We can substitute a deep tissue massage for the sports massage if you'd prefer. My hair stylist is ex-Army so he knows high and tight, like your cut. All on the house, of course."

"Crissy!"

"We made the deal when I first started out, remember? All those hours that you personally spent remodeling this place, I'd repay you in kind. So you're just letting me work off that debt. Any objections?"

"Uh, no, that'll be fine." He recognized the futility of arguing with her. And the more time he spent here, the happier she'd be squaring the old debt. "The gentleman's day package it is."

An hour later, Sean knew that he'd been suckered in by starting with the hydrotherapy. He'd had a lot of massages before while recovering from that back injury, including hydrotherapy. He'd even felt right stripping down to the buff, given the impersonal atmosphere here that reminded him of the hospital's physical therapists. Seawater had been a different touch but the basics had still felt familiar. He'd simply relaxed into the big tank, enjoying the jets of water pounding the muscle tension out of him.

It had left him so mellow, in fact, that he hadn't blinked when Joe produced the strange goop to rub on him. But he'd smelled enough to wonder what was going on.

Sean sniffed suspiciously. What was this stuff? It felt like honey but couldn't be.

"What are you using for the massage?" Was this the "body polish" step Crissy had mentioned? What the hell was a body polish? He tried to keep his voice casual.

"Dead sea salts, sir, mixed with aromatherapy oils," Joe answered quietly, his slender fingers kneading the stuff into Sean's shoulders.

"Sea salt?" Didn't Mike use that for cooking?

"A very special kind of sea salt, sir, imported from Israel just for this purpose. Folks have been swearing by this for thousands of years." He continued to work it into Sean's back.

Sean tried to figure out what was really going on. Joe was rubbing salt, mixed with smelly oils, into his entire body. What was the purpose? What man spent money for smooth skin?

"Please relax, sir," Joe asked, sounding as if he made this request every day.

Sean swore under his breath. Craziness but he couldn't walk out now. He began the breathing exercises he'd learned in the hospital until he was loose enough that Joe could go back to work.

Joe finally finished and left the room while the stuff worked on Sean's skin.

Sean closed his eyes and tried to sleep. Maybe this would be over sooner if he didn't think about what was going on.

Sean let himself quietly into the big old house, glad to finally be home. He'd been away on deployment for weeks, unable to see his lady. Thankfully, nobody'd gotten seriously injured and now he could finally relax. He dropped his duffel by the stairs and went hunting.

He spotted her from the kitchen windows, sunbathing face down in the backyard, her ivory skin gleaming in the dappled sunlight. She liked to soak up rays, covered only by her favorite rich lotion when it was this hot, protected from prying eyes by the old oak tree. Her back rose and fell slowly as she slept, her raven hair pulled away from her neck and one arm brushing the grass.

He was on her in seconds, his big body covering hers on the lounger and his hips snug against her sweet ass. He rubbed himself against her, tasting the outer approach to her hot crack that he'd soon invade.

"Damn, honey, you are so hot," he growled against her hair.

"Sean! You'll ruin your uniform! Get off me!" She bucked under him, trying to twist away from him.

He captured her hands and yanked them over her head, cuffing them in one of his big paws and leaving the other free to find her breast.

"You're mine, mine for fucking, mine for anything I damn well please."

Her skin was slick and greasy, making it difficult to hold her. He felt the oil soaking through his sleeve where it pinned her arm.

"Sean, the cleaners can't save your uniform!" She writhed harder, fighting to get free. His uniform's buttons rippled across her back as she slid away from him, nearly getting out from under him.

He snarled something anatomically impossible about the cleaners and dropped his entire body on to hers, controlling her by his weight. She still squirmed and argued but he smelled a new muskiness in her scent.

"Give it up, darling! Time for a good ride."

He nipped her neck, in the age-old greeting of a male to his mate, then explored the resulting marks with long, slow swipes of his tongue. She gasped and bucked again. But this time, her hips lingered against his, then wriggled.

"You're my bitch and don't you forget it," he growled. He nipped her again, drawing a drop of blood for the first time. She moaned and her hips circled under his.

He nipped and licked her again and again, unerringly returning to her most sensitive points. He kept her hands trapped while he rubbed himself over every inch of her back, setting his mark on her with the passage of cloth and metal over her soft skin.

"Please, you…you always know what I want," she sighed, her voice fading away.

"You're so sexy…Feel my cock fucking your back." He settled his bulging fly against the crack in her ass and rocked against her, letting the steady movements separate her and nestle him between her cheeks.

"Damn, my hand needs some of your action, too." He slipped a finger beneath her and rubbed her clit, rumbling in triumph at the countering surge of cream from her core. She quivered, driven beyond words, as her body answered him with its own rhythm.

"Yeah, wiggle for me," he murmured as his free hand quickly opened his uniform so his cock could find her.

"Feel how damn big you've made me." He slipped into her hot center slowly, luxuriating in her little whimpers and moans when he insisted on keeping to his pace, not her urgency. "So damn tight when your hot sheath grabs me. And those big beautiful tits of yours…"

He fed his hand under her and pulled her even closer to his chest, lifting her just a little so he could squeeze and roll her nipples. She sobbed in frustration, her inner muscles trying to pull him deeper.

"That's right, honey, that's right. Now, honey, now!" He settled fully into her at last and she climaxed, keening her release, when the zipper's base first rubbed her clit.

He continued moving, keeping her hot and eager so she couldn't ease too far down, relishing the waves rolling through her.

"Oh yeah, honey, you're so fine," he praised her, relishing the pulses gripping his cock and destroying any brains he had left. "Hot damn, honey! Gotta...gotta pump you." He adjusted his angle slightly, needing more from her. She gasped and shifted in response, tilting her hips, and he groaned.

"Hell, yes!" His cock settled into that perfect fit, where her hot depths enveloped every inch of him and he drilled her pleasure point at every stroke.

"Oh, goddamn fucking yes!" He grunted as he rode her hard, his mare to be enjoyed as he chose. Need built deep in him and he fought it, straining to make this last climb last as long as possible. She orgasmed again and again, her shockwaves ripping through him as if they truly were one body.

His head snapped back and he shouted as he pumped her full of his cream, then collapsed onto her back. After a long, sweaty moment, her head turned and Beth's chocolate-brown eyes smiled up at him.

"Missed you, darling," she sighed.

He'd sacrifice a uniform to this, any day.

Sean opened his eyes slowly and stared at the wall. It was the first time he'd seen the fantasy woman's eyes or heard her voice. Maybe pleasing Beth was reason enough to pull a stunt like this.

He faced Crissy warily at day's end, acutely conscious of how different his body felt under his usual work clothes. His skin was so soft now that he felt his jeans' crotch seam rubbing his ass. He felt good too, energized somehow, probably just from all the attention that folks had given him. Still, there were cheaper ways to get the same buzz.

"You look good, Sean. But are you pleased?" she asked shrewdly.

He shrugged. "I'm okay."

Crissy's mouth twitched. "Doing it for a lady? Don't worry; she'll like the effect. And you may change your mind about how much you enjoy it."

Sean didn't quite shrug, not wanting to disagree with Crissy.

"Besides, what's the harm in doing something just to feel good? If you've got the money, then go for it. A lot of my male clients come for themselves, not because their girlfriends tell them to."

Sean raised an eyebrow in disbelief. "Whatever floats their boat. But I don't think you'll ever catch me in a place like this again, just to suit myself. Thanks for everything though. I'm sure Beth will be pleased."

"Good luck, Sean." Crissy hugged him suddenly. Surprised, he put his arms around her and returned the embrace. "Just be sure to have a good time with Beth."

"Thanks."

Later that afternoon, Sean and Mike worked quietly to load the furniture into Sean's old pickup while Dudley ran alongside, barking when they left him inside.

To his embarrassment, Sean found himself using gloves to protect his hands. It seemed a pity to ruin all the effort that Crissy's staff had put into making them look good.

They finished the job by tying down a heavy tarp over the top, to keep the furniture and mattress dry until it could be delivered on Friday. Sean tossed a rope over the top to Mike, who caught it easily.

"Good catch!"

"No problem, Dad. Just the two Lindstrom men working together, right?"

"Of course, right," Sean laughed at the twist on their old saying. He'd first charged Mike with being a Lindstrom man at the age of five, asking him to look after his mother. They'd promised to always stand together when Mike ran afoul of the law, and sworn it would be despite all odds at the beginning of the custody fight. They'd kept their word, sticking together through thick and thin ever since.

"Bill Owens said his uncle's selling his old Range Rover. It's pretty worn out so he's not asking much," Mike said, as he helped put the last rope on.

"I thought Bill was going to buy it."

"No, it's in such bad shape that he can't afford the parts. But you might be interested."

"Yeah, I'll think about it. Maybe give him a call next week." He'd wanted a Range Rover ever since he'd seen the SAS driving them during the Gulf War. Their cost had always put them into the category of look but don't touch. Maybe Bill's uncle knew somebody who could rebuild it for him.

"Do you want leftover spaghetti for dinner, Dad?"

"How about Chinese instead? That might be fun and easier than cooking." They usually ate out on Sean's nights for dinner duty. But Thursday wasn't his night to provide a meal.

"Sure, I can go for that." Thankfully, Mike didn't ask why the unusual restaurant meal. Or why Sean was wearing gloves for this chore. He just whistled as he tossed a stuffed dinosaur for Dudley to fetch.

Sean wore gloves again when he helped Dave Hemmings rearrange Tracy's bedroom. First, they cleaned out the existing furniture, an odd mixture of bunk beds inherited from her brother and thrift store bargains that Deirdre had found.

"Sometimes the woman is a genius," Dave grunted, as they carried a remarkably ugly chest of drawers into the garage. "And sometimes, she just hasn't got a clue. Maybe I'll be lucky and somebody will buy this at her next garage sale."

Sean laughed, understanding the sentiment. His house was also furnished with bargains that he'd picked up over the years. He'd bought, fixed up what he could and sold what he couldn't, until all his furniture was at least comfortable. What would Beth think of the result? He turned from the thought that she'd probably never see his home.

"Do you want to put the bed in the same place as the old one?" he asked, returning to Dave's concerns.

"Yeah, that's the only place it'll fit."

Finally, the men stood back and considered the results. The white and gold furniture glowed in the sunlight. New curtains hung at the windows, perfectly matching bed's lace and pink ruffles. It looked like an enchanted cavern for a fairy princess, a very young fairy princess.

"I hope Tracy likes this," Sean said, thinking of the effervescent little girl.

"She'll love it," Dave said positively. "She drew a picture of what she wanted and this is it."

"Great."

"You want some coffee or maybe a beer?"

"Coffee would be good."

Dave smoothed the last wrinkled from top so it was perfectly smooth, sweeping his hand down the length of the bed, before standing up.

They were both cradling mugs, watching yet another storm blow in from Puget Sound, when Dave spoke again.

"Beth Nakamura is quite a lady. I've enjoyed working with her but it's been a challenge. Not much, if anything, gets by her."

Sean took a careful sip of coffee. "Yes, I've been very impressed by her."

"Yeah." Dave drank some more from his mug. "She's apparently a rising star at Treasury. Very few opportunities for somebody like her in Seattle."

"I can imagine. I'm sure she'll go a long way."

Sean's eyes met Dave's. Better set this straight now, if only to pour reality over his dreams.

"We're both adults, just having a little fun together. I know it'll end when she goes back to Washington. I'm okay with that."

"Fine. Just thought I'd mention what I've observed." Dave didn't sound entirely convinced but he didn't press.

The silence turned companionable in the kitchen's warmth, while the sky darkened outside.

At least Sean could look forward to forty-eight hours with her this weekend, and the freedom to try anything he wanted. No worries anymore about losing Mike if the court heard how he liked to be enjoyed by women.

Chapter Seven
Friday, 9:50 PM

Beth sat in the limousine and watched the clock. She had seen Sean walk in five minutes ago but she would wait until exactly ten PM. A Mozart violin concerto played softly in the background, chosen by the surprising chauffeur. Jason Birch was a slender, young African-American male who moved with the unconscious grace of a dancer or martial arts veteran and made easy small talk about the current opera season. Jenn would once have found his black eyes and café au lait skin irresistible.

She considered the implications of this weekend as she sipped her champagne. Jenn had made her opinion very clear, that this man meant more than a brief fling. Terror touched her again at the chance Jenn might be right. Surely she couldn't fall for a chance-met stranger from a bookstore.

What other judgment did she care about?

What would her father think of her spending a weekend with Sean, a man she knew little about except for their sexual chemistry? He'd probably understand. He always beamed quietly when his wife told the story of their first meeting, how she had asked the tall Japanese student for a dance at the Chemistry department mixer in London. He still blushed when his wife concluded the story by saying that she'd spent that night with him and every night since.

Well, perhaps love at first sight had worked for her parents but she'd never sought it. Formal introductions followed by a gradual building of trust and intimacy was more reliable. But a weekend fling would be a delightful way to unwind and renew herself, before seeking a more permanent arrangement.

She took a deep drink of the champagne, enjoying the bubbles fizzing against her palate. It would be fun to watch Sean's face, while she played oral games with that stunning cock of his. An ice cube perhaps, or menthol to slow his response, maybe a fizzy drink. Oh, the delight of slowly removing honey from him!

Time had passed too slowly since Wednesday's encounter with Sean. Even the intense financial negotiations, as the conference ended, hadn't distracted her from thinking about him. She'd thrown herself into shopping as she sought the items needed for the coming weekend. Jenn was a great help with clothing but Beth preferred to select her own playthings.

Sean's checklist had contained some surprises. He'd wanted some heavy sensation, which changed her choice of toys.

She enjoyed planning the games for such a responsive partner. It was amazing how well she meshed with Sean, how easily they moved with each other to create sensual magic, how intense the satisfaction was. After all, they were still almost strangers even if they did dance together well.

She ran her finger lightly around the rim of her glass, thinking about the clothes chosen for Sean. He had looked like a Viking just now, wearing a thick cable-knit sweater over jeans and boots. Silk would frame his delicious attributes marvelously.

Would he be uncomfortable in the unaccustomed confinement of underclothes, especially a silk thong? If he fidgeted, she'd just have to stroke that beautiful ass of his. Perhaps she'd calm him down but then again, perhaps not.

Finally she walked into the jazz club, raincoat over her arm, and saw him immediately. His face brightened and he came over to her. Beth leaned up for his kiss, deliberately deepening it when he would have kept the contact light enough for a public setting. He groaned and gathered her close against his big hard body. Finally she pulled her head back.

Beth wiped lipstick off his mouth carefully, delicately emphasizing her possession of him. His hand ran down over her back, lightly exploring the red silk shirt and black wool trousers under the black cashmere jacket, before dropping away.

"Let's go sit down, darling," Beth purred and Sean nodded. A few words to the hostess later, Sean and Beth followed the woman past the dance floor to a small, secluded booth. Beth slid in first and Sean sat down next to her.

She let the silence hold for a moment, relishing his tension, then turned to him. Why on earth had he worn something that hid his beautiful forearms? She'd have happily settled for a flannel shirt with the sleeves rolled up.

"Ready for inspection?" she asked. He nodded, looking slightly bewildered. She ran her fingertips along his jaw, testing for the facial. Lovely smooth skin greeted her, above the strong bones.

Sean watched her, frozen in place like a new recruit. Had he worn a similar look of disbelief during his first inspection at West Point?

"Hands?"

Sean promptly gave her his hands. Beth lifted one and studied the fingernails. She dropped a quick kiss on a scarred knuckle before releasing him. She gave his other hand the same scrutiny but lightly sucked a fingertip before releasing him. His quick intake of breath was clearly audible in the confined space.

"The scarf?"

Beth held out her palm for it and Sean held out the small bag he carried. Beth found the scarf, carefully bundled in protective tissue. She closed up the bag and set it aside.

"Very good, Sean. Have you been celibate for the past twenty-four hours?"

She ran her hand up his thigh and rested her fingers lightly over his fly. His hips jerked under the almost imperceptible touch.

"Yes, ma'am," he got out.

Beth tapped the hard ridge once and then rested her hand on his thigh, a few inches below that bulging crotch. "I can see that you're telling the truth."

Sean draped his arm around her shoulders and relaxed slowly.

The waiter appeared quickly and Beth ordered a club soda and lime, plus the same for Sean. Sean's eyes widened a bit when she ordered for him but he didn't object.

"How is your son?" Beth asked quietly, enjoying making him wait.

"Uh, Mike's doing well. His team won the game tonight. Did I tell you that he's the varsity quarterback for his high school?"

"Congratulations! You must be very proud of him."

Sean pulled his wallet out to show his prized cache. A few moments later, Beth was studying pictures of a young man who looked remarkably like his father.

"Mike's everything a fellow could hope for in his son," Sean said. He looked down at her and then went on, encouraged by her evident interest. "I'm very lucky to have him. He plans to go to West Point and I think he'll make it."

"West Point?" Beth was genuinely surprised. "Why? Because you went there?"

"I was released at the end of my first year when my girlfriend got pregnant."

"Did you regret being released? Sorry, I'm prying," she tried to shrug off the question. Why had she asked it? She didn't need to know that before spending a weekend with him. A voice in her head reminded her that her father liked to know career plans, past and present, of potential spouses for his children.

"I can talk about it if you want," he said easily. "I wasn't a good enough wrestler in high school to get a full scholarship anywhere, while the service academies would pay me to attend. My grandfather had been a Ranger during World War II so I chose West Point. As for being released, I got a son and a career out of it. I felt at home as a Ranger sergeant, so everything worked out."

"You were very lucky," she murmured and changed the subject to something less emotional. "That was a very nice bookstore where we met. Do you rent to other businesses like that or a variety of businesses?"

He raised an eyebrow at her but he followed her conversational lead.

"I own over a dozen commercial properties, all of which are currently rented. There's only the one bookstore that you saw. The rest are a variety of businesses, including some small offices and a couple of restaurants."

The waiter put their drinks down and disappeared silently. Beth slid a twenty-dollar bill onto the table and studied Sean again.

"How did you move to real estate from the Army?" Beth delicately trailed her fingernails over his thigh, enjoying the hard muscle under the denim. Social niceties were all well and good but it was time for a reminder of the weekend's agenda.

His answering quiver was delicious. Sean gulped a bit but answered.

"A buddy of mine, Adam..." He lifted his wrist and its burden of the black bracelet, so she could see the lettering. "I wear his bracelet in memory of him, ever since he died in the Mog. In Somalia, I mean."

"I've heard about the Rangers in Somalia, Sean. He must have been a magnificent soldier to be remembered so honorably," Beth offered. Sean's eyes flared in surprise.

"You've heard of it!" he breathed, before resuming his story. "Yeah, Adam was a great guy. He left the business to me, along with his life insurance and a small house in West Seattle. My wife died almost two months later, leaving me to raise Mike. That's when her folks filed the first lawsuit and I got a hardship discharge."

Beth frowned, surprised that a family member would attack Sean.

Sean went on, more slowly now as he reached the more private topics.

"Tiffany's dad threw her out when she got pregnant with Mike and wouldn't have anything to do with her, or Mike, afterwards. I notified him, of course, when Tiffany died."

"Of course," Beth agreed.

"When he heard that Tiffany was gone, he filed suit for sole custody of Mike. Said that I wasn't fit to raise a son and that he could do better, being a lay minister. And Mike was pretty wild then. Tiffany couldn't give him as much attention as he needed, with her strokes and paralysis and so on. I swear he knew every cop within ten miles."

He sipped his drink as he looked back, old agonies cutting deep into his face.

"I couldn't counter the lawsuit very well, not as a Ranger who had to be free to deploy at any time. I had friends who'd watch Mike while I was gone but the judge wasn't impressed by that. He gave me two weeks to make better arrangements so I left the Army and came here."

He stopped, seemingly embarrassed by his long speech. Beth patted his leg gently in reassurance. He gathered himself to go on.

"It's been a very good business for me. It pays enough to support the two of us and the hours are pretty much whatever I want. I've been able to spend all the time I want with Mike." Sean smiled, his eyes lost in happier memories.

"And Mike's grandfather dropped the lawsuit," Beth concluded.

"Not until Mike turned eighteen this year," Sean snorted. "The old fool even refused to see Mike if he couldn't have custody. He's missing out on a grandson, just because of stubborn pride."

Beth sipped her club soda, fighting the urge to rescue him. Dear heaven, the pain he must have known in his life. She wanted to hug him and assure him that he wouldn't be hurt again. She felt his body's heat flowing into her.

"What about you? What do you do when you're not browsing in bookstores?" Sean asked, pulling himself out of his reverie with an appreciable snap.

"Well, I was a currency trader for three years after I graduated from Harvard. Now I help the Treasury oversee that business." She kept the conversation to her work, as he had, rather than mention any hobbies.

"Currency trading? Is that like commodities trading? Where you bet on what the price of the stuff will be?" He shifted on the leather seat uneasily, trying to relieve his pants' tightness.

Beth chuckled at his situation. His description of her career was a little simplistic, but essentially correct.

"Yes, it's a lot like that. My first boss called it high-stakes gambling. I enjoyed it for a while but now I like having a different view."

Sean started to ask other questions but she put her finger to his mouth. She needed to touch him, if only the minimum contact allowed by a public place.

"Let's dance. It'd be a shame to miss out on a good band."

Sean opened his mouth to say something but stopped, his eyes wide and almost frightened before he controlled himself. How many times had he danced with a woman?

He led her to the dance floor with an elegant courtesy that pleased her. Beth would bet that his mother had taught him manners, along with morals. She immediately moved into his arms and they began to sway with the music.

Beth slid closer to Sean until her nipples brushed his chest and his leg was between hers. She could feel his erection and she leaned against it, enjoying how her body's slow dance movements caressed him. Her nipples were quite hard and she turned her face into his chest, tucking herself neatly under his chin. She stood eye-to-eye with most men but she felt like a little girl in Sean's arms. She purred as his hands stroked her back and ass.

The music changed and Beth blinked, looking at her watch.

"We'd better get going," she said regretfully.

"Whatever you say, ma'am," Sean said. "Although I could have stayed here a while longer."

Beth chuckled at that, enjoying how he'd changed his mind about dancing. "But wouldn't you rather go someplace private? Hmmm?"

She laughed at the look on his face as he steered her back to their booth, so they could retrieve their belongings.

The chauffeur was standing by the limousine and held the door for them to enter. Sean hesitated but recovered quickly, following her inside as if he rode in limos every day.

He openly studied the interior as the driver pulled out onto the road, his eyes finding every high-tech gadget. Beth ran her hand up his leg, deliberately distracting him, and rubbed his crotch seam, following it as it rose to meet the zipper.

Sean caught his breath and stared at her. She caressed his jaw, then moved in for a kiss. Their hands fed on each other as much as their mouths did, seeking skin to fondle and heat.

Sean made a wordless sound when his fingers cupped her breast. Her nipple tightened under the touch, stabbing his hand directly. He unbuttoned her shirt and Beth arched her back, silently encouraging him to look his fill. He cupped her breasts, rubbing his thumbs over the velvety nipples.

"No bra?"

"No underthings," Beth corrected.

"Shit." He closed his eyes for a moment and she waited eagerly. Then he bent his head to her throat.

"Oh yes, that's very nice," she approved, tilting her head back to open for him. His hands moved over her and Beth gasped, startled by how much he remembered of Wednesday's explorations. She moaned when he moved his mouth further down, tasting and teasing her until she was on fire.

"Please, Sean, do it!" she begged.

"No, not until we're someplace private." His eyes were fierce with the effort to control his own hunger.

She nodded slowly. There were hours yet to come when they could play all they wanted. Then she could bend his self-control to suit her.

Sean watched her acquiescence, then kissed her on the mouth, backing away from the previous urgency but still keeping her excited with hands and mouth.

That kiss lasted for a very long time. Finally there was a polite tap on the window and Sean lifted his head from Beth's breast. His blush was visible even in the dim light.

She stroked his back for a moment longer and then sat up, buttoning her blouse up quickly. Sean's condition appeared more respectable than hers after he fastened his shirt. At least he looked respectable above the waist; behind his zipper was another matter.

Sean came out of the limousine and froze, staring at the small private jet in front of him. Beth patted his ass.

"Come on, darling," she urged, smiling at his shock.

"Currency trading must have paid very well," Sean got out.

Beth laughed out loud, pleased at having surprised him.

"Oh it did, Sean, it truly did."

Moments later, they were aboard the jet and taking their seats. Beth glanced around, satisfied by what she saw. The plane was even more luxurious, with its rare woods and fine upholstery, than she had requested. The steward offered drinks but she motioned him away. Once they were in the air, Beth unbuckled her seat belt and stood up.

"Let's go explore the rest of this plane, darling."

She headed back, holding hands with him, and found the stateroom easily. A small display next to the door showed cruising speed and altitude.

Beth stepped inside and ran her hand over the silk coverlet on the enormous bed, its various shades of gold glowing against the wood paneling. That color combination was why she'd picked this particular jet: it should frame Sean's magnificent body like an altar cloth. She looked back at him as he braced himself in the doorway, eyes hot but body still leashed.

"Come on in, lover, and close the door. Don't you want to join the mile high club?"

Sean's eyes blazed and he kicked the door shut. He dived onto the bed, pulling her down with him. Beth laughed and caught his head in her hands as he leaned over her.

"You big beautiful Viking, you," she purred and arched against him. He caught her mouth with his and came down on top of her. Their tongues danced and dueled together as they relearned each other's taste. Beth caressed his neck, enjoying the strong cord of muscle and bone below those sensitive points.

Sean changed his angle and kissed her face, attending to her forehead, her cheeks. His tongue circled and explored her ears until she shivered and purred under the onslaught. He went lower still to mark the pulse points on her neck, exciting the sensitive points until she begged for mercy. Whatever else he did or didn't know, he was a genius at foreplay.

He rubbed her breasts through the thin silk, tugging at her nipples as they hardened. Then he licked them until the silk became a wet circle marking her body's need for him. Beth watched him, twisting restlessly as she tried to catch her breath.

He suckled her hard enough to pull much of her breast into his mouth. Beth choked at the hot, wet cavern he created and closed her eyes. She tugged at the bottom of his sweater, anxious to feel skin.

Sean straightened up, pulled the sweater over his head and tossed it aside.

"Shirt too," Beth panted as she sat up, peeling her jacket off with more haste than art.

"Okay but not yours."

"What?"

"Everything else but not your shirt." Sean paused to glare at her. "Understand?"

Just a red silk shirt? Her eyes lit at the possibilities. "Yes, sir."

She began to shed the rest of her attire as quickly as possible. A big arm wrapped around her and pulled her back across him and lying on the bed, just as she toed off her last shoe.

"Sean!" she protested laughing. "My trousers!"

"I'll show you how to take off trousers." He shoved his hand inside the waistband and down between her legs, forcing his way until his finger met her clit. She jumped and giggled, wriggling as he fingered her into a frenzy.

When he had her writhing on top of him and almost incoherent, he quickly pulled his hand out and unbuttoned her trousers. Two seconds later, her trousers were on the opposite side of the stateroom with his clothes. A quick roll put her under him on the big bed and he grinned in triumph.

"Is that how they taught you to wrestle in high school?" Beth gasped.

Sean laughed. "No, but it sure would have been nice to know how back then."

"Care to show me a few more wrestling moves?" she invited.

"Sure thing, ma'am," Sean agreed. "But maybe we should start with some cowboy moves, like how to ride a bucking bronc."

"I don't see any horses in here." Beth tried to be obtuse but her dancing eyes gave her away. "Maybe we should ask the pilot to land and fetch us some."

"Like hell! I'm sure we can find us some. Just have to know where to look, like here perhaps." He fondled her breast.

"Surely not there," Beth choked and gasped in earnest when his head dropped down to follow his hand. Her breasts quickly remembered all he had done before and became one giant, throbbing ache.

"Condoms in the nightstand," she moaned, just before his hand found her clit again and destroyed any pretense of conversation.

"Good girl," he praised, then brought her off hard and fast. Twice.

Beth opened her eyes, trying to recover. When was he going to put himself into her? His hand was nice but she wanted that big cock.

She found him standing by the bed, rolling on a condom with rather more skill than he'd shown before. Sweet baby, had he been practicing? Still, she liked his focus on the basics. Get her satiated and relaxed enough to take a cock of his size, then sheathe himself quickly before entering. Considerate to the end, that was Sean.

He blushed, then shrugged when he caught her watching. She smiled up at him, letting her genuine fondness show through as he knelt between her legs.

"Lift my legs up with your arms, darling, until they reach your shoulders."

"Can you do that?"

"I didn't learn yoga just to make conversation."

He grinned back at her and followed her suggestion. He pushed into her quickly this time, watching her face. Beth sighed as he reached even deeper than before.

"Very nice," she praised, settling herself around him for a welcoming wriggle. His eyes widened and he hissed at the sensation. "But I think we need one thing more."

"What?"

"What's the highest you've ever ridden a bucking bronc? Six thousand, eight thousand, maybe ten thousand feet? Think we can do better now?"

He caught the reference immediately and looked over his shoulder at the instrument panel.

"Welcome to the Mile High Club, cowboy," Beth purred.

"You are a wicked woman, ma'am," Sean drawled, his eyes alight. "Guess this cowboy will just have to show you how to ride a bucking bronc, no matter where it is." He circled his hips, pressing deeper inside her. Her eyes half-closed.

"Better teach me well, cowboy," Beth managed before he rode her in earnest. He dropped all pretense as soon as he started moving, thrusting into her as if heaven could only be found somewhere deep inside her.

The thought slid away from her as his body demanded her full attention. She watched the muscles rippling in his strong belly as his hips thrust and released. The strong shoulders and arms, beaded with sweat as they strained above her. The lovely forearms, with the elegant twisting veins standing out in fine relief, so close to her. The beautiful mouth, tight now in concentration, as he fought his instincts for a few minutes longer.

But his eyes trapped her. Those incredible blue eyes, half-veiled by long golden lashes, blazed down at her and held her. She caught fire from his need and became achingly conscious of just how much she wanted this man. Cream gushed forth, welcoming him, as her body transformed itself into an instrument focused solely on carnal satisfaction.

"That's it, honey," he grunted. "Come for me. Fuck, honey, come!"

She obeyed him, her hand dropping to rub herself and her eyes locked on his as the first pulses rolled through her body. Fierce satisfaction lit his face.

"Fuck!" he shouted, then again as he freed himself into orgasm. She locked herself around him, relishing his climax as if it was her own.

He collapsed afterwards, but managed to roll so that they lay side by side, his cock still throbbing inside her.

"Got any other wrestling moves, cowboy?" Beth managed. Best to keep this light.

"All the moves you want." To her shock, he stirred inside her. Dear heavens, he wasn't joking.

Hours later, Beth saw that the cruising altitude was falling. She leaned up on one elbow and looked down at Sean. His white skin glowed against the gold silk and she twined a lock of his hair around her finger. That golden pelt on his chest even looked magnificent when it was sweaty.

Sean's eyes opened slowly and he watched her for a moment then gently caressed her throat. Beth tilted her head, opening her neck to his touch.

"Ten minutes until landing, Ms. Nakamura," said a disembodied voice.

Beth closed her eyes. "Damn," she murmured.

Sean kissed the nape of her neck and then sat up

The steward imperturbably helped them strap in, calmly ignoring their barely respectable condition. Sean flushed a little at the conclusions that the steward had obviously drawn but stayed quiet.

Beth patted his leg after the steward left.

"Look out the window. Recognize where we are?"

Sean leaned over her and gazed out. Blazing lights danced in the darkness beyond. A single beam of light pointed straight up to the sky. He studied the incredible sight and then sat back in his seat.

"Las Vegas?"

Beth nodded.

"You flew us to Las Vegas for the weekend?" Sean's voice squeaked a little in astonishment.

"Sure did. It seemed like a good place to have fun with a beautiful man," she purred and stroked his arm. She smiled at his gasp but remained silent while they landed, letting Sean watch the sights.

Another limousine was waiting when the jet taxied to a stop. The chauffeur touched his hat and held the door for them to enter, which Sean didn't quite flinch at. They drove down the Strip and Beth opened the sunroof so Sean could see all the neon lights. Sean stayed silent, keeping his thoughts to himself.

The limousine turned off the Strip and down a large curving drive, before coming to a stop under a large portico. A uniformed bellman rushed forward to open the door and two men in suits, both slender and fit, followed him.

"Welcome back, Ms. Nakamura," said the taller of the two men, dressed in a gray suit with a very expensive tie. "This is your butler, Gianni Caraballo."

Gianni bowed, looking composed and elegant in his formal black suit.

"It's a pleasure to see you again," Beth said politely. "Sean, this is Paul Graziano, our host here. Paul, this is Sean Lindstrom, my guest."

Another round of handshakes followed before the men focused again on Beth, leaving Sean isolated on the periphery.

The two men kept up a steady stream of chatter as they led Beth and Sean to a private elevator, which deposited the party in an elegant foyer with only a few doors visible. The entire group moved out of the foyer and down a long corridor leading to a single door. Graziano opened the door and ushered Beth and Sean in.

Beth looked around at the suite. It was huge and incredibly opulent, with gold brocade and marble. Another hotel's lights gleamed outside the windows, with the desert sands and a mountain range shining beyond. Beth noticed that Sean had frozen beside her, when he saw the room, but she said nothing to him.

Gianni Caraballo, the butler, gave them a brief tour of the suite, emphasizing the amenities in its living room, master bedroom and bathroom. He assured Beth that the suitcases had been unpacked and everything was exactly as she had ordered.

Beth nodded and agreed that everything looked perfect, then showed the hotel's representatives to the door. She closed the door behind them and locked it, grateful for the silence. She stayed still for a moment, trying to gather herself before dominating Sean again.

"Strip," snarled a deep voice from directly behind her.

Beth choked and tried to turn.

A man's body immediately pressed her into the door and a single huge hand caught her wrists high above her head. She shook her head and he leaned into her harder until she couldn't move. After a few minutes, he shifted and quickly turned her to face him, still gripping her hands. His leg shoved between hers, opening her wide for him while pinning her to the door.

Beth stared at him, startled and a bit frightened by his change in behavior. Sean was an imposing figure, almost barbaric in his rough-edged simplicity against the intense adornment around him. He looked like a Viking taking stock of a palace and its ladies before ransacking it. A jolt of lust ran through Beth as she saw her fantasy come to life.

"No…" she managed to get out, as the fantasy demanded.

"Oh yes, foreign witch," he rumbled. Then he caught the front of her blouse and ripped it open. He shoved her shirt and jacket down her back so they trapped her hands behind her. Beth quivered as his fingers squeezed and stroked her breasts, then ran lower. He grabbed her hips and pulled her higher on his thigh. Her head fell back helplessly, offering herself to him.

Sean took advantage of the invitation and bent his head. Beth trembled when he nipped her.

He lifted his head and looked at her, his mouth curved in a cruel smile.

She stared back at him, seeing the hard line of his mouth marked by a single drop of crimson.

Very deliberately his tongue slid out and tasted her blood.

She swallowed convulsively.

"Please," she moaned.

His eyes flashed and he let her slide down his leg until she rested against the door. Beth watched him, caught by his leashed violence.

He bent and tore open her trousers. Another grab pulled them down to her ankles. Then he picked her up over his shoulder and started to walk. Beth struggled to get free, frightened and excited by his deliberate violence.

He dumped her on the big bed and she gulped for breath, her face pressed into the heavy brocade coverlet. She froze as a finger traced her spine lightly.

"Foreign witch, do you want to be a barbarian's plaything?" he growled. He pulled the clothing away from her wrists and the finger continued down, ending between her legs. She shuddered as it explored her slowly before another finger came to bathe in her cream. Then both fingers found their way inside her and she rocked against the pressure.

A moment's pause, then he pushed more strongly. How many fingers would her body welcome? She groaned again at her body's answer: four.

"Please, master," she choked as his hand shoved at her. Her muscles flexed and yielded to his demands.

Suddenly he ripped off her trousers, overcoming the slight resistance of her shoes by a stronger yank.

Beth heard a zipper's metallic snarl before his weight came down on her. She gasped, crushed between the harsh brocade coverlet rasping against her breasts and his fur-shrouded muscles. She tossed her head, gripping the coverlet, as she writhed under him.

"Do you want it, little witch? Do you want this big cock of mine?" Her hair rippled under his breath.

"Please, just take me!"

Sean's weight shifted and she shuddered as his teeth sank into the nape of her neck. He held her like that for a long minute, a tigress pinned for mating. Then he slammed into her to begin a long, hard ride.

She climaxed almost immediately but he ignored her stifled cry. He continued to pump her, pulling almost all the way out, then pounding his great length into her with all the force of his iron-hard body. He grunted rhythmically as he worked her cunt, angling his thrusts until he found exactly the right spot inside her.

Beth gasped and bucked against him, fighting for more.

"Fuck, fuck, fuck..." His words beat in her blood like the force of his cock savaging her womb. They drove thought out of her, to be replaced by animal need. She gripped and squeezed at him, striving to keep him inside her.

He bit her shoulder hard and she screamed, the sharp pain triggering ecstasy throughout her body. She shattered around him, every bone and muscle convulsing in an orgasm such as she'd never known before.

She heard him shout her name as he too found his release. Then she collapsed into unconsciousness under him.

Beth woke to see the sun peeping in past the curtains. She stretched slowly, feeling the answering soreness. Sean's body was like a furnace against hers, a welcome source of nighttime heat for a Viking's woman. His torso showed touches of red where she'd bitten and clawed him in passion. She purred at the memory of his response to those love marks.

His cock was warm against her, where it lay nestled between them. She petted it idly, comparing how cuddly it looked now to how ferocious it had stood the night before. Memories flowed stronger and she bent her head over him, laving it with her tongue before sucking gently. Its quick rise to greet her surprised her, given how hard and how often he had used it. She began to caress it more intensely, as she remembered her plans for the coming night.

Beth squeaked when Sean suddenly pulled her up. A quick roll trapped her under him and he gripped her wrists in one big hand. The other found a fresh condom in the litter on the nightstand.

"Witch," he muttered as he ripped the condom package open with his teeth.

Beth sighed happily and twined a leg around him.

Chapter Eight

Las Vegas
Saturday, 5 PM

Sean woke up when Beth touched his shoulder. She kissed him lightly on the mouth then moved away slightly.

"Time to get up, sleepy head. Your bath is ready."

Sean was surprised to hear of a bath. He'd hoped for a shower together but he quite possibly couldn't have taken full advantage of it, especially since his cock was rather sore at the moment. Beth undoubtedly had the experience to know when a man needed to soak his aches. But then, she also had an excellent eye for fun. Even breakfast had turned into a sexual delight with her.

He sat up and stretched before wandering into the bathroom. This weekend was turning out to be a bigger adventure than he'd hoped.

The bathroom was dimly lit by a single light over the tub itself and a few candles clustered at the tub's corners. Sean sniffed, trying to decide what smelled so good. It didn't smell like any of the few scented candles he'd smelled before or anything at the spa.

Shrugging, he turned the jets on and got into the bath. It was very warm and slightly oily, lightly scented to match the candles. His muscles began to relax and he slid down into the Jacuzzi, which was big enough to soak his entire body.

He was drowsy again within minutes, wondering what Mike was doing now before pulling his thoughts away. Mike would be fine. He had to start building a life without his son around all the time.

The water rolled against him and he opened his eyes to see Beth getting into the tub. Sean's eyes widened but he quickly shifted to make room for her.

"Just get comfortable, Sean. I'm going to wash you."

Sean nodded. A woman hadn't bathed him since he was a child.

"What are the candles scented with?" he asked, trying to find a distraction.

"Sandalwood, frankincense, bergamot. It's a blend of relaxants and aphrodisiacs I ordered just for us."

Sean's brain stopped working at the mention of aphrodisiacs. Beth's mouth twitched at the look on his face.

"Take it easy, darling. These are relaxants too. "

Sean nodded slowly and closed his eyes again.

Beth lathered a sponge and kneeled beside his hip. She circled his shoulder slowly, watching how the soap clung to his skin. Then she lifted his hand and cleaned his entire arm in a spiral movement flowing down from his shoulder to the tips of his fingers. She carefully separated his fingers and made sure that every inch was quite clean.

"Why are you washing me like this?"

Beth paused, still holding the tip of his thumb.

"What's the matter? Don't you like it?"

"Well, yes. But it's not like a regular bath." Sean's hand twisted under hers. She tightened her grip and he went still.

"Why should it be? I'm enjoying it," she answered calmly. Her eyes softened. "Just go with the flow and I promise that everything will work out."

"Okay then," Sean agreed, still puzzled but not inclined to argue more.

Then she rinsed out the sponge, applied more soap and cleaned first one leg then the other. Sean could only shudder when she attended to the crease between his torso and thigh. He looked away from her breasts, so enticingly close, and caught sight of her beautiful back in the mirrors, flexing as she worked over him.

She attended to his other arm before washing his face and chest. Sean felt the slow drag of the sponge through the thick hair and his nipples' rise to follow the motion. The sponge moved further down to where his cock reared in welcome.

He was slightly disappointed but said nothing when she simply washed it carefully, repeatedly soaping, rubbing and rinsing until every fold and wrinkle, every hard line, glowed clean and sweet. He tried some breathing exercises to control himself until he could lie acquiescent under her hand. He didn't dare look at her reflection.

"Roll over, darling. That's right; you have to kneel so I can wash your backside."

Sean closed his eyes and obeyed, praying that he wouldn't disgrace himself.

She started at the nape of his neck and worked down, attending to all the places that had been hidden before. The sponge felt rougher now or perhaps he was more aware of its feel.

He bucked, and then steadied himself when her sponge first traveled from his spine between his buttocks. She kept it there for a minute, letting him absorb the feelings of slickness and teasing roughness. Then she spread his buttocks with one hand and studied him.

His breath sighed out at her intent look. He nearly climaxed when her tongue tasted her lips. Then she cleaned him there too, welcoming every hidden inch with the same steady caresses that she'd used on his cock.

Beth wrung out the sponge and dropped it aside. Then she pulled out the small shower attachment and turned it on, testing its temperature. She met his eyes in the mirror with a smile.

"Time for some cooler temperatures, I think, darling."

Sean could only shrug in agreement.

She rinsed him easily, keeping the water barely warm enough to maintain his mood while still slowing him down. Then she stepped out and held a big bath towel for him to step into.

Before he had time to even pat himself dry, Beth had headed back into the bedroom. She beckoned him to follow and he went.

The bedroom was now dim as well, lit only by a few of the same scented candles. A single stick of incense sent lazy tendrils into the air. A futon was spread out on the floor to make a low flat bed, with cushions, sheets and towels scattered around. Small bunches of fresh flowers gleamed from vases around the room while a piano's voice ran through the room like a mountain stream. The room was warmer than before so that he felt hot in the towel.

"Lie down on the mat, Sean, on your back. I'm going to give you a massage."

Sean laid down immediately, a little surprised and confused but definitely hopeful. Maybe now she'd bring him off with her hand.

Beth kneeled next to him and removed the towel around his waist. His hand went to catch it but stopped. Naked was good; naked could be very useful for frolicking.

She placed cushions under his neck and knees. He relaxed, feeling secure and comfortable as he waited for her first move.

"Straighten your legs and relax your back. Very good."

Beth knelt behind his head and began to gently pluck the skin away from his face.

Sean closed his eyes, trying to understand what she intended. This felt like how his gym's masseuse worked out muscle tension. Not like the start of bedplay.

She worked down the front of his body to his hips and then sat back.

"Now roll over slowly and lie face down."

Beth readjusted the pillows and then sat next to Sean's hips quietly. He turned his head to watch her, still surprised by her ease with her own nudity. She looked like the goddess' handmaiden in an Eastern temple.

Beth poured some oil into her hand from a small jar and rubbed it into her hands slowly. Then she rested one hand between Sean's shoulder blades. It felt warm, like the heat from a baker's oven. Then she slowly began to rub his back.

She wasn't trying to excite him or release tension now. It felt as if she was just exploring the muscles in his body. He twitched, then rearranged his legs.

"Beth, please, can't you move a little faster?"

"No, darling. I'll move to the tempo I want."

She rubbed his back a little more. He couldn't imagine what she intended. He squirmed under her hands, trying to find a position that felt productive.

"Beth, what the hell are you doing? I can't lie here like this while you just, just play with me."

"What's the matter, Sean? Can't you let me have control?" Her voice was quiet and reasonable.

"It's not that! It's just that...well, how about letting me do something?"

"Isn't control the problem? I enjoy touching you." Her hands stopped. She looked down at him, her face very serious. "We agreed that you'd do anything I want this weekend. So what is your objection?"

He came up to his knees in a fury, staring at her. She looked straight back at him, entirely unruffled.

"What are you trying to do here? It'd be great if you were getting off, but you're not. And I'm not getting off either!"

"I told you my reasons: I am having a good time. That is all you need to know, in order to obey me." His dangerous lady looked straight back at him, as implacable as a samurai sword.

He glared, his fingers digging into the futon.

She raised the stakes. "Are you saying no, here at the first step on the road that I have asked you to follow? If you are saying no, then leave now. Forever. I have no need of your company on this road."

"I can't do this!" he roared. "There's no point!" He started to sit back on his haunches.

"I thought rangers never quit." Her voice was as soft as a sword leaving its scabbard.

He froze. How many times before had he heard that? How many times had he sworn he wouldn't give up, no matter what it took? But this was different, harder than ever before. This time he had to yield, lie passive, not take action. Not even know where matters were leading.

"Do you know how damn hard this is for me?" he asked in a much quieter voice.

"I know that I'm asking you to give up all influence, all control, even your knowledge of the outcome. You will do this because fulfilling my wishes, no matter what they are, is your reward." She waited for more objections. When he stayed silent, she went on. "So, will you do what I want or will you quit here and now?"

"I don't know if I can do this." His voice was very quiet in the dim room.

"Trust me, darling." Her voice softened but stayed resolute. "Just trust me."

Sean closed his eyes, shaking. He took a very deep breath before he lay back down on the futon. He relaxed cautiously, one reluctant muscle at a time. It was a long fight to calm his angry, whirling mind, which insisted on demanding why he couldn't do more.

He shivered once, when a draft touched his cooling body. Beth draped a towel over him and he steadily warmed up again, reminded of how she cared for his comfort.

"Concentrate on your breathing, darling," she whispered. She stroked him lightly, her fingers barely touching him, until he lay docile under her touch.

Then she began the massage again.

This time, he focused on her hands as they moved smoothly over him. The pattern was different than anything he'd experienced before, whether from a masseuse or a lover. Gradually, he realized that she was awakening his body, building a current that passed from her hands through his skin before diving into his bones. It was a dance of energy between them, which gave everything and asked nothing except enjoyment of the moment.

He forgot his confusion as he was drawn steadily into a world of sensuality. His breathing deepened as time ceased to exist.

She worked his spine thoroughly, pressing and stroking, sometimes just keeping her hand still. Sean began to feel both incredibly happy and relaxed at the same time. Strength flowed through him and he became more aroused. He heard himself purring like a cat.

Beth started to pound lightly on his spine, emphasizing various points as she worked. Heat built up and desire started to intensify. Then she stroked the length of his back, rocking Sean towards and then away from her. He shuddered when she reached the base of his spine.

"Relax, Sean. The massage is a gift for your sexual pleasure. All you have to do is enjoy."

He began to moan as his excitement built but he stayed receptive to her movements, as she taught him the sexual potential of his entire body. He had always focused primarily on his cock, sometimes on his nipples and anus. He had never imagined that there could be so much sensation found elsewhere.

Her hands circled his back several times before coming to rest at the top of his thighs. Then she rubbed his legs and buttocks until Sean's hips rocked.

Her hands left him briefly and he heard a packet rip. He opened heavy eyes and saw her pulling on a glove slowly, smoothing it down past her wrist with a slow, elegant sensuality.

"Gloves?" he whispered. She turned back to him and he shifted towards her hopefully. She chuckled softly.

"Take it easy, darling. I think you'll like this."

Her hands repeated their work on his legs, moving up to his buttocks until his hips repeated their earlier pleas. He needed more and this time she gave him the additional stimulus he craved. Her gloved finger circled his asshole, in an erotic dance that echoed through his body.

His hips swayed eagerly, intent on gaining more attention to this most neglected of erogenous areas. Would his lady accept him here too? His body shuddered in welcome and her finger slipped inside.

Taken at last by his dangerous lady.

He thought she groaned something but hearing was the least important sense at that moment. His previous experiences with his fingers or stolid sex toys were no match for this reality. Every fiber was concentrated on her single finger, so warm and supple, slender and elegant as she teased him. By the time her finger left, his hips were slamming against the floor and he could have screamed with lust.

Her strokes changed to a harsher movement, which pushed away sensuality. Her hands lifted briefly and the glove snapped as it came off, triggering a hot flash of disappointment.

Sean took a calmer breath as his arousal eased slightly. If this was the first step on the road, would he survive the rest?

"Roll over, Sean."

He obeyed, as if in a trance.

Beth placed her hand gently on his chest and simply kept it there for a long moment. Sean yielded to his trust in her and closed his eyes.

Beth showed the same skill and loving care on the front of his body that she had given his back. Chest, arms, legs, groin were all massaged. She dragged her hand over his body, towards his cock but never quite touching it, slowly marking all the points of the compass on his straining body. He couldn't have spoken, as his life force centered in his cock.

Then her hands worked over his cock, using strokes that built the energy and trapped it, repeating the pattern until he thrashed below her. She pressed hard between his legs and the surge stopped. He dragged oxygen into his lungs, trying to prepare for whatever came next.

Then she began again on his cock. This time, her hands demanded that he climax. He erupted like a geyser, slamming his hips up between her hands, screaming her name.

He recovered his senses to find her smoothing his face in a light massage. Then a large warm towel floated down over Sean and he mumbled his thanks before falling asleep in her arms.

"Wake up, Sean. It's time for dinner."

Beth lightly ran her fingers through Sean's hair as he blinked up at her. His eyes traveled downwards and he stared in shock at her attire. She was wearing a short black velvet dress that emphasized every line of her delicious body. The cloth wrapped around her neck and left her shoulders and back bare. He was acutely aware of her breasts moving behind the single layer of fabric.

Beth chuckled slightly and stood up.

"Your clothes are laid out on the bed. I'll wait for you in the living room."

Sean dressed very slowly. The first item was a black silk thong, soft as a lady's undergarments. He held it in the air studying it. He had heard of these but had never thought to wear one. He sniffed it suspiciously, finding the same scent as the candles and massage oil. He put on the thong, fussing and twitching until everything was in place, or at least as much in place as possible given the size of what the thong was supposed to contain.

He looked in the mirror at himself and blushed at its emphasis on his sexuality. He almost looked like one of those male strippers, except that none of them were as big and hairy as he was. Then he slowly reached for the other items.

Sean scrutinized himself in the mirror for a long minute. The single-breasted black suit, with its Italian label, was cut from the finest wool he'd ever seen. The matching vest framed the white shirt and the narrow line of black silk tie. Even the shoes fit perfectly in their glove soft leather. Money whispered from the beautiful cut and fabric, as well as the monogrammed gold cuff links and the gold watch on his wrist.

He tugged at the tie, very aware of the unfamiliar constriction. He felt as if he'd been tied up; silly thought, considering that this was less restrictive than his uniform had been. He was flying in some pretty high circles with his dangerous lady.

All of his embarrassment was wiped away by the look on Beth's face when she saw him.

"You look wonderful, Sean. Even sexier than I'd hoped." She leaned up and kissed him on the cheek. "Let's go have some dinner."

Sean offered her his arm and led her out, caressing her hand as it rested in the crook of his elbow. They strolled slowly through the casino, looking at the gamblers' restless attentions to the garish slot machines. A few people were playing blackjack and roulette.

"Crowds look pretty good tonight. I guess tourism seems to be coming back," Beth remarked.

"If you say so, honey. I've never been here before." Sean was much more interested in the slow rub of Beth's dress against him through his fine clothes.

The restaurant was small and exclusive, looking more like a private house than a large hotel. Oil paintings lined the walls, gleaming against silk wallpaper.

A waiter approached and asked for their drink order. Sean looked at Beth, waiting for her response. Was this behavior what she wanted?

She asked for the wine list and the waiter departed. He returned with another gentleman, who was introduced as the sommelier. The sommelier and Beth engaged in a lengthy conversation over the merits of various wines. The gentleman left, clutching the wine list and looking very pleased with Beth's decisions.

Sean sipped the chosen wine slowly, savoring the taste. He'd tried wine in Germany but only rarely. This was both light and complex at the same time, satisfying in its own right even while it hinted at complimenting foods.

"I thought you didn't like drinking, Beth," he remarked, glancing at her.

She raised an eyebrow at him and then smiled.

"I believe in moderation, Sean. It's best to be aware of what our bodies feel, not the chemicals in our blood. But one drink tonight, especially of wine, should just set the mood." Her eyes caressed his body for a moment and he blushed. She smiled and patted his hand on the table.

"Relax, Sean. Dinner and a little gambling should be fun."

He nodded and smiled back at her. Beth began to talk to him about his son, drawing out stories of Mike. Sean lost himself in recounting adventures and successes, paying little attention to the excellent food that Beth selected.

Beth told a few stories of her own childhood, lingering on her nieces and nephews' escapades. He laughed out loud over a tale of her nephew's misadventures at a Japanese kindergarten and answered with a story of his own time at West Point.

Finally Beth ran her fingers over his hand gently.

"Do you know how to shoot craps?" she asked. He nodded.

"Then let's go. You can show me how it's done." She rose to leave. The waiter bid them farewell, including a wish that they would look him up when they came back. Sean suspected that Beth had left a tip large enough to attract attention, even in this jaded town.

The casino was more crowded this time as they walked slowly through it, dodging other gamblers along the way. Beth attracted many envious stares as they went and Sean swelled with pride and possession. She led the way to a craps table in the middle of the high-stakes area.

Sean's eyes swept the room, managing not to stare at the intimate surroundings and exquisite décor. He stood for a few minutes, watching the action at the table. Matters were fairly quiet, as the players spent more time joking with the dealer than rolling the dice.

"Have you ever played craps before, Beth?"

"Once with my brother Jason, years ago. Neither of us knew what we were doing." She glanced over her shoulder and nodded to Paul Graziano, who'd come up beside her. His blue suit was just as immaculate as last night's gray. "Hello, Paul."

"Your usual stake, Ms. Nakamura. Is that enough?"

"Yes, that'll do for a start." She passed the chips over to Sean and signed the receipt quickly. He looked the chips over casually, then froze when he read the denomination. A thousand dollars per chip? He started to hand them back when she straightened up, but she refused them.

"Use these to start with, Sean."

"Yes, ma'am," he responded, recognizing an order however soft-spoken. He could follow her commands in this. He might not know how to read a fancy menu but he'd played craps more than once. He sent up a quick prayer that Lady Luck ride his shoulder tonight, as long as his dangerous lady was on his arm.

He began to bet on the action as Beth moved close to him. His pile of chips grew quickly and he took over the dice when the current shooter bowed out of the game.

Beth slid closer to him, near enough that he could smell her exotic perfume even in the crowd. He began to sweat but kept rolling the dice and winning, even while acutely aware of Beth's warmth and her bare back. He wrapped his arm around her, pulling her even closer, and grinned down at her.

"You're bringing me luck, lady!" Sean exulted and she laughed with him, her eyes dancing with excitement. A tremor slid through him, echoing her obvious delight in his actions.

The crowd kept building around them and Beth's dress rubbed against him, her body plastered to his. Sean managed to pay enough attention to the game that his bets made sense to the dealer, even while his head spun with her nearness. Her hand rested in the small of his back, lightly caressing him while she cheered him on.

Other people shouted and laughed around them, cheering and cursing the dice. Sean was only conscious of her and the dice as they rattled across the table.

Finally the pile of chips was a mountain in front of her and his cock was threatening to come out of that silk thong. Sean leaned down to Beth and kissed her on the cheek.

"Let's go, lady. It's time to play another game," he pleaded.

She kissed his mouth hard and fast, then drew back smiling.

"Okay, Sean, let's find something else," she agreed.

He gathered up the chips and they moved away from the table, leaving a trail of laughter and envious comments behind.

Sean offered the chips to Beth but she shook her head, rejecting them. She scanned the room quickly and Paul Graziano appeared next to her.

"You might enjoy the far table, Ms. Nakamura. The Chinese gentleman there is an excellent baccarat player," he suggested quietly.

"Thank you, Paul." Beth slid into the only available chair at that table and Sean took up position behind her. Paul Graziano produced more chips for her, before disappearing into the crowd.

The play began within moments and Beth focused strictly on the game. Sean watched her, admiring her coolness and command of herself. His arousal ebbed, replaced by pride in her ability to beat the other players at the game. Chips accumulated in front of her, always neatly stacked by her elegant fingers.

Finally there was only the Chinese gentleman playing against her, the table surrounded by a circle of quiet whispers. Sean tried very hard not to see the chips' denominations. The watchers' demeanor was more than enough to convince him that a large sum of money was at stake.

The final hand was dealt and the Chinese gentleman bowed in defeat. Beth bowed deeply in return. Both players rose from the table and Beth turned to Sean.

"Did you enjoy watching, Sean?"

"Yes, ma'am. It looked a bit like James Bond at the end though." Beth smiled at his reference to the most famous baccarat player on film and kissed his cheek.

"Let's go then," she smiled. "Paul, will you cash our chips in please?"

Paul took the proffered chips with a murmur of congratulations, which Beth acknowledged. She took Sean's arm and wandered towards the main casino area, glancing at other gamblers as she went. Sean resolved not to learn how much money had been at stake.

Paul caught up with them as they idly watched a roulette game and discreetly passed a stack of bills to Beth, which she promptly buried in her purse. Another stack went quietly to Sean. He glanced at Beth and she nodded her approval. He slid the bills into his pocket, resolving to give them to her later. A cordial goodbye followed and they strolled once again through the casino.

Beth stopped at the elevators and turned to face Sean.

"Sean, I need a copy of the Financial Times, an English newspaper. Bring it up to the suite in thirty minutes, won't you?" It was an order, not a request, although her voice was very unruffled.

"I'll bring it to you in thirty minutes, ma'am," Sean answered, wondering where he would find an English newspaper on a Saturday night.

Beth patted his cheek. "Empty yourself before returning, Sean. Can't have any distractions," she murmured and entered an open elevator.

Sean stared at the closing doors and swallowed hard. Then he started hunting for the newspaper.

Sean got off the elevator twenty-seven minutes after leaving Beth, newspaper in hand. He walked down the hallway and checked his watch, catching a whiff of that scent from his cuff. Adam's bracelet rubbed his arm under the fine cotton. For a moment, he saw Adam's eyes as they had been on that last night. " *Do it for both of us!*"

He snapped off a salute in response, promising silently, "*For both of us.*"

He knocked briefly on the door, precisely thirty minutes after leaving her. and went in at her assent. He stopped dead in his tracks when he saw what awaited him.

The suite was now lit entirely by candles, with curtains drawn against the neon lights beyond. A blaze of light came from a room on the far side, past a door that had always been closed before. Exotic music spilled out, evoking ancient passions with drums and a woman's voice. Indian music, perhaps. The aphrodisiacs' now familiar scent caressed him.

Beth watched him from the distant room, surrounded by light. Scarlet silk caressed her body like a lover, leaving one shoulder bare and showing a gleam of ivory leg. Her hair was twisted at the back of her head and secured by gold combs. More gold hung from her neck and wrists, delicate chains with hanging jade charms.

Sean's breath caught in his throat with a rasp.

"I am a priestess of the goddess Ishtar," Beth announced calmly. "I embody the goddess on earth at this moment. You are a warrior who has done well in the past. Now you must leave the mundane world behind, with its petty quarrels and dangers. Here you will be tested for your suitability to celebrate life with the goddess."

Sean nodded, overwhelmed by the appearance of his fantasy. The Twentieth Century disappeared and he became entirely a servant of the goddess, trusting the priestess to lead the way to fulfillment. The paper dropped unheeded to the floor.

"You will call me ma'am at all times. I will call you ranger."

"Yes, ma'am."

"Strip to the skin, ranger, and place your clothes neatly on the coffee table."

Sean obeyed promptly and then waited for the next order. All his blood seemed to be flowing to his crotch.

"You may approach me now, ranger."

Sean marched into the far room, careful to maintain a steady pace and keep his eyes in front. Old skills awoke and he observed as much as he could of his surroundings.

It had been a bedroom once but was now an exotic nest. Incense and red and white candles blazed, all casting the odors of musk and exotic flowers into the air together with their light. Red and white roses spilled across the bed and every other surface.

A dagger almost as long as his forearm lay, cradled in blood-red roses, on the table next to her. Candlelight danced along its slender, rippling blade and emphasized the cruel edge. Was it there for appearance? What if she used it to taste his blood?

Heat pooled in his groin at the thought.

"You are a warrior and must have a care for yourself, ranger, that you may serve the goddess again in the future."

Sean concentrated hard. What was she leading up to?

"If anything occurs to sound an alarm, then you must speak immediately, ranger. When you say the word "alarm," then I will stop your test and consider how best to proceed."

Safeword?

"Do you understand me, ranger?"

"Yes, ma'am." He saw no chance of opting out, not with Beth. She was too skilled and considerate for him to worry about harm.

"Listen up, ranger!" she snapped and he came fully alert to meet her admonition. "You have a duty to the goddess to speak if there is any chance of physical or emotional damage. A good warrior always warns of a threat. Stay silent and you will have failed. Do you understand me, ranger?"

"Yes, ma'am," he responded contritely.

"Now tell me how you will sound an alert, ranger."

"Alarm, ma'am."

"Very good." Beth pointed a finger at the floor in front of her. Sean promptly knelt at her feet, bowing his head to the ground, thankful that his years of martial arts training made this movement easy.

"Sit up, ranger, so that you may be attired suitably to serve."

He sat back on his heels but kept his eyes straight ahead, reflecting the attitude learned in the Army.

Beth held up a scarf for him to see and nodded approval, when recognition lit his eyes. It was the scarf that she had worn into the bookstore and that had pleasured them both. She wrapped it around his neck then tied it carefully in front with the knot against his Adam's apple. The soft silk caressed his throat from chin to collarbone, with the golden ends brushing his chest.

Then she tied a red and gold scarf around each of his upper arms. They hung down, stroking his arms while the delicate tips danced against his wrists.

"Now kneel down with your hips up in the air. Keep your knees spread."

Beth walked slowly around Sean and then knelt down behind him. She caressed him slowly, stroking his legs. Her touch traveled to the inside of his thighs. He choked back a gasp at a particularly intense sensation.

"Do not keep the sounds of your pleasure from the goddess, ranger," Beth snapped.

"Yes, ma'am," Sean answered, then sighed when her fingers stroked him again. He knelt in a trance of utter pleasure as her hand explored him, gliding forward to tickle his balls from underneath.

He shivered when a single oily finger prowled down his spine. A long slow pressure followed and he yielded readily to the finger's gentle foray into his insides. It felt even better than it had the first time.

"Tell me if anything hurts, ranger. This should only feel good."

More? Was she going to give him more fingers to twine inside him? He murmured an assent, focused only on the delights her hands were teaching.

He groaned a welcome to the second finger and quickly adapted to its additional pressure.

"Beautifully taken, ranger. You did well," she assured him. He murmured something in response, more concerned with her touch than the words' meaning.

He stretched eagerly for the third finger, savoring the hot agile massage traveling through his core. He rocked peacefully against their slow caresses, savoring the slow pulses that flowed from his prostate into his balls. How many times had he beat off, imagining being possessed by his woman in this way?

A brisk buzz stroked him and he pushed back against the steady vibration, circling near the fingers caressing his insides. Her hand slipped out and the vibrator slid into his anus on the same beat. It nestled against his spine, smaller than many of his collection at home, and its base settled neatly into the cleft of his buttocks. A butt plug, with a vibrator singing inside it.

"Thank you, ma'am," he groaned in welcome as her hand rested reassuringly on his hip.

He felt stuffed with sensuality, as if she'd gifted him with a key that could unlock marvels. This game would be played out with a living woman who wanted him, in the bright light of an open room. Not in the dark behind a locked door.

"Stand up, ranger, and face me."

Sean came to his feet carefully, acutely conscious of the effect his movements had on the throbbing pressure deep inside him. His erection was enormous, reflecting his body's enjoyment of that internal pressure.

He caught sight of the waiting dagger as he moved and hair lifted from his skin. He almost laughed at the familiar rush of adrenalin. This game would be played out in sensuality, in climaxes that racked his body to the bone. Not in blood or injury. This tide meant life, not death, to a warrior.

"Excellent. You look magnificent, ranger." Her low voice was husky and fired his veins like whisky.

Beth began to wrap lengths of black velvet ribbon around him, first around his waist and then between his legs to secure the butt plug. A few loops caught his cock and balls, lifting and separating them for display even while controlling them. A quick knot at the waist followed, leaving the ribbon's ends to float against his groin, every touch a reminder of Beth's control.

His eyelids drooped with pleasure as he gave himself to her handling. A single twist of her fingers left the vibrator silent. Sean mourned the lost stimulus, while he anticipated the slow buildup possible in its absence.

"See yourself in the mirror, ranger," Beth said quietly and stepped aside so he could see.

His body surged in response to the carnal image of himself, packaged and waiting for his woman's pleasure. He caught sight of Beth watching him, the dagger next to her hand and her eyes full of yearning. Something deep inside him snarled in triumph.

Chapter Nine
Sunday, 1 AM

Beth stared at Sean, hungering to taste him. He looked magnificent, a pagan in silks that only emphasized his masculinity. The narrow lines of ribbon called attention to his engorged cock, standing up proudly against his white groin.

She took a deep breath and savored the flow of energy that this scene was releasing, beginning when her first words had caught Sean into his fantasy's embodiment. He'd yielded himself readily to the plug's penetration, symbolizing her dominance while pleasuring him. Now he was dressed, with his cock standing at attention and a vibrator waiting inside him. Her terror at playing the scene well dissolved, leaving her free to concentrate on the rich chemistry between them.

She regally seated herself again in the big armchair. "You may give me a footbath now, ranger. You will find everything necessary through that door."

She nodded her head towards the bathroom and waited.

Sean's first steps were hesitant, clearly responding to the dildo shifting inside him. He soon found a steady pace and disappeared into the other room.

He returned with a laden silver tray, which held two basins and several small jars, and several towels neatly draped over his arm. He knelt silently in front of her, setting the tray next to him, and took her shoes off.

She sighed happily when he eased her feet carefully into the hot water.

He bathed each foot and then slowly rubbed it with the oil provided, which was similar to that used for his massage. His inexperience showed but so did his absolute absorption in the task. He carefully polished every inch to work out any aches, then attended to her ankles. His cock hardened further while he labored.

Beth leaned back in the chair, letting her eyes drift shut. She spoke when he hesitated at her knees.

"Work up my legs, then attend to my womanhood. Use your hands and mouth, ranger." The order sounded like the soft growl of a tigress in a temple courtyard.

Sean's eyes widened for a moment before he bowed his head in acknowledgment. "Yes, ma'am," he rumbled.

He kissed her feet, following the trail he had laid down in oil earlier. Then he moved up her legs with his hands first, closely followed by his mouth.

Beth closed her eyes in rapture. Tense muscles relaxed under the insistent caresses of his mouth and fell deeper into bliss with the soft brush of his hair between her thighs. Her legs fell open, inviting him closer. Her hips moved forward on the chair, seeking contact with his mouth.

She hummed when she smelled her own arousal. He answered with a delighted murmur, as his tongue first tasted her secrets. No need of a barrier now, given that they were both clean. No need of a barrier later to prevent pregnancy, after taking a birth control pill.

His attentions were slow and insistent as he pleasured her, taking her to many climaxes. Beth's hands moved in his hair, enjoying its feel against her skin, even while her clitoris shivered and danced under his teeth and tongue. But a corner of her mind kept touch with reality while her body melted for him.

Finally she pulled his hair abruptly.

"You have acknowledged the goddess well, ranger. Now you must be tested before true service can begin."

Sean bowed to the floor, then stayed kneeling on the floor with his head bent.

"Sit up, ranger, and look at me." Beth studied him, seeing the slow swirl of desire in his blue eyes. She took an item from a box next to her and held it out towards him.

"Do you know what this is, ranger?"

Sean stared at the small piece of metal with its narrow curves glittering in the light. Somewhere a drum pounded and tambourines danced. Recognition burned but he shook his head slowly. "Please explain to me, ma'am."

"It's a nipple clamp. It will test you with pain, ranger, even while it adorns your beauty."

Sean looked at the small object for another moment and then bent his head. A drop of sweat trickled down the center of his chest from under the scarf. Another drop echoed it from the tip of his cock.

Beth leaned forward and stroked his chest slowly, centering his blood and attentions where she wished. She put the clamp on carefully, watching his face.

Sean closed as his eyes but remained silent when the pain hit him. His breathing steadied after a moment and Beth took her hands away.

The other clamp went on with equal ease. Sean groaned softly and his breathing stayed slow.

Beth relaxed, knowing that he could tolerate the small pain. His cock gleamed as a thin trail of moisture slid down it.

"Close your eyes."

Sean complied immediately and she blindfolded him with a black silk scarf. He turned his head from side to side then stayed still. His mouth worked slowly, then relaxed as he accepted the loss of sight.

Beth stood up and took his hand.

"Come with me, ranger. Now lie down on the bed." The scent of roses strengthened when he sat down on the bed, crushing the delicate petals under his body.

"Put your hands over your head and spread them wide. Place your fingertips against the headboard, ranger."

Beth guided his hands into position, making sure that each finger touched the bed. Muscles and tendons stood out in sharp relief as his arms stretched and twisted to achieve the desired position.

"Very good, ranger. Now bend your knees and place your feet flat on the bed. Keep your legs spread wide. Lift your hips." She slid a pillow under him so that the soft skin between his legs was completely exposed. "Excellent."

Beth stepped back and studied him. His body lay like a banquet in front of her, with its most sensitive areas fully exposed for her handling. The tension necessary to maintain this position emphasized his muscles and made him look even more masculine.

"Now hear the rules of your test, ranger."

Sean's head turned towards her voice and his breathing seemed to stop.

"I am going to tease you with three fabrics. You must keep your fingertips and feet pressed firmly against the bed at all times, ranger. You will receive ten blows for every time your fingertips or feet fail to touch the bed. The goddess wishes you to move the rest of your body often. Do you understand?"

"Yes, ma'am." Sean's voice was very steady.

Beth looked him over again and then reached for the first fabric.

A long strip of silk velvet glided over Sean's face before gliding down to caress his shoulders. It traveled slowly across him, taking special delight in seeking out hidden places.

"One," came the count when it slipped under his arm and he shuddered as it found his pulse there.

The velvet embraced his nipples and danced with his navel. It sank against his ankles before sliding underneath his thighs. It melted against the ribbons where they bound his balls. He choked and shivered.

"Two."

It flirted with the plug's base. He trembled.

"Ma'am, please, oh Christ!"

"Three."

"Oh fuck!" he swore, hips jerking wildly.

"Four," as another tremor rocked his body. He grunted and bit his lip until blood dripped, as he mastered himself.

Finally the velvet moved away from him.

Beth explored Sean slowly with the Venice lace. It was soft, textured and seemed particularly good at lifting hairs away from his body.

He twitched when it dropped on his cock like a delicate hammer blow. "Shit," he hissed.

"Five."

Finally she dragged metallic tulle across him. It looked like a fine golden net, every wire standing in clear contrast to his white skin. It scratched him lightly, a harsher sensation that he obviously welcomed in his growing excitement. His cock stood stronger and his breathing deepened when she rubbed his nipples, his shoulders twisting to follow her hand.

"Six."

She slapped his cock lightly with the tulle and he bucked hard.

"Seven."

His hips writhed as they followed the tulle's path. The scent of his musk came clearly over incense. He kept his fingertips and feet in the required position despite the tulle's teasing. She finally lifted the bright web from his sweating skin, recognizing that he'd signaled how many strokes he wanted from the spanking.

"At ease, ranger."

Sean collapsed onto the bed and groaned softly. Beth gently stroked his arms and legs, easing circulation's return.

Then she snatched off one clamp, giving her warrior a faster release than normal. He yelped at the agony as blood rushed into his nipple. She bent her head and licked it carefully, covering the pain with pleasure.

Sean groaned and tossed his head from side to side. "Ma'am, please, oh ma'am, more please," he begged. The tulle had verified his checklist's claim: he liked strong sensation.

Beth removed the remaining clamp with equal speed and suckled him, binding the clamp's harshness to the wet heat of her mouth. He moaned happily and arched his back, shamelessly seeking more.

She lingered over his chest for long minutes, adorning the strong muscular curves with soft laving caresses before sucking and nipping his nipples. They shone brilliantly red against his golden pelt when she lifted her head. He was truly beautiful, flushed with heat in such delightful areas, as he quivered against the golden silk.

Her hand covered his face for a moment, warning him of the changed focus, before she pulled the blindfold over his head.

Sean squeezed his eyes shut and opened them slowly. He shuddered slightly and ran his tongue slowly over his lips, then straightened to his full length.

Beth seated herself in the armchair again, very pleased with her warrior. He could have wriggled less often if he wanted fewer blows. "Fetch me the gloves from the table, ranger."

Sean found a pair of fingerless, black leather gloves where she indicated. He bowed in front of her and lifted the gloves to her, spread across his hands. Beth accepted the gloves and pulled each one on slowly.

Sean watched her, spellbound and speechless. An occasional fine spasm ran through his body.

"Turn around, ranger, so you may be bound for your ordeal."

Sean spun in a single clean movement that screamed eagerness and Beth purred softly.

"Right hand first, ranger. Now the left." She efficiently wrapped black velvet ribbon around his wrists just above his wrist bone, so that each hand rested against the opposing forearm. He would be able to stay bound like this for a long time.

"Well done, ranger," she praised his acquiescence and he bowed his head in acknowledgment. "Now kneel down and bend over the bed, ranger, to receive your punishment."

Sean dropped to his knees smoothly and bent over as directed, quivering when her leather-clad hands caught and steadied him.

"You will keep your legs together at all times, ranger. It's the best way to protect your balls."

He flinched briefly. "Yes, ma'am."

"How do you give the warning, ranger?"

"I sound out the word, alarm, ma'am."

"Good lad." Her voice was a bit abstracted. She slipped a pillow under his chest for his comfort and stood back to consider his position. Long tremors flowed across him as he waited for her next move.

"May I speak, ma'am?"

"You have not been commanded to silence, ranger," Beth corrected him, dragging a fingernail down his spine in emphasis. He choked back a gasp and took a minute before talking again, turning his head against the golden silk to watch her.

"I would like to ask that you only count the good strokes, ma'am."

Beth's eyebrow lifted, considering his request. He wanted all seventy strokes to be heavy sensation? His eyes burned bright blue as he stared at her, silently begging.

"You have done well so far, ranger, and the goddess is pleased with you. You may have this boon."

"Thank you, ma'am!"

Beth trailed her fingers over one shoulder and down his arm to his palm, enjoying the shudder that flowed through him in response. She acquainted herself with his other arm in the same way, reminding him of the pleasure that her hands could bring. She visited his shoulders and spine, then his thighs, until he sighed and twisted under her touch.

Once she had returned him to sexual expectations, she dealt the first blow so it fell light as a raindrop. He hummed softly and waited patiently.

Beth smiled wryly. He would learn soon enough, especially when the plug started rocking between his tailbone and prostate and sent each swat dancing into his groin. How much of a sensual spanking would he enjoy? Would he be still be so willing when the seventieth blow fell?

She built the blows up slowly, always watching for his reaction to each increase in intensity. She stroked him where the blows landed, massaging the sensation into a broader area of skin as she kept him eager.

His arousal built as his skin heated and his hips began to twist and writhe. She dealt different types of swats, usually with the flat of her hand but sometimes only with her fingertips. She laid the blows evenly across his buttocks but emphasized the sweet spot above his thighs, where each contact sent a wave of pleasure through his pelvis and up his spine. She dealt a few swats to his shoulders, sending blood there to prepare him for the future.

She sharpened the tempo, pushing him to a higher level, and his arousal followed her lead. He moaned and wriggled under her hand, his ass clenching as the red heat built under his skin.

She smacked the plug lightly and he quivered in response before he begged her for more, pushing his hips up to meet her hand.

Her hand burned, matching his skin. The leather spread the blaze to every pore it touched, whether or not they'd felt his ass. She ran her hands down his back, driven to bring his heat into herself. He growled softly and arched against her palms, welcoming every touch. He was well started and now it was time to aim for more.

Beth found a soft deerskin flogger among her toys and came back to him. She laid the flogger against his back and slowly rubbed the soft leather tails against him, letting him feel the flogger first as part of her.

"Please, ma'am. Flog me, please," he sighed, his eyes drooping shut.

She dragged the tails over him until he hummed and twisted to follow the caress. Then she tapped him lightly, teaching him how a soft thud felt. He moaned happily and wriggled under the different sensation. She landed a stronger blow and he stayed with her easily as she built the intensity. It was the smoothest dance she'd ever had with a submissive.

After landing a few blows with real force, she ran an ice cube over his skin. He yelped in surprise but soon started purring as the ice eased the pain. She trailed ice over all of his shoulders and buttocks, letting him enjoy the contrasting sensations. The ice's meltwater carried subsequent blows' impact across still more skin, building bliss. He began to rub his cock against the bed seeking more stimulation.

She paused to admire him, licking her lips at his strong body twisted and bucked, displaying him in a frenzied ecstasy. His beautiful ass was as urgently colored as his cock before an eruption. He danced under her hand readily, erasing her anxiety at initiating a rookie and filling her with pride.

She dragged the overheated air into her lungs, letting his musk and sweat fill her nostrils like the blood pounding through his veins from her touch. It was all she could do not to roll him on the floor and take him.

She took another ragged breath and dropped her hand on him again, fiercely claiming him. He jerked then thrust himself up, wordlessly pleading for another touch of her hand. She caressed him again and again, his bliss sinking into her while she focused on his sexual pleasure. Over an hour had passed since the first swat had fallen.

"Ma'am, please, more...ma'am," he growled, making his desires quite clear.

Beth fetched her favorite Jay Marston flogger and let it fall through her fingers, as she considered where to strike first. It was heavier and broader than the last and would make the remaining blows fall stronger and firmer into Sean's rapturous body. She didn't think of it as Dennis' gift, from when she first learned to dominate a man; it was simply her most familiar friend, come to help her take Sean as high as possible.

She ran the tails over Sean's back and he sighed ecstatically, shifting himself to follow the new touch.

"Oh yes, ma'am. More, oh damn yes," he sobbed. A current ran through her at the rapture in his voice.

The last ten blows were the strongest but Sean was delighted. He pushed his hips back for each blow and laughed ecstatically when they fell. His cock was rich with blood, still lifting eagerly against his belly.

Beth tossed the flogger aside when she finished, shaking slightly. She caressed and kissed his back, feeding on his excitement until she wanted to sink her fingers into his bones to join them. He was well-marked but not bloody; he certainly wouldn't be able to sit down comfortably for a few days.

"Well done, ranger!" she praised him. "You mastered your ordeal like a veteran. The goddess is very pleased with you."

Sean laughed and looked up at her, his eyes bright as an archer's after winning the Olympics. "Thank you, ma'am, thank you!" he sang out. "Damn but I needed that!"

Beth chuckled softly, letting out the reins on her excitement.

"Lie down on the bed, ranger. On your back."

Sean stood up jerkily, obviously fighting for self-control. He stretched himself across the silk, displaying himself in a silent demand to be taken.

"Shit," he cursed softly as his weight pressed his sensitized back against the rough silk. He groaned again and let out a long slow breath. His cock shuddered under the black web. Heavy lids half-veiled the need burning in his eyes. His gaze lanced through her and shredded her self-control.

Experience meant nothing to her now, only the urgency to join him. But she had to play the game out and stay within his fantasy. She closed her eyes, building a priestess' command to a warrior.

"You did well, ranger, and have earned a reward. You will be permitted to celebrate life in the goddess' service."

Beth lifted the dagger from the table and held it up, letting the candlelight light flames in it.

Sean froze immediately, eyes wide and staring at the blade. He slowly dragged in first one breath and then another. His eyes lifted to meet hers and his mouth curled in the hard smile of a warrior eager to enter the mêlée.

"Take me, ma'am," he growled. "Let my blood flow like the roses. I will celebrate life in any way you command."

Beth inclined her head and glided towards the bed. She took a few minutes more to center herself until her hands were rock-steady. He watched her eyes throughout, full of the same clean-edged calm that had doubtless faced guns and missiles before.

"On your side, ranger, so your back faces me."

Sean's bound hands pushed hard against the soft bed and he arched into a roll, hips first. She caught him with her free hand and steadied him. She slid the dagger gently up his forearm until the tip caught under a ribbon. He stayed completely still as he waited for her, although she could feel his hammering pulse.

Beth eased the sharp edge further up his arm until the black velvet fell away soundlessly. He hissed at the returning sensation but didn't move. She rubbed his wrists quietly until he relaxed, while still sneaking in some caresses to his beautiful backside. He jerked when the vibrator began to sing again against his inner pleasure points.

"On your back, ranger."

He hissed briefly but quickly assumed another wanton posture, flaunting his assets and his eagerness. Beth's mouth twitched.

She laid the dagger along the vein in his groin, where the slightest pressure could kill or emasculate him. His heavy eyelids sank down for a long minute but his breathing never faltered.

"I beg of you, ma'am," he started, then stopped. "Please touch me with the knife."

A predatory smile touched Beth's lips. She slid the dagger up and teased a line of black velvet from his waist. His cock swelled harder against its black velvet web. She pressed harder and the ribbon ends fell back against him, one strand gone. He moaned and his cock jerked against its bonds.

Beth cut the remaining ribbons away from him with the same exquisite care she'd given the first strand. He watched every move, his eyelids drooping further while his cock grew larger. She cupped his balls, her thumb rising up his shaft and over the fat glans, watching his pre-come and sweat gild his cock. He moaned, his hips thrust restlessly and his tongue traced his lips. His eyes memorized every move of her hand.

Beth stepped back from the bed. He snarled but managed not to form a protest. His eyelids fell and then snapped up again, pleading with her.

She smiled, a very feminine promise of satisfaction. He shivered at the sight and his hands moved restlessly in the silk under him.

She slid the dress off her shoulder, letting the scarlet silk catch on her budded nipples. Her smile deepened when he hissed, his hips lifting as if to meet her. Her belly clenched as cream pooled between her thighs, ready to ease his way.

Then she slowly shimmied out of the dress, letting every wiggle reveal another taste of skin while pooling on another curve. His movements grew more and more restless, while his hands clenched and unclenched.

Finally, she wore only jade and golden chains to highlight her body's flushed eagerness.

"Please," he moaned, his eyes fixed on her and his body nearly frantic as it jerked restlessly. A continuous line of silver slid down his cock to brighten its black velvet ring.

Beth knelt beside him on the bed, taking one last taste of his beauty before allowing herself to lose control. She straddled his hips, keeping her cleft just beyond his cock. Then she stretched herself upon him and let consciousness of his body seep into every cell of her being. His chest fur pricked her nipples while his heartbeat echoed in her bones. He smelled richly masculine, as the scent of musk, sweat and aphrodisiacs wrapped her.

Beth nuzzled his shoulder, inhaling him further, then licked him, pulling his taste into her mouth and down her throat.

Sean growled at her possession of him, then he relaxed slowly and yielded himself to her. He shuddered at the pressure of her body against his erection.

"Ma'am, please, have mercy and fuck me," he begged shamelessly. He twisted impatiently and yelped when a particularly forceful move scratched his backside.

Beth settled deeper against him, deliberately reminding him of the marks that she'd already left, and he gasped. Then the hard ridge between their bellies grew harder and hotter as his hips circled under her, insisting on finding the ultimate satisfaction.

Beth caressed him restlessly as her blood seemed to seek him out with every pulse. Her breasts were full and flushed, her nipples burning where his chest fur rubbed them. She sank her fingers into his shoulders and rubbed her hips against him, as cream came forth in a match to the surging blood in her veins. Her foot kneaded his calf, desperately seeking the rough tickle of his hair.

"Ma'am, please! I want to give, I need to..."

Now. She needed him now.

She came up to her knees above him, letting his cock stand proudly free.

"Look at yourself, ranger. Your manhood is as naked as when it came from your mother's womb."

He moaned, his eyes seeking hers as his hips writhed.

"Now it will return to its rightful place inside a woman, cleansed by the proofs you have provided and tonight's ordeal." She wrapped her hand around his cock and squeezed it hard. He arched off the bed in response.

"Fuck," he groaned as more pre-come glided down the jutting length.

Beth smiled, a predator seeing the end game at last.

"I demand all of you, ranger! All your body, all your strength, now!" She rubbed the fat plum-shaped head through her folds until it gleamed.

"Fuck me," he groaned again as his head tossed. "Fuck..."

Beth leisurely claimed him, fiercely watching his eyes as he saw more and more of his cock vanish into her.

"Fuck," he mumbled, his eyes on stalks as he stared. "Oh shit..."

She wriggled her hips and sighed when his balls rested hard against her cleft. Her vagina was so full of his big horse cock that she felt barely able to contain their combined life force. She felt the fine tremors running through him from the vibrator deep in his ass. He rumbled his wordless encouragement.

She rose up again until he almost left her. She knelt tall and powerful above him, as his hips pushed off the bed in a quest to regain her.

"No, please!" he begged.

She caressed her breasts, rubbing and plucking at the tightly furled buds of her nipples. Then she swooped down on him and filled herself again.

"Yes, goddamnit, yes! Fuck me now!"

Beth groaned and slowed her thrusts, fighting to postpone her climax. He keened his hunger and grabbed the silk covers so tightly that his hands shone white. His cock traced circles inside her and she lost all sanity against his silent plea.

She moved faster and faster on him, seizing him ravenously. He matched her movements, hips pumping rapidly into her and his eyes shut. He yowled and hissed, snarled and grunted as he fought for more.

She twisted and danced above him, vitality filling her. Pulses built in her, starting deep and low, then pounding into her blood and bones. Her orgasm overwhelmed her and she abandoned herself to the flood, her senses tumbling into the light.

Sean's head snapped back as he finally launched himself into his own climax. He screamed her name over and over as he pumped his life's essence into her.

Chapter Ten
Sunday, Noon

Sean stared at himself in the big mirror over the sink. Another mirror in the opulent bathroom displayed his back, still marked by the night before. Bites and clawmarks showed clear against his skin, both in front and in back. Some of them were from Friday night when he'd joined the Mile High Club.

Red over his shoulders and lower asscheeks, with a few lines marking the flogger's fall. The real wonder was that none of them had hurt at the time. Shit, he distinctly recalled begging for more.

Three interlocked ruby circles, at the base of his cock and between his balls, showed where the black velvet had held him. He remembered clearly how she'd cut the ribbons off, using the bandage scissors very carefully. He'd stayed very still, as she asked. But he'd been too sated and sleepy, from that thunderous climax when she rode him, to do more than twitch under the bright blades.

Scissors...hell, even that little dagger she used, seemed dammed unimportant now, after watching her come to the most spectacular climax he'd ever seen in his life. And she'd had it with him, nobody else.

He traced a particularly vivid scratch across his pecs and shivered. He'd enjoyed the creation of all those marks. He'd even bit Beth hard enough to mark her a couple of times. She'd pulled his head closer and moaned when he did. And he'd laughed as he bent down to her again.

What the hell did that say about him?

Mrs. Wolcott had left marks on his ass after their night together, that had hurt like the devil for the first day. He'd wanted to go back to her bed but it had been simple to catch the bus, leaving her behind. He always knew she had no place in his future life, no matter how many times she walked in his fantasies.

Did he want to play like that again, make love so fiercely that pleasure and pain blended together into ecstasy? Or was it just for this one time only, then remember in dreams later? How would Beth treat him now that she knew so much of him?

Sunday morning and he had less than a day remaining with her. The center of the curtains glowed with light where they didn't quite close, providing just enough light to make the golden bedspread gleam. Beth slept soundly under it, her hair scattered across the pillow. A little snore escaped her.

Sean smiled at the sound. His dangerous lady wasn't perfect and she was here with him now. This was real life and he'd best take what he could, while luck still favored him.

He slid silently into the big bed and tucked her up close, careful not to wake her. Her nose twitched at the contact with his hairy chest and he froze. He calmed when she wrapped an arm around his waist and buried her face in his shoulder. No woman had ever trusted him enough to sleep with him the way Beth did.

A very old knot, too deep inside to be named, loosened and fell away.

Sean lay quietly and watched Beth sleep against him. He tucked a lock of raven hair back behind her ear and pulled the covers higher around her. His beautiful lady needed her rest, no matter what he wanted. A night like that one would wear anyone out.

Beth mumbled something and shifted closer. Her hand gently stroked his back and he pushed against it. A purr grew in his chest as her hand slowly moved up and down his spine. She rubbed her face in the hair on his chest, then nuzzled him until she was delicately licking his nipple.

He choked but kissed her hair. His hands began to revisit her favorite spots. She stretched to suckle his other nipple and his hand pulled her head closer. He slid his leg between hers as she reached up to meet his mouth.

"My turn," he murmured, tightening his fingers in her hair gently.

Beth looked up at him quizzically with her mouth still around his nipple. Then she released him gently and leaned her head against his shoulder. He tilted her head back and began to kiss her slowly. Their mouths played with each other like children exploring an ice cream cone.

Sean freed his mouth finally and began to gently work his way down her body. He cherished each bruise and mark with his mouth and hands, giving the softest massage to ease her aches.

Beth stretched her head back and abandoned herself to him, trembling when he kissed the bite marks on her thigh. She twisted against his hands as he lifted her hips to his mouth. She gripped his head to pull him closer and moaned when his tongue slipped inside. He savored the taste of her as she glided into her climax.

Beth stretched like a cat under him as he propped himself up on his elbows to look at her.

"Care to bring that marvelous mouth up here, lover?" she invited.

Sean smiled and slid to kiss her mouth. She returned his kiss with interest, one leg wrapping around his waist as she welcomed him. The kiss was deep and slow, like an opium poppy or his hips' rhythm as he worked his way inside her. She was entirely open and willing, as her hands urged him on with soft strokes over his shoulders. Even his climax was strong and leisurely as he lost himself in her.

A hunter's instinct stirred in the aftermath. She was still interested in him. It hadn't been an act, just to seduce him into letting her play games with him. What did that offer for the future?

Beth lightly ran a fingertip down a vein in his forearm.

"You're a wonderful lover, Sean," she sighed.

Sean's mouth twitched but he kissed her forehead.

"Maybe. Or maybe it's because you're such an inspiration."

"Maybe we should just agree that each other is incredible," Beth murmured and grinned up at him. Her stomach rumbled and she laughed openly. He joined in and hugged her, rolling across the bed.

"I ordered some breakfast for us, honey. It's waiting in the living room. Would you like a shower first?"

Beth looked at Sean, clearly surprised that he was taking charge of the arrangements, and then relaxed. "Shower and breakfast would be very nice," she agreed. "What did you order for breakfast?"

"Healthy stuff, mostly. Yogurt, granola, fruit. But there's coffee and sweet breads too," Sean confessed. Beth laughed and patted his cheek.

"I understand. Seattle boys need their coffee in the morning," she chuckled and sat up.

Sean relaxed slightly, pleased that she had accepted his decisions.

They showered together, playing in the water like children. First came little splashes as they tried to get each other wet enough to lather up, then greater bursts as they rinsed the soap off.

They managed to get the entire enormous shower stall wet until streams flowed down from the very top. The sight brought even more merry peals and Beth threw her head back, laughing like a toddler.

Sean settled his hands on her sides, rubbing her up and down as he joined in. Beth arched back against his grip, wriggling happily as the water bounced off her breasts and against Sean. She shimmied and chortled as she turned the shower into a fountain tumbling over him.

Sean laughed with her and shook himself like a dog, sending as much water back as he could. Drops fell from the tiled ceiling overhead, like a waterfall. One drop landed on his nose and he crossed his eyes at it.

Beth laughed so hard at the sight that she couldn't stand and had to lean back against the wall.

Sean frowned at her, in pretended hauteur, and she laughed louder. He pressed forward in a mock scolding, only to freeze when a drop fell down his forehead and into the corner of his eye.

She gulped back laughter and he advanced again, letting his own mirth ring out. Beth reached up and smoothed away the water above his eyes. He kissed her, sharing his enjoyment through the intimate touch of their mouths.

Beth drew him closer, wrapping her arms around his neck. Her leg slid up and down his before finally embracing his hip, in an echo of their tongues' dance.

Sean sighed happily and leaned against her, until the wet tile pressed her closer. She stretched up until her nether lips cradled his cock. He moaned and lifted her up, then slid her down onto him.

"Oh yes, darling," she purred as he kissed her throat. "Damn, but you feel good."

He rocked against her easily and slowly, memorizing the feel of her.

"Oh yes, oh my god yes," she breathed as his hands kneaded her ass. "You are fine."

She climaxed sweetly, her body rippling around him. He continued to thrust to the same slow steady beat and felt her reach for another orgasm.

"Good girl," he praised, somehow keeping his breathing as regular as his thrusts. "Let's see how many climaxes you can have before breakfast."

She found three more before his body finally arrived at one. He came heavily in deep shuddering spurts that tugged at his heart while they pulled the last drops from deep in his balls.

Beth blinked up at him afterwards, then licked her lips daintily.

"You really are fine, lover," she purred. He blushed, his legs barely able to support them, and let her slide down.

Dressed at last, Beth looked over at Sean, where he sat peeling a banana. The remains of breakfast were scattered across the table. "That looks good, darling. Can I have some?"

"Sure." He started to reach out to her but she jumped out of her seat and came over to him.

"Now how can I sit on your lap, Sean, when you're up against the table like that?" Beth teased him.

He pushed back his chair and stood up. She cocked her head inquiringly but he caught her wrist. He towed her over to a big chair by the window and sat down, pulling her down into his lap.

She promptly snuggled against him and he winced as her weight pressed him harder into the chair. But those marks would only be around for a few days to remind him of her.

He fed her pieces of banana, savoring the sweet warm weight of her while he could. She rested comfortably against him, watching his face and the Vegas skyline. Sean listened to his heart pound against her warmth.

"Did you enjoy last night, Sean? Are you comfortable with everything that happened?" Beth asked quietly and twisted her head up to see his face.

"Comfortable? Are you kidding? Beth, that was the most fantastic night of my life! And you were great, better than any fantasy I'd ever had of being used hard and well by a beautiful woman."

She smiled at his emphatic response and he kissed her hard on the mouth. Then his lips trailed over her face as he tried to convince her of his sincerity.

"Darling, I couldn't ask for anything more. But the best part was when you looked at me..." He stopped, overcome by the memory.

"What do you mean?"

"When you had the scarves on me and the ribbons... And the vibrator tickling my ass. I stood up and you looked at me like I was the greatest thing you'd ever seen. As if you couldn't wait to touch me." He paused, choking on emotion. "Sweetheart, I'd do anything to have you look at me like that again. I'd like it to happen often." His eyes met hers earnestly.

Beth searched his eyes and then closed her own for a moment. Had he frightened her?

"Let's go spend some vanilla time together," she said and stood up.

"Honey?" Hell, what had he said? Six years a widower, twelve years celibate, and now lunging at the first woman in his bed? Cool down, Lindstrom, and think with your head for a change.

"We're only together for a weekend, remember? And neither of us is ready for a replay of last night. So let's just hang out together." Her eyes were deep and still, implacable.

He had committed to only a weekend. His hold loosened on her and she stood up.

Beth tossed a leather jacket at him from the closet. He caught it and pulled it on, his mouth quirking at yet another display of her moneyed tastes. He was wearing designer jeans and an incredibly soft turtleneck sweater, both of which outlined every muscle. She'd called the sweater's wool alpaca and said it came from South America, an exotic item from an exotic lady.

The red silk thong underneath reminded him of its twin from the night before. Red, damnit. Red silk where nobody would see. She'd wanted him to remember passion, even while he looked as respectable as a banker.

Beth joined him, settling her own jacket around her shoulders. He purred to himself as he saw how much they looked like a matched set. Where did that thought come from? Damnit, did he want to rearrange his life for a woman again?

Beth calmed down slightly once they were out of the room. She even slipped her hand into his in the elevator and leaned against him. He kissed the top of her head, and followed her out when the doors opened.

They walked through the casino quickly, barely noticing the scattered gamblers. She led the way outside and waited for the light to change. Sean pulled her against him, putting himself between her and the traffic. Beth glanced up at him but said nothing about his protectiveness.

They crossed the street and walked up, past towering palm trees, into another casino, full of tropical plants and running water. They moved more slowly through this place, stopping often to compare it to where they were staying.

Beth was more relaxed now, talking easily of small things like the use of different color carpets to guide gamblers through the casino. They found a small set of shops that Sean eyed cautiously, wary of womankind's well-known urge to shop. The jewelry looked very expensive but no prices were visible. Still, he'd go in there with her if she wanted, even if a single item could easily cost as much as his pickup truck. Hell, most of the items probably cost more than his old pickup.

Beth moved past the shops without pausing and he allowed himself to start breathing again. He was even more relieved when they emerged outside.

An incredible swimming pool lay on one side, edged with bright umbrellas and centered on water flowing from rocks. It looked like someplace where you could play out fantasies for hours. They stood in silence for a while, studying it. Sean felt Beth's hand caress his hip and he kissed the top of her head.

"Do you want to sit down here?" he asked.

"No, let's go on further and see the white tigers. I've never seen them before."

"Okay, honey," Sean said easily and moved on with her. They strolled down the path and found the entrance. Sean paid the admission fee, stopping Beth's protest with a finger across her lips.

"Let me pay for this one, darling."

She shook her head at him then smiled ruefully. He dropped a quick kiss on her mouth, thankful that she was willing to accept his money.

The white tigers and their companions were scattered along the winding paths, screened by chain link fence, with few other people braving the brisk autumn air. Soon Sean and Beth found themselves alone at the end of a cul-de-sac watching three young tigers sleep.

"They are so adorable, aren't they?" Beth murmured as one tiger rolled over on his tree branch, somehow managing to stay on. "They remind me of children."

Children. Permanent relationships have to consider children. Did he want more? His heart pounded and he couldn't speak, seeing her eyes soften as she watched the tigers. She'd look like that with her own baby.

He wanted her to look at his child that way. Jesus. He closed his eyes against terror. He'd been interested in dating, especially fucking, but not marriage.

"Yeah, they're sure cute," he managed to say, hoping he didn't sound as stunned as he felt. Mercifully, Beth paid more attention to the tigers than him.

Finally, she put her hand on his elbow and started to stroll on. Sean stayed silent, watching her rather than the exotic animals behind the high fences. What the hell was he going to do?

She was quieter than usual; was she sad that this was their last day? Surely not. Her world was so much bigger and brighter than his, with lots of handsome young men begging her for a chance to worship at her feet.

He bit back a snarl at the thought.

They returned to the jewelry store but this time Beth stopped to glance at the display. Sean looked for the prices this time, considering what her toys had cost. What would it feel like, to buy something just because it felt good and you could afford it?

What the hell could he offer that might make her stay with him? He had money but not as much as the men she was used to. He tried to think of things he could do, put them together in a pretty speech.

Beth and Sean wandered silently through the casino with their arms around each other. They barely made it back to their casino in time to meet the limousine.

Sean raised an eyebrow at the two neat suitcases, shaken by the butler having packed them. But the butler had probably made a lot of other things possible this weekend.

In comparison, the private jet was nothing worth mentioning, just the same plane they'd flown down in. Sean followed Beth up the stairs and buckled in silently. Then he looked around the cabin, trying to memorize every detail for the long nights ahead. It had been a great weekend but there would be other chances with other women, women who would fit into his world.

Yeah, right.

Finally, the seat belt sign clicked off and Beth unfastened hers impatiently. She stood up and held her hand out to Sean.

"Come on, Sean, let's go back and lie down."

Sean's breath caught and he followed her quickly. Beth kicked off her shoes in the stateroom and lay down on the bed. Sean followed her lead and was rewarded when she came straight into his arms. He cuddled her, building memories in this refuge against the outside world. Her breath warmed his heart and he nuzzled her hair, catching her scent and holding it.

They lay like that for a long time, holding each other like two children afraid of the dark. Then she kissed his shoulder and rested her head against his arm. His mouth traveled through the heavy black silk of her hair. She turned to meet his kiss.

They kissed for a long time, trading touches and sighs like the air they needed to live. Contentment built into a smoldering flame and Sean left her lips to explore her face. He caressed her with his nose and tongue as much as his mouth.

Beth murmured something, maybe in Japanese, and opened herself to him, kissing him whenever his mouth came near. She slid her hand under his sweater and stroked his waist, in sweet echo of his caresses. His hand slid down her hip and back again, so that his fingers tucked themselves comfortably into the small of her back. At some point, first one sweater and then the other became too hot and had to be eased off with many kisses and murmurs of appreciation for the skin revealed.

Sean forgot who touched whom as he sank further into the welcome of her passion. He explored her body and tried to memorize every aspect with every sense he possessed, so he would still remember her on the long cold nights to come. She was still his to enjoy and to pleasure, until the clock struck ten.

Beth encouraged him with throaty little whispers that sent shivers running through him, rippling her body to beg for his caresses, and filling the air with the heady delight of her musk. Her skin was softer than her silk scarf, ivory behind the rose of her arousal, as she fondled him. He opened himself up for her bold touch and she purred, cupping his balls as if they were the greatest prize in the world. He groaned and stretched, watching her with heavy-lidded eyes, as she fondled him. She leaned down to kiss him and his hand came up to guide her home to his mouth.

They found many excuses to linger and pause on the slow climb to the top, both showing reluctance to end this moment. But finally the time came when he rolled a condom down his shaft, while Beth watched avidly.

"You're so beautiful," she murmured. He looked up at her quizzically, as he finished adjusting the latex.

"Women are beautiful. Sunsets are beautiful. I'm not," he corrected her.

"Yes, you are," she said, her eyes bright with a suspicious wetness. "I hate losing the sight of you for one instant to that latex, let alone the touch of you. But," she swallowed and went on more brightly. "On the other hand, seeing the latex means that party time is here."

She slid her fingers up his straining cock, playing him like a fiddle.

He choked but soon laughed. "Maybe I am beautiful, if it makes you touch me like that." He bit off the last word as her thumb rolled over his cock's head and circled the shaft.

"Oh hell, woman!" he growled and pulled her on to him. She came willingly and he rolled, settling her under him. She smoothed his head and smiled as his mouth found her again.

They kissed desperately this time and urgency built. He raised himself over her and entered her, watching every smallest twitch of her body as she accepted him. Christ, he felt like he'd come home.

He thrust hard and soon lost the errant thought in a haze of hormones. Their lovemaking was fierce now and wild. His climax seized him like lion taking a gazelle, leaving him spent afterwards as small tremors continued to course through him.

How could he leave her? Giving up moments like this was hell. Never hearing her laugh again or talking to her about books felt like loneliness.

A soft tap on the door sounded as he was trying to find words to say what he wanted.

"We'd better get up and get dressed," Beth said quietly. She sat up abruptly and started to find her clothes without another word.

She'd never said she wanted to stay. Time to keep the bargain they'd made, build a life without her.

"Here's the scarf, Sean. Keep it in remembrance." She held it out. His gut clenched; this scrap of black and gold silk was all he'd have of her tomorrow.

"Thanks." He tucked it into his pants pocket, hiding it like everything else that had captured his heart except Mike.

The same limo and driver, J. Birch according to his nametag, met them at the airport. But this time, Sean and Beth sat at opposite ends of the back seat, as separate as their universes.

He shoved his hands in his pockets, angry with himself for being dissatisfied with his world. It was a good life, with a fine son and good friends. More than enough money too, even if not as much as she was used to.

And no one who lit up like a firecracker when he walked into the room, as she had on Saturday night.

The scarf smoothed over his fingertips. He squeezed it into a ball and made up his mind. Damnit, he couldn't let her go.

"Do you like children, Beth?" Sean asked, beginning to campaign.

"I love children and I'd like to have some of my own," Beth admitted, turning to face him. He gently brushed a lock of hair away from her mouth.

"I'd like more children, too. But I'd like most of all to have a good marriage." He watched her cautiously. "A good loving, committed relationship with the woman I adore." He took a deep breath and then laid all his cards on the table. "I love you, Beth. I know that now. I want to build a long-term relationship with you."

Beth's jaw dropped and she stared at him.

"Sean, darling, you don't know me," Beth protested. "We haven't even known each other a week. Okay, so we had some great sex but that's not everything."

"No, it's not a guarantee but it's a damn good start, Beth. I'm willing to take the chance and work on it with you."

Beth started to speak but the rest of his speech kept tumbling out. Maybe he couldn't keep her in comfort but he could at least show her he cared by being with her.

"I'd be glad to move to Washington, DC to be with you. I can't do it until Mike graduates but then I'd move immediately. And in the meantime, I'd fly out every chance I could to be with you. And there's email to help us keep in touch."

"Sean, please calm down." She patted his knee like a maiden aunt. "We've had a great time playing together but that's all. You need to look for someone around here, someone who'll fit in your world and be a great wife for you."

"Is it the money?" He hated asking, feared hearing that the problem was something he couldn't counter, but he needed to know for sure.

"What?" Beth stared at him. "No, of course not! I earned my money by myself and I honor people who do the same." She was so emphatic that he believed her. She'd never lied to him and she wouldn't start now.

Sean tried to imagine what she objected to. If it wasn't his money, then what did she want? "What do you mean by fit in my world?"

"Sean, you can get involved with the local scene. Maybe pay a fem domme to spank you or tie you up. Keep it as private as you like. Not everyone tells their spouse so you don't have to. You can even find a nice vanilla wife, who'll adore you..." Her voice tightened and she broke off, blinking rapidly and her eyes suspiciously bright.

Sean frowned at her, trying hard to understand. Why was she talking about his sexual tastes? He tried to bring the conversation back to basics.

"I hid everything I thought and felt from Tiffany and I'm not doing anything like that again. I can tell you anything and I'd trust you with everything. It's a good start on a marriage, Beth. So will you let me see you again?"

"That would be very unwise, Sean." Tears choked her voice and she hunted for a tissue in the limousine's capacious cabinets.

Oh Christ, was she going to cry? What the hell did he do now? He tried again, more cautiously.

"Why not? What do you want, Beth? I'll give it to you. I swear I'll go out and get it. Anything you want, just name it."

"Sean!" Beth wailed and stopped. Driven by an instinct beyond thought, he reached out for her. She came easily, not seeking him but not fighting him either. She lay against him, shaking but silent, and he clumsily patted her back. He had no idea what to say.

He'd kill any man who'd do this to her but the fault was his. He was the one who had upset this dangerous lady. He felt like the lowest scum in the universe.

She sat up finally. Their eyes met and he remembered Tiffany's doctor at Walter Reed Hospital, talking about the blood vessels in Tiffany's brain that could rupture and kill her at any time. That man had worn the same sorrowful, resigned look that Beth had now.

Sean waited for her to speak, truly frightened now. He hadn't been this cold inside before, even when he waited to jump onto that heavily defended Panamanian airfield from less than five hundred feet.

"Sean, what I want isn't something you can obtain. You either have it or you don't."

"Beth honey, just tell me." He kept his voice low and soothing.

"You're a damn fine submissive male, Sean. Masculine and challenging. You're going to be a splendid sensation slut, devouring every impulse that comes in from your five senses. But that's not enough."

She swallowed hard before she continued.

"I want...no, need a switch. Someone who can do either dominance or submission. Someone who enjoys taking, just as much as being taken, just at different times."

He saw her face clearly in the reflected light from a streetlamp. Her eyes were implacable above the glimmering tracks of her tears.

"You're not a switch, Sean. You're marvelous, magnificent, superb. Some other woman will be very lucky to have you. But I'm not going to lie to myself again, as I did with Genichi, that only one side of my personality needs to be happy. I can't play the dominant all the time, even for you. Please forgive me for saying this; I don't mean to hurt you. But you're a submissive male, not a switch."

The last words hit him like bullets. His eyes narrowed. He'd never given up without a fight before. He damn well wasn't walking away this time, not when it mattered more than life.

"I can take you. Remember the first night?" Jeez, they fit together so well, no matter what they did. He'd had plenty of experience in the Army with teams that worked and ones that didn't work. He'd seen the results of both often enough to know how rare and priceless the right team was. Beth was the one woman for his future.

"Did you do that because you wanted to? Or because I goaded you into it, by flaunting my wealth and importance?"

"Does that matter?" He answered her question with another.

"I need a man who dominates me sometimes, just because he wants to. Not because he's trying to please me. Do you understand the difference?"

"Yes." He cursed his inability to make a pretty speech, now when it mattered so much. He'd always been better at actions. Hell, she probably took his silence as consent. His brain whirled while she went on. Jeez, how could he convince her?

"Even my ancestors are divided on this road to choose. My Japanese side says that a woman should always follow her man. My Scottish side says that a strong woman can be a partner and even take the lead."

The limo pulled to a stop and the driver got out. The clock said ten pm.

"Beth, we can work it out. I've mastered harder situations than this. I know we care about each other." He took her by the shoulders, willing her to trust him and his belief in the future.

"That's why we should say goodbye now, while we're still friends. I'm sure you'll have a great life without me." Her voice broke a little on the last two words.

The chauffeur opened the door and Sean shook her a little, desperate to crack her resolve.

"I don't know everything about you and you don't know everything about me. But you never do know everything about the other person! I'm sure that I can be the man you need."

"You haven't shown me that, darling. I'm sorry, truly I am! But if you want to do something for me, then find somebody else and be happy. Please." She put a finger over his mouth, stopping any words that he might find. Her throat worked convulsively before she went on. "Let's just call it quits before anyone really gets hurt. Now I'm going to visit my parents and you're going back to your son. You'll be happy, I know you will." She held out her hand, completely ignoring his fingers biting into her shoulders. "Good-bye, Sean."

"I love you." The words came without thought, blazing against the despairing agony that racked him. He'd been lonely for years and survived. He couldn't go back to that, now that he'd lived with true companionship.

She flinched, her hand falling back. She removed herself to the other end of the seat. He saw his future sliding out of his hands. "That's what you think now but you'll forget about me. You have to, Sean."

Sean looked into Beth's eyes one more time. He'd lost the opening salvo but the campaign had only just begun.

"Just remember that Rangers never quit."

Sean let go of her and climbed out of the limo. He turned back for a few last words from the sidewalk.

"I won't say good-bye, Beth, because I'll be seeing you again soon." Sean was more certain of that than what he'd do when they met. "Just, good night and sleep well."

She flinched and then held out her hand to him. "Do please take care of yourself, Sean."

He kissed her hand, pressing a soft nip against the vulnerable pulse on her wrist, and released her. The wind rustled down the sidewalk and brushed against him, its harsh cold a reminder of Alaska and his bleak future.

The driver closed the door and touched his cap to Sean.

"Good luck, man," the driver offered. "Better get going. It's due to start raining again any time now."

"Thanks," Sean responded. He watched, hoping against hope, as the limo pulled away from the curb, just in case she changed her mind at the last minute. Then it turned a corner and was gone.

He rocked back and forth on his heels briefly, considering his options. What the hell was he going to do now?

His pickup waited patiently across the street, its battered skin an emblem of what his life looked like. He frowned, then turned his back on it and started walking.

First, he'd buy that Range Rover. Something tangible, shiny and new like a future with Beth.

Second, he had to convince her that he was a switch. So he had to dominate her sexually. How? Whatever he did had to be something that would turn her on. He couldn't be a medieval knight like that fantasy of hers. So what else?

She'd fantasized about him playing the barbarian and they'd done that in Vegas. It hadn't convinced her that he was the right man so he needed something else, something stronger and more aggressive. The only other submissive fantasy mentioned being kidnapped and interrogated by the French Resistance. That was a lot easier to pull off than a scene involving a castle and horses.

Okay, he'd become a Frenchman. She hadn't given any details of exactly how this happened so he'd have to figure it out on his own.

What if he got it wrong? Well, at least he had her checklist, telling him what sorts of things she did or did not want to do. Christ, what if he did them wrong?

He shuddered at the thought. It was several minutes before he moved again, turning into the wind as he moved forward.

Nothing ventured, nothing gained. This was the best chance to win Beth and he'd take it.

That settled, Sean started considering what he needed. Someplace to enact her fantasy, of course. Someplace private near Berkeley. He knew a commercial real estate broker in Northern California who had a brochure of old warehouses. Maybe one of them would do.

What equipment did he need? There were all the things locked up in his bedroom that he'd never shown anyone before. What else had he played with, that could appear in daylight without notice? She liked leather so that was a good starting point.

Sean kept walking as he worked out the details of exactly how to kidnap Beth and enact her fantasy. He instinctively became a Ranger again as he did so, writing an operation order as he had so many times in the Army.

Situation. Enemy: Beth's belief that he's strictly a submissive, not a switch. Friendly: his collection of sex toys, California real estate broker, her checklist.

Mission. Obtain a commitment from Beth Nakamura to a long-term relationship.

Execution. Concept of operations: convince Beth that he's a switch by dominating her during an enactment of her French Resistance fantasy. Scheme of maneuver...

Rain splattered against his jacket as he finished the remaining sections: service and support, command and signal. Few standard operating procedures mentioned anywhere.

Then he started to test his operation order for flaws and found a big one.

He came to a full stop and stared ahead. He had reached an old commercial district leading down to the docks. Puget Sound lay ahead, whipped to a frenzy by the wind, with the lights of West Seattle beyond. His home was there, keeping Mike safe and warm.

If anything went wrong, he could be arrested and sent to prison for kidnapping. He'd never harm her but that didn't matter, not if the law found out. The world would know all about him.

He shuddered in horror but kept thinking. He had to bring Beth to him; she wasn't going to seek him out. He couldn't believe that love letters would succeed better than action in convincing her, even if he thought he could write them. The kidnapping and interrogation scene offered the best chance of impressing her.

Christ, he was cold with a chill that began deep inside. He recognized it as an old friend that he'd met before, the mind-numbing terror that comes just prior to combat. He fought it back as he had then: reminded himself of the objective, then analyzed the plan and tried to minimize the risks.

Beth was worth any risk. He had a chance of winning her, given the way she'd cried. His dangerous lady wouldn't break down if she didn't care.

The plan could easily go wrong but it was the best hope.

Now, reconsider the worst case: the world would know and Mike would know. Mike would believe that his father was a criminal jerk.

That's when Sean seriously considered not trying for Beth.

He couldn't live with that vision so he came back to the cost of winning her.

Mike was eighteen and he'd be out of the house in less than a year. Maybe he wouldn't be too upset since he wouldn't have to live with the scandal for very long. Maybe Mike was enough of an adult now that he could understand that grown men sometimes have to do things that sound foolish to an outsider. Maybe.

So the absolute foulest situation was neither Beth nor Mike in his life.

The wind bit into his face but he didn't hide from it.

Finally, he turned around and started walking back to his pickup.

* * * * *

Sean walked into the house at midnight and dropped his portfolio on the table, with its penciled ops plan inside. Dudley clattered down the stairs and woofed softly in greeting. Sean squatted down and hugged his old friend.

"Hello, Dudley. Did you have a good time in Portland?"

Dudley's brown eyes softened at Sean's tone. He licked Sean's face and pushed closer. Sean choked, then turned his face into the golden fur. Dudley always knew when a human needed some comfort.

Mike's arrival was quieter, especially since he kept his mouth shut, even when he stood motionless on the threshold. Sean stood up smoothly and acknowledged Dudley's help with a pat, ready to move into action.

"Hi, Mike. Have fun in Portland?"

"Yeah, it was decent. Tracy really liked the bed and sent a thank you note." He came into the kitchen cautiously, trying to act as if his father always blinked back tears.

"Care for a soda?" Sean invited, opening the fridge. This might be easier if framed as a man-to-man discussion.

"Sure. What's the occasion?" Mike sat down at the table and Dudley settled happily next to him.

"No celebration. Not yet anyway. Just wanted to say a couple of things and might as well do it tonight since you're up." And while he still had the courage. Damn, he'd rather face a Somali mob again, alone and unarmed, than do this.

He tossed a soda can to Mike and straddled a chair, opening another for himself.

"Shoot." Mike was now openly curious. He rocked back, lifting the chair's front two legs off the floor.

"First, please tell Bill that I'm not interested in his uncle's Range Rover." Start with the easy stuff first.

"Sure. Any particular reason?"

"I'm buying a new one for myself."

Mike's eyes widened. "What kind? A Discovery?"

If he was going to do this, then he sure as hell wasn't going cheap. Well, as cheap as a Land Rover came, any way.

"A Ranger Rover 4.6HSE. Black, of course." The Range Rover of his dreams would be a good symbol of his future with Beth.

"Tight! That's really tight. When?" Mike almost bounced in his seat and the chair wobbled.

"Tomorrow."

Mike lifted his drink in salute and Sean matched the gesture, before draining his dry.

"So we'll have it for the Thanksgiving hunting trip."

"Yes, we should be able to drive it off the lot." The Thanksgiving that he might be celebrating from a jail cell.

Hell, Beth was worth the risk.

Mike caught his mood and waited.

"Second, I may be going to jail."

Mike's chair thudded into place as Mike spewed soda across the table. He coughed and choked, but his words were still intelligible.

"Like hell you will! You'd never do anything illegal."

"FBI might not see it like that."

"No way. I'm the one who did all that shit until you straightened me out. I know you." Mike's eyes blazed angrily as he wiped up the sticky froth. He looked dangerous and years older than his age.

His son's faith warmed him but Mike needed to understand.

"Mike, I met a lady but she's not ready to think about marrying me. She could get upset by my methods of persuasion and call the police."

Mike snorted and relaxed a little. "Your lady? Any woman that catches your eye is smart and tough. Not the type to call the cops."

"She likes playing games." Sean hesitated, uncertain how to describe how he'd spent the weekend.

"BDSM, right?" Mike tossed his can into the recycling bin.

"What?" Sean's world spun and he set his drink down slowly; this wasn't the time for confusing his brain with caffeine. He'd always done everything possible to ensure that first Tiffany and later Mike wouldn't know what really turned him on, all the things that the big world disapproved of but he found exciting.

"You know, sex and power. Role playing, power exchange…" Mike shrugged, looking as casual as if he was trying to find words for the latest TV show. He looked straight into his father's eyes.

"Dad, I know what kind of books and videos you've got hidden away. It just makes sense that this lady likes the same stuff." He shrugged again, looking nervous. "I didn't mean to snoop in your stuff but I was looking for some of your old films from Ranger School. When I saw your cabinet was unlocked for once, I thought the movies might be in there. Kept locked up from Mom since she hated hearing about everything to do with the Army except the NCO Club and pensions. I'm sorry if you think I was spying but…"

"You wouldn't," Sean reassured him. "I know you didn't break into any of my things. You could have done so years ago, if you'd wanted to." Mike had been quite a burglar before Tiffany's death, breaking into houses but never stealing more than trifles, just enough to prove that he'd been there. It had ended surprisingly easily, after Sean's discharge and the move to Seattle. The police and courts had been right: Mike had needed consistent love and discipline to feel safe. He'd become a son to be proud of.

Mike relaxed with a sigh of relief, then stood up to fetch a clean glass from the cupboard.

"How long have you known?" Sean returned to his main concern as he tried to absorb the implications of Mike's awareness. Mike knew and wasn't disgusted by his father's sexual interests, even though they were outside the usual run of things. He still cared about his father.

"A year maybe." Mike poured himself a glass of water from the fridge, avoiding the soda like someone who needed to keep a clear head. "You keep it locked up pretty well."

"That long," Sean muttered. He hadn't seen any signs of a changed attitude in Mike. He really did respect his father, no matter what Sean kept hidden.

"So what are you planning?" Mike straddled another chair, facing his father as an equal.

"None of your business. No need for you to go to jail." Sean's attitude was firm.

"Dad, nobody's going to do jail time." Mike was patient and reassuring, as befitted a veteran of close encounters with the law.

"Worst case, the police find out. I won't have you involved so you don't need to know anything. Things go badly, you'd lose your shot at West Point and the Army." He stated the indisputable facts one more time.

"The Army doesn't matter, not if it means you're in trouble." Mike's voice was dead calm, as if he stated a fundamental truth.

"Mike, damnit, you've always wanted to be in the Army," Sean tried again to reach him.

Mike's eyes never flickered, his face set stone cold. "Family is more important than the Army. You proved that when you took that hardship discharge. I'll find something else, the way you did."

Christ, Mike was willing to give his dreams up for his father.

Mike considered that, swirling his water in the glass. Sean waited for him to try a different angle of persuasion. Mike was clever and charismatic; he'd be deadly as an officer. But the old man could still usually outsmart him.

"You know, Carol's uncle is a big-time stuntman in Hollywood. Arranges complicated stunts all the time. He's even directed a couple of cheap movies."

"So?" Where was this going?

"I talked to him some on Saturday night, while the ladies were getting dressed for the big dinner."

Sean nodded, waiting for Mike's real pitch.

"He said that he's helped couples pull off stunts that'd normally get them arrested. Things that they both wanted to do but outsiders wouldn't understand. Like kidnapping."

Sean came to attention, considering the possibilities. Somebody who could provide a good cover story might make this much less dangerous.

"How?"

"He tells questioners it's for a movie. Just need to have somebody around with a camera and the right permits. He bragged about how fast he can get a permit, especially when it's a student film."

"Perfect." Any amount of foolishness went on in the movies, so pretending to perform a scene from World War II shouldn't worry the police at all.

"When did you want to do this? He's only in town for a little longer."

"She's in Berkeley this week."

"Sounds like time's short so you'll need both Carol's uncle and me."

Sean slammed his fist down on the table. "Hell, no!"

"Dad, getting a filming permit usually takes time but it's faster for student permits. We can do it if you bring me in."

"Mike, we're talking serious jail time here. I wouldn't be a father if I let you anywhere near this."

"You got a student ID?" Now, Mike sounded like the one who'd thought things through.

"No! But you're too young to be involved." Sean fell back on the most basic fact, the one that he'd built his life around. Mike was his son and under his protection.

"You need my help, Dad. You've always done everything for me, no matter what it cost you."

"You don't need to pay me back, Mike. This is about me and you're better off staying out of it." Sean's voice was softer now but still firm. Mike had always been too old for his years, even when he was meeting all those cops.

"I want to do this for you, Dad, as a present. It's something only I can do. You don't get many chances to give something really unique." Mike leaned forward, willing his father to understand.

Sean hesitated, startled by the naked love in Mike's voice. Neither of them had every much mentioned their feelings for each other, of course. How could he refuse a gift from his son, given in full knowledge of the risks? He tried once again.

"Mike, I really don't think you need to. I'll be okay."

"Dad, we're doing this together. If you don't want to think of it as a gift, then just see it as the two Lindstrom men standing together, no matter what the odds. Okay?"

Sean froze, trapped by the old saying he'd first used when Mike was four. The two Lindstrom men always stood together, no matter what. He had no counter for this argument.

He glared across the table at the man sitting there, the adult he'd been privileged to sire.

Then Sean laughed and held out his hand for a high five. Mike had won by turning Sean's weapons against him.

The two Lindstrom men were going into battle together.

Chapter Eleven
San Francisco Airport
Monday, 9 am

Beth waited patiently for her parents to clear Customs, slightly apart from the rest of her family. Everyone was there: her three older brothers, their wives and all seven of their children. Even Kasey, Jason's very pregnant wife, had come to welcome her in-laws. They all carried a gift, flowers and balloons mostly. Beth had a box of her mother's favorite Belgian chocolates, miraculously produced by the concierge at her hotel.

She hadn't slept the night before. In fact, she'd spent most of the night pacing across her hotel room; it had seemed a better option than tossing and turning, crying in a lonely bed. Sean was the finest submissive man she'd ever played with. But she couldn't lie to herself again and say that only one side of her needed to be happy.

Little Hiroki, who considered himself quite the conqueror at not quite two, hurtled across the lounge towards the door. His father Conal broke off his discussion of the latest artificial heart technology and scooped up the toddler just before the door swung open. Sean would have moved as fast to rescue a child.

Tears welled up at the image. She needed to find something else to think about, something that wouldn't bring Sean to mind.

Suddenly the flow of emerging passengers opened up, showing Hiroki and Catriona Nakamura walking hand-in-hand behind a porter pushing a heavily loaded luggage cart.

The Nakamura clan burst into action as all members hurried forward. All was pandemonium as greetings were exchanged, children exclaimed over and gifts given. Beth hugged her mother briefly and stepped aside quickly as little Hiroki demanded attention from his favorite grandmother.

Beth would have liked to linger a bit longer near her mother, who was always ready to reassure and defend her children.

Somehow Beth found herself in the back of Jason's minivan with her father, heading towards the family home in Berkeley. Catriona was in the next row forward, catching up on the latest news of Kasey's condition.

Beth tuned the conversation out; all her brothers' wives wanted to talk about their pregnancies with Catriona, since she was an obstetrical surgeon. What would it be like to talk about her pregnancy with her mother?

"Your grandmother sends her congratulations, Beth."

Beth snapped her attention back to her father. "Forgive me, Father. My attention was wandering."

Hiroki's eyes searched hers briefly, seeing every detail. He patted her hand.

"I mentioned to her that you have achieved career status with the American government."

Beth nodded, trying to see where this was going. She now had a permanent job with the government, not something that could be ended at the government's convenience. So Father had bragged about Beth to his mother, after not publicly defending her a year ago. It sounded as if he'd undertaken a quiet campaign to recover Beth's status.

"The Nakamura clan is very proud of your achievements, Beth. My mother sends this in token of her regard."

Hiroki offered Beth a beautifully wrapped box and she opened it carefully. Inside the elegant wooden box lay a magnificent pearl necklace, composed of perfectly matched, graduated large South Sea pearls.

"The necklace was a personal gift to her from her grandmother, upon her graduation from college, the first woman in her family to achieve that. Now you are the first to serve the American government, a great honor for our family."

Beth's mouth worked but no words came out past the knot in her throat. Grandmother had just brought her back into the clan again. She managed to smile at her father.

Hiroki slid his arm around her shoulders and hugged her.

"I am so very glad to have you as my daughter," he said softly and kissed her on the cheek. "You have always been everything and more than I hoped."

"Oh, Father!" Beth gulped and yielded to tears. Hiroki pulled her against him and she cried into his shoulder, finding the comfort she had needed from him a year ago. His arms continued to shelter her while she mourned the loss of Sean.

* * * * *

The old pickup truck jerked to a stop. Beth was sprawled across the seat with her head in Sean's lap. The motion sent her feet to the floor but her mouth never lost contact with his cock. She swirled her tongue up his shaft and opened her mouth to take him deep again.

Sean jerked her up by the shoulders. She caught a glimpse of the world outside for a moment. They seemed to be in the alley behind a lumberyard. Not his house, not her hotel. That didn't matter; getting her hands on him was more important than finding a bed.

Then he dumped her onto the seat and came down on her. His tongue stabbed deep, claiming her. She responded fiercely, feeling teeth and lips grind as their tongues mated.

He growled and started fighting her pants' zipper. She lifted her hips for him and he yanked the denim down past her knees. They fought the confined space as much as the cloth, as both lovers tried to overcome the jeans' barrier. Beth banged her wrist against the steering wheel but finally succeeded. Her shoes and trousers dropped onto the floor under the brake pedal.

A moment later Sean's hot body covered her again. She nipped his shoulder in welcome, even as he plunged inside her. Lights burst behind her eyelids as she convulsed.

* * * * *

The alarm went off at precisely six am on Tuesday morning, as it had been told to. Time to rise so she could have breakfast with her father. Damn.

Beth rolled over and buried her face in the pillow. The dream had been so real that she could still see Sean in the light from the lumberyard. She was wet between her thighs and moved farther away from the matching spot in the sheets.

Beth sat up and hugged her knees to her chest. She rested her cheek on the tight knot of her limbs and rocked slowly, curled to comfort herself as she remembered old challenges.

She had always wanted to be a Japanese lady, her head bent meekly as she followed her lord. But she didn't fit in Japan, either physically or emotionally with her intense drive to reach the top and lead, both at work and in the bedroom. Genichi had been right about that, no matter how hurtful his words had been when she had broken the engagement.

She had never wanted to be a Scottish lady but she behaved, more than often not, as a strong, creative Scot. Was she asking too much for one man to be all, as Jenn said? Or was Sean right? Could he satisfy both sides of her dream?

No matter what she did, she kept thinking about Sean. He'd followed her into her sleep more than once. Even total exhaustion after playing with her nieces and nephews hadn't kept him away. She felt like a teenager daydreaming about the man who'd showed her carnal pleasure for the first time. Had Mother felt like this after she met her future husband?

She sighed and sat up. Thinking didn't change the fact that she'd sent Sean away and lost him. He wouldn't possibly want to see her again, after she'd dismissed him so completely.

Beth came into the kitchen after putting her sheets in the wash. The coffee pot was full and she checked the time in surprise. Her mother usually left for the hospital well before now, even on days without duty in the trauma department. Beth filled the waiting thermos and then started a fresh pot.

She sat on the chair, elbows on the counter, and contemplated the brewing coffee. She had never been a particular fan of coffee, seeing it as a survival necessity in the workplace rather than a pleasure.

But now the smell reminded her of Sean. She smiled, remembering how he drank his coffee as if every drop was necessary for life. She wondered if he had a pickup truck.

A door closed upstairs and Beth jumped. She quickly popped a bagel into the toaster.

"Good morning, Mother. Your bagel is almost ready and here's your thermos for the drive."

Beth noticed that her mother looked like the proverbial cat who'd caught the canary. And then spent the night playing with it.

For the first time, she wondered about her parents' sexual relationship. A quick glance at her father showed that he looked exhausted, sated and very content.

Beth turned to give her mother a hug and flinched inwardly at her mother's surprise. Years of squabbles and subsequent distances couldn't be erased in a minute but she could start now.

She hugged her mother again, turning the casual greeting into something more significant. It almost felt like embracing her own twin, given their matching height and build. But Catriona had blonde hair and blue eyes, while Beth had the black hair and eyes of her father's family.

"Thanks, Beth, for looking after me. I don't know where the time went. Guess I must have overslept." Catriona's voice was a little hoarse at first but quickly recovered its usual lilt.

She kissed her daughter's cheek and Beth responded with a clumsy peck. She needed to do this more so she'd become less awkward. Catriona was gone within seconds, after a brief discussion of dinner plans.

"Would you like a cup of coffee, Father? Or would you prefer tea?" Beth offered, returning to their usual custom. She and her father always shared a cup in the morning on her trips home, before he departed for his lab at UC Berkeley.

"Coffee would be fine, thank you. Perhaps you will join me on the deck?" Beth nodded.

They sat outside silently, enjoying the mugs' warmth between their palms while watching the morning sun burn through the fog. The Golden Gate Bridge would be visible later when the haze vanished.

But now the fog wrapped them intimately, even as it caressed the eucalyptus trees next to the deck. Hiroki Nakamura and his daughter sat in similar attitudes of contemplation, meditating on the scene before them.

"Father, may I ask you a question?"

He nodded calmly and waited, his expression open and relaxed.

"Were you surprised to fall in love with Mother?"

His eyes widened briefly at the question.

"Yes, I was very surprised to fall in love with Catriona. She was very different from what I'd ever considered finding in my life. But..." Never very articulate, he hunted for words to express himself. "She fulfills me. She fulfills needs I was unaware of. I knew within a day of our first meeting that I could not live without her. Knowing that made everything else easier to manage."

Beth nodded in understanding. Her parents' love and need for each other had been strong enough to build a good life together, despite the conflicts between their two totally different backgrounds. Two had become a strong whole. Could she build an equally satisfying world with Sean?

"Beth, life is not always what we want. It is often not what we would wish for our beloved daughter."

Beth smiled at him, misty-eyed. He had been so angry when Genichi had humiliated her, mincing no words in his denunciation. Memory of that unexpected torrent now overshadowed his subsequent patience with his mother, when he waited for a better time to overcome his mother's angry disappointment.

Hiroki went on slowly. "I pray that your life has not left you too scarred to try again. I pray that you will take a chance again on a man that you can love."

Beth put out her hand and slipped it into her father's. Maybe he could comfort her now.

"Father, I met someone that I'd like to tell you about."

* * * * *

Beth toppled her king, acknowledging another defeat at chess. Hiroki began to set the pieces up again without looking at her and she helped him, glad he didn't say anything about her lapsed concentration. If he did, she'd pretend she was thinking about her new assignment, which was something important.

Thursday noon. Eighty-six hours without Sean but who was counting?

"How are our birds doing?" he asked as he moved an ivory knight neatly into place.

"I don't know. I haven't been up to the park to watch them." She set the ebony queen next to her king. The sunroom, with its walls of windows showing yet another storm coming in across the bay, felt like a prison.

"I thought of them while I traveled, every time someone mentioned the weather." He turned the ivory queen so she was aligned identically to her king.

"Perhaps I should go check on them and make sure the storms haven't disturbed them." And try to think about something other than the mistake made with Sean.

"It is always good to know when loved ones are safe," Hiroki agreed, moving pawns smoothly into position.

Beth stood up, then gave him a quick, fierce hug. His hand closed strongly on her arm, returning her affection. Then he patted her hand. "Take your time visiting our friends, Beth. I have much to catch up on at home before your mother returns."

Beth started up the path with a hard stride, head up so she could taste the wind. She should be happy and excited to start her new assignment for the Treasury. Instead her thoughts revolved around a man that she'd left, quite deliberately, behind.

She turned past her parents' garden and up the hill, looking for the first vantage point where she could see the hilltop. The path took almost two miles to climb to the park, most of it spent skirting yards and cliffs. It crossed streets at only three points before it emerged into the grove.

Another bird watcher, a much more dedicated sort who kept his binoculars at the ready for minutes at a time, was visible from one of the few vantage points. He was a slender man, dark-haired, standing in the grove and sweeping the surrounding skies with his glasses.

Something in how he surveyed the scene reminded her of the bookstore clerk in Seattle, watching the sidewalk outside his store. What was his name? Gary. Why did she remember him so easily? Was she fated to remember everyone and everything connected with Sean?

She shook herself into action and continued walking. She hit the next incline in a burst of action that sent sparrows flying. She moved with the speed of long-familiarity under the trees, glad that they were recovering so well from the fire of a decade past.

She never saw Gary lower his binoculars, then speak quietly into a radio he produced from a pocket.

Beth paused at the first street, a narrow opening into a cul-de-sac that seldom offered any traffic. It was busier than usual today, with an ancient truck rumbling in the middle, that looked old enough to have welcomed De Gaulle into Paris. One man was under the hood with only his hips and legs visible. Another sat behind the wheel with his head out the window, listening to the mechanic's instructions. The mechanic's backside was as fine as Sean's, even in a rough leather jacket and baggy pants.

Two men fussed over a big movie camera on a tripod, set up on the street corner yard. The one facing Beth was young, tall and blond; he might grow up to be as attractive as Sean one day. The other man seemed familiar but he kept his back turned.

Beth swore silently. Was she doomed to look for Sean in every man she saw?

Time to go; there were two more streets and another mile before reaching home. She checked for traffic and then stepped out into the street.

Things happened swiftly after that. One moment, she was crossing a strip of California road. The next moment, she was standing in the middle of the street, staring into Sean's wary but determined eyes under a black beret. It lay flat on his head in the French style, hiding his American haircut. Was that a Luger pistol in her ribs?

What the hell was going on?

"French bitch," he snarled. "Did you think your German friends would protect you?"

Beth stopped breathing as she recognized the question. It was the first line of the submissive fantasy she'd sent Sean. Then her belly tightened and her heart started pounding against her ribs. Was he going to dominate her?

"How dare..." She wet her lips and tried again. "How dare you stop me? You are a fool to challenge the Nazis, rulers of all Europe. Now go home and don't bother your betters."

The truck's hood slammed down. Beth glanced around Sean's arm and saw...Dave Hemmings as the second cameraman? He watched her from beyond the camera, his face neutral. Its young operator definitely looked like Sean's offspring, as he recorded her reactions.

She could ask Dave for help if she wanted to. Kidnappings were dangerous, with their open invitation for police involvement. Her skin ran cold and then hot.

No. Dave Hemmings was her safety net; she could simply walk away with him and avoid any danger from Sean. If she didn't do that, then she consented to the fantasy being played here, taking the chance of submitting to Sean.

She would have no control once she left with Sean and would have to rely solely on him. She could be hurt physically or frustrated emotionally if he wasn't able to dominate her. She dismissed the first risk quickly; Sean would never harm her, although he must know that she could enjoy pain's vivid stimulation.

The second risk was more real; he'd never proven that he could top her in a way that placed his satisfaction before hers.

But this was her one opportunity to discover if Sean was a switch, capable of both taking and being taken. See if he really was the man of her dreams. Almost no chance but still, maybe it would work.

She looked back at Sean and swung her arm in a roundhouse swing at his face. "Imbecile!" she spat out the third line of her fantasy.

His eyes blazed down at her and he caught her hand, millimeters from his cheek.

"Foolish wench," he laughed and she felt the scene's energy snap into place between them. Her breasts tightened and dew beaded between her legs.

The truck kicked into a smooth rumbling purr, like all those old war movies. "Hurry up!" the driver called.

Sean twisted her arm behind her back and pushed her to the truck, the gun's barrel pressing into her back. Dave's face relaxed and he gave her a quick thumbs up.

Sean tossed her between the swaying canvas curtains into the back and followed her in a smooth dive. She found herself trapped between a blanket-covered hay bale and a very big man, who still had a gun in her ribs. There were crates of apples in old-fashioned wooden crates towards the front.

She trembled and grew wetter. The hay rasped her nipples through the blanket and her heavy field jacket.

The truck's doors slammed shut an instant before it pulled away from the curb. Beth didn't think of trying to guess its route or destination. This was now 1944 France and the Resistance would never let collaborators know their secrets. Her only hope was the man above her, with the hard ridge threatening to tunnel into her trousers.

He shifted himself, just enough to quickly buckle her hands into leather cuffs behind her back. Metal clanked and a chain slid into her palm. She tried to tug her wrists apart but the leather and steel refused to yield more than a few inches. She couldn't possibly free herself.

She cursed him, angry and excited.

Then he pulled her head up and smoothly gagged her with a silk scarf, a knot in her mouth to keep her silent. Another silk scarf covered her eyes in a blindfold and he tied her bootlaces together to hobble her.

Beth tossed her head from side to side, trying to orient herself in the new world composed only of sounds. The truck ran smoothly, taking the hills and curves easily if loudly. Its heavy engine sent a continuous vibration through its frame and into her body, triggering an answering throb from her shoulders to her hips. And into her core, which registered its opinions in the dampness of her panties. She could smell her musk begin to rise over the masculine scents of hay and engine oil.

He yanked her onto her back and she tried to roll away. He grabbed the neck of her jacket, stopping her easily. Then he ripped open her jacket with one brutal tug, sending buttons flying. She tried to scream, even as her breasts firmed in anticipation.

He ripped open her broadcloth shirt quickly and easily. Beth twisted under him, too anxious to stay still. Her chest rose and fell with her rapid breathing and her nipples were spikes of eager tension.

She froze when a knife slid up her bare midriff and teased her simple white silk bra. Her thighs tightened against her wetness. The knife felt like an extension of his touch, in the darkness behind the blindfold.

He cut the silk off her with a single smooth stroke and she moaned when his hand cupped her. He kneaded her breast hard, lifting it towards him. He chuckled wickedly when her nipples tightened further. His other hand played similar games until both breasts were throbbing and heavy.

"Such tempting morsels," he rumbled, dropping his head. If his hands had been inviting, then his mouth was irresistible. She writhed under him, as incoherent pleas formed behind the gag. But she couldn't talk and she couldn't see. She was free to respond to him, without worrying how to please him.

The truck's motion sometimes sent her closer to him but sometimes further away. The burlap was rough against her back, despite the protection of her remaining clothing, while the hay rustled with every movement. She could smell the hay's earthy scent and the apples' sweetness combined with her musk, as she grew wetter and wetter.

She tried to rub her legs together to relieve her tension but he blocked that by shoving his knee between her legs. She pushed her hips against his knee but his hands bit into her hips. She whimpered as she accepted his rules: he set the actions and the pace.

Thankfully, he returned to her breasts after her hips lay acquiescent against his leg. Perhaps soon he'd use his hand on her below the waist.

The truck stopped and he sat up. A whisper of cold air brushed her nipples, in stark contrast to his mouth's heated warmth. She listened hard, impatient for his return.

He cupped her breasts in his hands and she felt his avid gaze. She smiled under the gag when he pinched and twisted her nipples, enjoying the rapidly returning excitement. He focused his attention on one breast and its crowning bud until she was frantic.

Then he slowly, wickedly claimed that nipple with a sharp stab of pain. She recognized a Japanese cloverleaf clamp's wicked touch immediately and gasped, adjusting herself. Soon only a hard ache remained.

She arched eagerly when he rubbed cold metal over her other breast and moaned when the second clamp took it. She would be very sensitive when he removed them.

Chain crackled then lay across her abdomen like a lover as he linked the clamps. She was held captive by him, at her breasts, wrists and ankles.

He unzipped her trousers then yanked them down to her hips to free her mound. He cupped her and she sighed at the welcome warmth after cold air's snap. His fingers slid between her folds and she tried to open herself further, only to be stopped by the unyielding corduroy. A big finger stabbed into her, then another finger joined to screw into her.

Her belly tightened as her hips pushed up against him, desperate to find the climax that he was lifting her towards.

"Now, woman! Come for me now," he snarled as a rough finger rubbed her clit in exactly the stroke she loved. Her body exploded obediently and willingly.

She gasped for breath afterwards, feeling the last pulses die away. Then his mouth closed over one breast, immediately returning it to a state of pure excitement. She grunted behind the gag when his hand delved between her legs. Soon he demanded another climax of her and she gave it willingly, her body spasming under his wicked touch.

The drive went on forever as he fucked her with his mouth and hands. Or was it only a few minutes? They left the hills and drove across a city, full of dissonance as the route turned senselessly. The truck bumped across railroad tracks more than once, producing a change in his hands' rhythm, and over bridges.

His breathing was occasionally ragged but he never rubbed himself against her, never released his cock from its confinement into her welcoming warmth.

Sometimes his mouth used her breasts but sometimes it traded places with his hands. Sometimes he led her slowly from orgasm to orgasm but sometimes he took her at a gallop.

They stopped once, the truck idling while cars thundered overhead. He ran his hands over her, skimming from collarbone to pelvis as her body rippled in an echo of their passage. She hummed, trying to understand his new demands, as her body fell into a slower pulse of arousal. Then he circled her breasts until she sobbed her willingness. His hands cupped her nipples lightly, warming her as he hinted at his next move.

One hand delved below, gliding deep into her swollen folds. Her hips thrust into his touch as she obeyed his unspoken demand. Just before she eased into a new climax, he snatched one clamp off with practiced ease and simultaneously thumbed her clit. She screamed soundlessly as the two stimuli sent her body into a blinding orgasm.

She was still shaking when his mouth covered her other breast and his hand found her favorite pleasure point deep inside. He pressed firmly with his hand while he simultaneously sucked her breast deep into his mouth. He repeated the two demands until her body throbbed in response, waves flowing from her breasts to her cunt and back again. Her body bent into a great bow of arousal as it offered everything to him.

"Now, woman!" he snarled, snatched the last clamp off and thrust deep inside her. His insistence was a rare hint to her effect on him. She came in a thundering rapture that ran throughout her body, from both her clit and her cunt.

The truck rumbled back into life while she was trying to catch her breath. Rain fell as they left the overhead highway's protection, first as a steady mist but soon as a downpour. He swirled his tongue over her, lapping at her enflamed nipples like a rare appetizer.

The rain's drumming was an echo of her heartbeat before she satisfied yet another command to climax for him.

Finally the truck lurched its way down a railroad track and he stopped his assault on her senses, moving completely away from her. She was too sated to do more shiver as the cold air returned to her overheated body.

It bumped onto smoother pavement then stopped. Water poured over one side of the roof, indicating some shelter from the weather. The engine fell silent as the Luger returned to her ribs. A door opened and then slammed shut in the cab.

They had arrived. What did he plan now? Her pulse exploded into terror's trip-hammer beat. Or was it desire's rhythm? She struggled to think.

The truck's doors opened and the big man scrambled out, then turned to pull her after him.

He yanked her trousers up to her waist and pulled her jacket back to her shoulders again. She was hot, wet and swollen against cloth's steady rub and she twitched under the rough sensation.

He tossed her over his shoulder, paying no heed to her struggles, and ran into the building. An elevator, a freight elevator by the draughts brushing through it, lifted them up higher and higher. Somewhere far below, the truck came alive again before it faded into the distance.

He set her down on her feet, supporting her against his hard body. He unchained her cuffs then lifted first one wrist, then the other shoulder high.

Each wrist was anchored before her head stopped spinning. Her hands instinctively grasped the metal bar that separated them. Four staccato clicks announced her legs' separation and their attachment to another metal rod, her feet firmly planted in her hiking boots against the floor. She could stand like this for a long time.

He yanked the blindfold off so she could discover her new universe.

Beth blinked several times as her eyes adjusted to the filtered light coming through the banks of grimy windows and skylights. She saw an enormous room in a brick building, furnished with a big wooden swivel chair, a table with a chest to one side, and two ancient wood stoves that heated their surroundings to almost tropical warmth. The floor had been swept to a warehouse's idea of clean. She was spread-eagled against a set of pipes, a relic of the room's manufacturing past.

She felt totally exposed and helpless, despite her heavy clothing. She was completely at the mercy of the big man watching her from across the room, his blue eyes considering her in a predator's level stare. He was ferociously calm, in contrast to her body's throbbing sensitivity.

She trembled, the motion traveling deep and ending in a slow burn in her gut. She gathered herself to fight. Oral sex was well and good, but she could find that with another partner, as could he.

"Are you going to tell me where the art is, beautiful bitch?" he purred, prowling towards her. His eyes stripped her remaining clothes in an unspoken promise. "As soon as you tell me where the Nazis hid our treasures, then I'll let you go."

She shook her head violently. Never, she mouthed against the gag. She would play this scene out to the end.

He held his knife before her eyes, a big wickedly-sharp dagger that he'd looted from an opera-bound Nazi general. She managed to sneer, even though she trembled and her breasts hardened under her shirt's remnants.

He rubbed the flat of the blade over her cheek. She remained motionless and stared back at him. What the hell was he going to do?

"You should never have left us, your true people, for foreign men," he remarked, teasing the gag's edge with the dagger's tip. The silk shredded slightly but didn't tear. "You should have stayed where you belonged, with those who love you."

His eyes burned into hers but she managed to refuse again. Her insides were twisted together, while her cream now dripped onto her thigh. She tried to breathe.

"So you want to play this game, do you?" He caressed her neck with the dagger's sharp edge, so that her pulse beat frantically against it. "Then where is the art?"

In a move so fast that she had no time to respond, he cut the gag away and tossed it aside.

"Tell me or I'll pluck your clothes from you."

"No! You are nothing, compared to their mighty army." She found a laugh to throw at him. "They will hold Europe when you and your kind are long dead."

"Foolish woman, do you think you have experienced everything I can do to you?" He circled her, studying her closely. She snapped her head to follow him, growing more uneasy and excited with his every step.

He halted behind her and slid her hair away from her neck. He licked her nape and she jerked, then shrieked a little when he nipped her. He laved and nibbled on her sensitive points, until she trembled but remained stubbornly silent.

She was almost relieved when he left her and went to the table. But her eyes widened in shock when he returned with a pair of heavy scissors.

"You wouldn't dare cut my clothes!"

"I find that I prefer your nakedness. It offers so many opportunities," he purred. Her blood ran cold and then heated as her breasts tightened again.

Still, she gasped in outrage when he ran the scissors up her jacket and shirt sleeve to her neck. Now her only clothes above the waist hung by one shoulder.

He stood back, savoring the view. She burst into a string of curses, railing at him for destroying her warmest coat.

"How dare you cut it, you dirt-grubbing..."

He stopped her by the simple expedient method of kissing her. She fought and tried to wrench her mouth away from him. He trapped her head between his two big paws and continued to kiss her until she yielded to him. Then his tongue roamed her mouth like a ravenous army, conquering everything it touched. His hands kneaded her breasts until she moaned and twisted.

"Where is the art?" he breathed against her cheek.

"No," she stammered, dragging her few remaining wits back. "No, the Nazis would kill me if I told you."

"Little fool," he rumbled, "do you really want me to question you until you beg for mercy? You know what I can do and how dangerous I am." His eyes gleamed, sapphire-bright but still controlled, above his flushed cheekbones. He paid no attention to the bulge resting behind his fly, which seemed only mildly interested in Beth's potential. He looked like a lion considering how best to spring upon a gazelle.

"I will never tell!" Beth cried out.

He cut the jacket and shirt off her other arm and tossed the remains under the table. Dear heavens, what was he capable of?

"How dare you! Do you think that is enough to make me talk?"

"You should have remained home," he remarked, his eyes resting on her tightly furled nipples. Her breasts rose and fell frantically while her ruby-red nipples tightened more.

Did he mean that she should have remained with him? Was he looking for a pledge from her?

"No! I, ah, oh!" she gasped as his mouth welcomed her treacherous breasts. How could she resist him when they reacted like this?

He suckled her strongly and she writhed, grasping the handrails for support. "Damn you, how can you do this!"

His hand tugged at her other breast. She shrieked as he worked her breasts, using mouth and hands as each touch sent a jolt directly to her clit.

He stroked her back and his hand soon traveled over her derriere, first over the trousers then inside. Her head rolled back as he teased her. But the heavy corduroy trousers were too snug for the close contact he sought. He eased them open, while he marked her with small growls and nips.

She groaned when he rubbed her clit between her swollen folds. Her hips thrust convulsively as she sought to follow his fingers' steady probes inside her. Then he lifted his mouth from hers and yanked her trousers down to her knees.

She squeaked and opened her eyes, shocked by the cold air exploring her hot skin.

He walked around her again, studying every inch of her. She eyed him warily, starting to be very concerned about his plans. How far would he go to dominate her? The kind of oral sex they'd enjoyed in the truck should have been enough to make him use her like a ravenous stallion, leaving him spent and exhausted. Then she could have left him without promising any changes.

What had she said in that damn checklist that he could use on her now? She remembered mentioning nipple clamps, spanking, leather belt...What else?

"Too many clothes," he remarked and brought back heavy scissors.

"You ruined them!" she protested, as two efficient cuts left the trousers lying on the floor at her feet.

"You're not showing me enough yet," he remarked. He ran a possessive hand up her leg and cupped her mound. She jerked then rolled her pelvis into his grasp. "But you're starting to be wet enough."

She couldn't give him what he demanded. If she was right, then yielding would destroy them both in a failed union. The penalty for failure was huge.

She shuddered and tried to protest his hand's behavior but soon lost the ability to form words. She grew flushed and faint, frantic with the need for more. But he wouldn't tell her to come and she hovered on the verge.

He smacked her hard on the butt. She jerked but it felt good, so good to have the harder sensation. He smacked her on the other cheek and she yelped. He rubbed the spot hard before landing three more blows in quick sensation.

Beth cried out and wriggled as he fondled her. Had she mentioned spankings in that checklist? She tried to protest.

"What are you doing?"

"You've been a very bad girl and you still haven't told me what I need to know. Now where is the art?"

"I'll never tell!" She didn't remember why not, just that she couldn't talk. So she added a few words about his ancestry in a tone that made his eyebrow lift.

He spanked her hard after that, combining blows and caresses into a mixture that made her body writhe and her hips thrust into every touch. He visited much of her body, including her throbbing, sensitive breasts, until she keened her desire. He paused from time to time, to fondle her or kiss her. Once his groin brushed her hip with a hard ridge closely confined in his trousers.

But she never spoke of the art, or returning to the home that loved her.

She hung on the bars, eyes shut as she gasped for breath during a respite. His hand gently teased her erect clit while the other fondled her fiery ass. She sighed her approval before she registered the grease on the fingers sliding up and down the cleft between her buttocks. But the coolness felt so good.

A finger delicately teased her clit while another slipped into her ass. She welcomed both greedily, enjoying the lightly stretched feeling.

"Oh yes, please. Oh more, oh yes," she sighed, the first time she had begged.

He gave her more, gradually working until three very large masculine fingers stuffed her backside, while his other hand eased into her cunt. She rocked between his hands, moaning deep and low.

She floated in a haze when he left her, her eyes still shut. Then cold metal entered her ass and she shuddered at the size and weight. She'd taken jelly and silicon butt plugs before. But stainless steel? It was big, not the largest she'd ever carried, but enough to make her body stretch around it. And it was certainly heavier than anything she'd ever known before.

"What are you doing?" she whispered.

The big plug settled into place at last and her body clenched around the base, holding it close. Heat flowed between her breasts and her ass, encouraged by the finger circling her clit. She wouldn't be able to hold the weight long but her body fought to continue the sensation for the moment.

"Where's the art?"

"I'll never tell," she managed, more faintly than before. He had far more imagination than she'd given him credit for but she still couldn't take the chance.

"Little fool," he growled and pulled his belt free. Her mouth went dry at the familiar sound and she stared longingly at the wide strip of flexible leather.

But this was Sean, who protected women. He wouldn't use that on her, even though she was so aroused that she'd welcome it.

He doubled the belt and snapped it as a test. She shivered at the experience behind the casual motion.

"Talk to me, woman." His gaze was steady and controlled but her body heated under it.

She took a deep breath, fighting back the demand clamoring inside. She formed her answer very carefully.

"No."

He brought the belt down unerringly on her ass. She shrieked and rose to her toes in response, before settling back. The blow ran through her body like a call to arms.

"No," she said again. But the word was changing now to another meaning.

"You need a damned good hiding," he muttered, "for all the trouble you're causing."

"No," she said again. And she meant yes.

He tanned her backside a dozen times and she cried out in response every time. Heat rose through her like mercury in a thermometer. She lost the ability to form words when he rubbed the leather between her legs, then lightly tapped her pussy with it.

"No, please," she moaned then, uncaring now what he thought. She needed this, the belt's hard touch setting an answering pulse through her body. She wanted more, needed more.

Beth floated in an ecstatic haze when he stopped, her body alive as never before. Somehow her body still embraced the butt plug, while her nipples throbbed. She felt both grateful and vulnerable to him.

She opened her eyes finally and looked for him. She found him standing naked in front of a stove, rolling a condom down his straining, vibrantly alive cock.

What was he going to do? She couldn't suck him, not when she was bound like this. And he wouldn't fit into her cunt, not in this position with that enormous plug filling her ass. But she couldn't bear not holding every possible inch of him. She trembled with fear and arousal at the choices.

He studied her and smiled slowly, his eyes lighting in harsh triumph as he read her expression.

"What do you think I'm going to do now?"

"I don't know," she whimpered.

"Yes, you know," he corrected her. "Try again. What am I going to do? You said it in that damn limo once."

Beth sent her mind back to find the answer. "You're going to do exactly what you want, not what pleases me."

"Exactly right," he growled and came back to her. "What are you going to do?"

"Whatever pleases you," she said steadily, finally surrendering to him.

He probed her with the tip of his cock. She was wet, dripping with it. But how could she accommodate him and the plug?

"Ah, Sean," she moaned as his glans slid in, stretching her to the point of pain. He worked himself into her slowly and she yielded to him, easing her breathing so that she relaxed enough to accept him. It was very difficult and she burned with pain, tight as a virgin in this position with her legs spread just far enough to accept his hips.

She took a deep breath and filled herself with the scent of hungry male. Anything was worth it, if he was satisfied, even if she hadn't managed to accept every inch.

He stayed motionless, his eyes closed as if he was memorizing the feeling of her like this. Gradually she relaxed around him and softened in welcome.

"Oh yes," he murmured. "That's it, woman. Open for me."

Beth trembled as her body did exactly that. He slid into her up to the hilt. Then he locked his arms around her and started to move.

He fucked her long and hard, in deep piston strokes that almost took him from her before plunging inside again, driven by the power of his muscled legs. Her inner muscles gripped him when they could, caressing him as her hands and legs couldn't. She nipped his shoulder, holding onto as much of him as possible. She arched herself, abandoning herself to being fucked by the one man in the world who really mattered.

"Fuck yes," he groaned when he found a slightly different nook inside her. "Perfect. Oh fuck, fuck…"

He forgot his self-control and changed to swift strokes that pounded her deeply, without leaving her body. His voice deepened and roughened as it stopped forming words. She forgot everything except the magic of this moment.

He stabbed deeper and howled as his climax grabbed him. He yanked the plug out of her and a thrill blazed up her spine in response.

Beth exploded into ecstasy, everything in her convulsing in an agony of satisfaction. A scintillating pinwheel of light burst behind her eyes and she lost consciousness, anchored only by him.

She came awake slowly and found herself still possessed by his cock. His hand ran down her back and one finger slipped possessively into her ass. Her eyes widened at his dominance.

"Say the words, Beth." He watched her calmly then circled his finger inside her. Her hips quivered.

"Beth," he prodded but didn't move his finger.

Her mind stirred sluggishly before framing the truth.

"I should never have left." She closed her eyes, then forced them open. Time to yield, both in fantasy and real-life. "Please, I'll tell you where the art is, if you'll just come back to me. I need you more than life, my marvelous switch."

Sean kissed her deeply then.

"We're going to get married," he said finally, producing a small jewelry box from the back pocket of his pants. "I don't care where and I don't care when, as long as we both agree that we're engaged until then."

Beth stared as he slid an enormous square-cut sapphire engagement ring on her finger. She couldn't run away, given that she was still bound hand and foot to the pipes.

"I don't even care how we get married, as long as it's legal in the United States."

"Okay," Beth murmured, still pondering the ring's promises.

"Is that all you have to say?"

She stirred at the stern note in his voice and met his eyes. Time to claim her future with him.

"I love you, Sean."

"That's better." He kissed her, gently at first and mindful of her bruises, then more strongly as she answered him. "I love you. And you're going to dominate me again, you hear that?"

"When I want to," she shrugged, fighting to keep a straight face. He really was going to be a handful. Of course, she'd never wanted any other kind.

He eyed her suspiciously then relaxed when he read her consent. "Good enough." He began to untie her wrists.

"Father gave you his blessing. Yesterday, when he went on campus," she remarked, just to confirm her guess. How else would Sean have known when she was outside the house?

He stilled, going a little white, then relaxed and smiled at her. "Yes, he did. It felt real good to be accepted by your family. I didn't tell him everything I planned though." He gently rubbed the first freed hand.

Beth's mouth twitched at his concern. "Don't worry. You told him enough to make him happy or he'd never have helped you kidnap me."

"Yeah," Sean agreed and looked happier. "Yeah, you're right. He even welcomed me to the family."

Beth smiled, tears pricking her eyes. Sean must have greatly impressed her father, if he said that much.

"Your mother packed some of her clothes for you. They're in the desk."

Both parents had helped Sean. Tears of joy swam in her eyes.

"Scotland at Christmas," she murmured, flexing her hand to help the returning circulation. Time to start talking about the future.

"What?"

"My family always spends the week between Christmas and New Year's in Scotland. We can get married then."

His face lit up and he kissed her again. "Hooyah!"

"What?"

"Ranger talk. I'll teach you."

"Yes, dear." She rubbed his shoulder. "There is one catch though."

"Yes?" He was quite still as he watched and waited.

"You'll have to make the arrangements. I'm going to be busy, moving from DC to Seattle and starting a new job."

"Yes!" He caught her against him and laughed. "Treasury, right? Hunting terrorist money?"

"Of course!" Beth laughed with him, especially when a tug reminded him that her ankles were still shackled. She giggled as she watched him bend to free her.

* * * * *

The Seattle night was cold and clear, with a brisk wind blowing from the north, as Sean and Beth ran to the stadium from the parking lot. Mike had arrived earlier, at the time preferred by his coach. But they'd dallied in the new Range Rover until Sean's wristwatch sounded the alarm.

They reached the stadium just in time to stand at attention for the national anthem. Sean did so with the unselfconscious ease of long practice, while Beth settled beside him as if she'd always stood there.

Then whistles blew, cheerleaders yelled and boys ran out onto the field.

Beth put her hand up and touched Sean's neck where the black silk scarf barely showed above his parka. He smiled down at her.

"Come on, darling, let's sit down for the opening kickoff."

Dave Hemmings waved at them from the stands and pointed at the seats next to him, carefully marked by two very fancy stadium cushions. The cushions had pockets and even back rests. They also looked brand-new.

Beth chuckled and started up the steps behind Sean. Their progress was slow as people brushed past, anxious to run just one more errand before the game started. Beth amused herself by rubbing Sean's ass whenever they had to stop.

One pause was especially long while a woman standing in the aisle tried to get her daughter to decide which soft drink she wanted. The girl looked to be of high school age, too old for such nonsense, while the woman had truly appalling taste in clothes. Beth considered memorizing the outfit, in order to tell Jenn that you could mix shades of green in one outfit for a bilious effect, but dismissed the idea as too painful.

She slid her hand inside Sean's jeans and petted him gently. Not too much, really, since it would be hours before they could leave the stadium.

Then the woman saw Sean and her face brightened. She preened and shimmied towards him, bringing a stench of cheap perfume. He stiffened. Beth's hackles rose at the woman's possessive voice.

"Sean! Thank God you're back. When do you think we can get together?" Her voice died away as she stared.

Beth's left hand, with the enormous engagement ring on it, rested on Sean's shoulder. Her right hand gave his ass a firm squeeze, while she watched the woman coldly. Centuries of noblewomen looked down her nose, while samurai loosened their swords in her eyes. Sean choked.

"Uh, ah, Jean." He stopped, appalled. "I'm sorry, Linda! I don't know how I could forget your name."

Linda looked ready to kill him. Dave Hemmings was trying hard to keep a straight face in the row beyond, while his wife was suffering a coughing fit. Beth smiled politely, too pleased with Sean to need any other signs of triumph.

"Linda, this is my fiancée, Beth Nakamura. We're getting married next month," he managed. "Beth, darling, this is Linda Davison and her daughter Jenny. Jenny is a senior here."

The women murmured polite nonsense before Linda produced a sickly grin.

"Sorry but I really do need to get drinks. Excuse me." She brushed past Sean and Beth and hurtled down the steps like a runaway car. Jenny watched her mother go and shrugged slightly, before turning her attention back to the pimply boy beside her.

Beth finally found herself seated next to Dave Hemmings' wife, who he proudly introduced as Deirdre. Sean sat down beside her and produced a beautiful new blanket, which he carefully draped over their laps.

Beth wriggled slightly, testing the aftermath of Sean's courtship. Very little discomfort really so she'd be fine in another day or so. Hopefully next time he'd go a little farther.

Deirdre promptly demanded a close-up look at the engagement ring and Beth happily showed her.

"Beautiful!" Deirdre enthused. "It's just perfect for you. But I'd never have thought that Sean would spend..." She stopped and looked embarrassed.

Beth laughed. "Oh, Sean has surprising depths when you drag them out of him." She turned the conversation to an easier subject. "We're so glad that you and your family can come to the wedding."

"Oh, we wouldn't miss it! Especially since Dave said you're chartering a plane?" Deirdre's voice trailed off expectantly.

"Yes, we thought that would be easier for our friends than to fly commercially right now. One plane from Seattle and another from Georgia, which will also stop in DC," Beth elaborated.

Deirdre started to ask another question but her attention shifted to the cheerleaders as they began encouraging the team.

Beth's hand ran up Sean's thigh, under the blanket, and cupped his balls gently. She stroked them possessively as she leaned against him. Mine, her touch said. All mine.

Sean froze in surprise and then began to chuckle.

On the field, Mike gave him the thumbs-up sign. Sean returned it, grinning broadly, before putting his arm around Beth and pulling her closer.

"Ugh, Gary called today," Sean remarked hoarsely. Beth glanced at him, a little surprised by the topic. "He said that he just got a new shipment in of erotica. He's saved us some books."

Beth kissed Sean's cheek. "Maybe tomorrow, darling. Maybe tomorrow."

Can't wait to read the next book?
Don't fight traffic to get to the bookstore!
Paying too much for gas?
Stay at home!

Go to www.ellorascave.com

Try an ebook.
Over a hundred ready to download onto your computer.
Turn your pc into your own personal library!
Read in peace—people will leave you alone, they'll think
you're hard at work when you're really enjoying another hot
romance from…

Ellora's Cave Publishing, Inc

Printed in the United States
21271LVS00007B/295-387

9 780972 437714